Susanna Gregory was a police officer in Leeds before taking up an academic career. She has served as an environmental consultant during seventeen field seasons in the polar regions, and has taught comparative anatomy and biological anthropology.

She is the creator of the Matthew Bartholomew series of mysteries set in medieval Cambridge and the Thomas Chaloner adventures in Restoration London, and now lives in Wales with her husband, who is also a writer.

Also by Susanna Gregory

The Matthew Bartholomew series

The Thomas Chaloner series

SUSANNA GREGORY

AN ORDER FOR DEATH

sphere

SPHERE

First published in Great Britain in 2001 by Little, Brown
First published in paperback in 2002 by Time Warner Paperbacks
This edition reissued in 2017 by Sphere

1 3 5 7 9 10 8 6 4 2

A CIP catalogue record for this book
is available from the British Library.

ISBN 978-0-7515-6941-4

Typeset in Baskerville by Palimpsest Book Production Limited,
Falkirk, Stirlingshire
Printed and bound in Great Britain by Clays Ltd, St Ives plc

Papers used by Sphere are from well-managed forests
and other responsible sources

Sphere
An imprint of
Little, Brown Book Group
Carmelite House
50 Victoria Embankment
London EC4Y 0DZ

An Hachette UK Company
www.hachette.co.uk

www.littlebrown.co.uk

To Isobel Hopegood

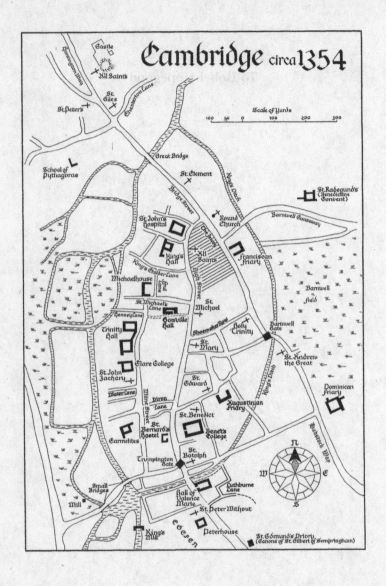

Cambridge circa **1354**

Castle
All Saints
St Giles
St Peter's
Huntingdon Road
Chesterton Lane

Scale of Yards
100   50   0   100   200   300

Great Bridge
School of Pythagoras
St Clement
King's Ditch
Bridge Street
St John's Hospital
King's Hall
All Saints
Round Church
St Radegund's (Benedictine Convent)
Barnwell Causeway
Franciscan Friary
King's Childer Lane
Michaelhouse
Foul Lane
St Michael's Lane
Trinity Lane
St Michael
Barnwell Field
Benney Lane
Gonville Hall
Shoemaker Row
Holy Trinity
Barnwell Gate
Trinity Hall
St Mary
St Andrew the Great
King's Ditch
Clare College
St John Zachary
Water Lane
Milne Street
Viron Lane
St Edward
Augustinian Friary
Dominican Friary
St Benedict
St Bernard's Hostel
Benet's College
Carmelites
St Botolph
Trumpington Gate
Luthburne Lane
Small Bridges
Mill
Hall of Valence Marie
St Peter Without
King's Mill
Peterhouse
St Edmund's Priory
(Canons of St Gilbert of Sempringham)
Barnwell Field

N
W   E
S

PROLOGUE

Cambridge, Christmas Eve 1353

YULETIDE WAS ALWAYS A MAGICAL TIME OF YEAR FOR Beadle Meadowman. He liked the crisp chill of winter evenings and the sharp scent of burning logs and of rich stews bubbling over fires in a hundred hearths. He loved the atmosphere of anticipation and excitement as the towns-folk streamed from their houses to attend the high mass in St Mary's Church at midnight, and he adored the candlelit naves and the heady smell of incense as it drifted from the chancel in a white, smoky pall.

He was in a happy mood as he strolled along Milne Street, holding his night lamp high so that he would not stumble in a pothole or trip over the mounds of rubbish that had been dumped by the people whose houses lined the road. A distant part of his mind registered that the gutters were blocked again, and that an evil yellow-brown gout of muck formed a fetid barrier that stretched from one side of the street to the other. He jumped across it, his mind fixed on the festivities that would begin when the bells chimed to announce that it was midnight.

He barely noticed the stench of rotting vegetable parings that were slippery with mould, or the odorous tang of animal dung and rotting straw that clogged the air. Instead, he heard the voices of excited children and saw lights gleaming from under the doors of homes that would usually be in darkness, and longed for his evening patrol to finish, so that he could join his family for the Christmas night celebra-tions. His sister had made a huge plum cake, which would be eaten with slices of the creamy yellow cheese he had

1

bought earlier that day, and there would be spiced wine to wash it down. And then there would be games – perhaps even a little dicing if the parish priest turned a blind eye – and the singing of ancient songs around the fire.

He reached the high walls of the Carmelite Friary and gave the handle on the gate a good rattle to ensure it was locked. Satisfied that all was in order, he walked to where Milne Street ended at Small Bridges Street and watched the glassy black waters of the King's Ditch for a moment. Only a few weeks before, a student-friar called Brother Andrew had thrown himself into the King's Ditch in a fit of depression, and Meadowman seldom passed the spot where the body had been found without thinking about him.

In the bushes at one side of the road, a man in a dark cloak waited until Meadowman had gone, and then emerged to walk purposefully towards the friary. He tapped softly on the gate, and was admitted at once by someone who owed him a favour. The same person had also been persuaded to leave inner doors unlocked and had arranged for the porter to be enjoying an illicit cup of Christmas ale in the kitchen. Without wasting time on pleasantries, the man in the dark cloak pushed past his unwilling accomplice and headed across the courtyard towards the chapel. Inside, a flight of steps led to a comfortable chamber on the upper floor, and at the far end of this was a tiny room with a heavily barred door and no windows. With a set of keys taken from the Chancellor's office in St Mary's Church earlier that day, the intruder opened the door and slipped inside.

Not many people knew that the University kept copies of its most valuable documents and deeds, and fewer still knew that these were stored in the large iron-bound box that stood in the locked room at the Carmelite Friary. Three years before, someone had broken into St Mary's Church and ransacked the University's main chest, which held its original deeds; since then the Chancellor and his clerks had been even more careful to ensure that the Carmelites received duplicates of everything. Aware that the bulging chest in St Mary's was an obvious target for thieves, the Chancellor had even taken to storing the odd silver plate and handful of gold at the friary, too. His proctors approved wholeheartedly of his precautions.

The man in the dark cloak knelt next to the chest in the Carmelite strong-room and lit a candle. The locks were the best that money could buy and would have been difficult to force, but he had the Chancellor's keys, and the well-oiled metal clasps snapped open instantly. Inside were neatly stacked rolls of parchment, bundles of letters tied with twine, and several priceless books. He sorted through them quickly, taking what he wanted and discarding the rest. Underneath the deeds and scrolls was a small box, the inside of which lit with the bright gleam of gold and silver when it was opened. The intruder glanced briefly at it, then flipped the lid closed and began packing his acquisitions into a small sack; he had not come for the University's treasure, but for something with a far greater value than mere coins.

He left the way he had entered, watchful for beadles or the Sheriff's soldiers, who would be suspicious of someone carrying a heavy bag around the town at the witching hour. But it was almost Christmas Day, and, for that night at least, most of the patrols were more interested in finishing their duties than in scouring the town for law-breakers.

Meanwhile, Beadle Meadowman had continued his rounds, and had passed through the Trumpington Gate in order to check the Hall of Valence Marie. Opposite was the dark mass of Peterhouse, while further up the road were the Priory of St Gilbert of Sempringham and the gleaming lights of the King's Head tavern. Meadowman had been called to the King's Head earlier that night, when a fellow beadle named Rob Smyth, full of the spirit of approaching Christmas, had drunk more than was wise. Smyth had picked a fight with a surly blacksmith, and Meadowman had been obliged to calm his colleague down and resettle him in a corner with another jug of ale.

Meadowman cocked his head and listened, but although drunken voices could be heard on the still night air, the patrons of the King's Head sounded more celebratory than antagonistic, and he saw no need to ensure that Smyth was behaving himself. He turned to cross the street. Ditches ran along each side of the Trumpington road, intended to prevent it from flooding, although in reality, the Gilbertine friars and the scholars of Valence Marie and Peterhouse tended to block them by filling them with rubbish, and they were really just a series of fetid, stagnant puddles. Storms sometimes washed them clean, but it had been a long time since there had been a serious downpour, and they were more choked than usual.

A dark shadow on the ground outside Peterhouse caught Meadowman's eye. He went to inspect it, and was vaguely amused to see a man lying full length on his front, arms flung out above his head, as though he had caught his foot in a pothole and had fallen flat on his face. As he knelt, Meadowman was not at all surprised to detect the powerful, warm scent of ale. One of the patrons of the King's Head had apparently had too much to drink, stumbled on the uneven road surface, and then gone to sleep where he had dropped. Meadowman recognised the greasy brown hood of Rob Smyth and, shaking his head in tolerant resignation, he turned his colleague over.

Water dripped from Smyth's face, drenching the fringe of fair hair that poked from under his hood and trickling down the sides of his face. Meadowman gazed at the blue features and dead staring eyes in sudden shock. Then he slowly reached out a hand to the puddle in which Smyth had been lying. It was shallow, no deeper than the length of his little finger. Meadowman realised that Smyth had drowned because he had been too drunk to lift his face away from the suffocating water when he had stumbled.

At Smyth's side was a pouch containing a letter. Meadowman frowned in puzzlement, wondering why his colleague should be carrying a document when he, like

Meadowman, could not read. It was written on new parchment, not on old stuff that had been scraped clean and then treated with chalk, so Meadowman supposed it was important. He pushed it in his own scrip to hand to the proctors later, then covered Smyth's body with his cloak. He stood, and began to walk back to the town, where he would fetch more beadles to carry the corpse to the nearest church, and where he would break the shocking news to Smyth's family. As he went, he reflected grimly that some people would not be celebrating a joyous Christmas that night.

The fields east of Cambridge, a few days later

A sharp wind gusted across the flat land that surrounded the Benedictine convent of St Radegund, rustling the dead leaves on the trees and hissing through the long reeds that grew near the river. The friar shivered, and glanced up at the sky. It was an indescribably deep black, and was splattered with thousands of tiny lights. The more the friar gazed at them, the more stars he could see, glittering and flickering and remote. He pulled his cloak tightly around him. Clear skies were very pretty, but they heralded a cold night, and already he could feel a frost beginning to form on the ground underfoot.

Against the chilly darkness of the night, the lights from St Radegund's Convent formed a welcoming glow. The friar could smell wood-smoke from the fires that warmed the solar and dormitory, and could hear the distant voices of the nuns on the breeze as they finished reciting the office of compline and readied themselves for bed.

And then the others began to arrive. They came singly and in pairs, glancing around them nervously, although the friar could not tell whether their unease came from the fact that robbers frequented the roads outside Cambridge, or whether they knew that it was not seemly to be seen lurking outside a convent of Benedictine nuns at that hour of the

5

night. He watched them knock softly on the gate, which opened almost immediately to let them inside, and then went to join them when he was sure they were all present.

The Prioress had made her own chamber available to the powerful men who had left their cosy firesides to attend the nocturnal meeting. It was a pleasant room, filled with golden light from a generous fire, and its white walls and flagstone floors were tastefully decorated with tapestries and rugs. The friar was not the only man to appreciate the heat from the hearth or to welcome the warmth of a goblet of mulled wine in his cold hands.

The nuns saw their guests comfortably settled, and then started to withdraw, leaving the men to their business. The Prioress and her Sacristan were commendably discreet, not looking too hard or too long at any of the men, and giving the comforting impression that no one would ever learn about the meeting from them. However, a young novice, whom the friar knew was called Tysilia, was a different matter. Her dark eyes took in the scene with undisguised curiosity, and she settled herself on one of the benches that ran along the wall, as if she imagined she would be allowed to remain to witness what was about to take place.

'Come, Tysilia,' ordered the Prioress, pausing at the door when she saw what her charge had done. 'What is discussed here tonight has nothing to do with us.'

Tysilia regarded her superior with innocent surprise. 'But these good gentlemen came here to visit us, Reverend Mother. It would be rude to abandon them.'

The friar saw the Prioress stifle a sigh of annoyance. 'We will tend to them later, if they have need of our company. But for the time being, they wish to be left alone.'

'With each other?' asked Tysilia doubtfully. Looking around at the eccentric collection of scholars and clerics, the friar could see her point. 'Why?'

'That is none of our affair,' said the Prioress sharply. She strode across the room to take the awkward novice by the arm. 'And it is time we were in our beds.'

6

She bundled Tysilia from the room, while the Sacristan gave the assembled scholars an apologetic smile. It did little to alleviate the uneasy atmosphere.

'I hope she can be trusted not to tell anyone what she has seen tonight,' said the man who had called the meeting, anxiety written clear on his pallid face. 'You promised me absolute discretion.'

The Sacristan nodded reassuringly. 'Do not worry about Tysilia. She will mention this meeting to no one.'

'Tysilia,' mused one of the others thoughtfully. 'That is the name of the novice who is said to have driven that Carmelite student-friar – Brother Andrew – to his death.'

'That is hardly what happened,' said the Sacristan brusquely. 'It is not our fault that your students fall in love with us, then cast themselves into the King's Ditch when they realise that they cannot have what they crave.'

'It seemed to me that Tysilia knew exactly what she was doing,' said the friar, entering the conversation. He disliked Tysilia intensely, and felt, like many University masters, that pretty nuns should be kept well away from the hot-blooded young men who flocked to the town to study. 'Her sly seduction of him was quite deliberate.'

'You are wrong,' said the Sacristan firmly. 'Poor Tysilia is cursed with a slow mind. She does not have the wits to do anything sly.'

'I do not like the sound of this,' said a scholar who was wearing a thick grey cloak. 'If she is so simple, then how do we know she can be trusted not to tell people what she saw here tonight?'

'Her memory is poor,' said the Sacristan, attempting to curb her irritation at the accusations and sound reassuring. 'By tomorrow, she will have forgotten all about you.'

'That is probably true,' said the man who had called the meeting. 'She certainly barely recalls me from one visit to the next.' He nodded a dismissal to the Sacristan, who favoured him with a curt bow of the head and left, closing the door behind her.

'We did not come here to talk about weak-witted novices,' said the grey-cloaked scholar. 'We came to discuss other matters.'

Despite the warmth of the room, several men had kept their faces hidden in the shadows of their hoods, as if they imagined they might conceal their identities. The friar shook his head in wry amusement: Cambridge was small, and men of influence and standing in the University could not fail to know each other; they could no more make themselves anonymous in the Prioress's small room than they could anywhere else in the town. The friar knew all their names, the religious Order to which they belonged, and in some cases, even their family histories and details of their private lives.

The man who had called the meeting cleared his throat nervously. 'Thank you for coming, gentlemen. I am sorry to draw you from your friaries, Colleges and hostels at such an hour, but I think we all agree that it is better no one sees us gathering together if we are to be effective.'

There was a rumble of agreement. 'There is altogether too much plotting and treachery in the University these days,' said the grey-cloaked scholar disapprovingly. 'God forbid that anyone should accuse *us* of it.'

The friar forced himself not to smile. What did the man imagine he was doing? Secret meetings with the heads of other religious Orders, to discuss the kind of issues they all had in mind when most honest folk were in bed, sounded like plotting to the friar.

An elderly man finished his wine and went to pour himself more, glancing around him as he did so. 'I do not imagine Prioress Martyn has allowed us the use of this chamber out of the goodness of her heart. Who is paying for her hospitality?'

The man in charge grinned, and held a gold coin between his finger and thumb, so that everyone could see it. 'I happened to be in the Market Square a few weeks ago,' he said enigmatically.

8

The others nodded their understanding, some exchanging smiles of genuine amusement as they recalled the incident when half the town had profited from an unexpected spillage of treasure in the stinking mud near the fish stalls.

'I saw it all,' said the old man bitterly. 'But I was not nimble enough on my feet to take advantage of the situation.'

The scholar in grey laughed from the depths of his hood. 'I wish I had been there! It is not that I have any special desire to take part in undignified mêlées and grab myself a handful of gold – although I confess I would not have declined the opportunity had it arisen – but I would like to have seen the effigy of Master Wilson of Michaelhouse dropped in the Market Square muck by irate peasants.'

'Wilson was an odious fellow,' agreed the old man. 'And his cousin Runham was no better. It was satisfying to see Wilson's effigy and Runham's corpse so roughly manhandled by the townsfolk. And it was even more gratifying to see the wealth that pair had accumulated through their dishonest dealings pour into the filth of the town's streets.'

'Not as gratifying as it was to seize some of it,' said the man in charge. 'And now I propose to put it to good use. It will pay for meetings such as this, so that we will all benefit from it.'

'Get on with it, then,' said the old man, refilling his cup from the wine jug yet again. 'I have other business to attend tonight.'

'I brought you here to discuss a murder,' said the man in charge. He gazed at each one of them, his eyes sombre. 'The murder of one of the University's highest officials.'

CHAPTER 1

Cambridge, March 1354

THE FIRST STONE THAT SMASHED THROUGH THE WINDOW of Oswald Stanmore's comfortable business premises on Milne Street sprayed Matthew Bartholomew with a shower of sharp splinters and narrowly missed his head. He dropped to his knees, ducking instinctively as a loud crack indicated that another missile had made its mark on the merchant's fine and expensive glass, and tried to concentrate on suturing the ugly wound in the stomach of the Carmelite friar who lay insensible on the bench in front of him.

Bartholomew's sister entered the room cautiously, carrying a dish of hot water and some rags ripped into strips for bandages. She gave a startled shriek when a pebble slapped into the wall behind her, and promptly dropped the bowl. Water splashed everywhere, soaking through the sumptuous rugs that covered the floor and splattering the front of her dress.

'Damn!' she muttered, regarding the mess with annoyance before crouching down and making her way to where Bartholomew worked on the injured man. She winced as another window shattered. 'How is he?'

'Not good,' replied Bartholomew, who knew there was little he could do for a wound such as had been inflicted on the Carmelite. The knife had slashed through vital organs in the vicious attack, and, even though he had repaired them as well as he could, the physician thought the damage too serious for the friar to recover. Even if the injury did heal, his patient was weakened by blood loss and shock, and was unlikely to survive the infection that invariably followed such piercing wounds.

'Shall I fetch a priest?' asked Edith, watching her brother struggle to close the end of the gaping cut with a needle and a length of fine thread. 'He will want a Carmelite – one of his own Order.'

Bartholomew finished his stitching and peered cautiously out of the window. A sturdy wall surrounded his brother-in-law's property, so that it was reasonably safe from invasion. It could still be bombarded with missiles, however, and the Dominican students who had massed outside were dividing their hostile attentions between the Carmelite Friary opposite and Stanmore's house – where they knew a Carmelite had been given shelter.

'Neither of us will be going anywhere until those Dominicans disperse,' he said, ducking again as another volley of stones rattled against the wall outside. 'They have the Carmelite Friary surrounded and I doubt they will be kind enough to allow one of the enemy out, even on an errand of mercy.'

'I will fetch a Franciscan or an Austin canon instead, then,' said Edith, gathering her skirts as she prepared to leave. 'This poor boy needs a priest.'

'You cannot go outside,' said Bartholomew firmly, grabbing her arm. 'I suspect the Dominican student-friars will attack anyone they see, given the frenzy they have whipped themselves into. It is not safe out there.'

'But I have nothing to do with the University,' objected Edith indignantly. 'No Dominican student – or any other scholar – would dare to harm *me*.'

'Usually, no,' replied Bartholomew, pushing her to one side as a clod of earth crashed through the nearest window and scattered over a handsome rug imported from the Low Countries. 'But their blood is up and they are inflamed beyond reason; I doubt they care who they hurt. The

11

Carmelites were insane to have written that proclamation.'

'A proclamation?' asked Edith warily. 'All this mayhem is about a proclamation?'

Bartholomew nodded. 'They denounced a philosophical belief that the Dominicans follow, and pinned it to the door of St Mary's Church.'

Edith regarded him in disbelief. 'The scholars are killing each other over philosophy? I thought academic arguments were supposed to take place in debating halls, using wits and intellect – not knives and stones.'

Bartholomew gave her a rueful smile. 'In an ideal world, perhaps. But factions within the University are always squabbling over something, and this time the religious Orders have ranged themselves on two sides of a debate about whether or not abstracts have a real existence.'

Edith's expression of incomprehension intensified. 'You are teasing me, Matt! People do not fight over something like that.'

'Scholars do, apparently,' replied Bartholomew, laying his fingers on the life pulse in the Carmelite's neck. It was weak and irregular, and he began to fear that the lad would not survive until the Dominican students grew tired of throwing stones at windows, and would die without the benefit of a final absolution.

Edith shook her head in disgust, and began to wipe the student's face with a damp cloth. Bartholomew understood exactly how she felt. For years, the various religious Orders that gathered in the University had bickered and quarrelled, and one of them was always attacking the views and ideas expounded by the others. On occasion, emotions ran strongly enough to precipitate an actual riot – like the one currently under way between the Black Friars and the White Friars in the street below – and it was not unknown for students to be killed or injured during them. It was nearing the end of Lent, and the students, especially the friars and monks, were tired and bored with the restrictions imposed on them. They were ripe for a fight, and Bartholomew

12

supposed that if it had not been a philosophical issue, then they would have found something else about which to argue.

He eased backward as another hail of missiles was launched, and cracks and tinkling indicated that more of Stanmore's windows were paying the price for Bartholomew's act of mercy in rescuing the Carmelite. The physician realised he had made a grave error of judgement, and saw that he should have carried the friar to Michaelhouse, his own College, and not involved his family in the University's troubles. He hoped the Dominicans' fury at losing their quarry would fade when the heat of the moment was past, and that they would not decide to take revenge on the Stanmores later.

'You should all be ashamed of yourselves,' said Edith, taking another cloth and trying without much success to wipe the blood from the friar's limp hands.

'I know,' said Bartholomew with a sigh. He felt the life-beat again, half expecting to find it had fluttered away to nothing. 'The current debate between the nominalists and the realists is a complicated one, and I doubt half the lads throwing stones at us really believe that nominalism is the ultimate in philosophical theories: they just want to beat the Carmelites.'

Edith continued to tend the unconscious man. Bartholomew had administered a powerful sense-dulling potion before he had started the messy operation of repairing the slippery organs that had been damaged by the knife, and did not expect the Carmelite to wake very soon – if at all. He laid the back of his hand against the friar's forehead, not surprised to find that it was cold and unhealthily clammy. So he was surprised when the friar stirred weakly, opened his eyes and began to grope with unsteady fingers at the cord he wore around his waist.

'My scrip,' he whispered, his voice barely audible. 'Where is my scrip?'

Edith looked around her, supposing that the leather

pouch friars often carried at their side had fallen to the floor. 'Where is it, Matt?'

Bartholomew pointed to a short string that had evidently been used to attach the scrip to the friar's waist-cord. It was dark with dirt, indicating that it had served its purpose for some time, but the ends were bright and clean. It did not take a genius to deduce that it had been cut very recently. Bartholomew could only assume that whoever had stabbed the friar had also taken his pouch, probably using the same knife. Bartholomew had found the injured friar huddled in a doorway surrounded by Dominicans; the scrip must have been stolen by one of them.

'Easy now,' he said gently, trying to calm his patient as the search became more frantic. 'You are safe here.'

'My scrip,' insisted the friar, more strongly. 'Where is it? It is vital I have it!'

'We will find it,' said Bartholomew comfortingly, although he suspected that if the friar's pouch had contained something valuable, then the chances of retrieving it were remote.

'You must find it,' breathed the friar, gripping Bartholomew's arm surprisingly tightly for a man so close to death. 'You must.'

'Who did this to you?' asked Bartholomew, reaching for his bag. His patient's agitated movements were threatening to pull the stitches apart, and the physician wanted to calm him with laudanum. He eased the friar's head into the crook of his arm and gave him as large a dose as he dared. 'Do you know the names of the men who attacked you?'

'Please,' whispered the friar desperately. 'My scrip contains something very important to me. You must find it. And when you do, you must pass it to Father Paul at the Franciscan Friary.'

'Do not worry,' said Bartholomew softly, disengaging himself from the agitated Carmelite and easing him back on to the bench. 'We will look for it as soon as we can.'

He continued to speak in the same low voice, sensing that the sound of it was soothing the student. It was not long before the Carmelite began to sleep again. Bartholomew inspected the damage the struggle had done to the fragile stitching, and was relieved to see that it was not as bad as he had feared. Still, he realised it would make little difference eventually: the friar was dying. His life was slowly ebbing away, and there was nothing Bartholomew could do to prevent it.

Outside in the street, the Dominicans continued to lay siege to the Carmelite Friary opposite, although their voices sounded less furious and the missiles were hurled with less intensity and frequency. Bartholomew risked a quick glance out of the window, and saw that the beadles – the law enforcers employed by the University – had started to arrive, and that small groups of Dominicans were already slinking away before they were caught. There was only so long they could sustain their lust for blood when the Carmelites were safely out of sight inside their property, and common sense was beginning to get the better of hot tempers.

'It will not be long now,' said Bartholomew, moving away from the window and kneeling next to his patient again, where his sister still sponged the pale face. 'The Dominicans are going home. We may yet be able to secure a Carmelite confessor to give this man last rites.'

'He will die?' asked Edith in a low whisper. 'There is nothing you can do to save him?'

Bartholomew shook his head. 'I have done all I can.'

Edith gazed in mute compassion at the friar's face. Bartholomew did not know what to say, and was frustrated that for all his years of training at Oxford and then in Paris, his medical knowledge still could not prevent a young man from dying.

'Richard is right,' said Edith bitterly. 'We always summon physicians when we are ill, but they make little difference to whether we live or not.'

'Richard has changed,' said Bartholomew, thinking about Edith and Oswald's only son. 'He is not the same lad who left for Oxford after the plague five years ago.'

'It is good to have him home again,' said Edith, declining to admit that her son had returned home lacking a good deal of his former charm. 'He plans to remain here for a while, to assess the opportunities Cambridge has to offer. He says he may have to go to London, because he is a good lawyer and he wants to work on expensive land disputes and become very rich.'

'He said that?' asked Bartholomew, startled by the young man's blunt materialism. He felt for the friar's life-beat again. 'I do not know why he wants to stay here anyway; he has done nothing but criticise everything about Cambridge ever since he returned.'

Edith did not reply, but Bartholomew sensed that she was as unimpressed by her son's behaviour as was Bartholomew. Richard had gone to the University of Oxford to study medicine, but had returned with a degree in law instead, claiming that a legal training would provide him with the means to make more money than a medical one. Although he disapproved of Richard's motives, Bartholomew knew the young man was right. Since the plague, there was work aplenty for those who were able to unravel the complexities of contested wills and property disputes arising from the high number of sudden deaths.

His lessons in legal affairs had done nothing to improve Richard's character, however. Although he could hardly say so to Edith, Bartholomew had preferred the cheerful, ebullient seventeen-year-old who had set off determined to learn how to heal the sick, than the greedy twenty-two-year-old who had returned.

'The streets are almost clear,' he said, glancing out of the window and then resting his hand on the Carmelite's forehead. 'I will leave in a few moments to fetch a confessor. Will you stay with him?'

'Of course,' said Edith immediately. 'This poor boy can remain here as long as necessary. Oswald will not mind.'

'He will,' said Bartholomew, imagining his brother-in-law's

disapproval. 'He will not be pleased to return from his business meeting to learn that I endangered his wife by bringing an injured Carmelite to her, or to see that his panes have been smashed by vengeful Dominicans.'

He edged nearer the window, so that he could see into the muddy road below. There were definitely fewer dark-robed Dominicans in Milne Street now, and he wished the remainder would hurry up and return to their own quarters on Hadstock Way.

'Look at him, Matt,' said Edith softly, sponging the hands of the injured Carmelite. 'He is about the same age as Richard.'

Bartholomew glanced down at his patient and saw that she was right. He had barely noticed the man's face. When he had first caught sight of the wounded student, clutching his stomach in a spreading stain of blood, all Bartholomew's attention had been taken with brandishing a hefty pair of childbirth forceps at the surrounding Dominicans and dragging the injured friar to the nearest safe haven. Then, once they had reached Stanmore's property, Bartholomew had concentrated on tending the wound and ducking the splinters of glass.

For the first time, he studied the friar. He had a pleasant face, with a mouth that turned up at the corners, although already it had the waxy sheen of death about it. His fingers were deeply ink-stained, suggesting that he spent at least some of his time studying or scribing, rather than wandering the town with his classmates looking for Dominicans or Franciscans to taunt or attack. His hair was light brown and smelled clean, and his habit, although blood-soaked and marked with the signs of a scuffle, was neat and showed evidence of recent brushing. Here was no lout, but a man who took care over his personal appearance. The only unusual thing about him was the pale yellow sticky residue on one of his hands. It looked like some kind of glue, although Bartholomew had never seen anything quite like it before. He supposed it was some new import from Spain

17

or France. Such items were becoming common again now that people were recovering from the impact of the plague and trade was resuming.

'I wonder what was in his scrip that was so important to him,' mused Edith. The sound of her voice pulled the physician from his reverie. 'Whatever it was, he considered it more vital than telling you the names of the men who stabbed him.'

'Perhaps he did not know them,' said Bartholomew. He glanced out of the window again. 'If I leave my Michaelhouse tabard here and borrow that cloak of Oswald's, I should reach the Carmelite Friary unmolested—'

'Matt!' whispered Edith urgently, jumping away from the Carmelite in alarm. 'Something is wrong with him!'

Bartholomew saw the friar's eyes roll back in his head as he began to convulse, thrashing about with his arms and legs and pulling open the sutured wound. With Edith exhorting him to do something, Bartholomew attempted to control the fit with more of his sense-dulling potions, but to no avail. Gradually, the uncontrolled twitching and shuddering grew weaker, along with the friar's heartbeat. The student was still for a few moments, gasping raggedly while the opened wound pumped his life blood into the rugs that covered the bench. And then he simply ceased to breathe. Edith took his hand and called out to him, but the Carmelite was dead.

'They killed him,' she said, tears welling up in her eyes. Unlike her brother, she was unused to the presence of sudden death and it distressed her. 'Those Dominicans murdered him.'

'They did,' agreed Bartholomew softly. He stood, feeling defeated. 'I will fetch one of the Carmelites to see to him.'

'Fetch Brother Michael first,' said Edith unsteadily. 'He is the Senior Proctor, and it is his responsibility to investigate University deaths. I want to see those murdering Dominicans brought to justice.'

'So will the Carmelites,' said Bartholomew grimly. 'I just hope they will not decide to do it themselves.'

Brother Michael, Senior Proctor of the University, Fellow of Michaelhouse and trusted agent of the Bishop of Ely, puffed across the yard of Stanmore's business premises with his Junior Proctor and a group of his beadles marching untidily behind him.

With one or two exceptions, the University's law-keepers were a rough, ill-kempt breed. They all sported coarse woollen tunics with scarlet belts that marked them as University officers, but underneath they wore a bizarre assortment of garments that gave most of them a very eccentric appearance. Some had donned the boiled leather leggings that suggested they had fought for King Edward in France before the plague had forced a truce, while others possessed an eclectic collection of articles passed to them as bribes from students they caught breaking the University's rules. A quick glance revealed a courtier's scarlet hose, a Dominican's cloak, a grey shirt that had probably been a Franciscan's undergarment, and a pair of wooden clogs that had doubtless belonged to a scholar from the north.

The Junior Proctor was a different matter. Will Walcote was dressed in the sober black habit of an Austin canon, and over it was an ankle-length cloak. His calf-high boots were of good quality leather, and although they were mud-stained from walking along the High Street, they had been carefully polished. He was of average height, had thick brown hair that was cut short above the ears, and had a thin, intelligent face. He was popular in the University, more so than his intrigue-loving superior, and already it was rumoured that he would be Michael's successor as Senior Proctor, although Bartholomew knew Michael had doubts about Walcote's suitability.

The untidy procession came to a shambling halt, while Michael looked around him imperiously. The yard was cobbled, and everywhere were threads of the cloth that had made Oswald Stanmore one of the richest men in Cambridge. The lean-to sheds were filled with bales of wool and silk, and even though the merchant himself was at a business meeting in another part of the town, his apprentices were busy loading and unloading carts, making inventories and carrying out his orders.

Michael presented an impressive figure in his billowing black cloak and the dark Benedictine habit beneath it, and several of Stanmore's apprentices faltered nervously when they saw him. The monk had always been large – tall, as well as burly – but contentment and self-satisfaction had added a further layer of fat around his middle. His thin, lank brown hair was cut neatly around his gleaming tonsure, and his flabby jowls had been scraped clean of whiskers. He and Bartholomew had been friends for some years, although Michael's post as Senior Proctor and the duties it entailed occasionally put a serious strain on their relationship.

Bartholomew watched the monk and his retinue enter the yard, then went to meet them. It was cold for March, and Michael's winter cloak was lined with fur to protect him from the bitter winds that shrieked across the Fens from the north and east. Despite the fact that it was Lent, and that the monk should have been fasting or at least abstaining from some foods, he looked a good deal better fed than most of his beadles, and his round face gleamed with health and vitality.

He spotted Bartholomew and Edith at the top of the short flight of steps that led to Oswald Stanmore's office, and strode to meet them. Walcote followed him.

'I heard there was a row between the Dominicans and the Carmelites,' said the monk, waiting for Bartholomew to descend the steps. 'My beadles acted immediately, and I thought we had prevented any serious trouble. Then I receive a message from you saying that someone has been killed.'

'It is true,' replied Edith, answering Michael's question before Bartholomew could speak. Her eyes were red from crying over the death of the young friar she had not known, and her voice was unsteady. Bartholomew fervently wished

20

he had taken the Carmelite to Michaelhouse, and had not involved his sister in the University's troubles. 'The Dominicans killed a Carmelite. He died right here, in Oswald's office.'

'How did he come to be there?' asked Michael curiously.

'Merchants like Oswald have bands of apprentices, and bands of apprentices love nothing more than lone scholars to fight – be they Carmelites or anyone else.'

'Matt brought him,' replied Edith. 'The apprentices did not approve, but they carried him upstairs, then stood watch to make sure no Dominicans broke through our gates. I suppose all the fuss has died down now, given that they seem to have gone back to work.'

'I suppose,' said Michael carefully, knowing it would take very little for trouble to ignite again. 'How did you manage to prevent your apprentices from rushing into the street and joining in the affray?'

'I forbade them to,' said Edith, surprised by the question. 'They did not like standing by while scholars threw stones that smashed our windows, but they did as they were told.'

'Would that all merchants had as much control over their people,' muttered Michael, impressed that Edith had been able to impose her will so effortlessly on a group of spirited young men. He had forgotten that dark-haired Edith, who always seemed so slight next to her younger brother, was a very determined woman. He turned to Bartholomew. 'Where is this poor unfortunate now?'

Bartholomew led him and Walcote to the office, while the beadles remained in the yard to be shown broken windows and scratched paintwork by the indignant apprentices. Edith had covered the body of the friar with a crisp white sheet, although a circular red stain had already appeared, a stark foretaste of what lay underneath. Gently, Bartholomew pulled the sheet away from the friar's face, so that Michael could see it. Both men turned in surprise when they heard Walcote's sharp intake of breath.

'That is Faricius of Abington,' said the Junior Proctor, gazing down at the body in horror.

'You know him?' asked Michael. 'Have you arrested him for frequenting taverns or brawling or some such thing?'

'Not Faricius,' said Walcote, clearly shocked. 'He was a peaceful and scholarly man. I met him at a lecture we both attended on nominalism. After that, we met from time to time to discuss various philosophical concepts. I liked and admired him.'

'Do you have any idea why someone might wish him harm?' asked Michael, watching Bartholomew cover the face of the dead scholar again.

Walcote's voice was unsteady when he replied. 'None at all. He was a good man, respected by the people who knew him. This is a vile town, if friars like Faricius are slain in broad daylight.'

'I agree, Will,' said Michael sympathetically, but rather condescendingly. 'But it happens occasionally, and it is our duty – yours and mine – to bring the culprits to justice. Matt, what were you doing in the middle of a fight between friars that ended in bloody murder?'

'I was visiting a patient, and heard the sounds of a brawl in the making on my way home. Then I saw a group of Dominicans standing around a bloodstained Carmelite lying in a doorway.'

Michael eyed his friend warily. 'How many Dominicans?'

'Half a dozen or so. The Carmelite was bleeding from a wound in his stomach, and I assumed he had been stabbed by them.'

'Lord, Matt!' said Michael, shaking his head in disapproval. 'Intervening was a foolish thing to do. One man against six is not good odds. What were you thinking of?'

'There was no time to consider the odds,' replied Bartholomew tartly. 'I only saw an injured man and thought I might be able to help him. I waved my childbirth forceps at the Dominicans and they dispersed readily enough.'

'I should think so,' said Michael, smiling wanly. 'Those

22

forceps are a formidable weapon if you know how to use them. I would think twice about taking them on, too.'

'I considered taking Faricius to Michaelhouse,' Bartholomew went on. 'But I was not sure if he would survive the journey. I brought him here instead.'

'So, did one of these six Black Friars definitely stab Faricius?' asked Michael. 'Did you see any of them holding knives or with bloodstained hands?'

Bartholomew shook his head. 'I am sorry, Brother. I was more concerned with taking Faricius somewhere I could tend him properly, and I did not notice much about the Dominicans. I would say that they did not look as though they were going to give him last rites, however.'

'Would you recognise them again?' asked Walcote hopefully. 'It was daylight, which is unusual. Most of these riots take place at night, when the perpetrators stand a better chance of escaping under cover of darkness once they have had their fill of violence.'

'Oh, yes,' replied Bartholomew. 'They were not happy to see their prey snatched from under their noses and told me so. We exchanged quite a few unpleasant words before I left.'

Michael's expression was dark with anger. 'They threatened you, did they? I shall see they pay for that with a few nights in the proctors' cells – whether they confess to murdering Faricius of Abington or not.'

'I cannot believe that the Dominicans and the Carmelites are behaving like this,' said Walcote, his eyes fixed on the still figure under the sheet. 'I know we Austin canons are no angels, and that there are occasional fights between individuals, but we do not march as a body on rival Orders.'

'Nor do we Benedictines,' said Michael in a superior manner. 'There are better ways of resolving differences than resorting to fists.'

'I am surprised their priors did nothing to stop it,' Walcote went on disapprovingly. 'Could they not see what consequences their students' actions might have – the damage that committing a murder might have on their community here in Cambridge?'

'They will see what the consequences are when I get my hands on them,' said Michael grimly.

Michael ordered four of his beadles to construct a stretcher of two planks of wood and some strips of cloth, and then instructed them to carry Faricius to St Botolph's, the church nearest the Carmelite Friary. Walcote was dispatched to fetch Prior Lincolne, which was no easy task given that the Carmelites were not currently responding to yells and bangs on the door. Once he had alerted Lincolne to the fact that one of his number was dead, Walcote was to go to the Dominican property on Hadstock Way, to ensure all the rioting Black Friars had returned home and were not still prowling the streets intent on mischief.

'This is a bad business, Matt,' said Michael, holding open the door to St Botolph's, so that the beadles could carry their grisly burden inside. Bartholomew noticed that Faricius was dripping blood, and that a trail of penny-sized droplets ran between the Stanmore property and the church. 'We have had no serious trouble since last November, when Runham dismissed my choir and attempted to cheat the workmen he had employed to rebuild Michaelhouse. I was hoping the calm would continue.'

'It has been calm because we have had a long winter,' explained Beadle Meadowman, struggling to manhandle Faricius through the narrow door without tipping him off the stretcher. 'It has been too chilly to go out fighting. Scholars and townsfolk alike would rather sit by their fires than be out causing mischief in the cold.'

Meadowman, a solid, dependable man in his forties, had been recruited by Michael as a University law officer following the dissolution of the hostel in which he had been a steward. He undertook the varied and frequently unpleasant duties of a beadle as stoically and unquestioningly as he had the orders of his previous master, a man

24

whose intentions were far from scholarly. Meadowman was a good beadle, and Michael was well satisfied with him.

'That is true,' agreed Bartholomew. 'The early snows and the frosts that followed killed a lot of people. It was especially hard on the older ones, like poor Dunstan the riverman. I did not think he would see another Easter, but he refuses to die.'

'But our students are not elderly men who need blazing hearths to warm their ancient bones,' said Michael. 'I was really beginning to feel that the worst of our troubles were over, and that the town and the University had finally learned to tolerate each other's presence – and that the religious Orders had learned to keep their quarrels for the debating halls.'

'You sound like Walcote,' said Bartholomew, smiling at him. 'He always seems horrified when the students fight, even though, as Junior Proctor, he is used to it because he spends most of his life trying to stop them.'

Michael frowned worriedly. 'Will Walcote is a good fellow, but he is too gentle to be a proctor. I was uncertain of the wisdom of the choice when he was appointed a year ago, but I thought he would learn in time.'

'And he has not?'

Michael shook his head. 'He tries, but he just does not have the right attitude. He is too willing to see the good in people. He should follow my lead, and assume everyone is corrupt, violent or innately wicked until proven otherwise.'

Bartholomew laughed. 'No wonder your cells are always full.'

'Do not tell Father William any of this,' said Michael seriously, referring to their colleague at Michaelhouse, who was determined to be a proctor himself. 'He will petition the Chancellor to have Walcote removed so that he can apply for the post himself. Although I may complain about Walcote's ineffectuality, William's ruthlessness would be far worse.'

'Do you think Walcote will resign when he realises he is not suited to the task?' asked Bartholomew.

Michael sighed. 'I doubt it, Matt. He has not taken any notice of my heavy hints so far.' He gave his friend a nudge with his elbow and nodded across the High Street to where two Benedictines walked side by side. 'But if he did, one of those two would be my choice as his successor.'

Bartholomew regarded him askance. 'Because they are Benedictines, like you?'

Michael tutted impatiently. 'Of course not. It is because they are exactly the kind of men we need to represent law and order in the University. Have you met them? Allow me to introduce you.'

Before Bartholomew could point out that it was hardly an appropriate occasion for socialising, with the body of Faricius barely inside the church and a murder to investigate, Michael had hailed his Benedictine colleagues. Bartholomew studied them as they walked towards him.

The taller of the two had light hair, a handsome face and large grey eyes. There was a small scar on his upper lip, and when he spoke he had a habit of frowning very slightly. The second had dark hair that fitted his head like a cap and blue eyes that crinkled at the corners. They seemed pleasant and affable enough, although Bartholomew immediately detected in them the smug, confident attitude of men who believed their vocation set them above other people.

'This is Brother Janius,' said Michael, indicating the dark-haired monk, before turning to the fairer one. 'And Brother Timothy here comes from Peterborough.'

'We have met before,' said Timothy, returning Bartholomew's bow of greeting. 'A few days ago, you came to Ely Hall, where the Cambridge Benedictines live, and tended Brother Adam.'

'He has a weakness of the lungs,' said Bartholomew, remembering Adam's anxious colleagues clustering around the bedside as he tended the patient, making it difficult for him to work. He vaguely recalled that Timothy and Janius had been among them, and that Janius had insisted on a lot of very loud praying, so that Bartholomew could barely hear Adam's answers to his questions. 'How is he?'

'He has been better since you recommended that lungwort and mullein infused in wine,' replied Timothy, smiling.

Janius gave his colleague an admonishing glance. 'He has been better since we began saying regular masses for him, Timothy. It is God who effected the change in Adam's health, not human cures.'

'Of course, Brother,' said Timothy piously. 'But it is my contention that God is working through Doctor Bartholomew to help Adam.'

Janius inclined his head in acknowledgement. 'God shows His hand in many ways, even by using an agent like a physician. But what has happened here?' he asked, glancing down at the ominous trail of red that soiled the stones in St Botolph's porch. 'I hope no one was hurt when the Dominicans marched on the Carmelites earlier.'

'Unfortunately, one of them was stabbed,' replied Michael. 'His name was Faricius.'

Timothy raised his eyebrows in surprise. 'Faricius? But he was no fighting man.'

'You know him?' asked Michael. 'How?'

'Faricius was a good scholar,' said Janius. 'Brilliant, even. He was one of the few Carmelites who came here because of a love of learning, rather than merely to further his own career in the Church by making useful connections.'

'We were near St Mary's Church when the Carmelites nailed their proclamation to the door,' said Timothy, still shocked by the outcome of the riot. 'I saw the Dominicans were furious, and it was clear that a fight was imminent, but I did not anticipate it would end quite so violently.'

'But do not blame only the Dominicans,' said Janius reasonably. 'I heard the Carmelites taunting them and daring them to attack. One side was every bit as responsible as the other.'

'As always,' agreed Timothy. 'These silly quarrels are invariably the result of two wrongs.' He leaned forward, rather furtively, and spoke to Michael in a soft voice. 'Is there any more news about your negotiations with Oxford, Brother? Forgive me for mentioning this in such a public place, but you told me Doctor Bartholomew knows your business, anyway.'

'He does,' replied Michael. 'But I am not expecting any progress on the Oxford matter until Ascension Day at the earliest – a good six weeks from now.' He turned to Bartholomew and lowered his voice conspiratorially. 'We are talking about my plans to surrender a couple of farms and a church to Merton College at Oxford University in exchange for a few snippets of information.'

'Right,' said Bartholomew carefully. He knew Michael had been engaged in a series of delicate negotiations with an Oxford scholar for several months, and that the monk tended to tell different people different stories about his motives and objectives. The arrangements were supposed to be secret, but a Michaelhouse scholar named Ralph de Langelee had made them public the previous year in an attempt to discredit Michael and prevent him from becoming the College's new Master. It had worked: Langelee had been elected instead.

'What happens on Ascension Day?' asked Janius curiously. He crossed himself and gave a serene smile. 'Other than the spirit of our Lord rising to heaven, that is.'

'Other than that, William Heytesbury is due to come to Cambridge to finalise our agreement,' said Michael. 'He is keen to secure the property for Merton, but he still does not trust me to deal with him honestly.'

'And does he have cause for such distrust?' asked Timothy bluntly.

Michael's expression was innocence itself. 'Why should he? I have two farms and a church that are nearer Oxford than Cambridge, and I propose to transfer them in exchange for a little information and a document or two. It is a generous offer. Those Oxford men are so used to dealing with each other, that they do not recognise a truthful man when they see one.'

28

Bartholomew, however, was sure Heytesbury had good cause to be suspicious of Michael's 'generous offer'. Whatever it entailed, the monk would make certain it was Cambridge that emerged with the better half of the bargain. He was surprised that Timothy, who seemed to know Michael well, should need to ask.

'Here comes Prior Lincolne,' said Timothy, looking down the street to where the leader of the Carmelite Order in Cambridge was hurrying towards them. 'We will leave you to your sorry business, Brother. Come to see us soon: you are always welcome in Ely Hall.'

'Thank you; I imagine I shall need a dose of sanity and calm after dealing with this murder,' said Michael, as the Benedictines walked away. He rearranged his face into a sympathetic smile as the Carmelite Prior reached him. 'Accept my sincere condolences for this dreadful incident, Father.'

Lincolne did not reply. His eyes lit on the spots of blood that splattered the ground, and he pushed past Michael to enter the church. Lincolne was a man of immense proportions. Bartholomew was tall, but Lincolne topped him by at least a head, a height further accentuated by a curious triangular turret of grey hair that sprouted from his scalp in front of his tonsure. The first time Bartholomew had seen it, when Lincolne had arrived in Cambridge to become Prior after the plague had claimed his predecessor, he thought a stray ball of sheep wool had somehow become attached to the man's head. But closer inspection had revealed that it was human hair, and that it was carefully combed upward in a deliberate attempt to grant its owner a hand's length more height. Lincolne was broad, too, especially around the middle, and his ill-fitting habit revealed a pair of thin white ankles that looked too fragile to support the weight above them.

He knelt next to Faricius and began to recite the last rites in a loud, indignant voice that was probably audible back at his friary. He produced a flask of holy water from his scrip and began to splash it around liberally, so that some of it fell on the floor.

'Do you have any idea what happened?' asked Michael, watching the proceedings with sombre green eyes.

'What happened is that the Dominicans murdered Faricius,' Lincolne replied, glaring up at Michael. Holy water dribbled from the flask on to Faricius's habit. 'Faricius was one of my best scholars and hated violence and fighting. I will have vengeance, Brother. I will not stand by while you allow the Black Friars to get away with this.'

'I would never do such a thing,' objected Michael, offended. 'I am the University's Senior Proctor, appointed by the Bishop of Ely himself to ensure that justice is done in cases like this.'

'I have been at the Carmelite Friary in Cambridge since I was a child,' Lincolne went on, as if Michael had not spoken. 'Yet, in all that time, I have never witnessed such an act of evil as this.'

'An act of evil?' asked Bartholomew, thinking it an odd phrase to use to describe a murder.

'Heresy,' hissed Lincolne, spraying holy water liberally over himself as well as over the dead student. 'Nominalism.'

'I beg your pardon?' asked Michael, startled. 'What does nominalism have to do with anything?'

Lincolne pursed his lips in rank disapproval. 'It is a doctrine that came from the Devil's own lips. It denies the very existence of God.'

'I do not think so,' said Bartholomew, surprised by the Carmelite's assertion. 'Nominalism is a philosophical doctrine that . . .'

He trailed off as Lincolne fixed him with the gaze of the fanatic. 'Nominalist thinking will destroy all that is good and holy in the world and allow the Devil to rule. It was because people were nominalists that God sent the Great Pestilence five years ago.'

'I see,' said Bartholomew, who had heard many reasons for why the devastating sickness had ravaged the world, taking one in three people, but never one that claimed a philosophical theory was responsible. 'So, you are saying that the plague took only nominalists as its victims? Not realists?'

'I think God sent the Death to warn us all against sinful thoughts – like nominalism,' declared Lincolne in the tone of voice that suggested disagreement was futile. 'And that wicked man, William of Occam, who was the leading proponent of nominalism in Oxford, was one of the first to die.'

'But so were a number of scholars who follow realism,' Bartholomew pointed out. 'The plague took scholars from both sides of the debate. That suggests a certain even-handedness to me.'

'Gentlemen, please,' said Michael impatiently. 'This is neither the time nor the place to be discussing philosophy. We have a dead student here. Our duty is to discover who murdered him, not to assess the relative virtues of realism and nominalism.'

'Then tell the Dominicans that,' snapped Lincolne. 'They are nominalists – every last one of them – and now a Carmelite lies dead.' He rammed the stopper into the flask's neck and heaved himself to his feet. He towered over Michael, and Bartholomew could not help but notice how the curious topknot quivered as if reflecting the rage of its owner.

'It was the proclamation you wrote and pinned to the door of St Mary's Church that precipitated this sorry incident,' said Michael sharply. 'And Faricius paid the price.'

'That is grossly unfair—' began Lincolne indignantly.

Michael cut through his objections. 'I sincerely doubt whether the student-friars – Dominican or Carmelite – genuinely feel strongly enough about a philosophical debate to kill each other: your notice was merely the excuse they needed to fight. And I will have no more of it. The next person who nails a proclamation to any door in the town will spend the night in the proctors' cells.'

'The Carmelites are a powerful force in Cambridge,

Brother,' said Lincolne hotly. 'We have forty friars studying here; the Dominicans only have thirty-three. You should think very carefully before you decide to take the side of the nominalists.'

'I am not taking any side,' said Michael firmly. 'Personally, I am not much interested in philosophy. And numbers mean nothing anyway. At least half a dozen of your forty are old men, who will be no use at all if you intend to take on the Dominicans in a pitched battle. They will, however, be valiant in the debating halls, which is where I recommend you resolve this disagreement.'

His green eyes were cold and hard, and even the towering Lincolne apparently decided Michael was not a man to be easily intimidated. The Prior knelt again and began to straighten and arrange the folds of Faricius's habit, to hide his temper.

'Now, I need to ask you some questions,' said Michael, seeing that Lincolne seemed to have conceded the argument. 'You say Faricius was a gentle man, but did he have any enemies? Did he beat anyone in a debate, for example?'

Lincolne glowered at the sarcasm in Michael's voice. 'I am aware of no enemies, Brother. You can come to the friary and ask his colleagues if you wish, but you will find that Faricius was a peaceable and studious young man, as I have already told you.'

'As soon as I heard that the Dominicans had taken exception to your proclamation, I sent Beadle Meadowman to tell you to keep all your students indoors until tempers had cooled,' Michael went on. 'So why was Faricius out?'

Lincolne glared at him. 'We have as much right to walk the streets as anyone – but we did comply with your request. I instructed all my students to remain indoors, even though it is Saturday and teaching finishes at noon.'

'Then why did they not obey you?' pressed Michael.

Lincolne seemed surprised. 'But they did obey me. None of them left the premises. It was not easy to keep them in, actually, given that the forty days of Lent have seemed very long this year, and everyone is looking forward to Easter next week. The students are excited and difficult to control.'

'So I gather,' said Michael wryly. 'But you have not answered my question. Faricius was found lying in a doorway on Milne Street. He was clearly *outside* the friary, not inside it. If none of your students left the premises, how did he come to be out?'

Lincolne frowned as he shook his head. 'When your beadle arrived to tell me that we should lock ourselves away when the Dominicans came, I rounded up *all* my students and took them home. Faricius was definitely inside when the front gates were closed. He could not have gone out again without asking me to open them – and he did not.'

'Did he sprout wings and fly over the walls, then?' demanded Michael impatiently. 'I repeat: he was found on Milne Street. Perhaps he did not leave through the front gate, but he was outside nevertheless.'

Lincolne's eyes flashed with anger. 'You are taking a very biased approach to this, Brother. It is not Faricius's actions that are on trial here: it is those of the Dominicans. They killed Faricius. Interrogate them, not me.'

'Oh, I will,' said Michael softly. 'I will certainly get to the bottom of this sorry little tale.'

When Prior Lincolne had completed his prayers over Faricius's body, two Carmelite students arrived to keep vigil. It was nearing dusk, and one had brought thick beeswax candles to light at his friend's head; the other carried perfumed oil to rub into Faricius's hands and feet, and held a clean robe, so that his dead colleague would not go to his grave wearing clothes that were stained with blood. One student was self-righteously outraged that the Dominicans had dared to strike one of their number, and complained vociferously about it to Michael; the second merely twisted the clean robe in his hands and said nothing. Michael homed in on the latter.

'What is your name?' he demanded.

The student-friar jumped nervously. He was about the same age as Faricius, and had a mop of red-brown hair that was worn overly long. A smattering of freckles across the bridge of his nose gave him a curiously adolescent appearance, and his grubby fingers had nails that had been chewed almost to the quick. There was nothing distinctive or unusual about him, and he looked just like any other young man whose family had decided that a career in the Church would provide him with a secure future.

'Simon Lynne,' he replied in a low voice, casting an anxious glance at the other student.

'What can you tell us about Faricius, Simon?' asked Bartholomew, in a kinder tone of voice than Michael had used.

'He was a peace-loving man,' stated the other student hotly. He was a thickset lad who was missing two of his front teeth. 'He would never have started a fight with the Dominicans.'

'We were not talking to you,' said Michael, silencing him with a cool gaze. 'We were speaking to Lynne.'

Lynne swallowed, his eyes flicking anxiously to Faricius's body. 'Horneby is right. Faricius was not a violent man. He came to Cambridge last September, and was only interested in his lessons and his prayers.'

'Do you know why he happened to be out of the friary when your Prior and I expressly instructed that everyone should remain inside?' asked Michael. 'Was he given to breaking orders?'

'No, never. He always did as he was told,' said Lynne.

'Then why was he out?' pressed Michael.

'He was not,' said Lynne unsteadily. 'He remained in the friary to read when the rest of us went with Prior Lincolne to pin that proclamation to the church door. After that, you ordered the gates closed and they did not open again until Prior Lincolne was summoned here.'

Michael was growing impatient. 'But if Faricius had been safely inside, he would not be lying here now, dead. At some point, he left the friary and was attacked. How? Is it possible to scale the walls? Is there a back gate? Are the porters bribable, and willing to open the gates for a price?'

'No,' said Lincolne immediately. 'All our porters are commoners – men who have retired from teaching and live in the friary at our expense. They are not bribable, because they would not risk being ejected from their comfortable posts by breaking our rules.'

'The walls, then?' pressed Michael irritably. 'Did Faricius climb over the walls?'

'Impossible,' said Lincolne. 'They are twice the height of a man and are plastered, so there are no footholds. And anyway, he was not a monkey, Brother.'

Michael sighed in exasperation. 'You are telling me that it was impossible for Faricius to have left your friary – more precisely, you are telling me that he did *not* leave your friary. But he was found in Milne Street at the height of the skirmish with the Dominicans. How do you explain that?'

'It seems we cannot,' said Lincolne, with a shrug that made him appear uncharacteristically helpless. 'You will have to ask the Dominicans.'

'You want me to enquire of the Dominicans how a Carmelite friar escaped from within your own walls without any of you knowing how he did it?' asked Michael incredulously. 'That would certainly provide them with a tale with which to amuse themselves at your expense!'

Lincolne grimaced, uncomfortable with that notion. 'Unpleasant though this may be for us, that is where your answer will lie, Brother.'

Michael closed his eyes, and Bartholomew expected the monk to show a sudden display of temper, to try to frighten the Carmelites into telling him the truth. It was patently obvious that Lynne was hiding something, and that even if he had not actually lied, he had certainly not told the complete truth. Whether Lincolne and Horneby were also lying was unclear, although Bartholomew found he had taken a dislike to the fanatical Prior and his gap-toothed novice for their uncompromising belligerence. Their reaction to Faricius's death seemed more akin to outrage that a crime had been committed against their Order, than grief for a man reputedly scholarly and peaceable.

But Michael had had enough of the Carmelites. He nodded curtly, and left them to the business of laying out their colleague and of saying prayers for him. Bartholomew followed him out of the church, and then stood with him in the grassy churchyard, where the monk took several deep breaths to calm himself. Walcote, who came to report that the Dominicans were all safely locked in their friary, joined them and listened to Michael's terse summary.

'One of their number has been murdered,' said Michael angrily. 'You would think they would be only too happy to co-operate and provide us with the information we need to solve the crime.'

'They probably thought they did, Brother,' said Walcote soothingly.

'They were hiding something,' snapped Michael. 'In the case of Lynne, I have never seen a more uncomfortable liar.'

Bartholomew agreed. 'Lynne was about as furtive a lad as I have ever encountered, but that does not mean to say he was concealing anything to do with Faricius's curious absence from the friary.'

'What do you think?' demanded Michael of his Junior Proctor. 'Why do you think the Carmelites would withhold information from me?'

Walcote shrugged. 'Something to do with this nominalism–realism debate, perhaps. It is possible that they intend to write further proclamations, and do not want the proctors to prevent them from doing so. It is also possible that *Lincolne* is telling the truth, but that Faricius's *classmates* were prevaricating because they do not wish to speak ill of the dead.'

Michael rubbed his chin thoughtfully. 'I suppose Faricius may have broken the rules and slipped out, and Lynne and Horneby do not want their Prior to think badly of him now that he is dead. But I am not convinced. Having spoken to Lynne, I think there is more to Faricius's stabbing than a case of a lone Carmelite being stupid enough to walk into a gang of brawling Dominicans.'

Bartholomew nodded slowly. 'So, we agree that Lynne was lying – although we cannot be sure about Lincolne and Horneby. *Ergo*, there are two possibilities: either Lynne was lying of his own accord and was uncomfortable doing so in the presence of his Prior; or all three constructed some tale between them that Lynne was uneasy in telling.'

'I am tempted to march right back in there and shake the truth out of them,' said Michael testily. 'But that would only convince Lincolne that I am determined to divert blame from the Dominicans. I shall have to catch Lynne alone, and then we shall see how his lies stand up to some serious prodding.'

'Was Faricius really the scholarly man they would have us believe?' mused Bartholomew. 'Or was he just like the rest of them – a lout in a habit spoiling for a fight?'

'He was scholarly, right enough,' said Walcote. 'I told you earlier that he attended lectures and that I admired his thinking.'

'You need to decide whether Faricius really did remain in the friary to read when the others went to watch Lincolne pin his proclamation to the church door, or whether Lynne has just been told to say he did,' said Bartholomew to Michael.

Michael smiled craftily. 'I am glad you seem interested in this crime, Matt. You can help me solve it, as you have done before.'

Bartholomew balked at this. 'No, Brother! I am too busy to spend my time chasing murderers with you. And anyway, that is why you have a Junior Proctor.'

Walcote shook his head. 'The last week of Lent is always busy for us. The students are restless, and we are anticipating more trouble. It will be difficult for us to solve murders *and* keep peace in the town.'

'And you are not busy at all, Matt,' added Michael. 'The first signs of spring have heartened people, so fewer of them are sick; it is coming up to Easter week, so we only teach in the mornings; and your treatise on fevers will never be finished. It is already longer than virtually everything written by Galen and you claim you are only just beginning.'

'And you *did* find the body,' Walcote pointed out.

'I found an injured man,' corrected Bartholomew. 'But I can tell you nothing relevant. I asked who had stabbed him, but he was more concerned with the fact that he had lost his scrip than in telling me who had prematurely ended his life.'

'Was that because he expected to recover?' asked Michael. 'Or because whatever was in his scrip was more important to him than seeing his killer brought to justice?'

'I do not know, Brother. Dying people react in different ways. He may have been delirious. He had certainly swallowed a good deal of the laudanum I give to very ill patients, and that can cause people to say odd or irrelevant things.'

'Pity,' said Walcote. 'If you had learned the name of the killer, you would not now be obliged to help us solve the crime. And I imagine it will take a while, because there are already questions regarding how it could have happened. I have the feeling this will transpire to be more complicated than a simple case of a Black Friar stabbing a White Friar during a riot.'

'I agree,' said Michael. 'I feel it in my bones, and I am seldom wrong about such things.'

Bartholomew looked from Michael to his deputy. 'You two have been in Cambridge too long! You are looking for complex solutions when there is a very simple one staring you in the face. Have you never heard of Occam's razor?'

Walcote said approvingly, 'Occam was a great man – a nominalist, like me.'

'*You* are a nominalist?' asked Michael, startled. 'What has induced you to follow a ridiculous notion like that?'

Walcote swallowed nervously, uncomfortable with Michael's

disapproval. 'It makes sense. It is a good way of looking at the universe.'

'So is realism,' countered Michael.

Walcote immediately backed down in the way Bartholomew noted he always did when faced with serious opposition. It was an aspect of the Junior Proctor's character that Bartholomew thought unappealing and Michael found aggravating. 'I suppose it is. They both are.'

'Actually, to be honest, I do not think one theory has any more to offer than the other,' Michael went on pompously, also noting Walcote's reluctance to stand up for what he believed. 'They are both pathetic, desperate attempts that try to allow us to comprehend a world that was never created to be understood. What we *are* meant to understand is people – the lies they tell and the plots they hatch.'

'As you say, Brother,' said Walcote, chastened.

'But we are not supposed to devise complex solutions to what are simple problems,' said Bartholomew, trying to bring the discussion back to his original point. 'That is the basis of Occam's razor.'

'What has Occam's razor to do with Faricius's death?' asked Michael irritably. He seemed disheartened by Walcote's meekness, and Bartholomew supposed he was questioning yet again the suitability of a man like Walcote to be a proctor.

'It says that the conclusion with the fewest assumptions should always be taken over the one with more,' said Bartholomew. 'The simplest, most parsimonious theory is always the right one. Therefore, I deduce that the Carmelites are lying because Lincolne does not want to appear as though he has no control over his friars. And that is all.'

'Believe what you will, Matt,' said Michael superiorly. 'You will find that you are wrong and we are right. It is too late today, but tomorrow morning you must come with me to the Dominican Friary to see whether you can identify these six student-friars you saw near Faricius before he died.'

'Do you not think it wiser to go now?' suggested Walcote timidly. 'Why wait?'

'Two reasons,' replied Michael. 'First, it is almost dark and friars will be preparing for compline. And second, because I want these Dominicans to reflect on what they have done. It may make them more willing to confess.'

'But what if they take the opportunity to run away from Cambridge?' asked Walcote uneasily. 'You may visit the Dominican Friary tomorrow and find they have fled.'

'I do not think so,' said Michael comfortably. 'The beadles will detain anyone attempting to leave Cambridge under cover of darkness, and to flee is a clear statement of guilt. We will have them either way.'

'If you say so, Brother,' said Walcote unhappily.

The Dominican Friary lay outside the town gates, to the east of the King's Ditch. The Ditch split away from the River Cam near the castle in the north, then it and the river encircled the town like a huge pair of pincers until they met again in the south near the Trumpington Gate. Not only were the waterways clear markers of the town's boundaries, but they provided a certain degree of protection. Few people were inclined to wade or swim across the sluggish, sewage-filled channels, so most traffic entering or leaving Cambridge went through one of its two gates or crossed one of its two bridges.

The oval-shaped area enclosed by the Ditch and the river was full to overflowing with buildings and tofts. This part of the town was little more than half a mile in length, and yet it boasted ten churches, several chapels, three friaries, St John's Hospital and six of the University's eight Colleges. In addition, there were about thirty hostels and halls, and a large number of houses in which the townsfolk lived. Some of these were grand and spacious, like the one that Bartholomew's sister and her husband owned, while others were little more than hovels, clinging to each other in a losing battle against gravity.

When the Dominicans had first arrived in Cambridge in the 1230s, they had decided against wedging themselves into a town that was already bursting at the seams, and had instead purchased a house and land on Hadstock Way. From these humble beginnings, the friary had grown into an assortment of handsome buildings enclosed by a sturdy wall. The wall was necessary partly because rival Orders occasionally physically attacked each other, and partly because the friary's location outside the town rendered it vulnerable to the attentions of outlaws.

Like Michaelhouse, the friary was built of a honey-coloured sandstone that had been specially imported from the quarries at Barnack, near Peterborough. There was a refectory with long tables where the friars ate, with a chamber above that served as their sleeping quarters. Then there was a separate kitchen block with an attic that provided accommodation for the servants, stables, and an elegant chapel and suite of rooms in which the Prior resided. A sizeable portion of the garden had been set aside as a graveyard – which Bartholomew recalled had seen a lot of use during the plague – and nearby were well-tended vegetable plots that provided cabbages, peas and beans to supplement the friars' meals.

It was mid-morning, and the sun was fighting against heavy grey clouds. A few bright rays had penetrated the east window of St Michael's Church that Palm Sunday morning, but by the time Bartholomew and Michael had eaten breakfast, any evidence of the approach of the long-awaited spring had been smothered by clouds that had blown in from the south west.

Normally, Bartholomew would have been resentful that Michael's request to help him solve a murder obliged him to miss teaching duties, but Palm Sunday heralded the beginning of Easter Week, when lectures were only scheduled for the mornings, ostensibly so that the scholars could spend more time in church. Students and masters alike were looking forward to Easter Sunday the following week, when

41

they would celebrate the end of the forty days of Lent with a feast. As Lincolne had noted, all the University's students were restless and fretful, and the masters were finding it increasingly difficult to force them to study or to hold their concentration.

When Bartholomew and Michael reached the Dominican Friary, the first thing they saw was a small group of sullen Carmelite student-friars, eyeing the tall walls resentfully and muttering to each other in low voices.

'And just what do you think you are doing?' demanded Michael, making several of the white-robed novices jump. They exchanged guilty looks.

'Nothing,' said the one with the missing teeth, whom Bartholomew recognised as Horneby. His friend, the freckle-faced Simon Lynne, was just behind him. 'We are just taking the air.'

'Well, you can "just take the air" inside your own friary,' said Michael sharply. 'Be off with you!'

Most of them, Lynne included, immediately began to slink away, but the fiery Horneby held his ground and the others hesitated, wanting to see what would happen.

'It is not fair!' Horneby burst out. 'The Dominicans killed Faricius, and yet nothing has been done about it. You do not care!'

Michael sighed. 'I can assure you that I have thought of little else but Faricius's murder since yesterday, and I care very much that his killer is brought to justice. I have my own reasons for leaving the Dominicans alone until this morning – all my experience and instincts told me that I would stand a better chance of forcing the killer to confess by waiting, not rushing.'

'We do not believe you,' said Lynne, almost tearfully. 'So, it is for us to avenge poor Faricius.'

'It is for you to go home,' said Michael firmly. 'Hurry up, or I shall fine the lot of you for attempting to cause a riot.'

'It is because *he* is a nominalist, like the Dominicans,' said Horneby bitterly to Lynne, casting a resentful glare in

Michael's direction. 'That is why he will do nothing about Faricius's murder—'

'What is nominalism, Horneby?' asked Bartholomew, cutting across Horneby's angry words. 'Explain it to me.'

Horneby gazed at him, and then shot a red-faced glance at his companions. Michael raised his eyebrows and hid a smile.

'What do you mean?' Horneby asked nervously.

'Define nominalism,' repeated Bartholomew. 'It is a perfectly simple request. Or tell me why you follow realism. I do not mind which.'

'Why?' demanded Horneby. 'Will you summon the Devil to refute my arguments?'

'I will refute nothing,' said Bartholomew. 'I will simply listen to what you say.'

He stood with his arms folded and waited. To one side, Michael leaned against the friary wall and watched the scene with amusement glinting in the depths of his green eyes. Horneby cast another agitated glance at his colleagues, hoping one of them would come to his rescue. None did.

'It is about whether things do or do not exist,' he stammered eventually. 'Some things do exist, and some things do not.'

'I see,' said Bartholomew. 'Can you be more specific?'

'No,' said Horneby. 'I do not choose to be specific.'

'I fail to see why everyone seems to have taken sides in a debate that so few people understand,' said Bartholomew, shaking his head in genuine mystification. 'You are prepared to lurk outside a friary filled with hostile Dominicans over something you cannot even define.'

'Prior Lincolne says that nominalism is heresy,' said Horneby sullenly.

'Lincolne is one of realism's most vocal proponents,' agreed Bartholomew. 'Everyone knows his feelings on the matter. But I do not understand why *you* have also embraced the philosophy. Is it just because he tells you to?'

Hornby glowered at him. 'God is on the side of the just,' he declared hotly. 'Numbers are irrelevant.'

'They are not,' Bartholomew pointed out practically. 'If the Dominicans decided to come out now, you would find yourselves outnumbered at least five to one. Go home, Hornby, and take your friends with you. This is no place for you.'

Michael watched approvingly as the White Friars began to walk away. An unpleasant incident had been averted, although he sensed that his friend's point was as lost on the Carmelites as it would have been on the Dominicans. As Bartholomew had explained to his sister the previous day, the debate itself was not important – it was simply an excuse for a fight.

'We should make sure they do not come back,' Michael said, beginning to follow them. 'They were unable to answer your arguments, but that will not stop them attacking any Dominicans they meet.'

But the Carmelites were aware of the stern eyes of the Senior Proctor behind, and they returned to their friary without further incident. Michael looked grim as he watched the door close, then turned to walk back to the Dominican Friary. As they made their way along the High Street, Bartholomew spotted his sister. Her cloak was damp and tendrils of dark hair escaped from what had probably been a neat plait earlier that morning. She seemed breathless and rather bemused.

'I have just ridden from Trumpington,' she explained, referring to the small village two miles to the south of Cambridge where her husband owned a manor. 'Richard accompanied me.'

'From your windswept appearance, I take it that he did so at a rather more brisk pace than you are used to,' said Michael, amused.

Edith nodded. 'It was a compromise. He wanted to ride like the wind, I wanted to walk. We settled on a brisk trot, which suited neither of us. Next time, I will ask someone else to escort me.'

'And how is Richard?' asked Michael. 'I have not seen him since his triumphant return to Cambridge with his new law degree.'

'He is well,' replied Edith, 'although I do not approve of that ear-ring he has taken to wearing. It makes him look like a courtier.'

'Perhaps that is the idea,' said Michael. 'I imagine most of our students would dearly love to sport gold bangles dangling from their lobes, but, fortunately, the University forbids such displays of fashion. It is a pity in a way: they would certainly provide a convenient handhold when their owners are arrested.'

Bartholomew winced at the idea. 'Why are you in town today?' he asked Edith. 'And how did you manage to prise Richard from his bed before noon?'

She smiled. 'I have come to collect butter for our dinner tomorrow celebrating Richard's return. You are still coming, I hope, Matt? He will be disappointed if you do not.'

'Of course I am coming,' said Bartholomew, looking away, so that she would not be able to read in his face that he had forgotten all about her invitation. 'What time did you say?'

'Evening,' said Edith. 'But before sunset. You do not need me to tell you that outlaws make the roads unsafe for a lone man at night.'

'What are you having to eat?' asked Michael keenly, in a brazen attempt to inveigle an invitation. The students were not alone in becoming bored with the endless Lenten fare of bean stews and stale bread, and the monk knew that Edith would prepare something special in honour of her beloved only son. 'Fish? Lombard slices?'

'River trout stuffed with almonds, raisin bread, and I have been baking pastries most of this week,' she replied, a little unsettled by the monk's intense interest. 'Meat is still forbidden, of course, but fish can be made interesting with a little imagination.'

'It certainly can,' agreed Michael vehemently. 'What kind of pastries?'

'There are your Benedictine friends,' said Bartholomew, uncomfortable that Michael was quizzing his sister about what was supposed to be a family occasion. 'Janius and Timothy.'

'I will see you tomorrow,' said Edith to Bartholomew. She nodded to the two Benedictines as they approached, and then was gone, carrying Michael's hopes for a good meal with her.

Timothy and Janius greeted Michael warmly, and Janius sketched a benediction at him. Both carried large baskets and said they had been distributing bread to the town's poor.

'Have you found your killer yet?' asked Timothy. 'The scholarly Faricius did not deserve to die in such a manner.'

'It is not pleasant to think of a killer walking the streets of our town,' agreed Janius. 'I hope it will not be long before he is apprehended.'

'So do I,' said Michael. 'Matt and I are going to the Dominican Friary now, to see whether he can identify the students who were near Faricius yesterday afternoon.'

'Can we do anything?' offered Janius. 'We remembered Faricius in our prayers, of course, but if we can do anything else, you must let us know.'

'I tried to help yesterday,' said Timothy, sounding uncomfortable at mentioning something that might sound boastful. 'Because I was keen to do all I could to avert bloodshed, I accompanied Beadle Meadowman to the Carmelite Friary to ensure that Prior Lincolne would admit him – I was afraid a beadle would not be granted an audience with an important man like a Prior.'

'I would fine any friary that denied access to my beadles,' said Michael. 'But thank you. I suppose the Carmelites could have declined to open the door.'

'Fortunately, Lincolne was wiser than that,' said Timothy. 'I heard Meadowman deliver your order that all Carmelites were to remain within their friary until further notice, and then returned to my own hall as quickly as I could. I did not want to add to your troubles by providing a lone

Benedictine for the Dominicans to vent their ire upon.'

'Actually, the Dominicans and the Benedictines have a truce at the moment,' said Janius. 'We both accept nominalism as a basic truth. But I do not think most students really care about the realism–nominalism debate. It is just a convenient excuse for a good fight.'

'That is certainly true,' said Michael. 'But I will have these six Dominicans under lock and key today, if I think they are responsible for Faricius's death.'

'Good,' said Janius. 'We will pray that justice is done. Now, in fact.'

He crossed himself vigorously and his blue eyes lit with pleasure as he sensed a cause that was worthy of his religious attentions. He bade farewell to Michael, and began to stride towards the Church of St Andrew that stood just outside the Barnwell Gate. Timothy followed him, his head already bowed as he began his own pious meditations.

'They are good men,' said Michael warmly, watching them go. 'And there are not many of those around these days.'

chapter 2

ON THEIR WAY BACK TO THE DOMINICAN FRIARY, Bartholomew and Michael met Walcote, who offered to accompany them with a pack of beadles, in case the Dominicans took exception to the Senior Proctor arresting some of their number. With Walcote and the men at his heels, Michael strode up to the friary gate and hammered on it. It was answered almost immediately by a strange-looking man, whose hair stood in an uncertain halo around his tonsure and who had a wild look in his eyes.

'Clippesby,' said Michael in surprise. 'What are you doing here? I thought you were at Michaelhouse, overseeing the polishing of our silver in preparation for Easter.'

'I finished that,' said Clippesby shyly. 'Then I offered to help the cooks shred the cabbage, but they were afraid I might cut myself, so I went for a walk instead.'

Then the cooks had been very tactful, thought Bartholomew, hiding a smile. It was well known in the town that the Dominican John Clippesby, Michaelhouse's master of music and astronomy, was not entirely in control of his faculties, and that he was always being given time-consuming and usually pointless tasks to keep him out of harm's way. The cooks would certainly not want him in the kitchen with a sharp knife in his hands.

'But what are you doing *here*?' pressed Michael, suspecting that Clippesby had somehow slipped past the porters, and that the Master of Michaelhouse did not know he was at large.

'I heard there was trouble between my Order and the Carmelites, so I thought I should come to see what was happening,' replied Clippesby. 'But I was just leaving, actually. For some reason, Prior Morden said he did not want me here, and suggested that I should go home.'

'I bet he did,' muttered Michael, who had been trying for some time, without success, to foist the unstable Dominican back on his own friary and out of Michaelhouse. Morden was no fool, however, and had no more wish to have a madman imposed on him than Michaelhouse had been.

'All the Dominicans are inside,' Clippesby went on. 'Prior Morden says that it is too dangerous for anyone to be out, although he said *I* would be safe, because I am a Michaelhouse man and do not live in the friary.'

Bartholomew felt a surge of anger against Morden. The Prior knew perfectly well that marauding Carmelites would not ask a man wearing the habit of a Dominican whether he lived at the friary or whether he was a member of a College. It would be irrelevant anyway: the Carmelites' antagonism was not aimed at the friary in particular, it was aimed at the Dominicans in general. Clippesby would have provided an ideal target for the little group of sullen Carmelites Bartholomew and Michael had just followed home.

'Wait here,' said Bartholomew, reluctant for Clippesby to be alone. 'We will walk to Michaelhouse with you after we have spoken to Morden.'

'I will be all right,' said Clippesby, beginning to move away from them. 'Saint Balthere appeared to me this morning and instructed me to pray for him in St Michael's Church. He would not have done that if any harm was due to befall me, would he?'

'Saint who?' asked Michael warily.

'That does not necessarily follow,' said Bartholomew, worried that the Dominican's unstable condition might be taking a turn for the worse. 'Wait here until we have spoken to Morden.'

But Clippesby was already wandering away down the road, and Bartholomew had glimpsed the distant look in his eyes that always appeared when the voices inside his head began to claim his attention. In the physician's opinion, the conversations seemed to be heavily one-sided, with Clippesby doing most of the talking. How the saints managed to make him shut up long enough to pass any kind of message to him was entirely beyond Bartholomew's understanding.

'He will come to no harm,' said Walcote reassuringly, seeing Bartholomew's concern. 'Everyone knows he is touched, and so will leave him alone. If the truth be known, I think he frightens people. They do not understand the things he says and does, and they are afraid of him.'

'They have good reason to be,' announced Michael. 'I am afraid of him myself.'

Still glancing uneasily behind him at Clippesby, who sauntered along Hadstock Way as if he had not a care in the world, Bartholomew followed Michael and Walcote across the Dominicans' courtyard to the Prior's lodging. They were hurriedly intercepted by a man with heavy brow-ridge, like an ape, who introduced himself as Thomas Ringstead, the Prior's secretary. He instructed them to wait until Prior Morden had been informed that he had visitors – something that invariably annoyed Michael, who liked to burst in on people unawares to see if he could catch them doing something he could use to his advantage.

After a chilly wait in the courtyard, where a sharp wind blew dead leaves from the previous autumn around in desolate little eddies, Ringstead came to tell them the great man was ready. Michael elbowed him aside and made his way to the Prior's comfortable office on the first floor, pushing open the door so hard that it flew back and crashed against the wall. The tiny man who sat writing at a table near the window almost jumped out of his skin.

'I wish you would not do that, Brother,' he complained in a high-pitched voice, almost like a child's. 'You do it every time you visit, and I keep telling you that the hinges are delicate.'

Ringstead inspected the wall behind the door, and clucked

softly at the plaster flakes that lay on the floor. Judging from the small cracks that radiated from a circular indentation at the level of the latch, either Michael had visited Prior Morden with some frequency, or the fat monk was not the only one who liked to enter the solar with a bang.

'Very sorry,' said Michael, not sounding in the least contrite as he strode across the room and placed himself in front of a blazing fire, depriving everyone else of the heat by blocking it with his bulk.

Prior Morden sighed irritably and put down his pen. If Lincolne of the Carmelites was a giant, then Morden of the Dominicans was an elf. His head did not reach Bartholomew's shoulder, and the physician noticed that when the Prior sat in the chair his feet did not touch the floor. He was dressed in an immaculate habit of fine black wool, and a delicate silver cross hung around his neck.

'I expected you yesterday,' said Morden, picking up a sheaf of parchments and shuffling them fussily. 'I heard what happened with that Carmelite, and I suspected you would come to try to blame his death on us Dominicans.'

'I am here to discover who killed Faricius of Abington, not to blame the innocent,' said Michael tartly. 'Do you have any idea what happened yesterday?'

'What happened is that the Carmelites challenged my student-friars to a fight, but then ran away like cowards to skulk within their walls when we responded,' stated the little man uncompromisingly.

'I see,' said Michael. 'The gathering of Dominicans in Milne Street, who threw stones – not only at the Carmelite Friary but at the houses of the merchants who live nearby – was the Carmelites' responsibility, was it?'

'Essentially,' said Morden, unruffled by Michael's sarcasm. 'Prior Lincolne wrote a proclamation saying that anyone who followed the theory of nominalism should be burned in the Market Square for heresy, and then had the audacity to pin it up at St Mary's Church. But it is the realists who should be burned for heresy!'

51

Michael cast a weary glance at Walcote and Bartholomew, and then turned to Morden. 'Has the whole University gone mad? I can accept that one or two misguided individuals feel that the known universe revolves around the realism–nominalism debate, but I am astonished that so many apparently sane people deem this issue so important.'

'Lincolne's act was a deliberate insult to us,' Morden went on. 'You see, our Precentor, Henry de Kyrkeby, is due to give the University Lecture in St Mary's Church on Easter Sunday, and his chosen subject is nominalism. Lincolne's proclamation was calculated to offend us specifically.'

'Kyrkeby?' asked Bartholomew in surprise. '*He* is lecturing?'

'Yes, why?' demanded Morden aggressively. 'Do you think him incapable of speaking at the University's most prestigious annual academic event?'

'Well, yes, actually,' said Bartholomew bluntly. 'He is a patient of mine, and for the last several months his heart has been beating irregularly. I recommended he should avoid anything that would make him nervous or tense.'

'It was a great honour when a Dominican was invited to speak at such an auspicious occasion,' said Morden indignantly. 'Of course he did not refuse the Chancellor's invitation.'

'He mentioned none of this to me,' said Bartholomew thoughtfully. 'No wonder he has visited me three times this week. It is apprehension that is making him ill.'

'I imagine he did not tell you because he knew you would advise against it,' said Walcote practically. 'Foolish man, to put pride above his health.'

'He has been working very hard on what he plans to say,' said Morden. 'For weeks, he has thought of little else.'

'Then I imagine it will be an entertaining occasion,' said Michael, bored with a conversation that had nothing to do with Faricius's murder. 'But I did not come here to talk about—'

'I only hope it will not be entertaining in a way that will

52

'prove detrimental to the friary,' interrupted Morden, pursing his lips worriedly. 'He read me parts of his lecture last week, and I confess I have heard stronger and more erudite arguments.'

'He has changed it since then, Father Prior,' said Ringstead reassuringly. 'I was very impressed with what he read me last night. Do not worry. Our Precentor will do us justice.'

'Are you sure?' asked Morden anxiously.

Ringstead nodded. 'The lecture is now a very mature and astute piece of thinking. Even the Carmelites will be stunned into silence with the eloquence and perceptiveness of his logic.'

'That assumes they are able to appreciate it – and I have seen no evidence that they can,' muttered Michael. He spoke a little more loudly. 'But whatever philosophical views are held on this subject, Prior Morden, it is no excuse for riotous behaviour – for Dominicans or Carmelites.'

'You do not understand the importance of this issue,' said Morden vehemently. 'Your Benedictine colleagues at Ely Hall do, though – they have ranged themselves on the side of nominalism. Brothers Timothy and Janius are shining examples.'

Michael gave a fervent sigh. 'I know that some scholars have strong views on the matter, but I do not think most of us care one way or the other.'

'That is not true,' objected Morden hotly. '*I* care very much.'

'And so does Lincolne,' said Michael thoughtfully. 'But do you care because you are a committed nominalist, or because you have a natural inclination to oppose anything upheld by the Carmelites? Everyone knows the two Orders have always despised each other.'

'Lincolne is a loathsome man,' declared Morden, indicating that the long-standing enmity between the two Orders was doubtless the real cause of the Dominicans' sudden interest in philosophy. 'But nominalism is a much more rational theory than realism. However, you are wrong to think that no one cares. Many people feel very strongly about this issue.'

'That is true,' said Bartholomew in a low voice to Michael and Walcote. 'This debate has provided the Orders with an excuse to re-address ancient grievances. You will find that most clerics have taken this debate very much to heart, and you will also find that they are doggedly aligning themselves on whichever side of the discussion their Order has deemed correct. There seems to be no room for individual thought on *this* matter.'

'Like sheep,' muttered Michael in disgust.

'Not entirely,' offered Walcote timidly. 'Many highly intelligent men have taken up this argument – and it is not purely the domain of louts spoiling for a street battle.'

'That is not how it appears,' said Michael. 'But this is not a new debate – it originated with Aristotle and Plato. Why should the two sides suddenly resort to violence over it?'

'That riot yesterday was not our fault,' stated Morden, breaking into the muttered conversation. 'What started it was the proclamation Lincolne wrote. It is *his* action that precipitated the incident in Milne Street.'

'I see,' pounced Michael. 'An "incident in Milne Street" is how you would describe the murder of a Carmelite, is it?'

'Dominicans are not the only ones who dislike the Carmelites,' retorted Morden. 'The Austin canons loathe them just as much – not to mention the Benedictines.' He gave Michael's own dark robe a meaningful glance and then looked at Walcote's Austin habit.

'It was not Benedictines or Austins that my colleague saw closing in on Faricius with malice in their eyes,' said Michael sharply. 'It was Dominicans. Even he can tell the difference.'

'Yes,' muttered Morden nastily. 'The Benedictines can barely rouse themselves from the dining table.'

Michael ignored the jibe. 'Matt saw six Dominicans advancing on Faricius intending mischief. I would like a word with them, if you please. And you need not concern yourself about their likely reluctance to give themselves up: he can identify them.'

Morden treated Bartholomew, and then Michael, to unpleasant looks. 'I am sure they meant Faricius no harm. Have you considered the possibility that they were trying to help him? Did you actually *see* them stab him?'

Bartholomew shook his head. 'But they are the ones who should be answering these questions, not me. Will you send for them or would you rather I picked them out?'

Morden's glower deepened. 'Everyone is in the refectory at the moment, eating breakfast as they listen in reverent silence to the readings of the Bible Scholar. Come.'

'Breakfast?' echoed Michael in astonishment. 'But it is almost noon!'

'The lateness of the meal would not have anything to do with that misguided group of Carmelites who were lingering outside your walls, would it?' asked Walcote with raised eyebrows. 'Were you preparing to do battle with them?'

'What Carmelites?' asked Morden with an air of assumed innocence that was patently false. 'Were there Carmelites outside our walls this morning? I did not notice.'

'It is just as well we moved them on,' said Michael to Bartholomew, not fooled for an instant by Morden. 'The last thing we want is a revenge killing. But let us go to see these students, eating their breakfast in the middle of the day.'

Bartholomew, Michael and Walcote followed Prior Morden down the stairs and across the yard to the largest of the buildings in the Dominican Friary. The door to the refectory was closed, but even so, Bartholomew could hear that the sounds emanating from within had nothing to do with the Bible Scholar. Morden gave an irritable frown before throwing open the door and stepping inside. Bartholomew ducked instinctively as a piece of bread whistled past his ear, although Michael was slower and received a boiled leek in the chest.

Morden gaped in horror for a few moments, before striding to the nearest table, snatching up a pewter cup and banging it against the wall. The din gradually faded to silence, and the student-friars, who had been standing to hurl their edible missiles, quickly took their places on the benches that ran the length of the room. Some had the grace to appear shamefaced as their Prior ran admonishing eyes over their ranks, but many made no secret of their amusement at having been caught.

'Where is Kyrkeby?' Morden demanded. 'He is supposed to be overseeing your meals today.'

'He is not here,' replied one of the student-friars, a smooth-faced, arrogant youth who Bartholomew immediately recognised as one of the mob that had been near Faricius.

Morden sighed. 'I can see that, Bulmer. But where is he?'

'We do not know,' answered another student. A green smear on the front of his habit and crumbs in his hair indicated that he had been in the thick of the mischief. 'Probably working on his lecture. He does little else these days.'

Bulmer walked to the door and then turned, pointing across the courtyard to a room on the far side. The distinctive bristle-head of Kyrkeby could be seen in the window, bent over a book. 'Yes, there he is. Working on his lecture, as usual.'

Morden glowered at the assembled students. 'I would have hoped that you would not require a nursemaid, and that you could be trusted to behave yourselves in a manner suited to men who have chosen to become friars. But I can see my faith in you was misplaced.'

'It certainly was,' mumbled Michael to Bartholomew, gazing around him in disdain. 'I have never seen such a deplorable spectacle among men of the cloth.'

Although a food fight was not something usually associated with friaries, the physician was aware that most of the religious community in Cambridge comprised young men – some only fifteen or sixteen – who had been sent to acquire

56

an education of sorts before they were dispatched to parishes all across the country. Young men in large groups, even clerics, would inevitably display some degree of high spirits, and the scene in the refectory had been exactly that. Still, he thought, hardening his heart, six of the faces that were turned towards their Prior had been responsible for more than a bit of horseplay involving a few vegetables.

'The proctors want to speak to those of you who were present when the Carmelite was killed yesterday,' announced Morden in his childish voice. 'I have been telling them that you are law-abiding men, but now I wonder whether I was wrong.'

'You are not wrong, Father,' said Bulmer. 'I was there, although I swear before God that we did not harm him.'

He met Michael's eyes steadily, and Bartholomew could not decide whether the young man's confidence was convincing bluster or genuine truthfulness.

'Thank you, Bulmer,' said Morden. 'And who was with you?'

Five others stood. Bartholomew recognised them all.

'What Bulmer says is true,' said a pink-faced boy with tightly curled fair hair. 'We admit we went to the Carmelite Friary after Horneby and Simon Lynne taunted us about the fact that Lincolne had written that proclamation and pinned it on the church door for all to see, but all the White Friars had fled inside their walls long before we could reach them.'

'And what about Faricius?' asked Michael coolly. 'He had not fled inside.'

Bulmer and his cronies exchanged a nervous glance. 'We were on our way home, when we saw a Carmelite lying in a doorway, so we went to see what he was doing. We saw he had blood on the front of his habit.'

'Because you had stabbed him,' said Michael flatly.

'No!' objected Bulmer. 'He was already bleeding when we found him. We were edging closer, to see what had happened, when your colleague arrived and took him away.

I am surprised you say he is dead – I did not know he was so seriously wounded.'

'Someone had driven a knife into his stomach,' said Bartholomew. 'He died from loss of blood about an hour later.'

'Well, it was nothing to do with us,' said Bulmer firmly. 'I admit that the sight of a white habit lying in front of us was a tempting target, but you drove us off with those horrible birthing forceps before we could even touch him.'

'If we had known he was badly hurt, we would have summoned help,' claimed the fair-haired student. 'But we only saw a White Friar lying in the doorway with blood on him. For all we knew, the blood might not even have been his.'

'Do not lie!' exclaimed Bartholomew in disbelief. 'The poor man was trying to hold his innards in. It was patently obvious the blood was his. And you can say what you like, but you were going to finish him off. You said as much when you tried to prevent me from carrying him away.'

'Those were words spoken in the heat of the moment,' said Bulmer defensively. 'We let you go, did we not? There were six of us, and had we really meant trouble, then you would not have left with him.'

Bartholomew wondered if that were true. He was not one of Cambridge's most skilled fighters, birthing forceps or no, and suspected that the six Dominicans had carried weapons that would have been much more efficient than a heavy lump of metal.

'It seems you must look elsewhere for your killer, Brother,' said Morden smugly. 'You heard these students: Faricius was already wounded when they found him. Perhaps they did mean to harm him when they saw his white habit, but they still allowed Bartholomew to carry him away. The Dominicans are not responsible for this crime.'

'Lord!' muttered Michael as he looked from the gloating features of the diminutive Prior to the calm gazes of the six student-friars who were protesting their innocence. 'What a mess! I do not know whom to believe.'

'Well, I do not believe any of them,' said Bartholomew firmly. 'I know what I saw.'

'You are right,' agreed Michael. 'So we will arrest the whole lot of them and talk about this in the proctors' cells – that should make them reconsider their stories and their lies and the threats they made to you.'

'You should take a horse, Matt,' said Michael, watching critically as Bartholomew prepared to visit his sister in her husband's country manor the following evening.

Bartholomew grabbed his warmest winter cloak and swung it around his shoulders. The pale spring sun that had cheered the town at dawn had long since slipped behind a bank of dense clouds, and a bitter wind had picked up. Now, as evening fell, it promised to be a miserable night, with wind and rain in the offing. Bartholomew did not feel like going out, but he had promised his sister he would be there. He would have gone earlier, but had been obliged to spend most of the afternoon tending the Dominican Precentor, Kyrkeby, whose frail heart and imminent lecture were making him breathless and feverish. Normally, Kyrkeby was a compliant and grateful patient, but that day he was agitated and moody, oscillating between angry defiance of the Carmelites and frightened tearfulness when he talked about the lecture that loomed on his horizon.

'I am pleased you plan to sleep at Trumpington tonight and not return here,' Michael continued, when the physician did not reply. 'But you should not walk there alone at this time of the day. You would be wise to take someone with you.'

'Cynric has promised to escort his wife to the vigil in St Mary's Church tonight,' said Bartholomew, referring to his faithful book-bearer. 'I cannot ask him to come with me.'

'Ask me, then,' offered Michael generously. 'Years of wrestling with recalcitrant undergraduates have honed my fighting skills, so that I am more than a match for most would-be robbers. I can protect you almost as well as Cynric.'

'But you have a murder to investigate,' Bartholomew pointed out. 'And anyway, I imagine you are also expected to take part in a vigil tonight. You are a monk after all, and Easter Week is an important time for clerics.'

'The Benedictines at Ely Hall plan to keep vigil in St Botolph's Church,' replied Michael, slightly disapproving. 'But so do the Carmelites, and I do not want to spend an entire night yelling at the top of my lungs in a futile attempt to make the prayers of a few Benedictines heard over four dozen bawling White Friars.'

'If the Orders confined their rivalries to who can shout the loudest prayers, Cambridge would be a nicer place in which to live,' said Bartholomew fervently. 'Then I would have been treating Faricius for a sore throat, rather than a fatal stab wound.'

'And I would not be thinking about how to solve the mystery surrounding his death: a man whose Prior swears he did not leave the friary and whose apparent killers claim he was already stabbed when they found him.'

'I suppose the Dominicans could be telling the truth,' said Bartholomew uncertainly. 'I did not actually *see* them stab him. But they certainly intended mischief when I caught them: they were advancing on him with undisguised menace as he lay helpless, and I am sure they planned to make a quick end of him.'

Michael agreed. 'Those student-friars we met yesterday – Horneby, Lynne and Bulmer – are the kind of men who turn small disputes between the Orders into violence. They are the younger sons of minor noblemen, who have been dispatched to the religious Orders to make their own fortunes in the world because they cannot expect an inheritance.'

'Like you?' asked Bartholomew, aware of Michael's own noble connections.

Michael regarded him coolly. 'In a sense, although I would hardly describe my family as minor. They are a powerful force in Norfolk. But lads like Horneby, Lynne and Bulmer are sent to Cambridge to form alliances with other men destined for high posts in the Church—'

'Not to study and receive an education?' interrupted Bartholomew. 'This is a University, Brother. It is a place of learning, not somewhere to develop business connections.'

'Do not be ridiculous, Matt,' said Michael dismissively. 'Many of these friars only stay for a term or two. How much learning do you imagine they absorb in that time?'

Bartholomew sighed heavily. 'Not all scholars are ambitious power-mongers, here only to further their careers.'

'No,' admitted Michael, after a moment of thought. 'There are exceptions, and you are one of them. The Benedictines at Ely Hall are also a sober group of men.'

'And there are others,' persisted Bartholomew. 'In our own College, Master Kenyngham is devoted to his teaching, and even Father William never misses a lecture.'

'But things are different in the friaries, Matt. The Orders are legally obliged to send one in ten of their number to Oxford or Cambridge, and the men who come are not necessarily endowed with a desire to learn. They see their time here as an opportunity to escape the rigours of living as priests, and to engage in the kind of fighting that most young men love. And that is what they are – young men – for all their habits and their cowls.'

'They certainly behaved like undisciplined louts two days ago,' said Bartholomew, thinking of the six Dominicans clustered around the injured Faricius, and of their sneering threats when he had driven them off.

Michael seemed to read his thoughts. 'I mean no disrespect, Matt, but had Bulmer and his cronies genuinely intended to kill Faricius, you would not have been able to stop them. If Cynric had been there, it would have been a different matter, but you were alone. And there is another thing that worries me, too.'

'What?'

'They all readily identified themselves. Murder is a serious offence: would they have leapt to their feet so willingly if they really had killed Faricius?'

'They knew I would identify them anyway,' said Bartholomew doubtfully. 'It would have done them no good to deny it.'

'They did not know that for certain. And if all had denied encountering you, it would have been the word of six friars against a lone physician, who had half his attention on a patient who was bleeding to death.'

'Then do you think they are telling the truth: that they saw a wounded enemy and did not know he was so seriously injured?'

Michael shook his head slowly. 'I do not know. Perhaps one of the six struck the fatal blow, and the others merely saw a wounded Carmelite. Then, when you came along, they decided that it was not worth a battering from your forceps and they let you both go.'

'So, how will you discover which of them was responsible?' asked Bartholomew. 'Will you interview them all separately?'

'Already done,' replied Michael. 'Walcote and I had them in the proctors' cells yesterday and today. They all said the same thing: they admitted that they were out looking for trouble, but maintained that when they found Faricius he was already bleeding. You did not actually see them stab him, and so there is insufficient evidence to charge them with his murder. I was forced to release them.'

'Then what do you think happened? Do you think one of Faricius's own Order harmed him?' asked Bartholomew, thinking about the peculiar story spun by Lincolne and his students that Faricius could not have left the friary.

Michael scratched his chin, fingernails rasping on two days' growth of bristles. 'It is odd. On the one hand, we have Prior and friends certain that an exit from the friary was impossible and that Faricius was inside; on the other we have the very real evidence of his corpse outside it. I cannot decide what the truth is.'

'Either they really believe what they say is true – even though it clearly is not – or they want to hide the real truth and have decided to do it by confusing you.'

'Well, it is working,' said Michael irritably. 'I *am* confused.'

'So, what will you do? Where will you start?'

Michael sighed. 'I can do no more to solve Faricius's murder today. I worked hard questioning those Dominicans and I am tired. I feel like doing something pleasant this evening – and I do not mean sitting in a freezing conclave with Michaelhouse's eccentric collection of Fellows after an inadequate meal.'

'Lent is almost over,' said Bartholomew, knowing that the miserable food was the real cause of the monk's discontent. Michael was usually perfectly happy to relax in the company of his colleagues, despite their peculiarities.

'And not a moment too soon,' said Michael bitterly. 'Lent is a miserable time of year. No meat to be had; church services held at ungodly hours; gloomy music sung at masses; everyone talking about abstention and fasting and other such nonsense.' He watched the physician swing the medicine bag he always carried over his shoulder as he prepared to leave. 'Going out alone when you have an offer of company is madness, Matt. Let me escort you to Trumpington.'

'I do not need an escort,' said Bartholomew. 'I walk to Trumpington quite regularly, and you have never expressed any concern before.'

Michael gave a long-suffering sigh. 'You are being remarkably insensitive, Matt. Edith told us what she planned to cook tonight, to celebrate Richard's return to Cambridge. However, the offerings at Michaelhouse are more of that revolting fish-giblet stew and bread I saw Agatha sawing the green bits from this morning. If you were any kind of friend, you would see my predicament and invite me to dine with Edith.'

'I wondered what was behind all this uncharacteristic concern for my safety. It is not my well-being that preoccupies you: it is Edith's trout with almonds, raisin bread and pastries.'

'You have convinced me to come,' said Michael, reaching for his cloak. 'I took the precaution of hiring a couple of horses yesterday. We will ride. It will leave more time for eating.'

'And what do you think Edith will say when she sees you have invited yourself to her family reunion?' asked Bartholomew, sure that his sister would not be pleased to see Michael on her doorstep determined to make short work of her cooking.

Michael gave a smug grin. 'She will thank me for my devotion to you – for accompanying the brother she adores along a dangerous road so that he can spend an evening in her company. And anyway, I want to meet your nephew again. It is five years since last I saw him.'

'He has changed,' said Bartholomew, walking with the monk across the courtyard to where Walter, the surly porter, was holding the reins of the two horses Michael had hired. 'He abandoned medicine to study law and it has made him pompous and arrogant. Perhaps he has just spent too much time with lawyers.'

'Or perhaps he has just spent too much time with that band of mongrels at Oxford who call themselves scholars,' said Michael with an unpleasant snigger.

'Brother Michael!' exclaimed Oswald Stanmore, as the Benedictine and Bartholomew walked into his manor house at the small village of Trumpington. 'What are you doing here?' His eyes narrowed in sudden suspicion. 'You have not come about the murder of that Carmelite, have you? Matt was wrong to have brought him to my property.'

Edith sighed crossly. 'Really, Oswald! What was Matt supposed to do? He could hardly carry Faricius all the way back to Michaelhouse.'

'But by taking him to my house, he endangered the lives of you and my apprentices,' said Stanmore sternly. 'It was a thoughtless thing to do.'

'I am sorry, Oswald,' began Bartholomew, knowing the merchant had a point. 'I did not—'

Edith raised a hand to silence him. 'Matt was right to do what he did, Oswald, and any decent man would have done the same. Those louts murdered a priest right outside our door. Would you rather he turned a blind eye to such an outrage?'

'From what I hear, the killers were priests, too,' retorted Stanmore. 'And so I imagine that turning a blind eye would have been a very prudent thing to do. But prudence is not something that runs in your side of the family, it seems. Thank God Richard does not take after you two.'

'No one could ever accuse me of imprudence,' said Richard lazily from his position in the best chair in the house – a cushion-filled seat that was placed so close to the fire that Bartholomew was surprised his nephew did not singe himself.

Bartholomew saw Michael regard Richard with interest. Richard had indeed changed from the gangling seventeen-year-old who had marched away to Oxford University some five years before with dreams of studying medicine. He possessed the same unruly black curls and dark eyes as Bartholomew, and had grown tall. But there the likeness ended. Richard's face was plumper than it should have been for a man of his age, and there were bulges above his hips that testified to too much good living. His hands were pale and soft, as though he scorned any sort of activity that would harden them, and there was a decadent air about him that certainly had not been there when he had lived in Cambridge.

His clothes presented a stark contrast to those of his uncle, too. Whereas the physician's shirt and tabard were frayed and patched, Richard's were new and the height of fashion. He wore blue hose made from the finest wool, a white shirt of crisp linen, and a red jerkin with flowing sleeves that were delicately embroidered with silver thread. On his feet were red shoes with the ridiculously impractical curling toes that were currently popular at the King's court, and in his ear was the gold ear-ring to which Edith had taken such exception. His beard was in the peculiar style that covered the chin and upper lip, but left the sides of the face clean shaven, and was so heavily impregnated with scented oil that Bartholomew could smell it from the door. The physician resisted the urge to comment on it.

'Well,' said Michael, wrinkling his nose and smothering a sneeze. 'You are not the awkward youth I remember from the black days of the plague.'

'And you are not the slender monk I once knew, either,' retorted Richard promptly, his insolent eyes taking in Michael's considerable bulk.

Bartholomew raised his eyebrows. 'If you recall a slender monk, Richard, then your memory is not all it should be. Michael has never been slender.'

'When I was a child, I was so thin that my mother was convinced I was heading for an early grave,' said Michael. 'She took me to see a physician, who bled me and dosed me with all manner of vile potions. I have spent the rest of my life ensuring that I never warrant such treatment again.'

'Most physicians are charlatans,' agreed Richard, throwing Bartholomew a challenging stare. 'They claim they can cure you, but their powdered earthworms and their lead powder and their paste of sparrows' brains no more heal the sick than do the expensive horoscopes they insist on working out.'

'You are right,' said Bartholomew, wondering why his nephew was trying to goad him into an argument when it would only spoil Edith's evening. 'I have long believed that horoscopes make no difference to a patient's health. However, I have also learned that a patient's state of mind is important to his recovery – if he believes a horoscope will provide a more effective cure, then he is more likely to get well if I use one.'

Richard yawned and reached out to take some nuts from a bowl that had been placed near him. 'If you say so.' He lost interest in his uncle and turned his languorous gaze on Michael. 'But what brings you to Trumpington on this cold and windy night, Brother? It would not be the fish-giblet stew that Agatha is simmering at Michaelhouse, would it?'

Michael regarded him coolly, and if he were surprised that Richard had guessed the real reason for his visit he did not show it. 'The Trumpington road is haunted by outlaws. I merely wanted to ensure that your uncle arrived safely.'

'So, will you be returning to Cambridge now?' asked Richard with feigned innocence. 'You have discharged your duty and he is here in one piece.'

'I thought I might stay a while – at least until the rain stops,' said Michael, smiling comfortably. Bartholomew knew that Michael allowed very little between him and a good meal, and it would take far more potent forces than the irritating Richard to make him abandon one. And Michael knew perfectly well that the rain had settled in for the night, and that it was unlikely to abate until the following day. 'You seem to have had an interesting sojourn at Oxford; I would like to hear more about it.'

'Perhaps later,' said Richard, reaching for more nuts. He smiled ingratiatingly at Edith. 'Is the food ready?'

Edith returned her son's smile. 'Almost. I will tell the servants that we have two more guests.'

'Two?' asked Bartholomew. 'Who else did you invite?'

'Not me,' replied Edith as she left the room. 'Richard asked a friend to come.'

'Who?' asked Stanmore of his son, surprised. 'You have only been back a few days, and you have spent most of that time in bed, recovering from your "arduous journey".'

'It is no one from Cambridge – and certainly no one from Trumpington,' said Richard, with a contrived shudder. 'I do not know why you live here, father. It is little more than a few hovels stretched along a muddy track, and it is occupied almost entirely by peasants. If I were you, I would live in the house in Cambridge.'

Bartholomew found he was beginning to dislike his nephew. The manor Stanmore and Edith occupied was luxurious by most standards and certainly by anything Richard

67

was likely to have experienced at Oxford, if Bartholomew's memories of the place were anything to go by. It was a large hall-house near the church, which looked out across strip fields and orchards. It had red tiles on the roof, and the walls were plastered and painted pale pink. Inside, the house was clean and airy. Wool rugs covered the floor, rather than the more usual rushes, and the walls were decorated with wall hangings. There were plenty of cushioned benches to sit on, and the table at which the Stanmores and their household ate was of polished wood – of the kind that did not puncture the diners' hands with splinters each time they ate, as at Michaelhouse. But it was the smell of the house that Bartholomew liked best. It was warm and welcoming, a mixture of the herbs Edith tied in the rafters to dry, of freshly baked bread from the kitchen, and of the slightly bitter aroma of burning wood. Bartholomew had spent his childhood at Trumpington, and the house always brought back pleasant memories.

That evening, the main chamber was even more welcoming than usual. Edith had decorated it with early spring flowers, and little vases of snowdrops and violets stood here and there, mingling their sweet fragrance with the scents already in the room. Because it was dark, lamps were lit, filling the room with a warm amber glow. They shuddered and guttered as the wind rattled the window shutters and snaked under the doors, sending eerie yellow patterns flickering over the walls.

Michael poured himself a goblet of wine from a jug that had been placed on the table, and went to sit in the chair opposite Richard. He took a sip, and then stretched his legs towards the fire with an appreciative sigh.

'It is cold out tonight,' he said conversationally. 'It is just as well we rode, Matt. Walking would not have been pleasant in this wind.'

'You rode?' asked Stanmore. He handed Bartholomew a goblet of wine and then sat next to him on the bench near the table, since Michael and Richard had already claimed the best places. He raised his eyebrows and regarded Michael with amusement. 'You anticipated that Matt would ask you to accompany him and took the precaution of hiring horses?'

'I am a man prepared for every eventuality,' said Michael silkily. He turned his attention to Richard. 'But tell me about Oxford. Why did you abandon medicine and embrace law instead?'

'Law is a nobler profession,' replied Richard. 'It is better to make an honest living than to practise medicine.'

'Law? Honest?' asked Bartholomew, too astonished to feel offended. 'Is that what they taught you at Oxford?'

Richard sighed irritably. 'I was educated just as well at Oxford as I would have been in Cambridge – better, probably.'

'It was not your allegiance to Oxford that startled him,' said Michael. 'It was your claim that law is an honest profession. Where did you learn such nonsense?'

Richard regarded him coolly. 'It is not nonsense. I decided it would be better than poking around with sores and pustules and suchlike. And then, when the Death comes again, I shall ride away as fast as I can, not linger to lance buboes and watch people die.'

'Running will not save you,' said Bartholomew soberly. 'There was barely a town or a village in the whole of Europe that escaped unscathed. The plague would just follow you. Or worse, you might carry it with you and spread it to others.'

'We are supposed to be celebrating,' said Stanmore firmly. 'We will not spend the evening dwelling on the Death. We all lost people we loved, and I do not want to discuss it.'

'Quite right,' said Michael, holding out his goblet for Stanmore to fill. He changed the subject to one that was equally contentious. 'I have never been to Oxford, but Matt tells me it is an intriguing place. Personally, I have no desire to see it. I imagine its greater size will render it very squalid.'

'It is not squalid,' said Bartholomew quickly, seeing Richard look angry. 'Well, not as squalid as some places I have seen.'

Richard glowered, and was about to make what would doubtless have been a tart reply when Stanmore cleared his throat noisily as Edith walked in.

'You still have not told us who you invited to dine tonight,' said the merchant hastily, to change the subject before Edith saw that they were on the verge of a row. 'When will he arrive?'

'He is here already,' said Richard. He gave an amused grin. 'I met him quite by chance in the town a few days ago. Apparently, he has business in Cambridge, and has been lodging at the King's Head.'

'Good choice,' muttered Michael facetiously. 'It serves both bad food and a criminal clientele.'

'We were delighted to run across each other,' Richard went on, ignoring him. 'I insisted he stayed with us for at least some of his visit, and I took him to the Laughing Pig when he accepted my offer today. Unfortunately, we both drank rather more than we should have done, and he went upstairs to sleep. He is a friend from Oxford.'

Stanmore pursed his lips in disapproval. 'Oxford. I might have guessed someone from *there* would not be able to pass a day without availing himself of a drink.'

'We were only toasting each other's health,' objected Richard. He uncoiled himself from his seat as someone entered the room – a courtesy that had not been extended to Bartholomew and Michael – and gave the newcomer a genuine smile of welcome. 'But here he is.'

Bartholomew and Michael stood politely as a shadowy figure entered the room. And then Bartholomew saw Michael's jaw drop in astonishment when he saw the man who stood in front of them. The newcomer seemed as discomfited by Michael's appearance as the monk was by his.

'William Heytesbury of Merton College,' breathed Michael, staring at the man.

'Brother Michael of Michaelhouse,' replied Heytesbury. 'What are you doing here?'

'You two have already met?' asked Richard, surprised that the Oxford scholar, who now reclined in the Stanmores' best chair with a brimming goblet of wine, should be acquainted with the likes of the obese Benedictine. 'How?'

'We are in the middle of certain negotiations,' replied Michael vaguely. Although his plans to pass two farms and a church to Oxford in exchange for information were not a secret, he was evidently not prepared to elaborate on them for Richard's benefit. He raised his cup to the Merton man. 'Your health, Master Heytesbury. I was not expecting to see you until well after Easter.'

'The roads have been dreadful,' replied Heytesbury, stretching elegant legs towards the fire. 'The snow and rain have turned them into one long quagmire from Oxford to Cambridge. I decided to start the journey early, so I would not be late for our meeting.'

'But that is not until Ascension Day,' said Michael, raising his eyebrows. 'Six weeks hence. The roads are not *that* bad!'

Heytesbury gave a small smile. 'True. But I have other business in Cambridge, besides the agreement I am making with you.'

'Such as what?' asked Michael, affecting careless indifference, although Bartholomew caught the unease in his voice.

Michael had already gambled a great deal on the success of his arrangements with Merton, and did not want them to fail. Bartholomew was hazy on the details, but he knew that the seemingly worthless information and documents Heytesbury would pass to Michael would eventually be worth a lot more than two farms and a church. Michael anticipated that he would be able to steal the patronage of some of Oxford's wealthiest benefactors, and that Cambridge would ultimately emerge richer and more powerful than her rival University. Bartholomew knew that Heytesbury was under the impression that the monk wanted the information simply in order to secure himself the post of Chancellor in a year or two. For all Bartholomew knew, there could be an element of truth in that, too.

Heytesbury was an influential figure in the academic world. He had written a number of books on logic and natural philosophy, and was a leading proponent of nominalism. He was also a member of Merton, one of the largest and most powerful of Oxford's colleges. Bartholomew recalled listening to lectures given by Heytesbury during his own days there.

He studied the Oxford man with interest. In the flattering half-light of the fire and the lamps, it seemed the years had been kind to Heytesbury. He had been an intense young man in his twenties when he had first started to make a name for himself with his scholarship, and Bartholomew supposed he must now be nearing fifty. However, his face had retained its smooth skin and his brown hair was unmarked by grey; these, combined with his slight, boyish build, had led many an academic adversary to underestimate him in the debating chamber. Such opponents did not make that mistake a second time. But despite his superficially youthful appearance, the physician in Bartholomew detected a certain pouchiness beneath Heytesbury's eyes and a slight tremble in his hands.

Heytesbury continued to smile at Michael. 'My other work involved meeting one of your scholars with a view to taking him to Oxford. It was nothing that would influence anything you and I have discussed, so do not be concerned.'

'Poaching,' said Michael immediately. 'It might not affect our agreement, but as Senior Proctor I cannot stand by and watch you entice away our best students.'

'As luck would have it, he proved unsuitable,' said Heytesbury. 'I will not be taking him with me after all.'

'What business could possibly bring a Cambridge monk and an Oxford philosopher together?' asked Richard curiously. 'Especially since Master Heytesbury told me today that he had never been to Cambridge before.'

Then Heytesbury was lying, thought Bartholomew, listening to the philosopher explaining to Richard that the correspondence between him and Michael had been by letter. Bartholomew remembered very clearly the last time he had seen Heytesbury – at a clandestine meeting on some wasteland in Cambridge the previous year. Heytesbury had been trying to learn from a mutual acquaintance whether Michael was a man to be trusted. Fortunately for Michael, the friend put allegiance to Cambridge above an ancient friendship, and had encouraged Heytesbury to proceed in his negotiations with the monk. Heytesbury, quite rightly, had been suspicious of an offer that seemed to favour Oxford, but the monk was hoping the man's natural greed would encourage him to sign anyway.

Bartholomew noted that Heytesbury was as vague about their business as Michael had been, and supposed such subterfuge came naturally to men like them. He wondered what would happen if Heytesbury discovered that a number of people in Cambridge already knew that something was afoot between Michael and the scholar from Merton. Michael had been discreet, but the news had been announced the previous November – when Ralph de Langelee had wanted to make sure Michael was not elected Master of Michaelhouse and had used the Oxford story to stain the monk's reputation – and it had not taken long for the word to spread. But Michael would not want Heytesbury to discuss the case with Richard, who knew that the monk was no bumbling incompetent whose sole ambition was for personal power, but a skilled manager of intrigues who would best even a clever man like Heytesbury, given the chance. Michael wanted Heytesbury lulled into a false sense of security, so that he would sign the agreement without his suspicions being raised.

'You have explained why you came to Cambridge,' said Michael, smiling politely at the Oxford man. 'But you have not told us how you know Richard.'

'I tutored him during his time at Merton,' replied Heytesbury. 'It was I who persuaded him to give up the notion of becoming a physician and to study law instead. It is safer than poking around with leprous sores and more stimulating than inspecting flasks of urine. And there is always a need for good lawyers these days.'

'Yes,' agreed Richard fawningly. 'Ever since the Death, large numbers of wills have been contested, and so there is always work for those who understand the law.'

The conversation turned to legal matters, although Heytesbury did not join in. It was clear to Bartholomew that Heytesbury was uncomfortable with the notion that Michael might cheat him, and so had travelled to Cambridge to make more enquiries before he accepted the terms the monk was offering. Michael also said little, although his eyes gleamed as he sensed Heytesbury was worried enough to try to investigate him. Bartholomew saw that the monk anticipated a challenge, and was relishing the prospect of locking wits with one of Oxford's greatest thinkers.

'The food is ready,' said Edith, entering the room from the kitchen, flushed from the heat of the fire that was roaring there.

'Then let us begin,' said Michael, rubbing his hands in gleeful anticipation. Bartholomew was not sure whether his words referred to the food, or to the impending battle of minds with Heytesbury.

Michael had been wise to inveigle an invitation to Edith's house that night: the fare she provided was infinitely superior to anything that would have been on offer at Michaelhouse. There was trout stuffed with almond paste, pike in gelatine surrounded by roasted vegetables, followed by fried fig pastries, raisin slices and butter custard.

Stanmore broached one of his barrels of best wine, a rich red from southern France, while Richard provided a flask of something that he claimed was the height of fashion in Oxford. It was a colourless liquid that tasted of turnips and that burned Bartholomew's throat and made him cough. He wondered whether Richard would sell him some to use on those of his patients with painful bunions.

'Is it true?' asked Michael of Heytesbury, tilting his goblet and inspecting the drink inside doubtfully. 'Do Oxford scholars really drink this?'

Heytesbury drained his cup in a single swallow. 'It is a brew the King is said to like.'

'Then no wonder the country is in such a state,' muttered Michael. 'I am surprised the man has any wits at all, if he regularly imbibes this poison. What is your opinion, as a medical man, Matt?'

Bartholomew shrugged, reluctant to engage in treasonous talk with Heytesbury present. For all Bartholomew knew, Heytesbury could be the kind of man to report any rebellious sentiments among Cambridge scholars to the King's spies, and Bartholomew had no intention of losing his Fellowship for agreeing that any man who regularly drank the potion Richard had provided was not fit to be in control of a plough, let alone a country. He was surprised that Michael was not similarly cautious.

'I always knew Cambridge men had weak stomachs,' said Richard, tossing back the contents of his goblet and then fighting not to splutter. 'We are made of sterner stuff in Oxford.'

'We will see about that,' said Michael, downing the remains of his own cup and then pushing it across the table to be refilled. 'Will you accept my challenge?'

'He will not,' said Edith firmly. 'This is supposed to be a pleasant family meal, not some academic drinking game. I do not want either of you face down on your trenchers or ruining the occasion for the rest of us by being sick on the table.' She snatched up the flask and rammed the stopper into it so hard that Bartholomew wondered whether Richard would ever be able to prise it out.

'You are quite right, madam,' said Heytesbury smoothly. 'I drink little myself and do not enjoy the company of those who lose their wits to wine and have no sensible conversation to offer.'

Bartholomew looked at Heytesbury's unsteady hands and the way the man was able to swallow Richard's poison as though it were water, and was not so sure. The fact that Richard claimed the first thing he had done when he had met Heytesbury was to visit the Laughing Pig indicated that Heytesbury was not being entirely honest. Bartholomew watched as the Oxford man took a small package from his scrip, pulled a piece of resin from it and stuffed it in his mouth. He saw Bartholomew watching curiously and slipped the packet across the table for him to see.

'Gum mastic,' said Bartholomew, inspecting the yellow substance closely. 'This has only recently come to England, but it has many uses. For example, it makes an excellent glue and is a powerful breath freshener.'

'Do not tell the students this,' said Michael, taking it from Bartholomew and regarding it without much interest, before flinging it back to Heytesbury, 'or they will all be swallowing it, and we shall never be able to prove that they have been drinking.'

Heytesbury caught the package deftly, and changed the subject. 'Tell me about Cambridge. Is it a pretty town?'

Michael gave Bartholomew a hefty kick under the table to attract his attention, then winked, letting the physician know that Heytesbury's untruthful statement about this being his first visit to Cambridge had not gone unnoticed. Bartholomew supposed that Heytesbury had no reason to know that the physician had personally seen him meeting scholars from Bene't College in a place where he assumed – wrongly, as it happened – they would not be observed. Michael's face was unreadable when Heytesbury looked at him, and Bartholomew saw the monk was content to let Heytesbury continue in his belief.

'Cambridge is God's own kingdom on Earth,' announced Stanmore warmly. 'I have lived here all my life, and I have never seen a lovelier spot.'

'Have you travelled much, then?' asked Heytesbury with polite interest.

Stanmore nodded. 'Yes, indeed. I have been several times to Saffron Walden – a good fifteen miles to the south – and once I went to London. But neither compares to Cambridge.'

'I see,' said Heytesbury. 'Have you ever been to Oxford?'

Stanmore shook his head, barely able to suppress a shudder. 'I was not pleased that Richard decided to study there when we have a perfectly good University here, but he was insistent. Still, I suppose his choice was a wise one, given that he is now a lawyer, rather than a physician.'

'At least I will make my fortune,' said Richard. His face was flushed and sweaty from drinking too much wine in a stuffy room. He began to remove his tunic, revealing an intricately embroidered shirt underneath with huge puffed sleeves. 'I would have been doomed to poverty had I pursued a medical career. Lord, it is hot in here!'

'Move away from the fire, then,' suggested Stanmore, a little acidly. 'You would not be so warm if you allowed some of the heat to travel to other people.'

'What,' demanded Michael suddenly and loudly, 'are those?' Everyone followed his eyes to the front of Richard's newly revealed shirt.

'They are called buttons,' said Richard haughtily, glancing down at them. 'Why?'

'I know what they are,' said Michael impatiently. 'But I have never before seen such monstrous examples of them – at least, not on a man. I understand the King's mother goes in for that kind of thing.'

Bartholomew could see his point. Buttons had only recently gained popularity, because it was said that the King approved of them. Most were made of bone or wood and were small, unobtrusive discs that performed the function of holding two pieces of material together without the need for elaborate systems of laces. Richard's buttons, however, were huge, almost the size of mushrooms, and were evidently made of some precious metal.

'They are the height of fashion,' said Richard defensively. 'Do you know nothing of the King's court?'

'They are ugly,' said Stanmore, eyeing them critically. 'But I doubt this modern liking for buttons will last long. They will never take the place of laces.'

'You should be careful if you ever need to run,' Bartholomew advised his nephew with a smile. 'If one of those things bounces upwards, it will take your teeth out.'

Michael regarded Richard with arched eyebrows. 'Do all Oxford scholars adorn themselves with these "buttons", as well as drink liquid that would be better employed in scouring drains? Or is it just confined to those people who study law?'

Richard bristled at the insult, but Heytesbury laid a soothing hand on his arm as he smiled at Michael. 'It is a passing phase, no more. You will find no buttons on me. I would not have expected you to negotiate with me if I had been covered in lumps of metal.'

'Speaking of our agreement, perhaps we should draw it up tomorrow,' suggested Michael hopefully. 'I am sure you need to be back in Oxford for the beginning of the new term, and if we finalise matters now, you will not be obliged to make a second journey.'

Heytesbury's smile was enigmatic. 'Patience, Brother. There is no hurry. I will stay here for a while, and visit your halls and Colleges to see how they compare to my own. There may be things for me to learn.'

The expression on his face made Bartholomew suspect that he had serious doubts on that score.

'I am sure the Chancellor would be delighted if you offered to lecture here,' suggested Richard. He turned eagerly to Bartholomew and Michael. 'Master Heytesbury is one of the leading authorities on the theory of nominalism.'

'I am not sure that is a good idea,' said Michael hastily. 'For some unaccountable reason, the religious Orders here have taken that debate very much to heart recently. I do not want a full-scale riot with the Carmelites, Franciscans and Gilbertines on one side and the Dominicans, Austins and Benedictines on the other.'

'Your scholars riot over philosophical issues?' asked Heytesbury in a contemptuous voice. 'At Merton, we tend to fight with our wits, not our fists.'

'Things have changed, then, have they?' asked Bartholomew archly, not prepared to let Heytesbury get away with that one. 'There was a good deal of fighting when I was a student there.'

'There are fights, of course,' said Heytesbury coolly, not pleased to be contradicted. 'But not over issues of philosophy. What kind of world would it be if the theory that gained predominance was the one that had the most aggressive supporters?'

'One that would suit a lot of the scholars I know,' muttered Michael. 'It would save them the embarrassment of exposing their inferior minds.'

'A lecture on nominalism by its leading protagonist would be a great thing for Cambridge,' persisted Richard. 'It would show them the nature of *real* scholarship.'

'We will see,' said Michael vaguely.

Richard was about to add something else, when there was a loud, urgent hammering at the gates. The merchant looked at his wife in surprise.

'Who can that be? It is late, and I am surprised anyone in the village is still awake.'

He stood abruptly when horses' hoofs clattered on the cobbles of the yard outside. Bartholomew heard Hugh the steward demanding to know the rider's business, but then there was the sound of approaching footsteps and the door to the hall was flung open. A cold draught swirled inside, making the fire gutter and extinguishing several lamps.

'I am sorry to intrude, Master Stanmore,' said Sheriff Tulyet, pushing past Hugh, who seemed about to make a more mannerly announcement. His cloak was sodden, and he was breathless from a hard ride against a fierce head-wind. 'But I must speak to Brother Michael.'

Richard Tulyet was small, with a wispy beard that gave him the appearance of a youth unable to produce the more luxurious whiskers of an older man. Only the lines of worry and tiredness around his mouth and eyes suggested that he was loaded with the considerable responsibility of main-taining law and order in a rebellious town where a signifi-cant portion of the population comprised young men.

'Me?' asked Michael, surprised. 'Why? What can have happened to induce the town's Sheriff to ride through such a foul night to seek me out?'

'Your University,' replied Tulyet, grim-faced. 'It is in uproar again. You must return with me immediately and take charge of your beadles, or we shall have no town at all by the morning.'

'Who is it this time?' asked Michael wearily, reaching for his cloak. 'Hugh, saddle up my horse, if you please.'

'The Franciscans have some Austin canons trapped in Holy Trinity Church,' replied Tulyet in some disgust. 'Apparently there was a dispute over who should preach the sermon. They tossed a coin, would you believe, and the Austins won. The Franciscans declined to listen to an Austin, and left.'

'So what is the problem?' asked Michael when the Sheriff paused. Stanmore poured Tulyet a goblet of wine, which he accepted gratefully. 'If the Franciscans went home, why are you here?'

'They did not return to their friary,' said Tulyet. 'Apparently, they made for the Cardinal's Cap, where they spent the evening drinking the poor taverner dry of ale – for which they still need to pay. And then they headed back to Holy Trinity Church.'

'Were the Austins still inside?' asked Stanmore.

Tulyet nodded. 'The Franciscans claim that neither I nor my soldiers have jurisdiction over them, because they are in holy orders – under canon, rather than secular law – and refuse to go home.'

'My Junior Proctor can deal with this,' said Michael impatiently. 'I left him in charge, and he knows what he is supposed to do if the scholars cause mischief.'

Tulyet sighed, his face sombre. 'That is the real reason why I am here, Brother. I am afraid I have some bad news for you.'

'What do you mean?' demanded Michael suspiciously.

Tulyet sighed. 'Will Walcote is dead. Someone hanged him from the walls of the Dominican Friary.'

CHAPTER 3

ONCE MICHAEL HAD LEFT WITH TULYET TO BEGIN AN immediate investigation into Walcote's death, Bartholomew did not feel like continuing with the celebrations at Edith's house. He offered to accompany the monk home, afraid that the murder of a close colleague would prove to be a harrowing experience, but Michael declined, muttering that he did not want to spoil Edith's party.

The physician did not enjoy the rest of the evening, and escaped to the bed in the attic that had been provided for him as soon as he could do so without causing offence. Meanwhile, Richard dominated the conversation, outlining his grand plans to amass wealth and fame. Bartholomew had encountered many greedy men in his time, but such brazen avarice was a quality he had never expected to see in his nephew. Heytesbury fell silent once Michael had gone, and stared into the fire, evidently lost in his own thoughts.

The following morning, just as the sky was beginning to lighten in the east, Bartholomew crept out of his room, and tiptoed downstairs and across to the stables. He thought he had succeeded in leaving the house undetected, and was surprised and not particularly pleased to find Richard waiting for him with a huge black stallion already saddled.

'What is that?' demanded Bartholomew, eyeing the vast beast uneasily.

Richard seemed startled by the question. 'It is a horse. What does it look like?'

'That is no horse; it is a monster,' said Bartholomew, hurriedly stepping back as the animal tossed its mighty head and pawed at the ground. 'Where did it come from?'

Richard patted the horse's neck fondly, although the animal did not seem to reciprocate the affection. 'He hales from the stables of the Earl of Gloucester, and has a pedigree of which any nobleman would be proud. I bought him two days ago from the Bigod family in Chesterton.'

'How did you pay for such an expensive item?' asked Bartholomew, astonished. 'You have only been in Cambridge a week or so. I had no idea practising law could be so lucrative.'

Richard shot him an unpleasant glance. 'I was doing well in Oxford, as it happens, but I am fortunate in having Heytesbury as a friend. He has recommended me to several of his richest acquaintances. But never mind me, what do you think of my horse?'

'Did you have to choose one that was so big?' asked Bartholomew, taking another step back as the horse, sensing that it was about to take some exercise, headed for the open door. Richard grabbed the reins, but the animal paid him no heed, and his tugs and curses were irrelevant to the course of its progress outside.

'I do not ride ponies,' retorted Richard haughtily, still hauling on the reins. 'And this beast suits my status as a lawyer. I cannot be seen mounted on something inferior, can I?'

'I suppose not,' said Bartholomew, saddling his modest palfrey. He hoped the looming presence of the black monster would not cause it to bolt, or, worse still, that it would not follow Richard's lead and thunder off down the dark track towards Cambridge at a speed that was unsafe. Bartholomew did not enjoy riding at the best of times, but doing so at a breakneck pace along a frost-hardened track in the near-dark was definitely low on his list of pleasant ways to spend a morning.

'The Black Bishop of Bedminster,' said Richard.

Bartholomew gazed at him uncomprehendingly in the gloom. 'What?'

'That is his name. The village of Bedminster, near Bristol,

83

is where he was bred. It is an impressive title, do you not think? It is fitting for a fine animal to have such a name.'

'I am sure it is,' said Bartholomew. 'I only hope it never runs away. I would not like to think of you wandering the town shouting "Black Bishop of Bedminster" as you try to lure it back.'

Richard scowled, and then swung himself up into his saddle. The horse pranced and reared at the weight, and Bartholomew was not entirely sure that Richard had the thing under complete control. He watched from the safety of the stables, noting that the saddle was a highly polished affair with a pommel that gleamed a dull gold in the first glimmerings of day. Such an object would have cost Bartholomew at least a year's salary.

Richard's clothes were equally expensive looking. He had abandoned the soft wool hose and buttoned shirt he had worn the previous night, and sported leather riding boots with silver spurs, a black tunic with flowing sleeves and dark grey hose, all topped off with a long black cloak that he arranged carefully over the back of the saddle so that it would show off his finery to its best advantage. The gold ring that pierced his ear gleamed even in the dim light of early morning, and the smell of the scented goose-grease, with which he had plastered down his unruly locks and beard, was strong enough to mask even the odour of horse.

'What do you intend to do in the town?' asked Bartholomew, wondering what the people of Cambridge would say when they saw such an elegant peacock strutting around their streets flaunting his wealth. Richard would be lucky if he survived the day without someone hurling a clod of mud – or worse – at such a brazen display of affluence. 'I have to attend mass at St Michael's Church, and then spend the morning teaching.'

'Perhaps I will accompany you,' said Richard thoughtfully. 'Your new Master, Ralph de Langelee, has connections at court, and would be a useful man to know. He is an 'unmannerly lout, but I will have to turn a blind eye to that, if I am to make my fortune in Cambridge.'

'It looks to me as though you have already made it,' said Bartholomew.

Richard grinned. 'I will do better yet if profitable business keeps coming my way. But I doubt I will stay long in Cambridge; it is too rural for a man like me. I will go to London soon – now *there* is a place for a man who intends to make his way in the world! Opportunities in London are like leaves on the trees.'

Bartholomew heartily wished his arrogant, ambitious nephew would take his black horse and ride to London that very morning. Eager to escape from the young man's company as quickly as possible, he climbed on a bale of hay and made an awkward transition from it to the back of the palfrey. Fortunately, Michael had selected a mount that was fairly tolerant, and although it was startled by the weight that suddenly dropped on to it, it stood its ground. Hugh the steward opened the gate, and Bartholomew and Richard began the short journey to Cambridge.

It was a Tuesday, and farmers and peasants were already making their way to the town with carts and sacks full of goods to sell in the marketplace. Six dirty-white geese were being herded along by a listless boy who wore a piece of sacking as a cloak; the birds honked balefully as faster-moving pigs were driven through their midst. Chapmen with heavy packs slung across their shoulders plodded through the mud left by the rains of the previous night, cursing as their feet skidded and slipped in the treacherous ruts that formed the road. Richard complained bitterly about the stench left by the pigs, and only stopped when Bartholomew lent him a thick bandage to wrap around his mouth and nose. Bartholomew had seen courtiers do the same, claiming to be more easily offended by unpleasant odours than the common folk. The physician supposed his nephew hoped to give the impression with his silly bandage that he, too, was nobly born.

They were just passing the Panton manor on the outskirts of Cambridge, when they saw a small group of nuns standing at the side of the road. The nuns' heads were swathed in white veils that were bright in the dim light, and their cloaks were splattered with muck from the road. One of them glanced up, and apparently decided that Richard's fine horse, elegant apparel and face bandage marked him as a man of breeding and wealth and therefore someone she might ask for help. A pale hand flagged him down. Richard's attempt to leap from his horse and stride boldly to her rescue was marred only by the fact that his spur caught in the stirrup: Bartholomew's timely lunge saved him from a tumble in the mud.

'How might we be of assistance, ladies?' Richard enquired suavely, unabashed by an incident that most people would have found acutely embarrassing. Bartholomew envied his resilience and confidence.

'It is our Prioress, Mabel Martyn,' said one of the nuns. She was a tall woman, with dark eyes and smooth brown hair that poked from under her wimple. She looked the splendid figure of Richard up and down in a brazen assessment of his physique. 'There is something wrong with her.'

'My uncle is a physician,' said Richard generously. 'He will heal her.'

'I thought you said physicians were charlatans, incapable of healing anyone,' muttered Bartholomew, pushing the reins of his horse at his nephew and walking to three other nuns, who were clustered around a figure on the ground.

'We are from St Radegund's Convent,' announced the young woman. 'We are nuns. Well, I have taken no final vows yet, so I suppose I am not.'

'I hope you do not decide upon a life of chastity,' said Richard gallantly. 'It would be a sin to shut away such beauty in a cloister.'

'I agree,' said the woman fervently. 'Although better that than being married to some old man with no teeth who sleeps all the time. I do not find gums very attractive.'

'Nor do I,' said Richard, apparently unable to think of any other response to her peculiar revelations.

She beamed at him, and Bartholomew realised that she was a little slow in the wits and that a cloister might be the safest place for her. He turned his attention to the Prioress, who lay semi-conscious in the long grass at the side of the road. Her wimple was askew and her breathing deep and loud. The unmistakable smell of wine was thick in the air around her.

'I think she had a sip too much at breakfast,' he said carefully. His natural good manners rebelled against bluntly announcing that Prioress Martyn of St Radegund's Convent was drunk.

'But we have not had breakfast yet,' objected the young woman, missing his point entirely. 'So you must be wrong.'

'Why are you out so early?' asked Richard, voicing what Bartholomew had also been wondering: it was unusual to see nuns travelling *towards* their convent at such an hour in the morning. 'Have you been to mass at Trumpington Church?'

'We have been nowhere,' said the young woman. 'We are still coming back from last night.'

Richard looked confused, and one of the others hastened to explain. She was tall and strong-looking, about forty years of age, with thick red hair and eyes that were too wise for a nun.

'We were invited to dine at the house of Roger de Panton yesterday. Time passed more quickly than we thought, and we have only just realised that we need to hurry so as not to be late for prime.'

Bartholomew pulled something from underneath the snoring Prioress and held it up for the others to see. It was an empty wineskin. He supposed that the Prioress's last tipple was more than her constitution could bear after what sounded like a heavy night.

'I told you to dispose of that, Tysilia,' said the older woman sharply.

87

Tysilia pouted sulkily. 'I did, Dame Wasteneys. I took it when she was in the latrine.'

'Perhaps she has more than one,' said Bartholomew, hauling the semi-conscious woman to her feet. She groaned, and opened bleary eyes. 'The walk in fresh air will do her good. When you arrive home, give her plenty to drink and make sure she has a good breakfast.'

'We can give her plenty to drink now,' offered Tysilia, brandishing the wineskin helpfully.

'I meant watered ale or milk,' said Bartholomew, regarding her askance. 'Do not give her wine; she has had more than enough of that already.'

'She is not drunk,' asserted Dame Wasteneys, regarding Bartholomew sternly. 'She is indisposed. I would not like it said that the Prioress of St Radegund's was tipsy before prime.'

'As you wish,' said Bartholomew, thinking that the walk through Cambridge with the Prioress staggering between two meaty novices would do more damage to her reputation than anything he could say. He knew that wine was sometimes more than just a pleasant beverage for some people, and the broken veins and slightly purple nose of the Prioress suggested that she was one of them. He handed Dame Wasteneys a packet containing some cloves, which he used for patients with toothache.

'Give her some of these to chew. They will mask the scent of the wine.'

'Thank you,' said Dame Wasteneys, sketching a brief benediction at him. 'You are very kind.'

Leaving the nuns to walk back to their convent, Bartholomew and Richard mounted their horses again. Bartholomew was sure that the sudden deluge of spray and pellets of mud that the Black Bishop of Bedminster kicked up with his hoofs, and that landed squarely on the startled Prioress, would do more to dispel the effects of wine than the coldest morning air. Oblivious to her indignant curses, Richard rode towards the town.

* * *

Bartholomew and Richard reached the Trumpington Gate, and waited for the guards to wave them through. The soldier on duty regarded Richard's snorting black horse doubtfully. Sergeant Orwelle was a thickset man with a limp from a wound received in the service of the King. Bartholomew had recently treated him for rotting teeth, and one of his first tasks as a physician, when he had arrived in Cambridge more than a decade before, had been to remove a horn drinking vessel from the man's nose, which had managed to become stuck there during some bizarre drinking game. Orwelle felt indebted to Bartholomew – not for the removal of the offending item, but for the fact that the incident had never been mentioned again.

'Tell Brother Michael I am sorry about his Junior Proctor,' said Orwelle, patting Bartholomew's horse on the neck. 'It was me who found him, you know. I was on patrol, when I saw him hanging. It was a sad sight.'

'Did you see anything else – such as who did it?' asked Bartholomew hopefully.

Orwelle shook his head. 'If I had, then that person would now be under lock and key. It does not do for scholars to flaunt their lack of respect for the law in the town. It sets a bad example.'

'How do you know Walcote was killed by a scholar, and not a townsperson?' asked Bartholomew curiously.

Orwelle regarded him as though he were insane. 'Of course it was a scholar. The townsfolk have nothing against the proctors – quite the opposite, in fact, because it is the proctors who punish students for misbehaving. We *like* the proctors.'

'Sheriff Tulyet said Walcote was hanged from the walls of the Dominican Friary,' said Bartholomew. 'Is that true? It is a very public place.'

'He was around the side,' explained Orwelle. 'The front would have been a public place, but Walcote was hanging from a drainage pipe that juts out from the north wall. A line of trees conceals it from the road.'

'How did you find him, then?' asked Bartholomew.

Orwelle looked shifty. 'Do not tell the Sheriff, but I slipped home for a cup of hot ale halfway through my patrol – it was a horrible night, with all that wind and rain. I live near the Dominican Friary, and there is a shortcut along the wall that I always take. I doubt anyone else uses it after dark, and it was lucky I found Walcote when I did, or he would have been there until this morning.'

'But he was dead when you found him?', asked Bartholomew. 'There were no signs of life?'

'None,' said Orwelle. 'And I have attended enough hangings at the Castle to be able to tell right enough. He was stone cold, too, so he had been hanging there some time before I came across him.'

'What time did you find him?'

'When the bells chimed for compline,' replied Orwelle. 'You and Brother Michael had left to go to Trumpington for the evening, and I suppose it was a couple of hours after that. Whoever killed him must have done so just after dusk – any earlier, and someone else would have found him; later, and he would have been warm.'

'Was there anything at all that might help Michael catch the culprit?' asked Bartholomew.

Orwelle shook his head. 'The good Brother has already asked me all this. There was nothing. I cut Walcote down, to make certain he was not still living, then I ran to the gatehouse for help.'

'And what about the trouble between the Austins and the Franciscans?' asked Bartholomew. 'Did they fight all night?'

'The Franciscans went home when it became clear the rain was not going to stop that evening. They do not dislike the Austins enough to endure a drenching. By the time the Sheriff arrived with Brother Michael, the Franciscans and the Austins were tucked up in their own beds.'

'Good,' said Bartholomew. 'I was expecting to hear that there had been a riot.'

'There is unrest because the University is only teaching

in the mornings this week,' said Orwelle knowledgeably. 'The scholars are bored – they do not know what to do with free afternoons, and so spend them looking for trouble. It is a good thing Lent is almost over.'

'It is,' said Bartholomew, hoping the problems would be resolved when lectures returned to normal after Easter.

Orwelle suddenly sniffed the air. 'What is that dreadful stench? Is there a whore among the crowd waiting to come in?'

'Not that I can see,' replied Bartholomew, hoping Orwelle would not associate the powerful smell with Richard's carefully greased hair. The physician moved backward as Richard's horse grew restless at the enforced delay.

'Make sure you keep that thing under control,' Orwelle instructed Bartholomew, eyeing the animal distrustfully. 'We do not want it stampeding around the town, upsetting carts and knocking people down.'

Bartholomew raised his hands, palms upward. 'It has nothing to do with me. Tell Richard.'

'Oswald Stanmore's boy?' asked Orwelle, peering up at the fine figure who sat on his horse with the bandage still around his nose and mouth. The old soldier gave a sudden beam of delight. 'You and my Tom used to go fishing together. You remember him.'

Richard gazed coolly at the sergeant. 'Actually, I do not. And I prefer not to dwell on such unsavoury matters as fishing in dirty water.'

Orwelle's honest face crunched into a puzzled frown. 'Of course you remember my Tom. It was just before the Death. You and him used to sit together on the river bank, and catch minnows.'

'I do not think so,' said Richard, spurring his horse through the gate and into the town beyond.

Shooting an apologetic grin at Orwelle, Bartholomew rode after him, balling his fists so he would not be tempted to knock his nephew from his fine saddle.

'What are you thinking of?' he demanded when he had

caught up, snatching the reins from Richard's hands to make him stop. 'You could have acknowledged Tom Orwelle's father. You and Tom were friends once.'

'I cannot afford to be seen cavorting with the sons of common soldiers,' Richard flashed back. 'I have an impression to make on this town. I hardly think people will want to employ me if they see me discussing old times with peasants.'

'You need not be concerned,' said Bartholomew, disgusted. 'Tom Orwelle died of the plague. His father only wanted a kind word from you about him – the sharing of a fond memory. You have changed, Richard, and I do not like what you have become.'

Richard's jaw dropped. 'But I . . .' he began.

It was too late. Bartholomew was already riding away up the High Street towards Michaelhouse, leaving his nephew stuttering an unheard apology.

Still angry, Bartholomew rode past the recently founded College of Corpus Christi and the Blessed Virgin Mary, or Bene't College as it was known to most people because it stood next to St Bene't's Church. Work still continued on the College, which seemed to grow larger every time Bartholomew passed it. It already had two courtyards and a handsome hall building, and was being furnished with more accommodation wings and a substantial kitchen block.

The church was an ancient monument with a square, almost windowless tower that many people believed had been built before William the Conqueror had claimed the English throne in 1066. It was set in a grassy graveyard, and its amber stones were shaded by yew trees. Diagonally opposite it was the Brazen George, a large tavern known for good food and clear ale, which was a favourite of Michael's. Rows of town houses followed, some grand and well maintained, like the one belonging to the locksmith and his family, and some in sore need of a new roof and a coat of paint, like the one where Beadle Meadowman lived.

Beyond that, the great golden mass of St Mary's Church rose out of the filth of the High Street. Its new chancel gleamed bright and clean, elegant tracery reaching for the sky like stone lace. Its tower was a sturdy mass topped by four neat turrets that could be seen from many miles away. In a room below the bells was a great chest in which the University stored its most precious documents. To many, the sumptuous church represented all they did not like about the University, and the building was often the target of resentful townspeople.

A short distance from St Mary's was St Michael's, a church that had been specially rebuilt by Michaelhouse's founder Hervey de Stanton to be used by the scholars of the College he had established. Next to the dazzling splendour of St Mary's, with its Barnack stone and intricate tracery, St Michael's was squat and grey. It had a low tower, barely taller than the nave, and tiny porches to the north and south. Its chancel was almost as large as its nave, a deliberate feature on Stanton's part, because he intended Michaelhouse's scholars to pray in the chancel, while any congregation or members of other Colleges or hostels would use the nave.

Bartholomew considered St Michael's chancel one of the finest in Cambridge. Its tracery lacked the delicate quality of St Mary's, but possessed a clean simplicity that Bartholomew loved. The great east window allowed the early morning light to flood in, although for much of the day the church was dark and intimate. A tiny extension to the south was called the Stanton Chapel, and housed the tomb of Stanton himself. Other tombs and monuments lay in peaceful silence among the shadows, with still figures in stone gazing heavenwards, occasionally lit by the odd beam of dusty sunlight.

Just to the left was St Michael's Lane, a muddy track that led down to the wharfs on the river. On the corner was the handsome red-roofed Gonville Hall, where scholars were already gathering in the street to process to St Mary's, to celebrate the beginning of a new day with a mass. Some of them nodded to Bartholomew as he passed. Usually, members of different Colleges tended to regard each other with hostility, but Master Langelee of Michaelhouse had recently sold Gonville Hall a piece of property for a very reasonable price, and the scholars of Gonville and Michaelhouse had established a truce. Bartholomew was grateful that at least some factions within the University were not at each other's throats.

The horse slowed when it was faced with the muck of St Michael's Lane, picking its way carefully and skilfully around the larger potholes and piles of rubbish. The walls of Gonville loomed to Bartholomew's left as he turned down the small runnel, appropriately named Foule Lane, on which the mighty front gate of Michaelhouse stood. He hammered on the door, and was admitted by a porter who took the horse, grumbling about the amount of mud that clung to the animal, which would have to be cleaned off.

Michaelhouse's scholars were already assembling in the yard to process to the mass at St Michael's, most of them yawning and still rubbing the sleep from their eyes. At their head was Master Langelee, a large, heavy man with no neck, who had decided to become a scholar because life as a spy for the Archbishop of York was not sufficiently exciting. Given that his predecessor had been murdered after attempting to oust Langelee himself from his Fellowship because of an annulled marriage, he had probably been right.

Langelee called an affable greeting to Bartholomew, then strode briskly along the line of scholars to ensure they were sufficiently smart to represent Michaelhouse on the streets of Cambridge. Bartholomew did not much like the burly philosopher, whose belligerence and single-mindedness also made him unpopular with the students, but he had to admit that standards had risen since Langelee had assumed the Mastership. Michaelhouse scholars were inspected each morning, and any student whose tabard was not clean and tidy and whose shoes did not shine to Langelee's satisfaction was fined fourpence. Scholars who could not afford or declined to pay were put to work as copyists, to add to Michaelhouse's expanding library.

It was not only outward appearances that had improved. Lectures always started on time, and meals were served promptly. Previously, evenings had been free for the students, but Langelee had initiated a series of discussion sessions that the Fellows took it in turn to lead. The students were obliged to attend at least four each week, and Langelee kept a careful record of anyone who absented himself without permission. The topics were usually light-hearted ones, such as whether worms when cut in half were two animals or one, or whether ale tasted better in the morning or the evening, but nevertheless were valuable practice for the more serious disputations that were a major part of academic life. As long as Langelee did not take part in the discussions himself – he was not possessed of the sharpest mind in the University, and even the rawest, most inexperienced student invariably bested him – Bartholomew felt the students were benefiting enormously. There was also the fact that their busy schedules allowed very little time for causing mischief in the town. It had been many months since the proctors had paid a visit to Michaelhouse in pursuit of a student who had misbehaved.

The Michaelhouse Fellows were already waiting in their places at the front of the procession. The fanatical Franciscan Father William was first, nodding approvingly as Langelee berated one student for having hair that was too long. William's habit was easily the filthiest garment in Michaelhouse, but even Langelee's heavy-handed hints could not induce the friar to wash it. Like all Franciscans' robes, the habit was grey, but William's was so dark that he was occasionally mistaken for a Dominican. William detested the Black Friars, and Bartholomew found it extraordinary that he would risk being misidentified just because he had an aversion to hygiene.

Standing next to William, and already muttering prayers

that would prepare him spiritually for the mass that was to come, was the gentle Gilbertine Thomas Kenyngham. Kenyngham had performed the duties of Master for several years, and had been a kindly and tolerant leader. However, Bartholomew was rapidly coming around to the opinion that the students fared better under the sterner hand of Langelee, although he was amazed to find it so.

Michael waited next to them, the dark rings under his eyes indicating that the previous night had not been an easy one for him. He gave Bartholomew a wan smile as the physician stepped into his place.

Behind Michael were the newest Fellows. The Dominican Clippesby stood with the Carmelite friar, Thomas Suttone. Clippesby was talking in loving tones to a dead frog he had somehow acquired, and Suttone was trying to wrest it away from him before Langelee saw it. Langelee was not particularly tolerant of the Dominican's idiosyncrasies, mostly because he did not know how to respond to them.

Suttone was a long, bony man with short white hair that contrasted oddly with Clippesby's wild locks. He had some of the largest teeth that Bartholomew had ever seen in a person, and was a sombre individual, wholly devoid of humour. He was not an unkind man, but his unsmiling demeanour did not make him popular with his colleagues. Even the dour, uncompromising William was not serious all the time, and enjoyed a little light-hearted banter of an evening, especially if it were at the expense of the Dominicans.

Suttone and Clippesby began a covert push–pull competition over the frog, determination to possess it clearly written in the features of both. Bartholomew and Michael watched the tussle warily, hoping that Clippesby would not have one of his tantrums if Suttone were the victor, because when Langelee locked Clippesby in his room 'for his own safety' the other Fellows were obliged to take over his teaching responsibilities. The struggle, however, ended abruptly when the frog broke in two. Clippesby regarded his part in surprise, and then generously presented it to Suttone, whispering that there was little anyone could do with half a frog and that Suttone should take both bits. Michael snorted with laughter as Clippesby clasped his hands in front of him in genuine innocence, while Suttone was left holding a mess of spilled entrails that he was unable to explain to the disgusted Langelee.

Considering that the Fellows of Michaelhouse comprised a Benedictine, a Dominican, a Franciscan, a Carmelite and a Gilbertine, the College was remarkably strife-free. Bartholomew sincerely hoped it would continue, and that his colleagues would not be drawn into the rivalries and disputes in which the religious Orders indulged. William posed the greatest threat, with his naked hatred of Dominicans, but, fortunately, Clippesby was not sufficiently sane to provide him with a satisfactory target. Sometimes he objected to the hail of abuse the Franciscan directed towards him, but most of the time he seemed unaware that there was a problem.

Thinking of the unease between the Orders reminded Bartholomew of why Michael had left Edith's house early the previous night. He glanced at the monk, noting again that he looked exhausted and out of sorts.

'Are you all right?' he asked, brushing mud from his tabard as they waited for the procession to move off. 'Sergeant Orwelle told me how he found the body.'

Michael shook his head slowly. 'Walcote was a good man, despite my complaints that he was too gentle. I shall catch whoever did this, and string them up, just as they did to him.'

'It was definitely murder, then?' asked Bartholomew. 'There is no possibility it was suicide?'

'His hands were tied behind him,' said Michael shortly. 'It was not suicide.'

'Did the Dominicans do it?' asked Bartholomew. 'It seems a little brazen to use their own walls as an execution ground.'

'They said it had nothing to do with them, and that the

97

first they knew about it was when Tulyet hammered on their gates and demanded to know why a corpse was dangling from their wall. Prior Morden maintains that the gates have been locked since the fight with the Carmelites.'

Bartholomew raised his eyebrows. 'Prior Lincolne claimed the Carmelite Friary doors were shut, and that Faricius could not possibly have left the premises. But Faricius still ended up gutted like a fish in a grimy alley. These locked doors have peculiar properties, it seems.'

Michael sighed. 'If I had a groat for every time a scholar claimed he could not have committed a crime because he was locked inside a College or a hostel, when all the time he was as guilty as sin, I would be a rich man.'

'So, do you think the Dominicans killed Walcote, then?'

Michael rubbed his eyes wearily. 'I have no idea. Walcote was hanged from a drainage pipe that juts out from the top of the wall. Anyone outside the friary could have flung a rope over it and hauled him up by the neck.'

'Walcote was an Austin. Do the Dominicans have a dispute with them?'

Michael sighed again. 'The reality is that, at the moment, the Dominicans seem happy to fight anyone – *anyone* – who is not from their own Order.'

'Then it is not safe for any non-Dominican to be out on the streets,' said Bartholomew. 'That is not a healthy state of affairs.'

'You do not need to tell me that,' said Michael. 'I thought the town was calm last night, or I would never have allowed you to persuade me to go to Trumpington. Priors Morden and Lincolne promised to keep their students in, and I thought the worst of the trouble was over.'

'So, do you have any idea who might have killed Walcote? Were there any clues with the body?'

'None. He was killed in a secluded spot, probably just after sunset, when no one would have been around. I doubt there are witnesses.'

'So, what will you do?'

Michael fell into step beside Bartholomew as Langelee led the procession out of the yard and into the street. 'I must be careful with this case, Matt. I liked Walcote, despite my reservations about his gentleness, and I am in danger of allowing affection to cloud my judgement. If that happens, the killer may go free.'

'Can you delegate the investigation to your beadles?' asked Bartholomew.

'I do not trust any of them with something this important. Meadowman shows promise, but he is inexperienced. I need you to help me, Matt.'

'I will examine Walcote's body for you,' said Bartholomew. 'But I am no good at hunting down criminals. And anyway, what about my teaching?'

'It is Holy Week, and you only teach in the mornings,' said Michael. 'Walcote's murder is not only a deep personal blow, it is a strike against the University. The proctors are symbols of authority and order, and killing one of us is a statement of chaos and anarchy.'

'I think you are overstating the case, Brother,' said Bartholomew reasonably. 'It may just be that Walcote was alone, and that the attack on him was opportunistic. Or maybe some resentful student – previously arrested or fined by Walcote – saw an opportunity for revenge. His death is not necessarily imbued with a deeper meaning.'

Michael turned haunted eyes on him. 'I hope you are right, Matt. But I need your expertise, and I need another sharp mind to assess facts that I may miss. Will you do it?'

'Very well,' said Bartholomew reluctantly.

The monk nodded his thanks, and they walked the rest of the way to the church in silence. Bartholomew's thoughts were full of foreboding when he saw that, yet again, he was about to be sucked into a world of treachery and violence that had already claimed the life of Michael's deputy. He hoped they would solve the matter quickly, so that his life could return to normal.

* * *

'Two murders,' said Michael, pacing back and forth in his room after breakfast that morning, his black habit swirling around his thick white ankles. A jug on the table wobbled dangerously as his weight rocked the floorboards, and Bartholomew was grateful he was not working in his own room below, attempting to concentrate over the creak of protesting wood.

Michael had directed his three serious-minded Benedictine students to read part of an essay by Thomas Aquinas, thus neatly abrogating his teaching responsibilities for the rest of the day. Bartholomew's pack of undergraduates were not quite so easily dealt with, and tended to be rowdy and difficult to control if he were not with them. Surprisingly, when he had learned why Bartholomew wanted to be excused, Langelee had offered to supervise them himself. Like Michael, the Master regarded the death of a Junior Proctor as a serious threat to the University on which he had pinned his personal ambitions.

'Find the man, Bartholomew,' he instructed. 'You are relieved of all College responsibilities until you have the culprit under lock and key – except for the mass on Easter Sunday, when all Fellows should be present.'

'I hope it will not take that long,' said Bartholomew. 'It is only Tuesday.'

'Then you will have to work quickly,' said Langelee, glancing down the hall, where Bartholomew's lively students were already beginning to make themselves heard as they waited for their lesson to begin. 'If people learn that the University's officers can be easily dispatched and the culprits never found, the town will erupt into chaos.'

Freed of his teaching, Bartholomew sat at the small table in Michael's room, and made notes on an oddly shaped piece of parchment from Michael's supply of scraps. Parchment was expensive, and scholars tended to recycle old documents by rubbing the ink away with sand, and then treating the surface with chalk. The piece Bartholomew had was wafer-thin from previous use, and whoever had last scraped it had done a poor job, because the words were still legible under the layer of chalk. On one side was a summary of payments for Michael's army of beadles, while on the other Walcote had made a list of items that had apparently been stolen from the Carmelite Friary a few weeks before.

'Two murders,' repeated Michael, gnawing his lip thoughtfully. 'Faricius of Abington and Will Walcote.'

'You are not suggesting the two deaths are related, are you?' asked Bartholomew, as he wrote down the few facts they had about Walcote's death, chiefly where it had taken place and that it had probably happened after sunset. 'I can see no reason to link them together.'

Michael rubbed the dark bristles on his chin. 'Faricius, a Carmelite, was murdered when the *Dominicans* went on a rampage. And now Walcote is murdered outside the *Dominican* Friary. There is your connection, Matt.'

'It may be a connection, but I am not sure it is a meaningful one. There is nothing nearby, other than that drainage pipe on the friary walls, that could be used for a spontaneous hanging. Perhaps that is all your connection means.'

Michael rubbed his chin harder. 'But what about all the questions we have regarding Faricius's murder? What about the fact that his Prior insisted he could not have left the friary? And what about the fact that we know the Carmelites are lying – or at least hiding the truth – about his death?'

'What about them?' asked Bartholomew. 'They neither prove nor disprove the connection you are trying to make. I think the best way forward is to treat the two deaths as unrelated events. Then, if we discover evidence to the contrary, we can look at them from a new angle, and try to see whether there are other links. Is that reasonable?'

Michael sat down so hard on a stool that Bartholomew was sure he saw the legs buckle. The monk rested his elbows on his knees and gave his eyes a vigorous massage. 'I suppose so. I find this very difficult, Matt. I have never investigated the death of anyone I liked before.'

'I thought you were dissatisfied with Walcote's abilities as a proctor.'

'I was, although they seem insignificant now that he is dead. Doubtless I will come to remember him as the best deputy I have ever had. But I liked him well enough. He could be a little secretive at times, but he was a pleasant fellow to work with.'

'We will find his killer,' said Bartholomew encouragingly, although he was not sure how they would even begin what seemed such an impossible task.

Michael gave a wan smile and climbed to his feet. 'I was right to ask you to help me; you have already made me feel more optimistic about our chances of success. Now, where shall we start? Will you look at Walcote's body? I doubt there is any more you can tell me that I do not already know, but it is as good a place as anywhere to begin.'

Bartholomew nodded reluctantly. He did not enjoy looking at corpses and, although he had inspected a great many of them, the frequency of the occurrence did not make the task any more attractive. He was a physician, and he considered his work to be with the living rather than the dead.

'And then I suppose we had better ask questions about Walcote himself,' he said.

'What do you mean?' asked Michael suspiciously. 'I do not want to pry into the poor man's private affairs now that he is not here to defend himself.'

'We need to establish whether his death was a case of an opportunistic slaying, or whether it was a carefully planned attack. We will not know that unless we investigate his personal life, to see whether he had angered someone sufficiently to make them want to kill him.'

'Well, of course he had enemies,' said Michael impatiently, beginning to pace again. 'He was a proctor. There are plenty of students who resented spending nights in our cells, and who objected to paying the fine that secured their release.'

'Most students accept the fact that they have been caught, and turn their minds to devising ways to avoid it next time,' said Bartholomew. 'And most students do not kill a man over the loss of a groat or two.'

'A groat is a lot of money to people with nothing,' said Michael. 'I have had my life threatened on a number of occasions for far less than a groat.'

'You have?' asked Bartholomew uneasily. 'Then perhaps you should not go out alone until this is resolved. I do not want to see you hanging from a pipe on the walls of the Dominican Friary – although it would take a lot more than a length of lead piping to hold up the likes of you.'

'There is no need for rudeness, Matt,' said Michael stiffly. 'And doubtless I shall lose a lot of weight now that I have all the anxiety associated with solving two murders; that should please you.'

'It did not stop you from making the most of breakfast this morning,' said Bartholomew critically, not even wanting to remember what the monk had packed away inside his substantial girth after mass that day.

'My meals are my affair,' said Michael irritably. 'But we should not be discussing them; we should be trying to find out who killed Walcote and Faricius.'

He gave a weary sigh as he stared at the piece of parchment on the table with its scanty record of facts. Bartholomew understood his apprehension. The few scraps of information written there seemed a very fragile basis on which to conduct a murder investigation.

'You will be needing my assistance,' came a booming voice from the door as Bartholomew and Michael sat staring at the parchment. 'I heard about the death of Walcote and have come to take his place.'

Bartholomew and Michael jumped. They had not heard Father William climb the wooden stairs that led to Michael's

103

room, and his sudden appearance startled them. Bartholomew immediately noticed that William had dropped a sizeable blob of his breakfast oatmeal down the front of his habit, making him appear even more dirty and disreputable than usual, a feat the physician had not thought possible.

'It is not my decision who to appoint as Junior Proctor,' said Michael, quickly and not entirely truthfully. Bartholomew knew perfectly well that his opinions counted for a great deal when it was time for nominations to be considered. 'I think the Chancellor has someone else in mind.'

It was not the first time the belligerent Franciscan had offered himself for the post, and it was not the first time Michael had declined. William was an honest enough man, but he seldom admitted he was wrong, and he was always accusing innocent people of heresy. He had spent some time with the inquisition in France, before his superiors had dispatched him to the University in Cambridge because of his over-zealousness. To give William's bigotry full rein by appointing him Junior Proctor would be in no one's interests.

'But that is not fair,' protested William, crestfallen. 'I have been waiting years to be appointed, and you must appreciate that I would be good at ferreting out criminals, killers and heretics. I am the right man for the task, and you know it!'

'You would make a memorable proctor,' said Michael ambiguously. 'I will tell Chancellor Tynkell of your interest. However, it is my understanding that he has promised the position to someone else.'

'Who?' demanded William. 'I warrant it will not be someone with my dedication and experience.'

'You are probably right,' said Michael soothingly.

William rubbed his chin thoughtfully, then apparently decided to make the best of the situation. 'But until this person has officially accepted the position, you will need someone to help you,' he said. 'It will be good practice for when the new Junior Proctor resigns and I take his place.'

'That will not be necessary,' said Michael hastily. 'Matt is assisting me, and I need no one else. And anyway, I anticipate that Walcote's replacement will take up his duties very soon.'

'You need me,' stated William uncompromisingly. 'You see, this is not merely a matter of hunting down some criminal who has killed a man – which is all you have done in the past. This is far more complex: it is a case of unmasking a heretic.'

'I see,' said Michael, as William folded his arms and pursed his lips in the way he always did when he thought he had made an astute revelation. 'And how have you arrived at this conclusion, pray?'

'It is obvious,' said William, inserting his solid form through the door and perching on the windowsill when he saw Michael was prepared to listen to him. 'Walcote was an Austin canon; Austin canons follow the theory of nominalism; nominalism is an heretical notion; heretical notions are upheld by agents of the Devil. *Ergo*, you need a man like me to discover the Devil's spawn who killed Walcote.'

'There is a flaw in your logic, Father,' said Michael. 'If Walcote were one of these so-called heretics, why would another heretic kill him? Surely, the killer would be more likely to strike at a realist than a nominalist?'

William's convictions began to waver. 'Not necessarily,' he blustered. 'Heretics do not think in the same way as you or I. They do not always act logically.'

'And neither do Franciscan fanatics,' muttered Michael, eyeing the friar in distaste.

'You are a realist, are you?' asked Bartholomew, surprised that William was prepared to take a stand on an issue that was so complex. Normally the Franciscan had little time for intricate debates that required serious thinking.

'We Franciscans always follow the path of truth,' announced William. 'Of course we support realism. You did not think we were nominalists, did you? My Prior told me that the Franciscans supported realism, and I always follow his lead in such matters.'

Michael gave a low snort of laughter. 'Only when it suits you. He told you not to fan the flames of dissent between your Order and the Dominicans last summer, and you were brought before him three times for disobeying his instructions.'

'That was different,' said William haughtily. 'And anyway, he now recognises that I was right. We should have driven the Dominicans out of Cambridge last year, when I suggested we should.'

'You mean we should suppress anything we do not agree with, and persecute anyone who holds a different opinion from us?' asked Bartholomew, raising his eyebrows in amusement.

'That is the most sensible suggestion I have ever heard you make, Matthew,' said William, oblivious of the fact that the physician had been joking. 'Then we would eradicate heresy from the face of the Earth.'

'Along with the freedom to think,' said Bartholomew. 'But why are the religious Orders laying down such rigid rules regarding the nominalism–realism debate? In the past, they have always permitted individuals to make up their own minds about philosophical issues.'

'Not everyone is equipped with the wits to make a rational decision,' said William in a superior manner. 'Like the Dominicans, apparently.'

'And why do you think nominalism is so wrong?' asked Bartholomew curiously.

'It is wrong because it is heretical,' said William immediately.

'Yes, but *why* is it heretical?' pressed Bartholomew.

'Because it is,' said William. 'Everyone knows that.'

'Not everyone,' corrected Michael. 'The Dominicans, my dead Junior Proctor and my own brethren at Ely Hall do not agree – to name but a few people.'

William stared straight ahead of him, suggesting that he

106

knew he had been bested, but did not want to admit it.

'A group of Carmelites gathered outside the Dominican Friary on Sunday, and were prepared to fight against highly unfavourable odds in support of realism,' said Bartholomew. 'But when I asked them what realism was, they could not define it. The debate is simply an excuse for restless students to fight each other.'

'Right,' said Michael, turning a wicked grin on William. 'So, tell us what you understand by nominalism, Father. I should like to know.'

'Nominalism is all about giving things names,' said William, after a few moments of serious thought and throat clearing. 'The very word "nominalism" comes from the Latin *nomen*, which means name. It is not right to name things, because God did that when He created everything. It says so in Genesis.' He shot Michael a triumphant glance, indicating that he thought he had already won the argument.

'That is not exactly right,' said Bartholomew, as Michael turned away in disgust.

'Yes, it is,' snapped William. 'So there.'

'Aristotle and Plato believed that the world contains abstract concepts – like the quality of blueness or beauty – that are actually real,' began Bartholomew, determined that if the Franciscan were prepared to take a stand on the issue, then he should know what he was talking about. 'They called these things "universals". They also believed that the world contains individual things that are blue or beautiful – like a blue flower – which they called "particulars".'

'I know, I know,' muttered William, who clearly did not. He regarded Bartholomew suspiciously. 'But what have Aristotle and Plato to do with nominalism?'

Michael sighed heavily at his lack of knowledge. 'They were the first realists. You should know this. It is what you claim is the non-heretical thing to think.'

'Nominalists believe that universals have no real existence,' explained Bartholomew, ignoring Michael's outburst. 'They say that blue things exist – like the sky, that bowl on

107

the table, the stone in Michael's ring – but the quality of blueness is an abstract and does not exist. So, universals are imaginary concepts, and only particulars are real.'

'Oh,' said William flatly, so that Bartholomew could not tell whether he had grasped the essence of the argument or not. 'Why are they called nominalists, then? This makes no sense.'

'It does. The word "men" describes a group of people. It is a name, a *nomen*. Nominalists say that "men" is not a thing that has an actual existence, it is only a *name* describing a group of individuals. A "man" is a real thing – a particular – and so exists; but "men" is a universal and so does not.'

William blew out his cheeks. 'This is all very complicated, Matthew. If you are going to explain it to your students, you will need to simplify it a good deal.'

Bartholomew caught Michael's eye and willed himself not to laugh. He had already simplified the debate and had not even begun to explain its ramifications for the study of logic, grammar and rhetoric. When the Dominican Kyrkeby gave his lecture on nominalism for the University debate the following Sunday, Bartholomew was certain the Franciscans would not be sending William to refute his arguments.

'And Plato and Aristotle thought all this up, did they?' asked William, after a moment.

'No, Plato and Aristotle were realists,' said Bartholomew patiently, not looking at Michael. 'Nominalism was revived a few years ago by William of Occam, who was a scholar at Oxford.'

'Shameful man,' pronounced William. 'He should have left things as they were.'

'Occam was a student of Duns Scotus,' said Bartholomew. 'Duns Scotus was a strong believer in realism, but Occam gradually came to disagree with his master.'

'Duns Scotus was a Franciscan,' said William smugly. 'That is why I know realism is right and nominalism is wrong. But I cannot spend all day lounging in here with you when there is God's work to be done. I have teaching to do. Let me know this afternoon what you want me to do to help you catch Walcote's killer.'

'You have wasted your time, Matt,' said Michael in disgust when the Franciscan had gone. 'You tried to teach him the essence of the argument, but he simply clung to his own bigoted notions that realism was propounded by a Franciscan and so must be right.'

'He is not the only one to hold views like that,' said Bartholomew. 'Although I suspect that most people can argue a little more coherently.'

'I hope so. But he was right about one thing,' said Michael, standing and reaching for the cloak that lay across the bottom of his straw mattress. 'We should not be wasting time here when we have murderers to catch.'

'Before we visit Barnwell Priory to examine Walcote's body, I think I had better see Chancellor Tynkell,' said Michael, as he and Bartholomew walked up St Michael's Lane towards the High Street. 'I do not want William visiting the man and demanding to be made Junior Proctor before I have informed him who to appoint.'

'You told William that Tynkell already has someone else in mind,' said Bartholomew.

'He does,' replied Michael with a grin. 'Only he does not know it yet.'

The Chancellor of the University occupied a cramped office in St Mary's Church, although he fared better than his proctors, who were relegated to a room that was little more than a lean-to shed outside. Tynkell glanced up as Michael walked into his chamber, and smiled a greeting. He was a thin man, who Bartholomew understood took some pride in the fact that he had never washed, being of the belief that water was bad for the skin. His office certainly suggested that there might be some truth in the rumour, because it was imbued with a sour, sickly odour. Tynkell attempted to disguise his unclean smell by dousing himself with perfumes, although Bartholomew thought he should use something much stronger, and seriously considered offering to find out from whom Richard Stanmore purchased his powerfully scented hair oil. The Chancellor laid down his pen and rubbed his eyes with his fingers, transferring a long smear of ink on to one cheek. Bartholomew wondered how long it would remain there.

'I suppose it is too soon for you to have any news about the murder of Will Walcote?' he asked. 'You have not had time to begin your investigation.'

'But I have thought of little else since last night,' said Michael. 'We are on our way to Barnwell Priory, to inspect his body and to ask among his colleagues whether he had any enemies.'

'I thought *you* would have known that, Brother,' said Tynkell. 'If Walcote had enemies, they were made while carrying out his duties as your deputy.'

'Speaking of my deputy, I would like you to appoint one of the Benedictines from Ely Hall as Walcote's replacement. Either Timothy or Janius would be acceptable.'

'Timothy,' said Tynkell immediately, taking up his pen and beginning to write the order. 'Beadle Meadowman informs me that Timothy was a soldier before he took the cowl, and that is exactly the kind of man we need as a proctor. Janius would also be good, but he is smaller and thus less able to wrestle with burly young students in their cups.'

'He is stronger than he appears,' said Michael. 'And he is very good at talking sense to people. On balance, I suspect he would be better than Timothy, who is slower and milder.'

'But Janius is so . . . religious,' said Tynkell, frowning.

'He is a monk,' interjected Bartholomew. 'He is supposed to be religious.'

But despite his flippant words to Tynkell, Bartholomew knew what the Chancellor meant. Janius could scarcely utter a sentence without mentioning matters holy, and even Bartholomew, who was usually tolerant of other people's beliefs and habits, found the force of Janius's convictions unsettling.

'There is a difference between the religion we all practise and the religion that Janius promotes,' said Tynkell. 'Janius always wears that serene smile that makes him appear as though he has been in direct contact with God, and that he knows something the rest of us do not.'

'Master Kenyngham is like that,' said Michael.

'It is not the same,' insisted Tynkell. 'Janius's religion is so intense and . . . preachy. I cannot think of another word to describe it. It makes me feel acutely uncomfortable and rather inferior.'

Bartholomew understood his sentiments perfectly. Kenyngham's devoutness was much more humble than that of Janius, and the elderly Gilbertine certainly did not give the impression that he knew he was bound for the pearly gates, although Bartholomew imagined he was more likely to be admitted than anyone else he knew. Janius, however, exuded the sense that he already had one foot and several toes through the heavenly portals, and that he felt sorry for everyone else because they did not. Timothy had a similar attitude, although it was less flagrant.

'You have a point,' said Michael. 'I always feel I should not swear when I am with Janius, which could prove tiresome in some circumstances. Very well: Brother Timothy it is. I shall go to Ely Hall immediately, and inform him of his good fortune.'

'Do you not think you should ask him first?' said Bartholomew, thinking that *he* would not be very pleased to be presented with a writ informing him that his days would now be spent visiting taverns to ensure they were free of undergraduates, or trying to suppress riots.

Michael waved a dismissive hand. 'He will be delighted to do his duty. Come, Matt. Let us go and give him the happy news.'

Ely Hall, where the Benedictines lived, was a large, two-storeyed house on Petty Cury, overlooking the Market Square and St Mary's Church. It was a timber-framed building, the front of which had been plastered and then painted a deep gold, so that it added a spot of colour to an otherwise drab street. The door was bare, but the wood had been scrubbed clean, and someone had engraved a cross and a rough depiction of St Benedict in the lintel.

Michael's knock was answered by Janius, whose blue eyes crinkled with pleasure when he saw Bartholomew and Michael. He ushered them inside, then preceded them along a narrow passageway to a large chamber at the back of the building, which served as a refectory and conclave. A flight of wooden stairs led to the upper floor, which Bartholomew knew from his previous visit had been divided into six tiny chambers where the masters and their students slept.

Several black-robed monks were in the refectory that morning, most of them reading or writing. Through a window that overlooked a dirty yard at the rear of the house, Bartholomew could see a lean-to with smoke issuing through its thatched roof; cooking often started fires, and the Benedictines, like many people in the town, had opted to do most of theirs outside their house. Meanwhile, a merry blaze burned in the hearth of the refectory, and there was an atmosphere of good-natured industry.

Brother Timothy was in one corner, reading a battered copy of William Heytesbury's *Regulae Solvendi Sophismata*. He frowned slightly, concentrating on what was a difficult text. Janius had apparently been sitting at the table making notes on Peter Lombard's *Sentences*, a text that, along with the Bible, formed the basis of theological studies at Cambridge. Sitting by the fire was another familiar face, that of Brother Adam, an ageing monk whom Bartholomew treated for a weakness of the lungs. They all looked up as Michael and Bartholomew entered the room. Timothy stood, and came to touch Michael on the shoulder in a gesture of sympathy.

'We were so sorry to hear about Will Walcote. We will say a mass for his soul later today.'

'Thank you,' said Michael. 'But I came here to ask you whether you would take his place as Junior Proctor.'

112

'Me?' asked Timothy, startled. 'But I could not possibly undertake such a task.'

'I told you,' muttered Bartholomew. 'You cannot expect people to abandon everything on your command.'

'To be called to perform such duties is a great honour for the Benedictines,' said old Adam from his fireside chair. 'You should accept Michael's offer, Timothy.'

Timothy shook his head, flushing red. 'I could never fulfil such duties as well as Michael has. I would be a disappointment to him.'

'It is true you would have high standards to aim for,' said Michael immodestly. 'But I feel you would be the ideal man for the post, and so does Chancellor Tynkell.'

'The Chancellor?' whispered Timothy, flushing more deeply than ever. 'But I scarcely know him. What have I done to attract his attention?'

'Accept, Brother,' said Janius, his eyes shining with the light of the saved. 'God has called you and you cannot deny Him.'

'I thought Michael had called you,' muttered Adam from the fireside. 'It is hardly the same thing, no matter what Michael thinks of himself.'

Janius ignored him, and gripped Timothy's arm. 'God wants you to serve Him and our Order. To have a senior and a junior proctor who are Black Monks will be excellent for the University, and it will go a long way to setting us above the disputes between the friars.'

Bartholomew was not so sure about that, and suspected that many people would see Timothy's appointment as favouritism on Michael's part, and as a deliberate move to secure the best positions in the University for men in his own Order.

'I cannot accept,' said Timothy, shaking his head and refusing to look at Michael.

'There is always Father William,' muttered Bartholomew wickedly in Michael's ear.

Michael's shoulders slumped in disappointment. 'Very

well. If you have teaching that you cannot escape, or other duties that are important, then there is nothing I can do to persuade you.'

'You misunderstand,' said Timothy. 'I cannot accept because I will not be good enough.'

'Is that all?' asked Michael relieved. 'Give me a week, and I will prove that you are perfect for the task. In fact, I anticipate that you will be the best Junior Proctor I have ever had – and I have had a few, believe me.'

Timothy still hesitated, and it was Janius who spoke up. 'We will undertake Timothy's teaching duties when necessary, and will do all we can to support both of you. It is God's will.'

Timothy sighed and then smiled at Michael. 'When would you like me to start?'

'Now,' said Michael briskly, apparently deciding that Timothy should be allowed no time to reconsider. 'I knew a Benedictine would be a good choice. The ink is barely dry on the parchment, and yet you are prepared to abandon your personal duties to help me in this difficult situation.'

While they were talking, Bartholomew crouched down next to Brother Adam. The monk was small and wizened, and the murky blue rings around his irises suggested failing eyesight, as well as extreme old age. A few hairs sprouted from the top of his wrinkled head, but not nearly as many as sprouted from his ears.

'How are you, Brother?' asked Bartholomew. 'It is good to see you out of your bed.'

The old monk grinned with toothless gums. 'The brethren do not normally permit themselves the indulgence of a fire during the day, but Janius always has one lit when he thinks I might come downstairs. He imagines I have not guessed why there is always a blaze in the hearth just when I happen to leave my room. His religion can be a little unsettling from time to time, but he is a good man, to think of an old man's pride.'

'And your lungs?' asked Bartholomew. 'Are you breathing easier now?'

'Your potion helps,' said Adam, 'although I long for warmer weather. Spring is very late this year, and Lent has been interminable. Still, as I am elderly and ill, Brother Timothy insists that I be fed meat at least three times a week.'

'Good,' said Bartholomew, thinking that Timothy was an enlightened man not to demand that the restrictions of Lent be kept by the old and infirm. Although the Rule of St Benedict suggested more lenient guidelines for the sick, not everyone accepted them. He was sure Father William would not be so compassionate. 'I hope you do not refuse it because meat is forbidden in Lent.'

The old monk raised his eyebrows and regarded him in amusement. 'I am no martyr, Doctor. If I am commanded to eat meat, then eat it I shall. And my brethren have always been good to me. I will not burden them by insisting on doing things that are bad for me and that make me ill. It would be very selfish.'

'I wish all my patients had that attitude,' said Bartholomew fervently. He stood as Michael and Timothy made for the door.

'If you are going to Barnwell, then I shall accompany you,' said Janius, reaching for a basket that stood in a corner. 'I have eggs and butter to take to the nearby leper hospital, so I can do God's work and enjoy your company at the same time.'

He took a cloth from a rack where laundry was drying, and covered the basket to protect its contents from the rain, then set out after the others.

CHAPTER 4

WALCOTE'S BODY LAY IN THE CONVENTUAL CHURCH AT the Austin canons' foundation at Barnwell. Barnwell was a tiny settlement outside Cambridge, comprising a few houses and the priory itself. Beyond it was another small hamlet called Stourbridge, famous for its annual fair and its leper hospital.

The priory was reached by a walk of about half a mile along a desolate path known as the Barnwell Causeway. Once the town had been left behind, and the handsome collection of buildings that belonged to the Benedictine nuns at St Radegund's had been passed, Fen-edge vegetation took over. Shallow bogs lined the sides of the track, and stunted elder and aspen trees hunched over them, as if attempting to shrink away from the icy winds that often howled in from the flat expanses to the north and east. Reeds and rushes waved and hissed back and forth, and the grey sky that stretched above always seemed much larger in the Fens than it did elsewhere. As they walked, more briskly than usual because it was cold, ducks flapped in sudden agitation in the undergrowth, and then flew away with piercing cackles.

'Damned birds!' muttered Michael, clutching his chest. 'No wonder people like to poach here. I would not mind taking an arrow to some of those things myself! That would teach them to startle an honest man.'

The Fens were known to be the haunt of outlaws, and Bartholomew kept a wary watch on the road that stretched ahead of them, as well as casting frequent glances behind. Since the plague had taken so many agricultural labourers, the price of flour had risen to the point where many people could not afford bread. Three well-dressed Benedictines and

116

a physician with a heavy satchel over one shoulder would provide desperate people with a tempting target.

Michael seemed unconcerned by the prospect of attack, and was more interested in outlining the duties of Junior Proctor to Timothy. Timothy himself was more prudent, and carried a heavy staff that Bartholomew was sure was not a walking aid. Janius was also alert, and Bartholomew could see that he possessed the kind of wiry strength that was easily able to best larger men. While Michael continued to regale Timothy with details of his new obligations, Janius fell behind to walk with the physician.

'I am still worried about Adam,' he said, fiddling with the cover on his basket of food for the lepers. 'He claims he feels better, and our prayers help, of course, but sometimes he seems so frail.'

'He is old,' said Bartholomew matter-of-factly. 'I can ease his symptoms, but he will never be well again.'

Janius gave a startled laugh. 'You do not mince your words, Matthew! I was expecting some comfort, not a bleak prediction. Have you no faith that God will work a cure if we pray hard enough?'

'No,' said Bartholomew practically. 'Adam is almost eighty years old, and the wetness in his lungs will become progressively worse, not better. Such ailments are common in men of his age, and there is only one way it will end.'

Janius shook his head and gave Bartholomew a pitying glance. 'Yours must be a very sad existence if you place no hope in miracles.'

'My experience tells me that miracles are rare. It is better to assume that they will not happen.'

'You should pray with us at Ely Hall,' said Janius, patting Bartholomew's arm sympathetically. 'You strike me as a man who needs to understand God.'

'Right,' said Bartholomew vaguely, determined not to engage in a theological debate with a man whose eyes were already gleaming with the fervour of one who senses a challenge worthy of his religious attentions. He knew from

117

personal experience that it was never wise to discuss issues relating to the omnipotence of God with men who had the power to denounce unbelievers as heretics, and he hastily changed the subject before the discussion became dangerous. 'Do you often deliver eggs to the leper colony?'

Janius seemed taken aback by the sudden change in topics. He tapped Bartholomew's arm a little harder. 'Remember my offer, Matthew. It may save your soul from the fires of Hell.'

Bartholomew was relieved when Janius made his farewells, and watched the pious monk walk briskly up the footpath to where the chapel of St Mary Magdalene dominated the huddle of hovels occupied by the lepers. The chapel was a sturdy building, pierced by narrow windows, almost as if its builders did not want the light to shine in on the people inside. The huts were flimsy wooden-framed affairs, with thatched roofs that allowed the smoke from a central hearth to seep out and the rain to seep in. Bartholomew had visited them on many occasions, usually to help Urban, the Austin canon who had dedicated his life to tending those people whom the rest of society had cast out. He saw Janius turn a corner, then ran to catch up with Timothy and Michael.

'Janius has a good heart,' said Timothy, who must have had half an ear on the conversation taking place behind him, as well as on Michael's descriptions of his new duties. 'His own faith is so strong that he longs for others to be similarly touched. I understand how he feels, although I am less eloquent about it.'

'Good,' said Michael fervently. 'I already wear the cowl, so you have no need to preach to me.'

'Just because you are a monk does not mean that your faith is not flawed,' began Timothy immediately, his face serious and intense. 'I have met many clerics who simply use their habits to advance their own interests here on Earth, with no thoughts of the hereafter.'

'And doubtless you will meet many more,' said Michael brusquely. Given what he had told Bartholomew about the reasons most friars came to Cambridge, the physician supposed that Timothy was likely to meet a lot of men who were more interested in the earthly than the spiritual aspects of their existence. 'But we have arrived. Here is the priory.'

Barnwell Priory was a large institution, and the fact that it stood in the middle of nowhere meant that it had been able to expand as and when its priors had so dictated. Its rambling collection of buildings sprawled along the ridge of a low rise that overlooked the river. It was in a perfect location – close enough to the river for supplies and transport, but high enough to avoid all but the worst of the seasonal floods. A substantial wall and a series of wooden fences protected it from unwanted visitors, although beggars knocking at a small door near the kitchens were often provided with a loaf of bread or a few leftover vegetables.

The conventual church stood next to the road, attached to the chapter house by a cloister of stone. To one side was a two-storeyed house, which comprised the canons' refectory on the ground floor and their sleeping quarters above. The Prior of Barnwell had his own lodgings in the form of a charming cottage with a red-tiled roof and ivy-clad walls. Smoke curled from its chimney, to be whisked away quickly by the wind. From the nearby kitchens came the sweet, warm scent of newly baked bread.

The canons were at prayer in their chapter house when Bartholomew, Michael and Timothy tapped on the gate and asked to see Walcote's body. An Austin brother named Nicholas, whom Bartholomew had treated for chilblains all winter, escorted them to a small chantry chapel. He then returned to his duties, while the two canons who kept vigil on either side of Walcote's coffin, climbed stiffly to their feet, and readily acquiesced to Michael's request to spend time alone with his Junior Proctor.

The noose around Walcote's neck had so distorted his features that Bartholomew barely recognised the serious man who had been Michael's assistant for the past year. His face had darkened, and his eyes were half open and dull

119

beneath swollen lids. A tongue poked between thickened lips, and a trail of dried saliva glistened on his chin. Michael declined to look at him, and retreated to the main body of the church where he pretended to be praying. Hastily following his example, and evidently relieved to be spared the unpleasant task of inspecting a corpse, Timothy went with him.

Suppressing his distaste at submitting to such indignities the body of a man he had known and liked in life, Bartholomew began his examination, using for light the two candles that had been set at the dead man's head and feet. There was no question at all that Walcote had been strangled. The vivid abrasions around his neck attested to that. Bartholomew turned his attention to the hands, and saw that Michael had been right: more stark circles indicated that Walcote's hands had been tied, and he had evidently struggled hard, because he had torn the skin in his attempts to free himself. His feet had been tied, too, perhaps to prevent him from kicking out at his killer or killers.

'What can you tell me?' called Michael from the shadows of the chancel. 'Look at his fingernails. You always seem to be able to tell things from nails. And I want to know whether he was hit on the head and stunned. It would be a comfort to know that he was unaware of what happened to him.'

It was a comfort Bartholomew could not give, however, and it was apparent that Walcote had known exactly what someone intended to do to him, because he had struggled. The fact that he had been strangled by the noose, and that it had not broken his neck as was the case in many hangings, suggested it had not been an especially speedy end.

To humour Michael, Bartholomew inspected Walcote's fingernails, but they told him little. They were broken, which implied that the Junior Proctor had started his bid for freedom before he had been trussed up like a Yuletide chicken. The only odd thing was that there was a sticky, pale yellow residue on one hand, just like the stain Bartholomew had seen on Faricius's hand. He frowned, wondering what, if anything, it meant. He replaced the shroud, put the dead man's hands back across his chest as he had found them, and left Walcote in peace. Michael and Timothy followed him out of the shadowy chapel, both clearly glad to be away from the unsettling presence of untimely death in a man they had known. Timothy heaved a shuddering sigh.

'Nasty,' he said unsteadily, although Bartholomew was not sure whether he meant the manner of Walcote's death or the fact that he was now obliged to pay close attention to such matters.

Outside the church, Nicholas was waiting for them, clutching a bundle that he proffered to Michael. 'These are Will's clothes,' he said shyly. 'He was wearing a habit, a cloak and boots, all of which I removed when his body was brought here. I suppose we should distribute them to the poor, but it is hard to part with this last reminder of him. Will you do it?'

'Keep them,' said Michael, who like Bartholomew had noticed that Nicholas's own robe was pitifully threadbare and that he wore sandals, despite the fact that there had been a frost the previous night. Bartholomew thought it was not surprising he had chilblains. 'Will would have wanted them to be given to his friends.'

Nicholas swallowed hard. 'We all liked Will, and were proud that an Austin was a proctor. We hoped he might even become Senior Proctor one day.' He flushed suddenly, realising that for that to happen, Michael would have to be removed. 'I am sorry, Brother. I did not mean . . .'

He trailed off miserably, and Michael patted his shoulder. 'It is all right. I had hopes for Will's future, too. He was a good man.'

'Yes, he was,' said Nicholas, tears filling his eyes. He gave them a surreptitious scrub with the back of his hand. 'Laying out his body was the least I could do.'

'You did that very carefully, but there is still a patch of something yellow on one hand,' said Bartholomew. 'What is it, do you know?'

Nicholas sniffed, hugging Walcote's belongings to him. 'I have no idea, but it would not wash off. The same substance was on his habit, too. Look.'

He freed a sleeve from the carefully packed bundle, revealing a patch of something that was sticky to the touch, slightly greasy and pale yellow.

'How much of it was there?' asked Bartholomew, touching it with his forefinger.

'Just the patch on his hand and the little bit on his sleeve,' said Nicholas. 'It seems to repel water. I borrowed some soap from Prior Ralph, but it still would not come off.'

'I need to see Ralph,' said Michael. 'I have a few questions to ask.'

Nicholas went to fetch him, leaving Bartholomew, Michael and Timothy standing in the cloister alone.

'What is that stain exactly?' asked Timothy, bending to touch the residue on the garment Nicholas had put carefully on a stone bench.

'I have no idea,' replied Bartholomew. 'The only other time I have seen it was on Faricius.'

'So is that why you imagine it to be significant?' asked Timothy, straightening to look at him. He gave an apologetic grin. 'Forgive my questions. I am just trying to learn as much from you as I can, so that I can fulfil my new duties. But if you do not know what this yellow slime is, then how can you be sure that Walcote and Faricius did not acquire it quite independently of each other?'

'I cannot be sure,' said Bartholomew. 'But it is a peculiar substance, and I think it odd that it should appear on two corpses that were killed within a couple of days of each other.'

'But Faricius was stabbed during a riot in broad daylight, and Walcote was hanged in the shadows of dusk,' pointed out Timothy. 'I can see nothing that connects them.'

'You are probably right,' said Bartholomew. 'It is doubtless irrelevant.'

But something in the back of his mind suggested that it

was not, and that it was an important clue in discovering who had killed a studious Carmelite friar and the University's Junior Proctor.

Bartholomew shivered as he waited for Nicholas to fetch Prior Ralph de Norton. It seemed colder at Barnwell than it had been in Cambridge, and the wind sliced more keenly through his clothes. The cloisters, lovely though they were, comprised a lattice of carved stone that did little to impede the brisk breeze that rushed in from the north east. Bartholomew had heard that the wind that shrieked across the Fens with such violence every winter came from icy kingdoms above Norway and Sweden, where the land was perpetually frozen and the rays of the sun never reached.

'I wondered when you would visit us, Brother,' said a fat man with large lips and very protuberant eyes, who followed Nicholas through the cloister towards them. 'I am so sorry about Will Walcote – sorry for the loss to my priory as well as the loss to you.'

Michael inclined his head. 'I will find whoever did this, Prior Ralph. Believe me, I will.'

'I do believe you,' said Ralph softly. 'I have heard that you and Doctor Bartholomew make a formidable team when it comes to solving murders.'

Bartholomew was not sure he liked being known as a solver of murders: he would have preferred his name to be associated with his work as a physician, which, after all, claimed most of his time. Still, he thought optimistically, perhaps the appointment of Timothy would mean he was obliged to help the monk less frequently in the future. Timothy seemed more proficient and eager than most of Michael's junior proctors. When Ralph's bulbous eyes shifted questioningly to Timothy, Michael introduced him as Walcote's successor.

'Good God!' breathed Ralph, horrified. 'You do not waste any time! Will is barely cold, and yet you have already appointed a Benedictine in his place. I was going to suggest

123

you took another Austin canon – Nicholas, for example.'

Nicholas was mortified, and hung his head in embarrassment. But Timothy was unabashed, and rose to deal with the issue with cool dignity.

'I appreciate that my appointment must seem sudden, but that happened only because the Chancellor is determined to catch the monster who killed Will. If you, or anyone else, is dissatisfied with my performance once the culprit is caught, I will willingly resign and someone else can take my place.'

Ralph relented in the face of Timothy's disarming graciousness. 'I am sure that will not be necessary. I am sorry, Brother; I was merely taken aback by the speed with which Will was replaced.'

'Do you know anyone who had a grudge against Will?' Michael asked, finally getting down to business. 'I hate to ask such a thing, but we must leave no stone unturned, if we are to bring his killer to justice.'

Ralph appeared surprised by the question. 'I thought you would be better placed to answer that. I imagine many people objected to the long arm of the law as personified by Will.'

'I meant here, in the priory,' said Michael. 'Of course we will be reviewing his recent cases, but we need to know whether anyone had taken against him at his home.'

'Of course not,' said Ralph, a little offended. 'He was not here much, despite the fact that he enjoyed our company. He always said that walking home to us after a day of chasing miscreants and malefactors around the town made him feel as though he were properly escaping from his duties for a few hours.'

'That is how I feel about Michaelhouse,' said Michael, blithely ignoring the fact that his beadles regularly visited him there, and that he was constantly at their beck and call. 'So, there is no one at Barnwell who you think might have been jealous of his success or resentful of his connections with the University?'

124

'No,' replied Ralph smugly. 'We Austins are not given to jealousy and feelings of resentment against our fellows.'

Michael gave a snort of laughter. 'Do not take me for a fool! I am a cleric myself, do not forget. There will be resentment and jealousy wherever there are gatherings of people, and religious Orders are no different from secular folk.'

'Well, I can assure you that no one here minded Will's success,' said Ralph coldly. 'Indeed, it was generally assumed that it was good for us, because through him we had a certain degree of influence in the University.'

Bartholomew could see that Ralph genuinely believed what he was saying, and the more humble Nicholas had said much the same. It seemed Walcote was exactly as he had appeared – an affable, somewhat quiet man who had probably not enjoyed his duties, but who had continued to perform them to the best of his ability because his priory gained prestige from his appointment.

Bartholomew supposed that Michael would have to look into Walcote's recent cases, and see whether any of the scholars he had caught or fined might have had a reason to kill him. His heart sank at the prospect. Students were a rebellious lot, and he imagined that Walcote would have dealt with a good many of them over the last year. Cambridge possessed a very transient population, and it was even possible that someone might have returned to the town specifically to exact revenge for some past incident, and had already left.

Ralph began to recite a long list of Walcote's virtues, to which Michael listened patiently and politely. It was clear the Austin Prior had nothing more to say that could help them, and after a while Michael suggested, very gently, that they should be on their way to continue their investigation in the town. Ralph agreed, and left the shuffling Nicholas to see them out. Timothy walked with him, asking him for his own impressions of Walcote, while Michael nodded approvingly at his new deputy's initiative.

As they headed towards the gate, a bell chimed to

announce the midday meal. The canons began to converge on the refectory building, some spilling out from the chapter house and others coming from the gardens or the nearby fields. All walked briskly and purposefully, suggesting that breakfast had been a long time ago. A few chattered together as they walked, but most were silent, their dark robes swinging about their legs as they hurried towards the delicious buttery smell of baked parsnips and pea soup. Bartholomew spotted a familiar figure with tousled hair and a liberal collection of freckles.

'Look!' He grabbed Michael's arm and pointed. 'It is Simon Lynne. Remember him? He is one of the Carmelites we questioned about Faricius's murder.'

'So it is,' said Michael thoughtfully. 'Only those are not a Carmelite's robes he is wearing. That is the habit of an Austin canon.'

'He cannot be both,' said Bartholomew, puzzled. 'What can he be thinking of?'

'I do not know,' said Michael, watching the youth disappearing inside the refectory. 'But we shall find out.'

'Now?' asked Bartholomew, pausing and preparing to visit the refectory there and then.

'In my own time, when I know exactly what questions to put to him. It seems I was right after all, Matt. There *does* seem to be a link between the murder of Faricius and the murder of Walcote.'

Michael stepped outside the gates of Barnwell Priory and gave a sigh. The wind had sharpened since they had been inside, and a blanket of thick grey clouds made midday feel like evening. It had started to rain, too, unpleasant little splatters that had the bite of ice in them and that stung uncovered hands and faces.

'Well, that was a waste of time,' he said irritably, hauling his cowl over his head and drawing his warm cloak tightly around his shoulders. 'It is a long walk here, and I expected to gain more than you telling me that Walcote had been hanged – which I already knew – and that I must look outside Barnwell to uncover the identity of his killer.'

'That yellow stain might be important,' said Bartholomew. 'It may have been left there by his killer, and could help us identify the culprit.'

'Perhaps,' mumbled Michael ungraciously. 'Although we do not even know what it is, so I cannot see how it will help us to track down the murderer. If you said it was something used by tanners or by parchment makers or some other tradesman, then we might have been able to act on it. But all we know is that it is a yellowish sticky grease of unknown origin.'

'The Franciscan friars know a lot about peculiar substances,' suggested Timothy. 'Their rat poison is famous from here to Peterborough, so perhaps one of them might be able to identify it.'

Michael rubbed his eyes tiredly. 'I hope it was not a Franciscan who killed Walcote and Faricius. They are at loggerheads with the Austins at the moment, because of this damned philosophical debate, so I suppose it is possible. But the Franciscans will not take kindly to being accused of harbouring a killer.'

'Then we shall have to be more circumspect,' said Timothy earnestly. 'Ely Hall has mice, so I shall visit the Franciscans on the pretext of asking for a solution. While I am there, I shall have a good look for that yellow stuff. If I see any, I shall report back to you, and we can then decide how to proceed.'

'Good,' said Michael, approvingly. 'That may lead somewhere, and if it does not, we will have antagonised no one.'

'And what about the presence of Simon Lynne here and at the Carmelite Friary?' asked Bartholomew.

'That will probably amount to nothing,' said Michael gloomily. 'I wanted to find *real* clues. I was hoping to discover who killed Walcote quickly – today.'

'At least we have been thorough,' said Timothy encouragingly. 'We needed to inspect Walcote's body and we

127

needed to visit his priory, just to be certain we had overlooked nothing. Just because we learned little does not make it a waste of time.'

Michael looked as though he disagreed, but the priory door opened, and Nicholas sidled out, casting a quick and agitated glance behind him before he closed it. He was already wearing Walcote's boots, although they were too small and meant that he walked with a peculiarly mincing gait.

'I know something that may help you,' he said in a whisper, even though it was unlikely that he could have been overheard through the thick gates. 'I did not want to mention it at first, because I promised Will I would tell no one. But then I decided I should tell you anything that might prove relevant to his death, although you probably know what I am going to say anyway. But I thought I should mention it, just in case you did not.'

'I want to know *anything* that could have a bearing, however remote, on Will's murder,' said Michael, intrigued by Nicholas's rambling discourse.

'I do not know whether it has a bearing,' said Nicholas. 'It involves certain women, but I am sure you know what I am talking about.'

'Women?' asked Michael, mystified. 'With Will? I always understood his affections ran in other directions – in yours, to be precise.'

Nicholas lowered his eyes and gazed at the ground. 'We did have a certain understanding,' he said. 'We have been close since he arrived at Barnwell ten years ago. But that was not what I meant. Will had dealings with the nuns at St Radegund's convent. Did you know about that?'

'What kind of dealings?' demanded Michael, indicating that he did not. 'They were certainly not romantic ones. He was too devoted to you to indulge in that sort of thing.'

More tears brimmed in Nicholas's eyes. 'Thank you for saying that. But I do not know the nature of his business with the nuns. He never told me. I assumed it was something he was doing in relation to his duties as Junior Proctor, which is why I thought you would know about them.'

'Well, I did not,' said Michael shortly. 'What makes you think these "dealings" had anything to do with the proctors' office?'

'Everyone knows that the students tend to congregate near the convent from time to time,' said Nicholas. 'I suppose they find a gathering of ladies irresistible. I assumed his business was related to preventing that from happening.'

'Did you ask him about it?' said Michael.

Nicholas glanced at the fat monk with haunted eyes. 'Of course I did. He merely treated me to that enigmatic smile of his and said it was better for me not to know too much about what transpired at the convent.'

'What did he mean by "better"?' pressed Michael. 'Safer? Or was he suggesting that it was so secret that not even his closest friend could be told?'

'I do not know,' said Nicholas. 'It had nothing to do with you, then? It was nothing you had asked him to do as Junior Proctor?'

'No,' replied Michael. He looked thoughtful, trying to guess what arrangement his Junior Proctor might have had with the nuns of St Radegund's that was so secret he would not even tell his lover. 'Thank you for telling us this, Nicholas. If everyone is as helpful, we might yet have this killer in front of the King's justices.'

Leaving Nicholas to slip back into Barnwell Priory unnoticed, the monk turned on his heel and began to stride down the Causeway with Bartholomew and Timothy following. It was a miserable journey. The rain had turned to sleet and drove into their faces, and the wind sliced through Bartholomew's cloak so that he wondered whether there was any point in wearing it at all. Even the uncharacteristically brisk pace set by Michael did not serve to warm him. The countryside was grey, dead and dismal, and there was not the merest trace of spring buds or leaves on the stunted trees.

Michael, however, seemed cheered by Nicholas's intelligence, and walked purposefully, oblivious to the inclement weather that buffeted him. He declared that a visit to the good women of St Radegund's Convent was in order, and instructed Timothy to begin his covert search for the yellow substance in the Franciscan Friary, while he and Bartholomew undertook the more pleasant task of asking the nuns about Walcote's business with them. Obediently, Timothy hurried back to the town, while Bartholomew and Michael turned towards the convent.

The convent had suffered a serious fire in 1313, and everything had been rebuilt. The small community of Benedictine nuns now enjoyed a comfortable range of buildings that included a pleasant solar, a refectory with a substantial hearth so that they seldom ate in the cold, and a church that possessed some of the loveliest wood carvings Bartholomew had ever seen. All were linked by a cloister, which meant the nuns were not obliged to walk in the rain when they made their way to and from their offices.

Unfortunately, the reputation of St Radegund's had suffered badly under the leadership of some of its prioresses. The one who had ruled during the Death had not been popular or pleasant, but she had at least maintained a degree of order over the women in her care. Her successors had not, and the convent had been visited by a number of bishops and other important Benedictines to investigate allegations of dishonesty and loose behaviour.

Personally, Bartholomew had little cause to deal with the nuns, and so had no idea whether the accusations were true or not, although his suspicions had been aroused when he had seen the state of Dame Martyn that morning. Michael, whose calling as a Benedictine meant that he was privy to information about the convent that was not widely available, cheerfully maintained that the allegations were entirely true. Bartholomew did not know whether to believe him or not, given that the monk was not averse to flagrant exaggeration and that the notion of a convent of

130

willing ladies was something that appealed to his sense of humour.

Michael strode up a path that wound through an attractive grove of chestnut trees, and tapped on the gatehouse door. Bartholomew followed him slowly, the once familiar track bringing back uncomfortable memories. The last time he had visited St Radegund's was during the plague, when he had been betrothed to a woman named Philippa Abigny. Philippa had been deposited in the convent for safe keeping by her parents, although Bartholomew had visited her regularly. Once the Death had moved on, leaving the survivors to deal with its ravages as well as they could, Philippa had decided not to take an impoverished physician as a husband after all, and had married a wealthy merchant instead.

Bartholomew wondered how different his life would have been had he taken a wife. He would have been forced to resign his Fellowship, since Fellows of the colleges were not permitted to marry, and there would have been no teaching and no students. But there would have been compensations, such as a family and a real home. A sudden vision of Philippa entered his mind – tall, fair and lovely – and he experienced a sharp pang of loneliness. His painful reminiscences were interrupted when a metal grille in the door clicked open in response to Michael's knock, and a pair of dark eyes peered out at them.

'Yes?' asked the owner of the eyes expectantly. Bartholomew recognised her as the novice who had been so blunt about her Prioress's condition earlier that morning; he also recalled that her name was Tysilia. 'What can we do for you?'

Michael sniggered and waved his eyebrows at her. 'Let us in and I will tell you.'

The grille snapped shut and Bartholomew shot the monk a withering look, seeing that Michael's inappropriate flirting had lost them the opportunity to talk to the nuns about Walcote's death. They were hardly likely to admit such a flagrant lecher into their midst. So Bartholomew

131

was startled when the door was flung open, and Tysilia swung her arm in an expansive gesture to indicate that they were to enter.

'Come in, then, good scholars, and tell us what you had in mind,' she said, giving Michael an outrageous wink. 'Do not keep us wondering.'

Michael shot through the door, leaving Bartholomew to follow more cautiously. 'I have a bad feeling about this,' he muttered. 'Perhaps we should have Edith with us, or Matilde . . .'

'Oh, yes, we should have brought Matilde,' Michael whispered back facetiously. 'It is always a good idea to bring a prostitute to a convent as an escort, Matt – although I confess that, in this case, I do not know who would be protecting whom.'

'Well?' asked Tysilia, hands on hips as she looked the two scholars up and down appraisingly, as a groom might survey a horse. She no longer wore the cloak that had covered her that morning, and Bartholomew was surprised to note that her black Benedictine habit was fashionably tight, cut rather low at the front, and sported a large jewelled cross that was a long way from the simple poverty envisioned and recommended by St Benedict. 'What do you want?'

'We have questions of a confidential nature that pertain to a delicate investigation I am conducting,' said Michael pompously.

'Eh?' said Tysilia, a blank expression on her pretty features. 'What are you talking about?'

'We want to speak to the Prioress,' translated Michael.

'Oh! Why did you not say so? Come upstairs, then. I expect our Prioress will not mind a couple of guests. She likes surprises.'

'Perhaps you should announce us first,' suggested Bartholomew tactfully. 'It is time for sext, and she may not want to be disturbed at her offices by unexpected visitors.'

Tysilia and Michael regarded Bartholomew as if he were insane.

132

'Follow me, then,' said Tysilia, after an awkward silence. 'Everyone is in the day-room.'

'I believe "solar" is the fashionable way to refer to that chamber these days,' said Michael conversationally, as they walked with her through a narrow slype between the church and a parlour to reach the cloister. 'I have not heard anyone referring to a "day-room" for years. Even my grandmother does not use such an antiquated term.'

'I keep forgetting it,' said Tysilia. She gave a weary sigh. 'There is such a *lot* for a young woman to remember these days – like threading a needle with silk *before* starting the embroidery; not wiping my lips on the tablecloth at meal-times if anyone else is watching; and going to church occasionally.'

'It must be very taxing for you,' said Michael sympathetically, his eyes fixed on her swaying hips as she preceded him through the cloister. Aware of his attention, she lifted her robe higher than was necessary to keep it from trailing in the puddles on the paving stones, revealing a pair of shapely white calves and some shoes that were ridiculously inadequate for anything other than lounging indoors.

'I am Tysilia de Apsley,' she said, glancing around to give Michael a smile that had the undeniable qualities of a leer. Her disconcerting behaviour confirmed the impression Bartholomew had that morning: that she was not clever, and that she was being trained to hide the fact by flaunting her good looks. She certainly knew how to charm Michael. 'I expect you have heard of me.'

'I hear a great many things,' replied Michael ambiguously, stepping quickly around her to open a door before she reached it. She disappeared inside, and then gave a shriek of delighted indignation. Bartholomew glanced up just in time to see Michael returning his hands to their customary position inside their wide sleeves. 'But just remind me in what context I might have heard a pretty name like Tysilia de Apsley.'

'My uncle is the Bishop of Ely,' she said, her voice echoing

133

back down the stairs as she climbed them. 'Thomas de Lisle.'

'Damn!' muttered Michael to Bartholomew. 'I would not have done that, had I known. Still, I think she enjoyed it.'

'And what did you do exactly, Brother?' asked Bartholomew.

Michael chuckled softly. 'Nothing I would recommend you try, now that we know who she is. I should have remembered she was here. My lord Bishop told me that he had placed his wanton niece at St Radegund's out of harm's way; I recall telling him it was a very good place for her.'

Bartholomew glanced sharply at him. 'Do you mean it is good because it is a convent and will cure her indecent behaviour, or because she will probably feel at home in an institution with a reputation like St Radegund's?'

Michael's smile was enigmatic. 'What do you think?'

'I do not know,' said Bartholomew. 'But it is unwise to trust someone like her with gate duties. It seems to me that she will allow anyone inside as long as he is male.'

'The Sacristan, Eve Wasteneys, is no fool,' replied Michael ambiguously. 'I expect she knows what she is doing, although I cannot say the same for that sot who is currently drinking her way through the convent's once-impressive wine cellars.'

'Do you mean Prioress Martyn?' asked Bartholomew, recalling that she was happy to avail herself of other people's wine cellars, too, if her collapse at the side of the road that morning had been anything to go by.

'Have you met her?' asked Michael. 'I suppose you have been called to give her cures for over-indulgence, although the nuns usually try to conceal her excesses.'

'You look familiar,' said Tysilia, turning to Bartholomew with a slight frown marring her pretty features. 'I think I have seen you before.'

'This morning,' said Bartholomew. 'You were on your way home from the Panton manor, and your Prioress was taken ill.'

'She was not ill; she was drunk,' stated Tysilia uncompromisingly. 'But, yes, I think I remember you. However, you wore a pretty ear-ring this morning. What happened to it?'

'An ear-ring?' queried Michael, startled.

'That was my nephew,' replied Bartholomew.

'Your nephew is an ear-ring?' asked Tysilia, frowning harder than ever.

'Lord help us!' breathed Michael, regarding her uncertainly. 'No wonder the Bishop wanted her out of the way.'

'I am sorry I am confused,' said Tysilia, looking anything but contrite. 'But all men look the same to me when they wear black. If they wear pretty colours, I recall them better, but there is nothing memorable about black.'

'That must be awkward for you, considering men of your own Order wear black habits,' said Michael dryly.

Tysilia giggled, then pushed open a door at the top of the stairs. 'It has proved embarrassing on occasion. But here is our day-room – I mean our . . . what did you say it was called again, Brother? I have forgotten already.'

Bartholomew gazed at the scene in the solar, and fought hard not to gape in open-mouthed astonishment. A large fire burned in the hearth, and so that the room was warm to the point of being overheated. A number of nuns were there, some sitting at a large table and engaged in communal embroidery, while others lounged on cushion-covered benches or were comfortably settled in cosy window-seats. Two things caught Bartholomew's eye immediately. The first was that not all the nuns were fully clothed, although they did not seem to be especially discomfited by the sudden presence of two men in their midst; the second was that they were not alone.

Simon Lynne was there. He sat near a window, his freckled face flushed and his mop of thick hair tousled and unruly. He regarded Bartholomew and Michael warily, then rose slowly to his feet. The physician was not surprised that the Carmelite student-friar was red and tangle-haired, given that he must have run very quickly from Barnwell Priory to reach the convent before Bartholomew and Michael. He wondered whether Lynne had overheard Nicholas telling Michael about Walcote's mysterious visits to the convent, and had determined to ask his own questions before the Senior Proctor could – or perhaps he had even come to warn the nuns that Michael was heading their way.

'You arrived here remarkably quickly, Lynne,' said Michael coolly. 'But it is good to see you, nevertheless. There are a few questions I would like to put to you.'

'Another time,' said Lynne rudely, reaching for his cloak. 'I am late for my duties and must go.' He gave a brief nod to the nuns, who watched the exchange with amused detachment, and headed for the door. He was stopped dead in his tracks by a hand that was as expert at grabbing recalcitrant students as it was at making passes at Bishops' nieces.

'Then you can tell your Prior that you have been with me,' said the monk. 'What were you doing at Barnwell a few moments ago?'

'You are mistaken, Brother. I have not been at Barnwell,' replied Lynne hesitantly. 'And I do not have time to discuss it with you. I am late.'

'You can discuss it here or in my cells,' said Michael sharply, and the icy gleam in his eye made it clear that he was not bluffing. 'It is your choice, Master Lynne.'

'Really, Brother,' came a slightly slurred voice from one of the couches near the fire. 'Can a lad not even visit his aunt without being questioned by the Senior Proctor these days?'

'Not when that lad knows something that may be of relevance to a murder enquiry, Dame Martyn,' said Michael, not relinquishing his grip on Lynne. 'And you have never mentioned a nephew before. Is it true? Or is it a convenient lie told for this little tyke's benefit?'

'Of course it is true,' said Dame Martyn, not sounding particularly offended that Michael had effectively accused her of being a liar. 'And do call me Mabel. You know I am not a woman for unnecessary formality.'

136

'Are you feeling better?' asked Bartholomew, thinking that she did not look it. Her heavy face was unnaturally ruddy, and there was a bleariness about her eyes that spoke of poor health.

'Better than what?' she asked blankly.

'The doctor stopped to help us this morning when you were taken ill,' said the Sacristan, Eve Wasteneys, tactfully. Although almost all the other dozen or so nuns in the solar had followed Dame Martyn's example of shedding unwanted clothes, Eve remained fully dressed, with a starched wimple cutting uncomfortably into her strong chin.

'When you were drunk,' supplied Tysilia, less tactfully.

Dame Martyn shot the younger woman an unpleasant look. 'Go back to your mending, Tysilia. And this time, remember that the large hole at the top of a glove is to allow the hand to go in. You do not sew it up.'

'I will remember,' said Tysilia brightly, making a show of sitting on a stool and arranging her habit so that it revealed a good part of her long slim legs. She picked up the glove and immediately began to hem across the top with large, uneven stitches. Bartholomew watched her uncertainly, wondering if her action was a deliberate rebellion against the Prioress's authority, or whether Tysilia was so slow-minded that she did not realise what she was doing.

Dame Martyn smiled weakly at Bartholomew. 'So, it was you who came to my assistance this morning. I am grateful to you – for your discretion as well as for the medicine you gave me.'

'The cloves,' said Bartholomew.

'Cloves? For being in her cups?' asked Michael, amused. 'Perhaps your nephew Richard is right about physicians being charlatans after all.'

Dame Martyn ignored him. 'Unfortunately, we are poor, and I am unable to pay you for your services. I assume that is why you are here? But perhaps we can come to some arrangement.'

'What kind of arrangement?' asked Michael, before

Bartholomew could tell her that payment was not required.

Dame Martyn gave a leering smile that rendered her wine-ravaged features more debauched than ever. 'Well, I could—'

'We are excellent needlewomen,' said Dame Wasteneys hastily to Bartholomew. The Prioress seemed startled by the interruption, while Michael raised his eyebrows, royally entertained by the whole conversation. 'We will mend that tear in your cloak. Perhaps that will repay you for your kindness.'

'I will do it,' offered Tysilia.

'Not if he ever wants to wear it again,' said Michael. 'Look what she is doing to that glove.'

With a tut of annoyance, Eve Wasteneys snatched the glove away from Tysilia, and handed her a discarded offcut of material instead. 'Sew that,' she instructed. Tysilia's sulky pout vanished, and she began to adorn the hapless patch with her large, ugly stitches without seeming to understand that it was a pointless exercise. Bartholomew and Michael exchanged a bemused glance. Was Tysilia's behaviour an elaborate performance for their benefit?

'Will you accept our offer of darning, Doctor?' asked Eve. 'Or would you rather have a cabbage from the gardens?'

'I do not like cabbage,' said Michael, as though the offer was being made to him. 'But we have not come to haggle over greenery. We are here on official business.'

Dame Martyn reached out a plump hand and filled one of the largest wine goblets Bartholomew had ever seen, the contents of which she then drank so fast that Bartholomew was certain they did not touch the sides of her throat. 'What do you mean?' she asked. 'What sort of business?'

Michael looked significantly at Lynne and then back to Dame Martyn. 'Since I have not had occasion to visit you for several weeks, I assumed you had taken my Bishop's advice, and concentrated on your religious vocations rather than your more secular pastimes. But now I find you entertaining a student.'

'He is my nephew,' said Dame Martyn with a weary sigh, feigning boredom with the conversation. 'My sister's boy.'

'If you want to question Master Lynne, perhaps you could do so outside,' suggested Eve, apparently deciding that it would be better for all concerned if the monk and his friend went away, leaving the nuns of St Radegund's to their own debauched devices. 'Take him back to Cambridge with you.'

'But it is so much more pleasant here,' said Michael immediately, settling himself on a bench. He addressed the sullen student. 'Now, Lynne, why are you here? Did you run all the way from Barnwell?'

'I told you, I have not been to Barnwell,' said Lynne. His uneasy gaze shifted to Dame Martyn. 'I am here visiting my aunt.'

'Do not lie to me,' said Michael impatiently. 'I saw you at Barnwell Priory with my own eyes. You are a Carmelite; you should not have been at a convent for Austin canons. You know very well that the properties of rival Orders are out of bounds for student-friars.'

'It must have been my brother you saw,' said Lynne challengingly. 'People are always confusing us. Is that not true, Aunt Mabel?'

'Eh?' said Dame Martyn, caught in the act of taking another substantial draught from her jug-sized cup. 'Oh, yes. Peas in a pod, Brother.'

'I see,' said Michael flatly. He leaned back against the wall and treated the student to a long, cool stare. 'Be off with you, then. I shall have words with your Prior about your insolence, and then you will learn that it is not wise to play games with the Senior Proctor.'

Lynne needed no second bidding to take his leave. He shot down the stairs, and they heard his feet clattering on the cobbles of the courtyard as he ran towards the gate.

'You did not have to be so hard on the boy,' said Dame Martyn, bringing her red-rimmed eyes to bear on Michael. 'He was telling you the truth.'

'I have warned you about this kind of thing before,' said

Michael sternly. 'Believe me, Dame Martyn, you do not want our undergraduates to consider your convent to be a place that always gives them a warm welcome. Even your energetic ladies would find it too much.'

She sighed tiredly. 'You seem determined to disbelieve me, Brother. I assure you, we were doing nothing untoward. Look at us. We are scarcely dressed for receiving guests.'

'Some of you are scarcely dressed at all,' remarked Michael, casting an assessing eye around the gathering. 'And why are you all in here anyway? You should be celebrating sext.'

'The church is too cold,' said Dame Martyn in a voice that had a distinct whine to it. 'I do not want my poor ladies made ill by standing in a frigid church for hours on end.'

'So much for a life of religious contemplation,' muttered Michael. Bartholomew sensed that even he was a little taken aback by Dame Martyn's irresponsible attitude towards the offices she was supposed to oversee.

'During Lent, we have a longer terce than usual,' said Eve Wasteneys hastily, seeking to minimise the damage her superior was causing with her careless replies. 'And then we begin nones early, so missing sext is not as serious as you seem to think. But why did you really come, Brother? Was it only to criticise us for changing our offices?'

'I have a more pressing matter than that,' said Michael, considering his own investigation more important than the prayers the nuns had taken vows to undertake. 'Perhaps we can discuss it privately?'

'In my parlour, you mean,' said Dame Martyn with the kind of grin that suggested Michael had discussed 'pressing matters' in the privacy of her parlour before. Bartholomew decided that he really did not want to know any more about it.

'Your parlour will do nicely,' said Michael. 'Lead the way, Dame Martyn.'

'Mabel,' corrected the Prioress.

* * *

Dame Martyn's parlour was an airy room on the upper floor of the gatehouse. The shutters were open, and daylight streamed in through the glassless windows. A breeze rustled the parchments that lay on a table, which were prevented from blowing away by a selection of heavy metal ornaments. Unlike the solar, there was no fire, and although the room was light, it was very cold. It was very much like Bartholomew's own room at Michaelhouse, and he did not blame the Prioress for preferring the debauched cosiness of the solar.

'The Bishop of Ely granted Tysilia the right to gather firewood from the land he owns to the south,' explained Eve Wasteneys, who had followed them from the solar, doubtless unwilling to entrust the convent's reputation to her Prioress. 'But the grant is for wood for her personal use only, and it does not allow us to heat the entire priory. So, while we have plenty of warmth in the solar and the dormitory, the rest of the place is freezing.'

Michael frowned in puzzlement. 'You are being very scrupulous about this. Why not take what you like? I doubt the Bishop would find out if you did it discreetly.'

Eve gave a weary smile. 'You have met Tysilia, Brother. She is pretty, but somewhat short on wits. When de Lisle last visited us, Tysilia mentioned how pleasant it was to have a roaring fire in every room, and he guessed they were fuelled by his wood. He was furious, and threatened to take her from us if we abused her privileges again.'

'So, because we cannot trust that silly little fool, we are obliged to be honest,' said Dame Martyn, her disapproving voice indicating that she found such a position objectionable.

'Would it be such a bad thing if Tysilia were removed?' asked Bartholomew. 'I cannot see that you would miss her incisive wit and lively conversation of an evening.'

Eve smiled. 'We would not, although her lack of intelligence does provide us with a certain degree of entertainment. But it is not her we will miss: it is the money the

Bishop pays us to look after her. Despite what you may think, St Radegund's is poor, and we need her fees.'

Bartholomew recalled that Dame Martyn's predecessor had also been desperate for the money paid by boarders' wealthy parents. His fiancée Philippa had been considered a source of valuable income for the convent, and the then Prioress had watched over her like a hawk. Because Philippa's marriage would mean the end of the payments, the Prioress had gone to some lengths to keep her and Bartholomew apart.

'The Bishop will remove Tysilia anyway, if he thinks you are entertaining scholars in an improper manner,' warned Michael sternly.

Eve raised her eyebrows, and a smile of genuine amusement played about her lips. 'I had credited you with more insight, Brother. The Bishop knows exactly to what depths we are sometimes forced to plummet to make ends meet, and believe me, Tysilia was no innocent when he brought her here. She was with child.'

'Was?' asked Bartholomew. 'Then where is it?'

'It was born before its time and died,' replied Dame Martyn. 'We sent her back to Ely after she had recovered, only to have her foisted on us a second time for the same reason within a few months. She had already forgotten what we had taught her about how to avoid becoming pregnant.'

'We have tried all manner of diversions to distract her from men,' continued Eve, sounding exasperated. 'Only last week I took her with me to Bedford. I thought the journey might keep her out of mischief.'

'And I assume, from the expression on your face, that it did not,' said Michael.

Eve shook her head. 'She was the model of virtue on the outward journey, but there was a young man in our party on the way home, and I was hard pressed to conceal her indiscretions from our travelling companions. I suppose she just likes the company of men.'

'Have you considered giving her a task other than that

of gatekeeper?' asked Bartholomew curiously. 'Only I would not be so sure that she will allow the right people inside.'

'We are not too fussy about that,' mumbled Dame Martyn, settling herself in a cushioned chair with her monstrous cup in one fat-fingered hand.

'What other task did you have in mind?' asked Eve of Bartholomew, giving her Prioress a sharp glance to warn her against making flippant remarks. 'Work in the kitchen, where there are knives to injure herself on? In the gardens, where there are sharp tools? In the chapel, where sacred vessels need to be treated with respect and care?'

'Surely she cannot be that bad,' said Bartholomew.

'She is something of a liability, actually,' said Eve. 'And not only is she difficult to control, but she is a thief.'

'How do you know?' asked Michael immediately. 'Have items gone missing?'

Dame Martyn scowled at her Sacristan. 'You should not have mentioned that, Eve. It is a convent matter and none of Brother Michael's business.'

'It may be my business if I learn that her stealing is related to the death of Walcote,' warned Michael. 'So I suggest you be sensible about this and answer my questions honestly. Now, how do you know Tysilia is a thief?'

'The stealing has nothing to do with Walcote,' snapped Dame Martyn, finally nettled out of her half-drunken insouciance. 'She is a stupid girl who cannot resist anything that glitters. She seldom removes anything of worth.'

'That is not true,' contradicted Eve. 'She has a penchant for gold, and sometimes she takes items that are extremely valuable and that we cannot afford to lose. But Dame Martyn is right about her stupidity: Tysilia has not yet learned that in order to be a successful thief, it is necessary to steal when there are no witnesses and that you should not hide the proceeds of your crime in your own bed-chest.'

'Why not confront her about this?' asked Bartholomew. 'Tell her not to do it any more.'

'We have tried,' said Eve. 'But she simply denies

143

everything. When we point out that she was seen, or that the evidence of her guilt is concealed among her belongings, she merely claims we are mistaken.'

'So, with her stealing and her promiscuity, she is not an easy charge,' said Bartholomew, beginning to feel sorry for the nuns.

'She is not,' agreed Eve fervently. 'If I were a more cynical person, I would wonder whether the Bishop had given us his niece just so that he will have an excuse to suppress us at some point in the future.'

'Are you suggesting that my Bishop would deliberately foist a wanton woman on you, so that he could then accuse you of unseemly behaviour?' asked Michael, sounding shocked. Bartholomew thought that the wily Thomas de Lisle could well have formulated exactly such a plan, and imagined that Michael knew so, too.

'We do not mind licentious behaviour as such,' said Dame Martyn, treating Michael to a conspiratorial smile. 'We just prefer it to be conducted with sensitivity and tact.'

Warning bells began to jangle in Bartholomew's mind. Was Tysilia really just an empty-headed flirt, whom the Bishop had sent to destroy the reputation of a convent already in trouble over its secular activities? Or was she very intelligent, and merely pretending to be stupid for reasons of her own? Perhaps it was Tysilia with whom Walcote had had his secret business. Bartholomew wondered whether the Bishop might have charged her with some task, using a member of his family to act as his agent, much as he used Michael. He decided it was a distinct possibility, and determined to watch Tysilia very closely.

'The Bishop is behind with his payments,' said Eve to Michael. 'He now owes us for three months and five days of Tysilia's company. Would you mention it, if you happen to meet him?'

'No,' said Michael, wisely determined to stay well away from the dangerous business of informing a Bishop that he was in debt. 'But I am not surprised. De Lisle is not a wealthy man.'

'He is wealthy enough when it comes to his own comforts,' remarked Eve, a little bitterly.

'We should address the real purpose of my visit,' said Michael, abruptly changing the subject from de Lisle's dubious finances. 'Time is passing, and I do not want Walcote's killer to enjoy a moment more freedom than necessary.'

'Why do you think we can tell you anything about Will Walcote's murder?' asked Dame Martyn, sounding a little startled. 'We barely knew the man.'

'He visited you here on a regular basis,' stated Michael, although Nicholas had made no such claim. 'I want to know why.'

'You would ask me to reveal the personal secrets of a man who is now dead?' asked Dame Martyn, her red-rimmed eyes wide in feigned shock. 'That would not be a kind thing to do.'

'Do not lie to me,' snapped Michael. 'We both know perfectly well that he did not come here to avail himself of the services that your nuns like to offer. He was not that kind of man.'

'No,' said Eve, suddenly bitter. 'None of them ever are. But that does not stop them from coming to us and taking advantage of our poverty to snatch what they want. And then they return to their wives and their children, and pretend that they are good and honourable – not "that kind of man", as you put it.'

'That is not what I meant at all,' said Michael. 'Walcote was engaged in a relationship with one of his brethren, and was not interested in women. I know he did not come to you with the intention of romping in your dormitories.'

Dame Martyn regarded him craftily. 'Then I can tell you nothing more. I am under the sacred seal of confession.'

'Do not be ridiculous!' Michael exploded. 'Are you claiming that *you* were Walcote's confessor? I have never heard anything more outrageous in my life! Now, what was his business here, Dame Martyn? You will tell me, or I shall

145

make a personal recommendation to the Bishop that he removes his niece from you with immediate effect.'

Dame Martyn hastened to make amends. She evidently knew Michael well enough to guess that he would do what he threatened. 'Actually, we have no idea what Walcote did here. And that is the truth.'

'I see,' said Michael coldly. 'Shall I station my beadles here, then, to question anyone who comes or leaves? That would certainly deter visitors. Your happily married men will not like revealing the nature of their business *here* to interested beadles.'

'You are a hard man, Brother,' said Eve, when Dame Martyn seemed at a loss for words. 'But the reason we cannot tell you what Walcote did is because we really do not know. As I mentioned earlier, times are hard, and we are obliged to raise funds in any way we can. One method is to rent this room for meetings that people would rather did not take place in the town.'

'Do not tell him!' cried Dame Martyn in horror. 'The reason people come here is because they know they can rely on our discretion. Without that, we have nothing.'

'Are you telling me that your convent is used as a venue for criminals?' asked Michael quickly, as he saw Eve hesitate. 'Men gather here to plan crimes and other evil deeds?'

'We do not know what they plan,' said Eve with blunt honesty. 'All we do is make this parlour available to anyone who pays us four groats – no questions asked.'

'And Walcote hired this room from you?' asked Michael.

Eve nodded, while the Prioress looked disgusted at what her Sacristan had revealed.

'How often? Once a week? More? Less?'

Eve Wasteneys regarded Michael for a moment, and then shrugged, looking at her Prioress as she did so. 'Walcote is dead, Reverend Mother. He will not be paying us for any more meetings, and so we have nothing to lose by being honest with Brother Michael.'

'But one of the others might pay us instead,' said Dame Martyn plaintively. 'There is no reason these gatherings should stop, just because one of their number is dead.'

'They were Walcote's meetings,' said Eve. 'He paid us and he organised them. That source of income is finished, and it is in our interests to co-operate with the proctors now. We do not want his beadles stationed at our gates, and we cannot afford to lose Tysilia – assuming the Bishop pays us eventually, that is. We have no choice but to tell Brother Michael what he wants to know.'

'How often were these meetings?' repeated Michael, breaking into their conversation.

'Irregularly,' replied Eve, while Dame Martyn shook her head angrily and turned her attention to the dregs at the bottom of her cup.

'But how frequently?' pressed Michael. 'What were the intervals between meetings – days or weeks? And how many times did they occur?'

'He hired the room perhaps eight or nine times,' replied Eve, frowning as she tried to remember. 'The first two or three meetings were last November or December – around the time the Master of Michaelhouse was murdered, if I recall correctly.'

'You do not recall correctly,' said Michael immediately. 'When I was conducting that particular investigation, Walcote was in Ely. I remember quite distinctly, because there was a spate of crimes at that time, and I could have done with his help. He only arrived back in Cambridge the day Runham was buried and his cousin's effigy was smashed in the Market Square.'

That particular incident was vividly etched in Bartholomew's mind. 'He was one of the throng who managed to grab a handful of the coins that were hidden inside Wilson's effigy, and that spilled out when the thing broke.'

'She said *around* that time,' said Dame Martyn, showing a remarkable clarity of mind for someone who was drunk. 'She did not say *exactly* at that time.'

147

'I know I am right,' said Eve. 'I was also one of the fortunate people who managed to seize a couple of gold coins. We used them to repair the leaking roof in this room. Walcote commented on it when he next came, which was after Christmas.'

'So, the roof leaked the first time Walcote was here, but it was repaired by the time he next visited,' said Michael. 'So, his first meeting may have been *before* Master Runham died.'

'Not necessarily,' said Eve. 'We did not acquire the money and have the roof mended the next day. It took some time to reach an acceptable arrangement with a thatcher, and so Walcote's first set of meetings could have occurred just before or after the effigy incident.'

'But suffice to say he had two or three meetings in November or December and one after Christmas,' said Dame Martyn, raising one hand to her lips to disguise a wine-perfumed belch. 'I remember the Christmas meeting, because we spent the four groats he gave us on wine to celebrate Yuletide.'

'I bet you did,' muttered Michael, regarding the nun and her cup with rank disapproval.

'And you do not keep records?' asked Bartholomew hopefully. 'You do not write that kind of income in your accounts?'

Eve regarded him with weary amusement. 'Brother Michael is probably right: the people who hire our room do not do so for legal purposes. Since we do not want to be accused of complicity in any crimes they commit, of course we do not keep records of when these meetings took place.'

'Three meetings in November or December and one at Christmas is four,' said Michael. 'You said there were eight or nine. When were the others?'

'Recently,' said Eve. 'They were not on any particular day, and they were all late at night.'

148

'And who did Walcote meet?' pressed Michael. 'Were they local men or strangers? Did you recognise any of them?'

'No,' said Dame Martyn immediately. Michael raised his eyebrows.

'Once I thought I glimpsed William de Lincolne, the Carmelite Prior,' said Eve, who, unlike the Prioress, saw that it was unwise to play games with Michael.

'Lincolne,' said Michael casting a significant glance at Bartholomew. 'I knew there was something odd about him. Who else?'

'Possibly William Pechem, the warden of the Franciscans,' said Eve, ignoring Dame Martyn's angry signals to say nothing more.

'A Carmelite and a Franciscan?' asked Michael, surprised. 'They always give the impression that they dislike each other, and that they would never meet on friendly terms.'

'I do not know whether their meetings were friendly or not,' said Eve. 'And I cannot tell you whether they were both present at the same meetings.'

'What do you mean?' asked Michael.

Eve sighed impatiently. 'Exactly what I say, Brother. I think I saw Pechem, and I think I saw Lincolne, but I do not remember whether I saw them both on the same night. I cannot tell you whether Walcote's meetings were always with the same people.'

'That is interesting,' said Michael.

Eve went on. 'If you ask me to swear that it was definitely these men I saw I cannot do it – not because I mean to be unhelpful, but because I am simply not sure. As I said, it was dark.'

'I saw no one,' slurred Dame Martyn. She slipped suddenly to one side, so that she sat at an odd angle in her chair.

'That I can believe,' said Michael regarding her in disdain. He turned to Eve. 'Who else?'

'One other,' said Eve nervously. 'Although I do not know whether I should mention it.'

'You should,' declared Michael. 'Who was it?'

'Master Kenyngham of Michaelhouse.' She watched Michael's jaw drop in patent disbelief. 'See? I knew I should not tell you.'

chapter 5

'I KNEW THERE WAS SOMETHING MORE TO FARICIUS'S murder than a simple stabbing,' said Michael, as he and Bartholomew walked the short distance from St Radegund's Convent back to the town.

The day had grown even darker since they had been in the convent, and black clouds slouched above, moving quickly in the rising wind. Rain fell in a persistent, heavy drizzle that quickly soaked through Bartholomew's cloak and boots. He was shivering by the time they reached the King's Ditch, and longed to return to the comparative comfort of Michaelhouse, even if it were only to a room that was so damp that the walls were stained green with mould.

'I said those Carmelites were hiding something,' Michael went on, warm and snug inside his own oiled cloak and expensive boots. 'Now I learn that the leader of the Carmelites and the leader of the Franciscans – sworn enemies – were having clandestine meetings with my Junior Proctor.'

'Eve Wasteneys said she was not sure whether the two were at the same gatherings,' Bartholomew pointed out.

'But she did not say they were not,' said Michael.

'Do you believe her?' asked Bartholomew. 'She and Dame Martyn have no reason to be truthful with you. You threatened them, and they have good cause to dislike you.'

Michael shrugged. 'Dame Martyn might try to fool me, but Eve is a practical woman who knows that lying to the Senior Proctor is not a clever thing to do. I believe what she said. Also, the fact that she was a little vague about some of the details gives her story a ring of authenticity, as far as I am concerned.'

'I wonder what Walcote could have been discussing with

them,' mused Bartholomew, trying to imagine the kind of business that would bring the leader of the Franciscans, the fanatical Prior Lincolne and the gentle, unworldly Kenyngham together in the depths of the night at a place like St Radegund's Convent. 'Perhaps he was trying to resolve the conflict between the Orders.'

'No,' said Michael, after a moment of thought. 'Eve said the first meeting was in November or December, and there was no trouble to speak of between the Orders at that point. It has only come to a head during the last few weeks – since the beginning of Lent.'

'But that is when Eve claimed there were several more meetings,' said Bartholomew.

Michael rubbed his hands together in sudden enthusiasm. 'This is more like it, Matt! I thought at first that Walcote's death was a simple case of some embittered student striking a blow at the University's authority. Now I discover that he was organising secret meetings, and that he had been doing so for months.'

Bartholomew regarded him doubtfully. 'Why should that make you feel better about his murder? And you do, Brother; you are looking pleased with yourself.'

'Because this is the kind of mystery that I am good at solving. I possess a cunning mind, and am far better at resolving complex plots than I am at uncovering random acts of violence. We will get to the bottom of this, and we will see Walcote's death avenged. Now I know that a plot involving the University lies at the heart of it, I am more hopeful of success.'

'Well, I am not,' said Bartholomew gloomily. 'The webs of deceit and untruths spread by scholars are often extremely difficult to unravel. We might still be looking into this at Christmas.'

'Nonsense, Matt,' said Michael confidently. 'We will have this solved by Easter Sunday.'

'In five days?' asked Bartholomew uncertainly. 'I do not think so!'

'We will. I wager you a fine dinner – with as much wine as you can drink – at the Brazen George that by Easter Sunday we shall have this resolved. Do you accept?'

'Murder is hardly a matter for betting,' said Bartholomew primly. 'You are wrong, anyway. It will be impossible to solve this muddle in five days.'

Michael slapped him on the shoulders. 'You will see. But one of the first things we shall do is visit the Carmelite Friary. I want to inspect Faricius's belongings, to see if there is something to indicate that he was not the hard-working, scholarly man everyone seemed to admire. And then I shall ask Lincolne what he was doing with my Junior Proctor at St Radegund's Convent.'

'What if he denies it? Eve Wasteneys said she could not be certain.'

Michael rubbed his chin. 'You are right. Perhaps a full-frontal assault on the man would not be wise, given that we do not have a witness who is prepared to be unequivocal. It may warn him to be on the alert, or he may tell his co-conspirators. I shall have to be a little more circumspect.'

As they entered the town through the Barnwell Gate and started to walk down the High Street towards the Carmelite Friary, they met Brother Timothy, who had completed his business with the Franciscans. His covert search for the curious yellow substance that Bartholomew had seen on Faricius and Walcote had been unsuccessful, although he carried a bag of ominous-looking black powder that he was assured would rid the Benedictines of their mice.

'Nothing?' asked Michael, disappointed.

The Benedictine shook his head. 'I had my fingers in all manner of jars and bottles, so that even the herbalist, who loves to talk about his potions and concoctions, was beginning to grow suspicious. I pretended that my spare habit had a yellow stain that I was keen to remove, but I am sure he genuinely did not know the nature of the substance we saw on Walcote.'

'Did he suggest anyone else who might?' asked Michael.

Timothy scratched his head. 'I did not want to press him too hard, because Franciscans are intensely loyal to each other. If the herbalist thought we believed one of his brethren to be involved in a crime, he would close ranks with his colleagues, and we would never be allowed inside the gates again.'

'Never mind,' said Michael, not sounding surprised that the yellow stains had led nowhere. 'We are going to inspect Faricius's belongings. Perhaps they will yield some kind of clue.'

The Carmelite Friary was a compact institution on Milne Street, the buildings of which were smaller than those of the Dominicans, but which boasted a large and pleasant garden that ran down to the river near Small Bridges Street. Like the other friaries, it was dominated by a two-storeyed building that had a refectory on the ground floor with a dormitory on the upper floor. With it, stables, a kitchen and a chapter house formed a neat quadrangle, while the Prior's house was a pleasant extension that jutted out to the south. The Prior's quarters boasted a private chapel on the ground floor, with a chamber on the upper floor that was an office during the day and a bedchamber for Lincolne at night.

When they were shown into his chamber, Prior Lincolne was standing on a stool with a stick in his hand, making lunging swipes at the cobwebs that hung in silken threads from the rafters. Already several large splinters of oaken beam lay scattered across the rugs, where he had been overly rough with his cleaning.

'Spiders,' he announced as they walked in. 'I hate spiders. I do not like the way their webs entangle themselves in my hair.'

Looking at Lincolne's peculiar topknot, Bartholomew understood why. The tuft of hair barely cleared the lowest of the beams, and would have acted like a magnet to anything hanging from them. The physician imagined that it collected all manner of dirt as it rubbed its way across the ceilings in the various rooms Lincolne would have been obliged to enter during the course of a day.

'We would like to inspect Faricius's belongings, if we may,' said Michael, flinching backward as an especially vigorous poke from Lincolne brought down a shower of plaster. He pursed his lips in disapproval. 'Do you not have servants for that sort of thing?'

'We do,' replied Lincolne, stepping down from the stool, but still towering over his three visitors. 'However, I have exacting standards, and they seldom reach them. You want to inspect Faricius's belongings, you say? Why?'

'We are taking his death very seriously,' replied Michael. 'And we want to leave no stone unturned. It is possible that there is something in his possessions that may throw light on the identity of the killer.'

'Are you saying that your other enquiries have come to nothing?' asked Lincolne astutely. 'What about the Dominicans? You would be better concentrating your efforts there, as I have told you before.'

'And so we will,' said Michael. 'But first, I want to see Faricius's cell.'

Lincolne sighed impatiently. 'Very well, then. Come with me.'

'I am sure you have more important things to do than accompany us,' said Michael. He glanced up at the ceiling. 'There are spiders to declare war upon.'

'They can wait,' said Lincolne, casting a venomous glower at the hapless beings in the rafters. 'Perhaps the respite will lure them out, and I shall be able to catch them when I return.'

They followed him across the yard to the dormitory. It was afternoon, and a time when the friars were accustomed to a period of rest or private prayer before attending vespers, so a number of them were in the dormitory, some sleeping and some reading. The dormitory comprised a large room that was blocked into tiny cells just large enough to house a mattress, a prie-dieu and a couple of hooks on the wall.

Lincolne led the way to a cell near a window that overlooked the street.

'This was Faricius's bed. As you can see, he owned very little, but what he had is here.'

The cell was spartan, as a friar's home was supposed to be, unlike most of the others they had passed, which boasted rugs on the floor and colourful blankets. A bloodstained cloak, that was evidently the one Faricius had been wearing when he died, hung on one hook, while a spare habit adorned the other. A simple wooden cross had been nailed to the wall and a psalter lay open on the bed, as though Faricius had been reading it before he took his fateful last journey.

Michael knelt and peered under the bed, reaching out to withdraw a rough chest that was stored there. Inside were several clean shirts, some woollen undergarments, a spare scrip, and several pens and some parchment. There was also a much-fingered copy of William Heytesbury's *Regulae Solvendi Sophismata*. Lincolne gave a gasp of horror and snatched it from Michael's hands.

'What is this work of the Devil doing in our friary?' he demanded. The fury in his voice brought the resting friars, including the gap-toothed Horneby, scurrying to see what was happening.

'Ah, Horneby,' said Michael with a predatory smile. 'Just the man I wanted to see. You do not know where I might find young Simon Lynne, do you?'

Horneby looked furtive. 'He is probably in the garden, praying.'

Even Lincolne looked doubtful. 'He will be in the friary somewhere,' he said to Michael. 'I have been keeping our students in, because I do not want them attacked by violent Dominicans.'

'Then I want to speak to Lynne,' said Michael. He flicked his fingers at a youngster with bad skin. 'Fetch him, if you please.'

'Never mind Lynne,' said Lincolne, turning his attention

back to the book, away from the student who scrambled to do Michael's bidding. He held the tome carefully by one corner, as if it were a dead mouse. 'I want to know what this filth is doing in my friary.'

'I imagine Faricius was reading it so he could refute Heytesbury's arguments,' said Horneby, although he was unable to disguise the doubt in his voice. 'It is difficult to prove someone wrong if you are unacquainted with the essence of his argument.'

Lincolne thrust the book into Horneby's hands. 'Burn it,' he ordered uncompromisingly.

'We have just returned from St Radegund's Convent,' said Michael, in the silence that followed. Evidently, none of the student-friars was easy with the notion of burning Faricius's property. Horneby certainly did not hurry away to do his Prior's bidding; he stayed where he was, cradling the book in his arms, although at the mention of St Radegund's, he shot Michael one of the most furtive looks Bartholomew had ever seen, so that the physician suspected the student knew exactly where his friend had been. Lincolne merely seemed surprised by the monk's statement.

'What were *you* doing there?' he asked in distaste. 'It is not a place frequented by decent men.'

'What do you mean?' asked Michael innocently. 'It is a community of Benedictine nuns.'

'It is a community of loose women who wear Benedictine habits,' corrected Lincolne. 'Why the Bishop does not expel them and donate the buildings to the University is quite beyond me.'

'Have you never been there, to observe the nuns at prayer?' asked Michael casually, although Bartholomew was aware of the intense interest behind his seemingly careless question.

'That would be an impossibility,' said Lincolne, taking Michael quite literally. 'I hear they do not keep their offices – or rather, they keep their offices at times that suit them, rather than when they are supposed to be.'

157

'Do you know this from personal observation?' pressed Michael, still trying to ascertain whether Lincolne was prepared to admit that he had been to one of Walcote's nocturnal gatherings.

'I know from rumours,' replied Lincolne, frustratingly obtuse. 'I say all my offices here or in the chapel. But you have not told us what took *you* to such a place, Brother.'

'Matt was called there to physick the Prioress,' lied Michael.

'What was wrong with her?' asked Lincolne. 'Was it anything to do with the fact that she had to be carried through the streets of Cambridge in a drunken stupor just after dawn this morning? What did you recommend, Doctor? A dish of raw eggs and pepper, and that she should be more abstemious in the future?'

'Is that what the Carmelites use?' asked Bartholomew, answering with a question because he was reluctant to discuss the Prioress's medical details with Lincolne.

Lincolne nodded, unabashed by the implication that his colleagues should require such a remedy in the first place. 'And if we have no pepper, we use salt.'

Michael clearly wanted to press the matter of St Radegund's further, but was aware that if he pushed it too far, Lincolne would grow suspicious, which might prove unproductive in the long term. He sighed and turned his attention to the open psalter, instead. At that moment, the boy with the bad skin returned to say that he could not find Lynne. Horneby's unease visibly increased, although Lincolne did not seem particularly concerned.

'He will be hiding up a tree or in an attic somewhere. He will turn up when he is hungry.'

Bartholomew was watching Horneby, who fidgeted and shuffled under his penetrating gaze. 'What do you think, Master Horneby?' he asked, making the young man squirm even more. 'Will Lynne appear at dinnertime?'

Horneby nodded quickly, casting quick, agitated glances at his friends. Bartholomew was about to pursue the matter

158

when everyone jumped at a loud, startled exclamation from Timothy.

'What is this?' demanded the monk, straightening from where he had emptied the contents of Faricius's spare scrip on to his bed. Everyone craned forward to see what he had found. Between thumb and forefinger, Timothy held a large ring with a heavy stone that looked as if it were a ruby. Lincolne seemed astonished; Horneby, however, lost some of his ruddy colour.

Bartholomew thought back to when Faricius had died: the student-friar had been almost desperate to locate his scrip. Was it because he thought it contained the ruby ring – that he had forgotten he had left it in his chest at home? The strings that attached the scrip to Faricius's belt had been cut, and Bartholomew had assumed the scrip had been stolen by whoever had killed him. However, although the cut marks appeared recent, there was nothing to say that they had been made at the time of his death. Perhaps it had happened the previous day, or even earlier.

Or was there a simpler, more sinister explanation: that whoever killed Faricius and stole his purse had replaced the scrip, complete with ring, among the dead friar's personal possessions? Bartholomew supposed it was not impossible that some colleague, overwhelmed by guilt at what he had done, had sought to make amends by putting back what he had stolen. But that meant Faricius's murderer was a Carmelite, the only ones to have free and unlimited access to the cells in the dormitory.

While the others clustered around to look at the ring, Bartholomew picked up the purse. Its strings were old and worn. There was nothing to suggest they had been cut, and nothing to suggest that the killer had been clever and had replaced the newly cut thongs with old and dirty ones. The leather ties were of an identical colour to the purse, and had frayed in such a way that Bartholomew was fairly certain they were the originals.

He rubbed a hand through his hair. What did this mean?

That someone *had* stolen Faricius's other purse, and that his personal possessions ran to more than one valuable ring? That Faricius was delirious when he had urged Bartholomew to locate his scrip, and that he had forgotten the one that held the ring was safe in his friary?

'It is a ring,' said Lincolne, stating the obvious as he took it from Timothy. 'We do not encourage our friars to keep this sort of thing for themselves. I imagine he was given it, and that he intended to pass it to the friary's coffer, but his murder meant that he could not do so.' He slipped the ring into his own scrip.

'Do you now?' said Michael, raising his eyebrows to indicate that he was not so sure. He turned to the students. 'And who gave this pretty bauble to Faricius for the Carmelite coffer?'

'We have never seen it before,' said Horneby immediately. 'We do not know where it came from.'

'What about the rest of you?' asked Michael, glancing around at the assembled students. 'Does anyone know who might have given Faricius this ring? It looks valuable, and I cannot see that he would have mentioned it to no one.'

The chorus of denials was accompanied by shaken heads. Bartholomew studied the students carefully. Some appeared to be surprised by the find, while others were more difficult to read. Horneby licked nervous lips, and his eyes could only be called shifty. While Bartholomew could not be sure that he was actually lying, it was obvious that there was something about Faricius's death that was making him anxious and even a little frightened.

'How remarkable,' said Michael mildly. 'Faricius was presented with a valuable gift for the friary, and yet he shared news of his good fortune with none of you. Was he always so secretive?'

'Perhaps the Dominicans put it there,' suggested Horneby. 'They want you to question Faricius's good character, so that you will not blame them for his murder.'

'And how do you imagine they got in?' demanded

Timothy, who clearly thought Horneby's suggestion ludicrous. 'Surely, in a busy place like this dormitory, it would be extremely difficult for a stranger to enter and start tampering with people's private possessions?'

Lincolne intervened. 'Horneby's suggestion was meant to be helpful, but we can all see it is implausible. But perhaps the ring had some sentimental value for Faricius, and he decided to keep it, rather than forfeiting it when he was ordained.'

'He would never have broken the rules of our Order in that way,' said Horneby hotly. 'He was a good and saintly man.'

'Keeping a ring from a loved relative does not make him wicked,' said Lincolne gently, to calm him. He turned to Michael. 'But it does not give a Dominican the right to murder him, either.'

'No,' said Michael. 'It does not.'

Bartholomew, Michael and Timothy left the friary none the wiser regarding Faricius's death, Lynne's mysterious behaviour or what Horneby was so clearly hiding, and began to walk back along Milne Street. Bartholomew told them what he had reasoned about the purse, and the two Benedictines seemed dispirited that there were more questions than answers. Dusk came early, because of the rain, and Michael announced that he was tired and that it was time to go home. Timothy returned to Ely Hall, while Bartholomew walked with the monk along Milne Street towards Michaelhouse.

'There is Matilde,' said Michael, pointing out a slender, elegant woman who was picking her way carefully among the piles of refuse that lined the sides of the road. 'I wonder if she knows that the nuns of St Radegund's are plying their trade in her line of business. Matilde! Hey!'

His stentorian roar drew several startled glances from onlookers, and more than one of them smiled at the sight of the fat monk hailing a prostitute so brazenly on one of the town's main thoroughfares. Matilde was also surprised

161

to be addressed at such a volume, but her face lit with pleasure when she saw that Bartholomew was with Michael.

'Matthew,' she said warmly, as she waited for them to catch up. She looked at his wet cloak and the clay that clung to the bottom of his boots. 'Where have you been? Visiting the lepers?'

'Not today,' replied Bartholomew. 'I examined them about a month ago, and found them as hale and hearty as can be expected. Unfortunately, there is little else I can do for them.'

'You ease their discomfort,' said Matilde. 'That is more than they expect. But the sisters tell me that you have more murders to investigate – including poor Will Walcote's.'

'The sisters,' mused Michael, using the term Matilde always employed when discussing the town's prostitutes. 'It is odd you should mention sisters, Matilde. Matt and I went to St Radegund's Convent this afternoon.'

Matilde's pretty face hardened. 'Why were you there? It is no place for decent-minded men.'

Coming from a courtesan, this was damning indeed. Bartholomew stared at her. In his eyes, she was the most attractive woman in Cambridge, and possessed a sharp mind that he greatly admired. So far, their relationship had remained frustratingly chaste, and was confined to occasional evenings spent in her house with some of her 'sisters' for company, or the odd stroll in the water meadows near the river. The more Bartholomew came to know her, the more he liked her, and he was under the impression that she no longer practised her trade. No one ever claimed to secure her favours, and he suspected that her position as unofficial spokeswoman for the town's whores left her little time for physical liaisons with customers.

'You know about the activities of the nuns at St Radegund's?' asked Michael.

'I imagine those will be known from here to Ely,' replied Matilde dryly. 'But the sisters are not concerned. Most men are uncomfortable with employing nuns for those sorts of services, and find it disconcerting to beckon the woman of their choice from her prayers in the church.'

'I did not see much praying when we were there today,' said Michael. 'They claimed the church was too cold.'

'Cold or not, that is where you will find them of an evening. The church is always open for "parishioners", so the men can walk in and signal to whoever it is they want.'

'How sordid,' said Bartholomew in distaste.

Michael nodded agreement. 'That sort of thing is much more pleasantly conducted in the conducive surroundings of a tavern. Churches are too stark for it.'

'Thank you for that, Brother,' said Matilde. 'It is always good to know the views of monks on these matters. But not everyone at St Radegund's is a nun, you know. Some are the daughters of noblemen, who have been left in the Prioress's care until they can be married off.'

'Most of them will be an unsaleable commodity if they remain there too long,' said Michael with a chuckle. 'It is scarcely a safe repository for virtuous young ladies.'

'The worst of them all is that Tysilia,' said Matilde disapprovingly. 'I suppose men find her attractive because she is stupid. Presumably, her appalling lack of wits makes them feel superior.'

'I take it you do not like her?' asked Bartholomew mildly.

'No,' said Matilde shortly. 'And if you meet her, you will see why. But I do not want to spoil a nice day by discussing her. What induced you to go to St Radegund's in the first place? It is too early to secure the nuns' personal services, although I am sure Tysilia would make an exception.'

'I was following a clue regarding the murder of Will Walcote,' replied Michael.

Matilde nodded slowly. 'Yolande de Blaston – you remember her; she is married to the carpenter who worked at Michaelhouse last year – saw his body being cut down on her way home from the Mayor's house. Poor Walcote. He was a good man.'

'He was,' agreed Michael. 'Yolande did not see anything

163

else, did she? Did she spot anyone who should not have been out at that time?'

'No one should have been out at that time – including her,' said Matilde. 'It was well past the curfew. She did not mention anyone else, but I will ask. But this does not explain why you went to look for answers at St Radegund's Convent.'

'We learned that Walcote had a series of secret meetings with various scholars,' said Michael vaguely. 'They were held at the convent.'

'Oh, those,' said Matilde. 'Yolande has a long-standing arrangement with Prior Lincolne of the Carmelites, but he cancelled her twice to attend these meetings.'

'But *I* have only just learned about them,' said Michael, astonished that Matilde should be in possession of information to which he had not been privy. Bartholomew smiled, amused that Lincolne should be so damning of the nuns' behaviour when he had a 'long-standing arrangement' with one of the town's most popular prostitutes.

'I have known about the meetings for months,' said Matilde carelessly. 'The first one must have been around the time that Master Runham of Michaelhouse was buried, because I recall Yolande telling me that Lincolne later gave her one of the coins he had retrieved from Wilson's effigy, to compensate her for the inconvenience of being postponed.'

'How much later?' asked Michael. 'I want to know exactly when the first meeting took place.'

Matilde gave an apologetic shrug. 'I am sorry, Brother, but I doubt whether Yolande will remember that. It was November or December.'

'I do not suppose Lincolne told Yolande what was discussed at these meetings, did he?' asked Michael hopefully.

Matilde frowned as she tried to remember. 'Not precisely, but I know the leader of the Franciscans was there. And dear old Master Kenyngham from Michaelhouse. If Kenyngham were present, then you can be assured that nothing untoward was afoot.'

'Nothing untoward involving Kenyngham,' corrected Michael. 'But Kenyngham is not one of the world's most astute men, and he has a dangerous habit of assuming that everyone has good intentions. They have not. Kenyngham may not have understood what he was getting into.'

'There is no suggestion that these meetings involved anything sinister,' said Bartholomew. 'They could have been discussing the term's debating titles for all you know.'

'In a convent that has a reputation for lewd behaviour? In the middle of the night? Without informing the Senior Proctor?' Michael gave a snort of derision. 'Do not speak drivel, Matt!'

'Whatever it was must have been important,' said Matilde thoughtfully. 'Why else would such men risk going to a place like that at night? Still, I suppose it has the virtue of being the last place anyone would think of looking for them.'

'Ask whether Yolande can recall anything that may help me,' instructed Michael. 'This case is quite baffling, and any information would be gratefully received.'

'I can do better than that,' said Matilde. 'I have been feeling tired and bored lately, and I am in sore need of something to stimulate my wits. I think a brief sojourn at St Radegund's might be exactly what is required.'

'I do not think so,' said Bartholomew uneasily. 'It is not the kind of place you would enjoy at all. And anyway, I thought you did not like Tysilia.'

'I do not,' said Matilde. 'And that is even more reason for me to pit my wits against hers and see whether her appalling stupidity is genuine.'

'What do you mean?' asked Michael.

Matilde spread her hands. 'What I say. I find it extraordinary that someone could be so dim-witted, and I cannot help but wonder whether it is a ruse to hide a very cunning mind.'

'I thought the same thing,' said Bartholomew. 'I was even considering the possibility that she played some kind of role in these nocturnal meetings.'

'I hardly think so!' exclaimed Michael in disbelief. 'Such as what?'

'I do not know,' said Bartholomew. 'But she is the Bishop's niece, and the Bishop would not be averse to using a relative to help him in his various plots.'

'True, but not someone who genuinely believes that the moon is made of green cheese and that leaves fall from the trees in autumn because they are tired of holding on to the branch,' said Michael. 'She is just *too* stupid – an intelligent person would *know* she was overacting and moderate her performance to one that was more plausible.'

'I disagree,' said Bartholomew. 'I think she is sitting in St Radegund's at this very moment laughing to herself, because she thinks she has fooled you.'

'Absolutely,' agreed Matilde. She beamed suddenly, and clasped her hands in front of her. 'But she will not fool *me*, and this is just the kind of challenge that will provide me with the kind of diversion I need. It is an excellent idea. I wish it had occurred to me earlier.'

'It is a terrible idea,' said Bartholomew firmly. 'Michael is right: the time and place of these meetings suggests that they were not held to discuss something innocent, and that is precisely the reason why you should not go.'

'They probably will not let you in, anyway,' said Michael. 'Even St Radegund's cannot risk having the unofficial spokeswoman of the town's prostitutes as a guest.'

Matilde grinned conspiratorially. 'Do you recall when you invited me to the Founder's Feast at Michaelhouse a couple of years ago, Matthew? You should remember – we were virtually the only ones who were sober at the end of it.'

Bartholomew smiled, although most Founder's Feasts at Michaelhouse ended with everyone face down on the table, and his memories of them tended to blend together. But he recalled this one. 'You dressed as an old woman called Mistress Horner, because you did not want anyone to know who you were.'

Matilde raised her eyebrows. 'I disguised myself because

you were worried about inviting a courtesan to dine in your college, and because you had invited that murdering Eleanor Tyler as well. She abandoned you for the more appealing attentions of your students, if I recall correctly.'

'All right, all right,' grumbled Bartholomew, not wanting to be reminded about that particular adventure. 'What has the Founder's Feast to do with you going to St Radegund's?'

'It is not I who will sojourn there,' said Matilde simply. 'It is Mistress Horner.'

'No!' exclaimed Bartholomew. 'It is too dangerous. What if they intrude on you while you are in bed and learn that Mistress Horner's ample middle owes itself to a couple of cushions, or that her wrinkles disappear in water?'

'I will make sure that does not happen.'

'The good nuns might not want fat old ladies in their convent,' Michael pointed out.

'They will accept my offer of five groats for board and lodging,' said Matilde mischievously. 'They would agree to anything for five groats.'

'That is true,' admitted Michael. 'They would.'

'You cannot do this,' said Bartholomew firmly. 'If we are right, and Tysilia's stupidity conceals a cunning mind that is involved in the murder of Michael's Junior Proctor, then it is simply too risky. I cannot let you do it.'

'Are you concerned for my safety, Matthew?' asked Matilde playfully. 'Or for my virtue?'

'Your safety,' replied Bartholomew immediately. He faltered when he realised what his words had implied, and flushed when Michael and Matilde laughed at him.

'Are you sure you do not mind doing this?' asked Michael of Matilde. 'I cannot see how else I will be able to cut through the veil of secrecy and lies that those nuns have thrown over their activities. They may be perfectly innocent – well, as innocent as running a brothel in a convent can be – and we may be on the wrong path altogether.'

'Then I will find out,' said Matilde confidently. 'And I will expose that Tysilia as a liar and a cheat, if that is what she is.'

'I cannot believe you are encouraging her to do this,' said Bartholomew to Michael.

Matilde sighed, and laid an elegant hand on Bartholomew's arm. 'Do not worry so, Matthew. I will be perfectly safe. As a fat and unattractive matron, I am unlikely to be invited to take part in anything too exotic, and all I plan to do is listen and watch. It will only be for a few days, anyway.'

'If you discover anything, tell us immediately,' advised Michael. 'Do not deal with it yourself. Matt or I will visit St Radegund's every day, and you can indicate then whether all is well.'

Matilde's eyes gleamed at the prospect of an adventure. 'Do not ask to see me personally, or they will be suspicious. I will pretend to be deaf, so that they will think they do not need to lower their voices around me. So, if you see me cupping both hands around my ears, you will know it is a sign that I have nothing to report; if I fiddle with a ring on my finger, it means I wish to speak with you privately.'

'I do not like this at all,' said Bartholomew. 'If Tysilia is the kind of woman we suspect she is, then you will not be safe; she will quickly guess what you are doing. There must be another way to look into her dealings.'

'I can think of none,' said Michael. 'And time is passing. The longer we take to apprehend this killer, the less likely it is that we shall catch him. Do you want Will's murderer to go free?'

'Of course not, but—'

'I will be perfectly all right,' said Matilde. 'And, as I said, such an adventure will help me rouse myself from the lethargy that has been dogging me since the beginning of Lent. I am feeling better already: I have a challenge to rise to, and Easter is almost here.' She stood on tiptoe and quickly kissed Bartholomew's cheek. 'I promise to be careful, and you must promise to do the same. But together, we will see Will's killer brought to justice.'

She was gone in the gathering dusk before Bartholomew could voice any further objections, and he suspected they would be futile anyway. Matilde had made up her mind, and he knew that there was nothing he could say or do to prevent her from going ahead with her plans. He watched her walk away, thinking about how dear she had become to him over the last few years.

Michael yawned hugely. 'It has been a long day, and I am exhausted. Tomorrow, we will interview Morden of the Dominicans – I want to know more about those six student friars whom you drove away from Faricius – but tonight I only want a decent meal and a good night's sleep.'

'And we should talk to Prior Pechem of the Franciscans, too,' said Bartholomew. 'He may tell us why he was at these meetings.'

Michael rubbed his chin. 'I agree. But we must do so with care. I do not want to alarm this coven into silence. I was afraid to question Lincolne too vigorously about the meetings, and I am reluctant to interrogate Pechem for the same reason. If they close ranks, we might never have the truth from them. To find out what we want to know, we shall have to be circumspect.'

'Not necessarily,' said Bartholomew thoughtfully. 'We could just ask Master Kenyngham. He may tell us what we need to know without resorting to trickery.'

'Oh, yes,' said Michael softly. 'I have not forgotten Master Kenyngham.'

Bartholomew slept badly that night, his dreams mingling unpleasantly with his waking concerns for Matilde and his sadness over the sudden death of Walcote. He tossed and turned, and when the tinny bell finally clanked to inform scholars that it was time for mass, he had only just fallen into a deep sleep. He splashed himself with cold water in an attempt to render himself more alert, grabbed his clothes from the wall hooks, and pulled his boots on the wrong feet before realising his mistake. He was the last to join the procession in the yard, earning a warning glance from Langelee for his tardiness.

After the service, as he was walking back to Michaelhouse, a plump, crook-backed woman nodded soberly to him, and he felt his stomach churn when he recognised the bright, clear eyes of Matilde. She rode a small palfrey, and was already heading to St Radegund's Convent to begin her adventure. He considered calling out, but knew that to expose her disguise in the High Street would put her in even greater danger. With a heavy heart, he followed Langelee back to Michaelhouse, where he ate a bowl of grey-coloured oatmeal that tasted of sawdust.

Leaving Langelee to ensure that his students read a tract from Theophilus's *De Urinis*, Bartholomew set off with Michael to visit the Dominican Friary, where the monk intended to ask Prior Morden for more details about the six students Bartholomew had encountered near Faricius. Bartholomew fretted about Matilde as they walked, although Michael claimed he was being overprotective and that she knew perfectly well how to look after herself.

It was another murky day, with leaden skies filled with fast-moving clouds, and only the faintest hint of pink glimmering in the east. It had been a wet night, and the streets were clogged with rain-thinned horse manure that seeped through shoes and clung to the hems of cloaks.

When they arrived at the Dominican Friary, the priests were just finishing a hearty meal of coddled eggs, fresh bread and dates, the smell of which made Bartholomew hungry again. Ringstead, the Prior's secretary, came to greet them, but said that Morden had gone to see if he could locate his Precentor, Henry de Kyrkeby, who had not been seen since Monday afternoon.

One of the six students that Bartholomew had driven away from Faricius – the one whom Morden had called Bulmer – came to stand next to Ringstead, his demeanour hostile and sullen. Bartholomew wondered whether Bulmer was habitually disagreeable, or whether it was just the early morning visit from a proctor that prompted his unfriendly attitude. The physician hoped Bulmer was bound for a career at court, and that the Dominicans would not foist the ill-tempered lad on some unsuspecting village as parish priest.

'We are terribly worried about Kyrkeby,' said Ringstead. 'He has never been missing for two days before.'

'Have you reported his absence to the proctors' office?' asked Michael, irritable that he had yet another problem to solve. 'I have beadles who are paid to hunt down missing scholars.'

Ringstead nodded. 'Beadle Meadowman took details yesterday, and said he would ask the others to look for him on their patrols. Meanwhile, Prior Morden has gone to check the churches, to see if Kyrkeby is praying and has lost track of time.'

'Is he a visionary, then?' asked Michael, raising sceptical eyebrows. 'Two days is a long time to be unaware of the passing of time. I would expect hunger to drive him from his prayers and back to his friary.'

'Not all men are ruled by the calls of their stomachs,' said Bulmer rudely, looking meaningfully at Michael's ample girth.

'Kyrkeby is a saintly man, and he might well be lost in contemplation somewhere,' said Ringstead hastily, seeing Michael's eyebrows draw together at the insult. He was older than Bulmer, and had the sense to realise that it paid to stay on the right side of the Senior Proctor. 'He often wanders off to sit in churches.'

'Of course, it is possible that the Carmelites have done something to him, in revenge for Faricius,' said Bulmer, gazing at Michael with defiant eyes.

'And what *did* you do to Faricius?' Michael pounced.

Bulmer said impatiently, 'That is not what I meant. We did nothing to him, but the Carmelites probably do not believe that.'

Michael sighed heavily. 'Have you looked at Kyrkeby's belongings, to see whether anything is missing? If he is as other-worldly as you say, he may have wandered off

171

somewhere and simply forgotten to mention it to anyone.'

'It was the first thing we did when we realised he was not here,' said Ringstead. 'There is nothing to indicate that he planned to leave the town. Quite the contrary, in fact: as we mentioned when you last came, he is due to give the lecture in St Mary's Church on Sunday. He is looking forward to it enormously.'

'He is going to speak in defence of nominalism,' said Bulmer, throwing out the information in much the same way as he might a challenge to a fist fight.

Michael rubbed his chin. 'So I understand. It is a rather controversial subject to choose.'

Ringstead raised his hands, palms upward. 'That should not deter a good scholar, Brother. Indeed, controversial subjects must be better argued than dull ones, because there are more people looking for flaws in your logic.'

'That is true,' agreed Bartholomew. 'My best-argued lectures are on medical issues that are new or unusual.'

'But to choose nominalism, when there is already trouble between the Dominicans and the Carmelites, is irresponsible and self-indulgent,' said Michael disapprovingly.

'Scholarly disputation should never be a victim to narrow-minded bigotry,' retorted Bulmer. 'Just because the Carmelites are traditionalists and unwilling to change does not mean that reason and learning should stand still to accommodate them.'

'I agree,' said Bartholomew, neatly taking the wind out of his sails. 'We would never progress in our understanding of the world if we were all too afraid to embrace new ideas.'

'So when was the last time anyone saw Kyrkeby?' asked Michael, impatient with the discussion and wanting to move on.

'Monday afternoon,' said Ringstead promptly. 'He was working on his lecture, and had been avoiding a lot of his duties and obligations because of it. His absence in the refectory was what allowed the students to escape and march on the Carmelites last Saturday.'

'I saw him on Monday afternoon,' said Bartholomew. 'He was ill, and I was late going to Edith's house, because I was tending him.'

Ringstead nodded. 'After you left, he continued to work on his lecture, and that was the last anyone saw of him.'

Michael sighed. He wanted to talk to Morden, not investigate the disappearance of a cleric who would undoubtedly show up when it suited him. 'Show me Kyrkeby's cell,' he said reluctantly. 'Perhaps you missed something that may give me a clue as to his whereabouts.'

Ringstead led the way, with Bulmer trailing them like some aggressive guard dog. Bartholomew glanced uneasily behind him, half expecting to feel teeth sink into one of his ankles.

Like the Carmelites' dormitory, the Dominicans' was divided into tiny cells, some more homely than others. Bartholomew supposed that it was difficult to impose too much poverty on ambitious young men destined for high positions in the King's court or their Order, which explained why most of them boasted quarters that were so much more luxurious than his own.

Kyrkeby's cell was larger than the others', as befitted a man of his elevated office, and contained a handsome iron-bound chest as well as a bed, a chair and a small table. Notes were scattered across the table, and a quick glance at them told Bartholomew that Kyrkeby had been working on his lecture there. Judging from the amount of crossings out and corrections on the numerous scraps of parchment, it was not something that had flowed easily.

Michael's confidence in his ability to glance at a man's possessions and identify his whereabouts was misplaced. There was nothing to indicate why – or even whether – Kyrkeby had disappeared, and Bartholomew wondered if the man realised that he had bitten off more than he could chew with his impending lecture, and had left the town before he could make a fool of himself. Perhaps his attack of illness on Monday had frightened him so much that he had decided not to risk his health further by going through

173

what promised to be a tense and unpleasant occasion. He had certainly been agitated and out of sorts that day.

'Does anyone know whether there is anything missing?' asked Michael, becoming frustrated by the passing of time and the lack of progress. 'Are all his clothes here, for instance?'

'As far as we can tell,' said Ringstead. 'One of his cloaks has gone, but that tells us nothing, since he would wear it even if he were only going to the nearest church.'

'He owns a lot of jewellery,' added Bulmer irrelevantly. 'Rings, crosses and so on.'

'Does he?' asked Michael. 'And why would a Carmelite have "rings, crosses and so on"?'

'He has no more than anyone else,' said Ringstead briskly, so that Bartholomew had the impression that Bulmer had just been told to shut up. Ringstead was in a difficult position, with his Prior and Precentor absent, and the reputation of the friary in his inexperienced hands.

'And is any of this jewellery missing?' asked Michael.

Ringstead opened a small drawer that was partly concealed under the table. In it were several rings, a jewelled hair comb and a fine selection of silver crosses.

Michael's eyes were wide as he inspected them. 'This is an impressive collection to be owned by a priest sworn to poverty. But you have not answered my question: is any of it missing?'

Ringstead shrugged. 'I have no idea. You will have to ask Prior Morden that. He knows Kyrkeby better than I do.'

'I expect Kyrkeby will turn up,' said Michael, rubbing his hands together as though he imagined that was the end of the matter. 'I will instruct my beadles to pay special attention to the churches tonight, and if he is in one, then they will find him. Perhaps he was so disappointed with the behaviour of his novices on Saturday that he wants nothing to do with you all.'

Since Morden was absent, Michael quizzed Ringstead about the characters of the six Dominican students he had arrested – and released – in connection with the death of Faricius. But Ringstead was a poor source of information: he was not inclined to regale Michael with any illuminating gossip about the six, and was reluctant to answer any meaningful questions while his Prior was absent. Bartholomew did not blame him. Michael was a clever man, adept at latching on to seemingly insignificant sentences and reading into them whole chapters of information. Quite understandably, Ringstead did not want to be the cause of further arrests and suspicions.

With a sigh of exasperation, Michael curtly instructed Ringstead to keep the students inside the friary until further notice, and took his leave. Rain still fell, and everything dripped. The eaves of houses, the leaves of trees and bushes, and even the signs that swung over the doors of merchants' shops released a steady tattoo of droplets that drummed, splattered, clicked and tapped on to the mud on the ground. Thatches were soaked through, and the plaster walls of the houses along the High Street were stained a deep, dreary grey. Everything stank of dampness and mould.

Michael was keen to visit the Franciscans, to ask their Prior why he had been among those attending Walcote's meetings, but Bartholomew remembered that Faricius was due to be buried that day, and recommended that they go to the Carmelite Friary first.

Reluctantly, Michael trudged after Bartholomew along Milne Street. They arrived to see the massive form of Lincolne, with its curiously short habit, leading the way from the friary to St Botolph's Church, where a requiem mass was to be said. Immediately behind Lincolne was a crude wooden coffin, which had such large gaps in it that the dead man's fingers poked through one. Bartholomew supposed Faricius was lucky to have a coffin at all: since the plague, wood and carpenters were expensive, and most people hired a parish coffin, reclaimed when the funeral was over. Horneby was among the pall-bearers, while behind them trailed the other Carmelite masters and students.

'We need to talk, Brother,' said Lincolne in a low voice as he passed. He continued to walk, so Michael and Bartholomew fell into step next to him.

'Very well,' said Michael. 'We have more questions to ask anyway, but they will wait until you have finished your sorry task here.'

'My business is more urgent than yours,' said Lincolne presumptuously. 'I am worried about Simon Lynne: he has not been seen since Monday and his friends say they do not know where he is. I should have realised something was amiss yesterday, when you asked to speak to him and he could not be found.'

'Why are you concerned now?' asked Michael, seeing an opportunity to solicit information before telling Lincolne that he had seen Lynne himself only the previous day. 'Do you think he might have come to some harm? Or is it that his disappearance has something to do with the fact that he is clearly hiding something relating to the death of Faricius?'

Lincolne shot him an unpleasant look. 'It is far more likely that the Dominicans have threatened him in some way. It would be typical behaviour for men who profess to be nominalists.'

'The Dominicans' philosophical beliefs are hardly the issue here—' began Michael.

'Of course they are the issue,' snapped Lincolne, cutting him off. 'They are heresy!'

Michael refused to be drawn into a debate. 'I do not care. I am only interested in who killed Faricius. You claim that Lynne might be in danger from the Dominicans. Why? Has he done something to wrong them?'

'You seem very willing to believe the worst of us, Brother,' said Lincolne coldly. 'It is most unjust. The Dominicans march on our friary, Faricius is murdered and Lynne is missing, yet you seem to hold *us* responsible.'

'When did *you* last see Lynne?' asked Bartholomew, wondering whether the student-friar might have inflicted some harm on the missing Henry de Kyrkeby and then run

176

away. It had been bad luck on Lynne's part that he had chosen St Radegund's as his haven when the Senior Proctor had visited it, and worse luck still that the foolish Tysilia was on gate duty. Any sensible nun would have checked with her Prioress first, before showing unexpected guests into the heart of the convent, and then Lynne could have slipped away unnoticed by Michael and Bartholomew.

'He attended the evening mass in St Mary's on Monday, but I have not set eyes on him since then. I assumed he was walking in our grounds – to be alone with his grief for Faricius – but when we searched, there was no sign of him.'

'Monday night,' mused Bartholomew softly. 'It seems a lot happened on Monday night: Kyrkeby and Lynne went missing, and poor Walcote was murdered.'

'Well, you have no cause to worry,' said Michael to Lincolne. 'I saw Lynne myself only yesterday, enjoying the dubious hospitality of the nuns at St Radegund's Convent.'

'St Radegund's?' echoed Lincolne in disbelief, stopping abruptly and stumbling when the coffin thumped into the back of him. He glared at the pall-bearers, who shifted uneasily, and then turned his attention back to Michael. 'What was he doing there?'

'What many other young men do, I imagine,' said Michael blithely. 'Confessing his sins to the Mother Superior.'

'That Tysilia is at the heart of this,' said Lincolne bitterly. 'She is poison. Why she was not strangled at birth, I cannot imagine.'

'That is not a very friarly attitude,' said Michael, amused. 'What do you have against her?'

'She is a danger to men,' said Lincolne uncompromisingly. 'She uses her womanly wiles to seduce them into breaking their vows of chastity, and then, when they have betrayed themselves and God, she moves on to her next victim, leaving them with nothing.'

'She has made herself available to other Carmelites, then, has she?' asked Michael astutely.

Lincolne nodded. 'My friars do their best, but they are

177

young men when all is said and done, with young men's desires.'

'You cannot blame Tysilia because your friars cannot control their passions,' said Bartholomew. 'That is unfair.'

He recalled a suicide just before Yuletide, when a Carmelite student-friar had thrown himself into the King's Ditch. The note the young man left Lincolne indicated that the source of his deep unhappiness was the unrequited affection of a nun. The sad little letter had not mentioned Tysilia by name, but clearly Lincolne had drawn his own conclusions.

'Tysilia is not like other women,' insisted Lincolne. 'She is . . .' He gestured expansively, almost knocking the coffin from the shoulders of the pall-bearers as he sought to find the appropriate words to describe the Bishop's niece.

'Wanton?' suggested Michael. 'That is the term her uncle favours.'

'It is more than that,' said Lincolne. 'Would you believe she even tried her charms on Master Kenyngham of Michaelhouse? She claimed to be in pain and insisted that he place his hand on her chest so that the warmth would heal her. Kenyngham, who hates to see people suffer, obliged, then when he was leaning over her she made a grab for him so that they both tumbled to the ground.'

Michael started to laugh. 'Are you serious?'

'I am quite serious,' said Lincolne sternly. 'And it is no laughing matter. But I should not be standing here in the middle of the street looking as though I am telling jokes when I should be leading Faricius to his requiem. We will speak later.'

Bartholomew thought that he and Michael should attend Faricius's requiem, to see whether they could gather any clues regarding the student-friar's death, but Michael demurred. He took Bartholomew's arm and the physician found himself being steered in the direction of the Brazen George, the large and comfortable tavern on the High

Street, where Michael was sufficiently well known to be able to commandeer a private chamber at the rear of the premises whenever he liked.

'Just some warmed ale,' Michael told the surprised taverner, who had come expecting to serve a sizeable meal. 'Nothing else. We will not be here long.'

'Are you sure?' asked the landlord, wiping his hands on the white apron that was tied around his waist. 'My wife baked some Lombard slices today, and I know they are a favourite of yours.'

Michael smiled. 'You are kind, but I will just take the ale today, thank you.'

'Well, I would like some,' said Bartholomew. 'I am starving.' He reached across the table and felt the monk's forehead with the back of his hand. 'You are not ill, are you?'

Michael pushed him away as the landlord left to fetch their order. 'I do not spend all my time eating, you know. And I am growing tired of constant allusions to my girth. Even people I barely know have started to do it – like that Bulmer.'

'You do not usually care what people think,' said Bartholomew. 'Are you sure you are well?'

Michael sighed, his large face sombre. 'No murder is pleasant to investigate, but Walcote's is more personal than most. I sense it will take all my wits to best the cunning mind responsible for it and it is a heavy responsibility.'

'You were confident enough yesterday,' said Bartholomew. 'What has changed your mind?'

'Lincolne,' said Michael gloomily. 'And the missing Kyrkeby. And Lynne and Horneby and Bulmer and anyone else who either tells us lies or declines to tell us the complete truth. How can we hope to come to grips with this when no one is honest with us?'

Bartholomew tapped Michael lightly on the arm. 'We will get to the bottom of it.'

'It is all very odd,' said Michael, taking a sip of the ale

that the landlord had brought. 'I *knew* the deaths of Walcote and Faricius were connected; I just knew it. First, there was that yellow stain you found on both their hands, and then we saw Faricius's friend Lynne lurking around Barnwell Priory – where Walcote lived. You were wrong when you said they were unrelated.'

'In my experience, killers keep to one method once they have met with success. Faricius was stabbed, but Walcote was hanged – two very different modes of execution.'

'Perhaps one was spontaneous and the other planned,' said Michael. 'You cannot decide to hang someone on the spur of a moment unless you can lay your hands on a piece of rope.'

'Several pieces of rope,' said Bartholomew, selecting one of the Lombard slices – a mixture of figs and raisins wrapped in pastry and fried in lard. He took a bite and put the rest back on the platter. They were rich, not for wolfing down quickly, and now that he was not in competition with Michael for them, he could afford to eat at a more leisurely pace. 'Rope was needed for his hands and feet, too. Also, although Walcote was not particularly big, he was fit. I do not think it would have been easy for one person to overpower him and string him up.'

'It probably would not have been easy for two,' said Michael, staring thoughtfully at the Lombard slices before reaching out and taking one. He stuffed the whole thing in his mouth.

'Perhaps someone who lives near the Dominican Friary heard Walcote shouting for help,' suggested Bartholomew.

'Beadle Meadowman has already investigated that possibility,' said Michael, taking another pastry and treating it to the same fate as the first. 'He reported to me late last night, when you were in bed. No one heard anything or saw anything.'

'I suppose people's window shutters would be fastened,' said Bartholomew. 'It was cold, wet and windy that night. Shutters not only stop you from seeing out, but they muffle sounds.'

'That tale Lincolne just told us about Kenyngham and Tysilia was revealing,' said Michael. 'Kenyngham is no longer a young man, and he seldom ventures further than Michaelhouse or his own Priory of Gilbertines on Trumpington Way. So, how did he come to meet her? The answer is that he went to St Radegund's, just as Eve Wasteneys and Matilde told us.'

Bartholomew nodded. 'And for Lincolne to have witnessed this exchange means that *he* must have been at St Radegund's, too. Again, just as Eve and Matilde told us.'

'I wonder how Walcote induced all those men to go to a place like St Radegund's in the dead of night. It makes no sense. And why did he not tell *me* what he was doing?'

'You really have no idea?'

'None at all,' said Michael bitterly. 'I trusted Walcote, and often told him my secret plans. I am hurt that he did not see fit to reciprocate.'

'Did you tell him everything?' asked Bartholomew.

Michael regarded him as though he were insane. 'Of course not. I do not even tell you everything. But I did confide a great deal to Walcote. I am astonished that he had business with important men like Lincolne, Pechem and Kenyngham, and yet said nothing to me.'

'Perhaps he was planning to surprise you with something,' suggested Bartholomew.

'Such as what? I do not like surprises – especially ones that involve secret meetings in a place like St Radegund's. It sounds more like a plot than a surprise.' He punched Bartholomew on the shoulder, his previous low spirits revived by the ale and his determination to discover what his Junior Proctor had been doing without his knowledge. 'But we will find out whatever is afoot and we will solve these two murders.'

Bartholomew reached for the rest of his pastry to find it had gone. 'I thought you had lost your appetite,' he said as the monk swung his cloak around his shoulders. 'I was the one who was hungry.'

'How can you be thinking about food when we have a murderer to catch?' demanded Michael accusingly. 'Come on. Faricius's requiem will be over now. We should talk to Prior Lincolne.'

Bartholomew refused to return to the Carmelite Friary until they had fulfilled their promise to visit Matilde at the Convent of St Radegund's. The monk complained bitterly about the brisk walk along the Barnwell Causeway, but it was too cold to travel at the ambling pace he usually favoured. When they arrived at the convent, and had made their way through the dripping vegetation to the front gate, Michael was puffing and panting like a pair of bellows, although it had still not been fast enough to drive the chill from Bartholomew's bones. Shivering, and with a sense of foreboding, he knocked on the door.

The grille snapped open, and the bright black eyes of Tysilia peered out at them. Before he could announce their business, the door had been opened, and Michael pushed his way across the threshold, still grumbling about the speed of the walk.

'Do come in, Brother,' said Tysilia to Michael's back, as the monk headed towards the solar. Bartholomew glanced at her sharply, but could not tell whether she was being facetious, or merely reciting the words of welcome she had been trained to say.

'We would like to speak to Dame Martyn,' he said, feeling obliged to make at least some effort to explain their presence. 'Is she in her quarters?'

'Everyone is in the refectory,' replied Tysilia, as she closed the door behind him. 'We are having breakfast.'

'Breakfast?' asked Bartholomew, startled. Michael overheard and veered away from the direction of the solar to aim for a substantial building to his left. 'But it is almost midday.'

Tysilia seemed surprised. 'It is only midday if you rise at dawn. None of us do, I am pleased to say, and so for us it is breakfast time.'

'But what about matins, prime and terce?' asked Bartholomew. 'How do you keep those offices, if you wake so late?'

Tysilia waved a dismissive hand. 'We leave those for the friars and monks to say. We are doing God a favour, actually. Can you imagine what it must be like to have all those voices clamouring at you at certain times of the day? I am sure He is grateful to us for our conflagration. Or do I mean for our condescension? All these long words sound the same to me.'

'I imagine you mean "consideration",' said Bartholomew, eyeing her warily. He tried to read some expression in her dark eyes, but although they sparkled, they did so with a brilliance that was only superficially shiny, like a pair of Richard's buttons. He could not tell whether a clever mind was thoroughly enjoying itself by presenting a false image to the world, or whether what he saw was all there was.

'Have you caught your killer?' she asked. 'Is that why you are here again?'

Bartholomew glanced at her a second time, wondering whether her question was more than idle curiosity. He thought he glimpsed a flicker of something in her face, but then wondered if it were merely a trick of the light. He did not know what to think.

'No,' he replied shortly, not wanting to give away details to someone who might have more than a passing interest in the matter.

'We have a fat woman staying with us,' Tysilia chirped conversationally, as they walked towards the refectory. She did not seem to find his curt reply to her question worthy of comment. 'She is paying five groats a day to escape from her demanding husband.' Her pretty features creased into a moue of disgust. 'I hope my uncle will not foist one of those on *me*. I am happier changing my lovers each week.'

'Each week?' asked Bartholomew, trying to keep the surprise from his voice at her unusual choice of topics. He wondered whether she was trying to shock him, and he did not want to give her the satisfaction of seeing he was embarrassed. 'Do you not keep them longer than that?'

'No,' she said airily. 'You see, the first few times a lover meets you, he is affectionate and only wants physical favours. But after about a week, he wants more than a romp between the covers, and likes to talk and ask questions. I cannot be bothered with all that.'

'You mean you disapprove of conversation and discussion?' asked Bartholomew.

'I do not know about that, but I dislike talking,' replied Tysilia, opening the door to the refectory and ushering her guests inside. 'I talk and listen all day with the nuns. I do not want to do it during the night, as well. I am sure you know what I mean.'

She gave him a hefty nudge with her elbow that all but winded him, but he was spared from the obligation of supplying her with an answer by Eve Wasteneys, who came forward to greet them.

The refectory was warm and comfortable, and the hum of voices and laughter indicated that Dame Martyn did not insist upon silence or Bible-reading at meals. Breakfast comprised baked eggs in addition to bread and oatmeal, and Bartholomew was certain he saw Dame Martyn slide a large piece of ham out of sight under her trencher. Ham was not an item that should have been on the breakfast table during Lent, and so she was wise to hide it from the sight of her unexpected visitors. The Prioress smiled a greeting at Bartholomew and Michael, and then raised a large cup of breakfast ale to her lips, drinking long and deep, as if she imagined she might need the fortification it provided.

'Where is my ham?' demanded Tysilia petulantly, as she sat down at her place. 'It was here when I went to answer the door. Who took it?'

Dame Martyn and Eve exchanged a weary glance, and Bartholomew saw the plump, wrinkled woman who sat to one side raise her napkin to her lips so that no one would spot her smiling. Bartholomew was relieved to see her, knowing that if Matilde was sitting at the breakfast table and was amused by Tysilia's antics, then she was not yet in any danger.

'We do not eat ham during Lent, Tysilia,' said Dame Martyn meaningfully. 'You know that.'

Tysilia gazed blankly at her. 'But it is not Lent. We were eating ham this morning, so Lent must have ended.' Her eyes narrowed, and she pointed an accusing finger at Matilde. 'I bet *she* took it. She is so fat that she ate my ham, as well as her own. I will tell my uncle about this!'

'Have mine,' said Dame Martyn tiredly, seeing that placating the woman was the only way to shut her up and prevent her from further insulting their paying guest. She retrieved the meat from under her trencher and passed it to Tysilia, who began to gnaw at it like a peasant, pausing only to wipe her greasy fingers on the tablecloth.

'We start working on table manners tomorrow,' said Eve Wasteneys flatly, watching Tysilia's display of gluttony with disapproval. 'One thing at a time. But what can we do for you, Brother? Have you caught Will Walcote's killer?'

'Not yet,' said Michael. 'We came to ask whether you recall any more details about these meetings. I am sure they are significant, so anything you can tell us might help.'

'We told you all we knew yesterday,' said Eve. 'And we also told you that it was dark and late, and that we could not be certain about the identities of the men who came.'

'Perhaps Tysilia can help,' suggested Michael. 'She is the gatekeeper, after all. She must have admitted these men to the convent when they attended these meetings.'

'What meetings?' asked Tysilia, speaking without closing her mouth, so that the scholars were treated to the sight of a half-chewed slab of ham. 'I do not know about any meetings. We all went to bed early last night, because it was raining – the men tend not to come here when it is wet.'

'I see,' said Michael. Bartholomew saw that Matilde was having a difficult time controlling her mirth at Tysilia's brazen revelations, and at the embarrassment of the two senior nuns as their secrets were so mercilessly exposed. 'But I was referring to meetings that took place further back than yesterday – some of them before Christmas.'

'I remember Christmas,' said Tysilia brightly. 'Dame Wasteneys took her bow and shot some duck for us to eat.'

'Poaching on the Bishop's land, were you?' said Michael, raising his eyebrows in amused surprise, while Eve closed her eyes in weary resignation. 'But never mind that. Do you recall letting any men into the convent at about that time?'

'Oh, yes,' said Tysilia casually. 'Lots of them, all dressed in dark cloaks and hoods, so that no one could see their faces.'

'But did *you* see their faces?' asked Michael. Bartholomew heard the sudden hope in his voice.

Tysilia nodded. 'I could not see to their needs while they wore their hoods, could I? There was Sergeant Orwelle from the Castle; there was that silly Brother Andrew from the Carmelites, who made a nuisance of himself until he fell in the King's Ditch and drowned – good riddance, I said; then there was Mayor Horwoode, who comes when his whore Yolande de Blaston is unavailable . . .'

'That is enough!' snapped Eve sharply, apparently deciding to act before Tysilia destroyed the reputation of every man in the town. Dame Martyn had her nose in the breakfast ale again, and seemed too horrified to intervene. Eve turned to Michael apologetically. 'These are not the men who came to the meetings Walcote arranged.'

'But how do you know?' asked Michael. 'You said they were at pains to conceal their identities from you. How can you be sure that the Mayor and Sergeant Orwelle were not among those Walcote invited to his gatherings?'

'Because the folk Tysilia mentioned are regular attendees here, and I know who they are no matter how far they draw their hoods over their faces. But the ones who came with Walcote were not the same.'

'Walcote's meetings certainly did not involve that rough

Sergeant Orwelle,' offered Dame Martyn. 'He was not the kind of person with whom Walcote had business.'

'Believe me, you would be wise not to trust anything Tysilia dredges up from that muddy nether-world she calls her memory,' said Eve in an undertone, regarding the novice disparagingly. 'Her memories of yesterday are hazy, let alone from four months ago.'

'Are you gentlemen returning to the town?' asked Matilde in a slow, croaking voice, fiddling with the ring on her finger to indicate that she wanted to speak to them. 'If so, I have a message to send to my kinsman. Would you be so kind as to deliver it for me?'

'I suppose so,' sighed Michael ungraciously. 'Hurry up, if you want to write it. We have a great deal to do today and we cannot wait for long.'

'I do not write,' said Matilde, in the tone of voice that suggested she considered literacy akin to some disgusting vice. 'I will whisper my message and you can deliver it personally.'

'I will do no such thing,' replied Michael haughtily, playing his part well. 'You can mutter any message you have into the ear of my friend here. He is a physician, and much more used to the ramblings of old women than I am. He will carry your message.'

'And God bless you, too, Brother,' retorted Matilde as she eased herself off the bench with a great show of making it look like a painful and laborious business.

Tysilia watched her with open curiosity. 'She is fat,' she declared uncompromisingly. 'Fat women are ugly, and the Death should have taken them all.'

'Tysilia!' exclaimed Dame Martyn, genuinely aghast. 'You really must keep such hostile thoughts to yourself. It is not becoming.'

'I will never be fat,' continued Tysilia, tearing off another lump of ham with her sharp white teeth, like a carnivorous reptile. 'Men tell me I am a goddess, with my fine slim limbs and my smooth skin.'

187

'Beauty fades,' said Eve softly. 'And then what will you have left?'

'My mind,' said Tysilia proudly.

'Is she serious?' asked Bartholomew of Matilde, as she made her clumsy way towards him, so they could speak without being overheard.

Matilde leaned close to him, and pretended to be reciting her message. 'I still have no idea whether she is the cleverest woman in the country or the most stupid. But I overheard Eve Wasteneys and Dame Martyn talking about those meetings this morning. I am fairly sure they are telling you the truth when they say they do not recall which other men were involved.'

'What makes you say that?' asked Bartholomew.

'Because they were trying very hard to remember, and they could not. I think they wanted something with which to bargain, so you would leave them alone. I am not surprised that Dame Martyn recalls nothing; she is drunk most of the time. Meanwhile, Eve is so busy trying to keep the convent from falling about her ears that she is too overwhelmed to recall things like the names of men who visited the convent months ago.'

'But this was not months ago,' said Bartholomew. 'They told us last time that some of the meetings were comparatively recent.'

'A week or ten days,' confirmed Matilde. 'Although the first ones were held in late November. But they came cloaked and hooded, and the nuns deliberately did not pay them too much attention, because these men clearly did not want to be identified.'

'I bet they did not,' said Bartholomew.

'That is why Eve and Dame Martyn honestly do not know the identities of these people, other than the few who stand out physically – Lincolne because of his size and funny hair; Kenyngham because he had forgotten to cover his face; and Pechem because only Franciscans wear grey. Incidentally, the earlier gatherings were better attended than the more recent ones.'

'Why? Because to be caught at one might be dangerous?'

'The nuns do not know. They were concerned that dwindling attendance might cause Walcote to stop holding them, which would have meant the loss of four groats.'

'Are you all right?' asked Bartholomew anxiously. 'Does anyone have the slightest idea as to who you are?'

'Of course not,' said Matilde, her eyes gleaming through her mass of painted wrinkles. 'And I am thoroughly enjoying myself, so do not worry. Even if I were not trying to help you, Tysilia would present an interesting and amusing problem. She is the most brazen of thieves. She stole a pendant from me last night – a worthless bauble as it happens, but mine nevertheless. She took it when she thought I was asleep.'

Bartholomew was horrified, visions of Matilde being smothered with pillows or knifed as she slept rushing through his mind. 'She wanders unsupervised at night? But she may harm you when you are least suspecting it.'

'No,' said Matilde with a confident smile. 'I will lock the door tonight. She will not hurt me. But you should go now, or they will wonder what we are talking about.'

'You say your nephew is Robin of Grantchester, Mistress Horner?' asked Bartholomew loudly, stepping away from her. Matilde's eyes opened wide with horrified amusement when she heard he had chosen the unsavoury town surgeon as her fictitious relative. 'I shall see that he has your message this morning.'

Rain continued to fall heavily as Bartholomew and Michael walked back to Cambridge; by the time they arrived, they were soaked. Michael was disappointed that Matilde had nothing to report, and was not particularly comforted by the notion that Dame Martyn and Eve Wasteneys had actually been telling the truth when they said they could not

189

recall which men had had business with Walcote. He claimed he would rather they had been lying, because then there would have been a chance of learning the identities of the men involved.

'There is still Pechem of the Franciscans to interrogate,' suggested Bartholomew. 'Eve Wasteneys claims he was one of these mysterious midnight guests.'

'He is visiting the Franciscan house at Denny and will not be back until tomorrow,' said Michael with a sigh. 'He seems to be elsewhere every time I ask for him. I wonder if that is significant. Still, unless he plans to evade me for ever, I shall run into him sooner or later.'

'Then we should talk to Kenyngham,' said Bartholomew. 'He would never lie. He will tell us who the others were.'

Michael gave a hearty sigh. 'Really, Matt. Do you think that had not occurred to me? But Kenyngham is locked away in the Gilbertine Friary, engaged in some kind of prayerful fast for Lent. He is due to finish tomorrow, but until then, the Gilbertines will not interrupt him.'

'That sounds like Kenyngham. Now that he is relieved of his duties as Master of Michaelhouse, he can fast and pray as much as he likes.'

'True,' agreed Michael. 'But it is a wretched nuisance when I need his help so urgently. I tried every way I could think of to inveigle my way into the Gilbertines' chapel, but they were immovable. I have the feeling they regard him as a saint in the making. If it were anyone but Kenyngham, I would question such religious fervour as suspect behaviour.'

Bartholomew laughed. 'For a monk, you are remarkably intolerant of men whose lives are ruled by their religious beliefs.'

'Everything in its place, Matt,' replied Michael. 'I am extremely tolerant, actually. What I am *in*tolerant of is men who use religion to further their own ends – men like Prior Lincolne, who state that nominalism is heretical because he happens to be a realist; and men who believe they are God's chosen, and that everything that happens occurs for their benefit.'

'Like Timothy and Janius, you mean?'

'Especially Janius. I like them both, but their fanaticism unnerves me. It is dangerous to believe God controls everything to the point where you think what people do is irrelevant.'

Bartholomew agreed. 'Some of my patients are the same. Sometimes I wonder whether it is just so that they will not have to make difficult decisions or come to terms with things they find painful.'

'We could be burned in the Market Square for having this kind of conversation,' said Michael, jabbing his friend playfully in the ribs with one of his powerful elbows. 'To say we believe God is not directly responsible for everything that happens, and that humans have a choice, would be considered heresy by some.'

'Only because they have not thought it through,' said Bartholomew. 'If *everything* that happens is God's will, then we may as well abandon this investigation of yours, because anything we do is irrelevant to the outcome.'

'Now you are going too far. Next, you will be telling me you are a nominalist.'

'There is a great deal to recommend nominalism,' said Bartholomew defensively. 'Especially when you apply it to natural philosophy. For example, Heytesbury's *Regulae Solvendi Sophismata* says that variations in the intensity of a velocity increase with speed, just as the redness of an apple increases with its ripeness.'

'I see,' said Michael, nodding. 'Velocity, like redness, is a universal and not a particular.'

'Exactly,' said Bartholomew, warming to his theme. 'So, a body, starting from rest or a particular speed, would travel a certain distance in a specific unit of time. Thus, if the same body were to move in the same interval of time with a uniform velocity equal to the speed acquired in the middle of its uniform acceleration, it would travel an equal distance.'

'If you say so,' said Michael, bored by the sudden delve into natural philosophy, and not making the slightest effort to follow Bartholomew's reasoning. 'Heytesbury worked all this out, did he?'

'It is a very clever piece of logic. I am surprised you have never discussed it with him. There are many scholars who would love such an opportunity.'

'I met Heytesbury only once before our encounter in Trumpington, and then we were more concerned with sizing each other up than with arguing about uniform acceleration. And I am not interested in his ideas about movement and motion anyway, only in what information I can persuade him to part with that will be to Cambridge's advantage and the detriment of Oxford.'

'And you accuse Janius of being single-minded,' said Bartholomew, smiling. They reached the Barnwell Gate, and nodded to Sergeant Orwelle as they passed through. Seeing a familiar figure nearby, Bartholomew grabbed Michael's arm and pulled him into the shadows of the guardhouse. 'Speaking of Heytesbury, there he is. What is he doing?'

'He is with Prior Morden of the Dominicans,' said Michael, watching the two men, who were talking earnestly under the shelter of the west door of Holy Trinity Church. 'I wonder what could draw those two together.'

'Nominalism, probably,' said Bartholomew. 'As I have just told you, there are many scholars who would love an opportunity to cross intellectual swords with Heytesbury. Morden is doubtless one of them.'

'Morden is a decent administrator, and rules the Dominicans well enough,' said Michael. 'But he is scarcely one of our most astute thinkers. Have you noticed that is often the case? You have only to look at Michaelhouse to see that we have fared better under someone who is good at organisation but weak on wits.'

'You approve of what Langelee has done?' asked Bartholomew, surprised. 'I thought you were still angry with him for ruining your own chances of becoming Master.'

'I am,' said Michael stiffly. 'And I, of course, would prove that it is possible to have a brilliant mind *and* run an efficient College. But I admit Langelee is doing better than I imagined, and he is very tolerant of my duties as Senior Proctor. He allows me whatever freedom I need, and never asks me to explain my absences.'

'Perhaps he did you a favour, then,' said Bartholomew. 'At the next election, you will inherit a College that is in much better condition than the one he took over.'

Michael smiled. 'True. But we should not linger here reviewing my career. I wish I knew what Heytesbury and Morden are discussing.'

'It is nothing of relevance to you, your negotiations with Oxford, or your investigation, Brother,' came a rather sibilant voice from behind them. Bartholomew almost leapt out of his skin, unaware that anyone had been close enough to hear what they had been saying. Michael merely smiled as he recognised the smooth black hair and twinkling blue eyes of Brother Janius.

'Have you been listening to Heytesbury and Morden?' he asked.

Janius nodded. 'Now that God has seen fit to appoint Brother Timothy as Junior Proctor, all us Benedictines feel obliged to be watchful, so that we can gather information that you may find helpful in your duties. That is why God appointed Timothy – because He knew he would make a good and honest servant for the University.'

'But it was *I* who appointed Timothy,' said Michael. 'God had no feelings on the matter one way or another.'

'How do you know?' flashed Janius, anger flashing briefly in his blue eyes. 'God is all powerful, and determines every aspect of our lives.'

'Then tell me what He permitted you to overhear of the conversation between Morden and Heytesbury,' said Michael, apparently deciding that argument was futile in the face of such rigid conviction.

Janius brought his ire under control, and the serene

expression returned to his pale face. 'I was praying in Holy Trinity Church – God drew me there, so that is how I know He wanted me to eavesdrop on the discussion – and I heard Morden inviting Heytesbury to the Dominican Friary next week for a private discussion about nominalism.'

'Is that it?' asked Michael disappointed. 'That is rather mundane.'

'Not for the Dominicans,' replied Janius. 'They consider it a great honour, and plan to have a feast to celebrate the occasion. I wonder whether Heytesbury might consider coming to visit the Benedictines of Ely Hall. We will not be able to fête him in the same lavish way as will the Dominicans, but we can offer stimulating conversation and keen minds.'

'Then do not invite me, please,' said Michael. 'I cannot think of a more tedious way to spend an evening. Matt has just been telling me all about accelerating bodies and uniform velocity, and I have no desire to hear any more of it.'

Janius smiled at Bartholomew. 'I have heard your lectures on the physical universe are complex and not for novices. Were you telling Michael about Heytesbury's mean speed theorem?'

Bartholomew nodded enthusiastically. 'And just four years ago, Nicole Oresme devised a geometrical proof for the intension and remission of qualities based on Heytesbury's—'

'You mentioned yesterday that you planned to attend Faricius's requiem mass, Janius,' interrupted Michael loudly, deciding he had heard enough of nominalism as applied to the laws of physics for one day. 'Did you go? Can I assume that your presence here means that it is over?'

'It was over at midday, and the afternoon has been spent in private prayer for his soul,' Janius told him. 'That was why I was in Holy Trinity Church. But he is due to be buried about now, and I was on my way back there when I met you.'

'Good,' said Michael. 'I want to talk to the Carmelites,

194

and if they are all gathered together at Faricius's mass, I will not have to hunt them down individually.'

'You would not have to do that anyway,' said Janius. 'Since Faricius's murder, most of the Orders are keeping their students inside. No one wants a retaliatory killing.'

'There are those that would disagree,' said Michael. 'But it is cold standing here. Let us be on our way to this burial. Such an occasion will suit my mood perfectly.'

chapter 6

FARICIUS'S REQUIEM MASS HAD BEEN A GRAND AFFAIR. Prayers for him had been said in the church all afternoon, and the rough wooden coffin was being carried back to the friary, where there was a small graveyard in the grounds near the river. Bartholomew and Michael joined the end of the procession, which comprised mainly White Friars, but also a smattering of scholars from other hostels and colleges who had met Faricius and been impressed by his scholarship. Both Timothy and Janius were among the mourners, as was Heytesbury, although he at least had the good sense to keep his face hidden in a voluminous hood.

'What are you doing here?' Michael asked the Merton man in a soft whisper. 'A procession of realism-obsessed Carmelites is no place for the country's leading thinker on nominalism. Are you mad?'

'No such restrictions apply in Oxford,' replied Heytesbury testily. 'And I met Faricius once. I had the greatest respect for him, and wanted to persuade him to study with me at Merton.'

'I doubt he would have taken a nominalist master,' said Bartholomew. 'Have you not heard how the Orders have ranged themselves around this debate? The Carmelites have decided that realism is the ultimate truth.'

'Why should that make any difference?' demanded Heytesbury. 'The great nominalist William of Occam was a student of the equally great realist Duns Scotus. Faricius had an excellent mind, and I would have welcomed the opportunity to help him hone it, no matter what his beliefs.'

Bartholomew gazed at him, and wondered whether Oxford was really so different from her sister university. In his own experience, Oxford scholars were every bit as belligerent and aggressive as those in Cambridge, and just as prepared to prove their academic points with their fists. But given the strength of the feelings the debate seemed to have engendered that Lent, he could not imagine a Cambridge nominalist being willing to train a realist student, who in time might use that training against him and the beliefs he held dear. He wondered whether Heytesbury was a man of integrity who was devoted to scholarship in all its forms, or simply a fool.

The sombre procession passed in silence through the Carmelites' orchard and into the small plot of land that had been reserved for burials. It was a pleasant place, sheltered by chestnut trees and overlooking the water meadows that stretched away to the small hamlet of Newnham Croft. Several grassy mounds already graced the area, along with a sizeable knoll that Bartholomew knew was where the friary's plague victims had been laid to rest.

Under a spreading cedar tree was one of the town's curiosities. In 1290, a man named Humphrey de Lecton had been the first Carmelite to take a doctor's degree in Cambridge, and later became the first Carmelite to lecture for the University. When he died, he had been buried with some pomp and ceremony, and his grave was marked with an impressive piece of masonry: a disconcertingly realistic coffin with a likeness of Lecton etched into the top, covered by a four-pillared canopy that had once been painted. Wind and rain had stripped it of its colours, but the tomb still dominated the Carmelites' peaceful burial ground.

A rectangular hole had been prepared for Faricius near Lecton's monument, with a mound of excavated mud piled to one side. Water had collected in the bottom of the grave, and the coffin landed with a slight splash as it was lowered inside. Rain pattered on the wood and on the bowed heads of those who gathered around as Lincolne said his final words. Bartholomew saw Horneby standing next to his Prior, scrubbing at his eyes with the sleeve of his habit; the expression on his face was a mixture of anger and grief. Lincolne's peculiar turret of hair had escaped from under his cowl, and rose vertically from his forehead. Droplets of rain caught in it, so that it glittered in the dull light of the gloomy March afternoon.

'The Dominicans will pay for this,' Bartholomew heard Horneby mutter.

'Faricius was a peaceful man who abhorred violence,' said Brother Timothy gently. 'He would not have wanted his friends to indulge themselves in a rampage of hatred on his behalf.'

'He would not have wanted the Dominicans to murder him and then laugh about it,' snapped Horneby. 'They are in their friary celebrating what they have done. Look! They have even sent one of their number to observe his funeral and then report the details back to them.'

All eyes followed his accusing finger, and Michael was astonished to find himself the object of their scrutiny.

'I am not Dominican,' he said, aggrieved, pushing back his cowl to reveal his face. 'I am a Benedictine, as well you know.'

'Oh, it is you, Brother Michael,' said Lincolne. 'In this poor light it is difficult to tell Dominicans from Benedictines. Both wear black cloaks.'

'Rubbish,' said Michael brusquely. 'Anyone with the merest glimmer of sense can tell a mendicant from a monastic. I am a monk, not a friar.'

'One look at his girth should tell you that,' Bartholomew thought he heard Heytesbury mutter. 'Only Benedictines grow to such a size.'

'Have you come to tell us that you have arrested Faricius's killer?' asked Lincolne, in a tone of voice that suggested he did not think they had. 'It would be a fitting tribute at his funeral.'

'I have come to ask more questions,' said Michael. 'But I am a good deal wiser about this case now than I was yesterday. The truth will prevail, have no doubt about that.'

Bartholomew hoped the monk's confidence would not turn out to be a hollow brag. As far as he could see, they were even further from an answer, because all they had learned indicated that there was more to Faricius's death than they had first thought.

Lincolne did not look as if he believed it, either. He turned to the watching mourners with a few words of dismissal. 'Thank you for coming. It is gratifying to see that a Carmelite commanded such respect among so many people.'

The mourners began to move away in respectful silence. Heytesbury and Janius went with them, so that soon only Lincolne, Bartholomew, Michael and Timothy remained under the cedar tree. Horneby and several of his friends worked nearby, shovelling sodden earth that landed with hollow thumps on top of Faricius's coffin. Horneby's face was wet, although from the rain or from bitter tears, Bartholomew could not tell.

'The proctors have more questions to ask!' the student-friar jeered, shovelling hard at the earth. 'There have been more than enough of those already. What we want now are answers.'

'I would not need to ask more questions if you had told the truth,' snapped Michael, rounding on him. 'How can you expect me to catch your friend's killer when you were dishonest with me?'

'I was not—' began Horneby, startled by the attack.

'You told me it was impossible for Faricius to have left the friary, and yet he was found dead outside,' Michael continued relentlessly.

'I only said—' attempted Horneby.

Michael cut through his words. 'You are a fool, Horneby. I will find out what happened to Faricius, and I will discover how and why he happened to be outside when the rest of you were in here. But, by not telling me the truth, you are running the risk that the culprit may have fled the town before I uncover him. Is that what you want?'

'No! Of course not. But—'

'Then tell me what you know,' said Michael, in full interrogatory mode. Even Bartholomew felt intimidated by the flashing green eyes and the unwavering gaze. A mere novice like Horneby was helpless under the monk's onslaught.

'Nothing,' stammered Horneby, casting an agonised glance at Lincolne that would have told even the most inexperienced investigator that he was lying.

'Why was Faricius out?' repeated Michael. He appealed to Lincolne. 'Are we to stand here all day waiting for this half-wit to speak? Instruct him to answer me immediately, before any more time is wasted on his petty deceits.'

'You had better tell him what you know, Horneby,' said Lincolne tiredly.

'But we decided to keep it a secret,' wailed Horneby miserably, looking at his fellows, who seemed as unhappy as he did.

'What are you talking about?' asked Lincolne, bemused. 'Keep what a secret?'

'About Faricius,' said Horneby. 'What he was doing had no bearing on his death, and we decided it was better the secret died with him. There was no point in telling the Senior Proctor.'

'Worse yet, it will lead the investigation in the wrong direction,' said one of the others, appealing to his Prior. 'It is entirely irrelevant, and we decided Brother Michael would have a better chance of catching the killer if the waters were not muddied by what we know.'

'What is it?' demanded Michael. 'I am quite capable of deciding what is and what is not relevant to a murder investigation. I was solving crimes such as this while you were still mewling and puking on your mothers' knees.'

That was not strictly true. Michael had held his appointment as Proctor only since the plague, although he had been an agent of the Bishop of Ely before that.

'What is all this about?' demanded Lincolne, growing impatient. 'What are you not telling Brother Michael?'

'There is a tunnel,' said Horneby unhappily. 'It allows us to come and go as we please. Of course, we use it very rarely,' he added when he saw Lincolne's jaw drop in horror.

'A tunnel?' demanded Lincolne, appalled. 'What do you think this is? Some dungeon where prisoners must dig for their freedom?'

'We did not make it,' said Horneby defensively. 'It has been here for hundreds of years – ever since our Order moved to Cambridge, in fact.'

'That was in 1290,' Timothy pointed out pedantically. 'The Carmelites were granted land in Milne Street in 1290 by the Archdeacon of York, which is why Humphrey de Lecton was buried here. It was certainly not hundreds of years ago.'

'Well, it has been here a long time,' said Horneby, dismissive of such details. 'Each year, new students are shown the tunnel, then made to swear an oath that they will never tell anyone about it. The masters are never informed.'

'Why did you not mention this before?' demanded Michael angrily. 'You must see that this has a bearing on our enquiries. It explains how Faricius left the friary without using the gates.'

Horneby cast a nervous glance at his Prior. 'No masters are ever told, and you have always questioned us when Prior Lincolne was present. And anyway, Walcote knew about it. We assumed he would tell you.'

'Walcote is dead,' said Michael harshly. 'And why are you so sure that he knew, anyway?'

'He caught Simon Lynne using it a few days ago,' replied Horneby reluctantly. 'He was furious, and ordered us to close up the entrance immediately. He said he would return in a week, and if it were not blocked, he would report all of us to Prior Lincolne.'

'And I assume he did not?' asked Michael.

'He died,' explained Horneby. 'The week expired today. We were going to obey him, but when we learned he was dead, we saw we would not have to. You clearly did not know about it, or you would have guessed how Faricius left the

201

friary on the day he was murdered. Walcote was as good as his word when he promised to tell no one if we did as he ordered.'

'That is outrageous!' exploded Lincolne, his topknot trembling with anger. 'Such a tunnel is a breach in our security, and it was extremely foolish of you to keep it from me.'

'But we have not always been at loggerheads with our rival Orders,' Horneby pointed out. 'It is only a security problem if we are under attack, and that has not happened until recently.'

Lincolne favoured him with an icy glare. 'Perhaps that is so during the few months that you have graced us with your presence. But in past years there have been nasty incidents – perhaps not with other Orders, but with the Colleges and the hostels – where such a tunnel might have been very dangerous for us. Where is the damned thing, anyway?'

Horneby walked to the tomb of Humphrey de Lecton and pulled back a nearby tree branch to reveal a sinister black slit.

'Here it is. You slide through this hole, make your way forward on your hands and knees for about the length of a man, then a short tunnel leads to the garden of the house next door. You climb the wall, which is lower than ours and easier to scale, and you are in Milne Street.'

'I could not fit down that,' said Michael, eyeing it doubtfully.

'No,' agreed Horneby, looking him up and down. 'It would be much too tight for you. But most of us students have done it at various times.'

'Why?' demanded Lincolne. 'What would you leave the friary for?'

Horneby had the grace to look sheepish, and one of the younger novices was unable to prevent a nervous giggle escaping from his lips. Lincolne glowered at him, and the boy shrank backwards in abject embarrassment.

'To do what most young men do of a night, I imagine,' said Michael, seeing that none of the student-friars were

202

prepared to furnish their Prior with an honest answer. 'The taverns and the town's women are an enticing proposition compared to an evening seated in a cold conclave with someone reading from the Bible.'

'But that is against the University's rules,' cried Lincolne, appalled.

'Yes,' said Michael dryly. 'So, I recommend that you seal up this hole before any more of your students clamber through it and pay the price. But you still have not answered my original question, Horneby. I want to know what Faricius was doing outside the walls, not how he got there.'

Horneby exchanged more glances with his fellows, some of whom Bartholomew saw were shaking their heads, warning him not to tell. Michael saw them, too.

'Enough of this!' he snapped angrily. 'Faricius is dead. He was stabbed in the stomach and he bled to death with no priest present to give him spiritual comfort. It was a brutal, violent end for a man you say was gentle and peace-loving. If his memory means anything at all to you, you will tell me why he happened to be outside at the wrong time.'

'Was it a woman?' asked Lincolne, more gently. 'It seems that is the main reason most of you slip away from your duties and obligations.' His eyes narrowed in sudden suspicion. 'It is not that Tysilia, is it? I warned you all about her, after what happened to Brother Andrew.'

'Do you mean the Brother Andrew who drowned himself in the King's Ditch just before Christmas?' asked Timothy curiously.

'Yes,' said Lincolne. 'Tysilia stole his heart and then refused to see him. We told people his humours had been unbalanced and that he was ill when he took his own life – which was certainly true after he had encountered that witch.'

'Faricius was not seeing a woman,' said Horneby. 'Not even Tysilia. We all kept our distance from her, just as you ordered, Father.' He smiled ingratiatingly.

'Do not think that obeying him over this one woman

redeems you,' said Michael, seeing that Lincolne was vaguely mollified by Horneby's claim. 'Personally, I do not believe it should be necessary for a Prior to issue such a warning to men of the cloth.'

'Do not be so pompous, Brother,' muttered Bartholomew in Michael's ear. 'The chances are that some of your own escapades with women are known around the town. You will look foolish if they challenge your right to ask such questions.'

Michael ignored him. 'And do not try to change the subject, Horneby. I want to know why Faricius left the friary.'

'He was writing an essay,' said Horneby reluctantly.

'An essay?' echoed Michael, surprise taking the anger from his voice.

Horneby shot an apologetic glance at Lincolne. 'I am sorry, Father, but Faricius's essay was in defence of nominalism and supported the controversial theories of the Oxford philosopher William Heytesbury. Faricius was a nominalist.'

'An essay on nominalism?' asked Michael, looking around the assembled scholars in wary disbelief. 'Is that what this great secret is? Is that why Faricius risked life and limb to go outside when it was obvious he should have remained here?'

Horneby nodded unhappily, while the other students shook their heads in disgust that Horneby had betrayed their dead colleague's trust.

'Faricius was a nominalist?' whispered Lincolne, aghast. 'If only I had known! I could have used my powers of reason to show him that he was wrong, and that nominalism is heresy.'

'No,' said Horneby. 'He was quite certain of his beliefs and he argued them convincingly. You would not have dissuaded him. We all tried and were unsuccessful.'

Michael scratched his chin, a puzzled frown creasing his fat features. 'Nominalism is a complex theory. I cannot see

204

that a mere novice would provide us with any new insights, and so I fail to see why this essay is important.'

'Faricius could have provided you with new insights,' argued Horneby. 'He had a brilliant mind, and spent a good deal of time honing his debating skills. We were proud of him, but afraid for him at the same time.'

Bartholomew suspected that Horneby was right. Walcote, Timothy and Janius had all claimed to admire Faricius's thinking, while the great William Heytesbury had even offered to take him as a student. A man like Heytesbury could choose any scholar he wanted, and that he was interested in Faricius was revealing. Bartholomew realised that Horneby and his cronies were not the only ones who had maintained their silence about Faricius's beliefs: Heytesbury had also declined to enlighten Michael with what he knew of the Carmelite friar murdered at around the time he had arrived in Cambridge himself.

'And all of you knew about Faricius's philosophical leanings?' asked Michael, looking around at the other students. They nodded reluctantly, casting guilty glances at each other.

'Yes,' said Horneby. 'But he talked to other scholars in the University known to support nominalism, too, so that he could learn from them.'

'Such as whom?' demanded Michael.

'I cannot remember precisely,' said Horneby, a little testily. 'Half the town believes in nominalism, so he was not exactly strapped for choice.'

'Henry de Kyrkeby, the Dominican precentor, is due to give the University Lecture on nominalism,' suggested another student, more helpfully. 'I think Faricius waylaid him and discussed his ideas once. Then there is Father Paul of the Franciscans, who is a tolerant and kindly man. And I saw Faricius in deep discussion with your Junior Proctor on several occasions.'

'Brother Timothy?' asked Michael, regarding doubtfully the Benedictine who stood behind him. 'You have not mentioned this before.'

'My discussions with him were of a more general nature,' said Timothy, surprised by the student's assertion. 'We did not talk about nominalism.'

'Not Timothy, the other one. Will Walcote,' said the student.

'Unfortunately, Will Walcote is dead,' said Michael. 'I *do* recall him saying that he had met Faricius, however, and so I know you are telling the truth on that score. Who else?'

'I cannot remember,' said Horneby again. 'It was not something he discussed with us. He knew we did not agree with his ideas, and so he tended not to tell us about them.'

'Where is this essay now?' demanded Lincolne, still angry. 'And what do you think it had to do with his death?'

'Quite,' said Michael. 'I am no nominalist myself, and I appreciate why many people find its tenets heretical. But I cannot see why writing about it should result in anyone's demise.'

'I disagree,' said Lincolne. 'Nominalism poses one of the greatest threats to our Church and our society since the pestilence. It causes people to question basic truths like the manner of the creation and the nature of God. It is dangerous, and I will have none of it in my friary.'

'Because we all know you feel that way, Faricius could not keep his essay here,' explained Horneby to his Prior. 'He always left it in a crevice in the wall that surrounds the Church of St John Zachary. When he heard that the Dominicans were coming, he went to fetch it.'

'Did you see this essay when you found him?' asked Michael of Bartholomew.

The physician shook his head, but thought about Faricius's desperation when he had learned that his scrip was missing. Bartholomew had been wrong. Faricius had not been delirious or confused about which of his scrips he had carried, and it had not been the ruby ring that he had been thinking about: his scrip must have contained his precious essay.

'I suppose this means he was killed on his way to fetch the thing,' surmised Michael.

Bartholomew shook his head. 'Given his frantic desperation when he learned his scrip was missing, I think it more
likely that he had collected the essay and was on his way
home with it.'

'You had better show me this hiding place in the churchyard of St John Zachary, Horneby,' said Michael tiredly. 'It
is possible that the essay – or a copy – is still there.'

'Lynne and I have already looked,' said Horneby,
exchanging a glance with his friends. 'We went on Monday
night – we did use the tunnel, before you ask – but it had
gone. The stone had been replaced in the wall, and the
branches of the nearby bush arranged to hide evidence of
chipped mortar. Faricius always did that. I suppose he
intended to use it again once the riot was over.'

Michael sighed. 'What a mess! I wish you had told me all
this before. It might have saved a good deal of time.'

The students hung their heads, and none would meet
the eyes of their Prior, who glowered at them in silent fury.
Bartholomew could not decide whether Lincolne's anger
was directed at them for keeping secrets and delaying
Michael's investigation, or whether he was merely indignant that they had helped to harbour a heretic in their
midst.

So, had Faricius's controversial essay brought about his
death? Recalling his horror when he learned that his scrip
had been stolen, Bartholomew was certain it had played
some role. Faricius had been so concerned about its loss
that he had even failed to reveal the identity of the person
or people who had stabbed him. Bartholomew supposed it
was possible that the killers were men Faricius had not
known, although if the essay were at the heart of the matter,
that seemed unlikely.

As far as the physician could see, there were two possible
explanations for why Faricius had died. First, he might have
been murdered by a realist, who was afraid that a clever
thinker like Faricius would promote the cause of nominalism
to the detriment of realism. If this were true, then it was

likely that Faricius's killer was a Carmelite. Had one of his colleagues killed him, to protect the theory that the Carmelite Order had chosen to champion? Bartholomew gazed at Horneby and his friends, and wondered whether one of them still knew more than he had told. But Horneby suggested that Faricius had talked to lots of people, including the missing Dominican Precentor, about his affinity with nominalism. Was Kyrkeby's absence related to Faricius's murder? Had Kyrkeby committed the crime, then fled the town? But Kyrkeby was Bartholomew's patient, and the physician knew Kyrkeby's weak heart would not have permitted him to engage in a violent struggle with a young and healthy man. Yet how fit did one need to be to slide a sharp knife into someone's stomach?

The second possibility was that the killer knew an essay was in the making, but had made the assumption that it was in support of realism: because Faricius was a Carmelite, it was not unreasonable to assume that he had followed his Order's teaching. Therefore, the suspects were the nominalists, who would not want a brilliant essay in defence of realism circulating the town. Faricius's killer could therefore be a Dominican or someone who was a professed nominalist – like Walcote, for example.

'You should block this tunnel as soon as possible,' Michael advised Lincolne, as he moved away from the graveyard and began to head towards the front gate. His voice brought Bartholomew out of his reverie, who realised he was cold, wet, tired and ready for his dinner. 'It is too dangerous to leave as it is, given that you have this silly feud with the Dominicans.'

One of the students had lit a lamp, and Lincolne took it from him to inspect the dark entrance to the tunnel, shaking his head in disapproval and casting angry glances at his charges. He leaned forward and put his hand inside it, poking at the damp earth and announcing that the structure was unstable and that his students were lucky it had not collapsed on them. Suddenly, Horneby released a piercing cry of horror that made everyone jump. Bartholomew spun around to look back at him.

'What is wrong with the boy?' Michael whispered testily, his hand on his heart. 'Has he seen a dead worm? Or worse, has he found Faricius's "heretical" essay?'

'Brother! Come quickly!' cried Lincolne in a wavering, unsteady voice, as his students clustered around him to see what had so distressed Horneby.

Michael elbowed them out of the way and craned forward to where the lamp illuminated the inside of the tunnel. Meanwhile, Horneby held a black leather shoe in his hand. Bartholomew peered over Michael's shoulder, and saw that the shoe had been pulled from a foot that lay white and bare just beyond the entrance of the tunnel. He reached in and touched it, trying to determine whether it belonged to someone he could help, but it was unnaturally cold and still.

'Well?' asked Michael in a low voice. 'Is he alive?'

'I think you have another death to investigate, Brother,' said Bartholomew softly, so that only Michael could hear. 'I suspect Horneby has just located the missing Henry de Kyrkeby.'

'What in God's name is it?' wailed Prior Lincolne, as Bartholomew reached down inside the tunnel and tried to secure a grip on the white-soled foot. 'It looks like a corpse!'

'It *is* a corpse,' snapped Michael impatiently. 'And judging from the bit of black habit that I can see, and the fact that the shoe you are holding is made of the black-dyed leather favoured by the Dominicans, I would guess that this is one of them.'

'A Dominican?' squeaked Lincolne in alarm. 'Who? One of the louts who murdered Faricius, and who then decided he had a taste for Carmelite blood and was on his way to claim more of it?'

'I sincerely doubt it,' said Michael. 'The body is wet, and looks to me to have been here for some time. Given that

209

we have only one missing Dominican, I imagine this is Henry de Kyrkeby.'

'Kyrkeby?' shrieked Lincolne in agitation. 'But what is he doing in our tunnel? Was he trying to leave? Or was he trying to come in?'

Bartholomew began to pull on Kyrkeby's foot, and succeeded in freeing one leg. But the body was stuck fast, as if something was pinning it inside its gloomy resting place.

'Or has someone just used the tunnel as a convenient place to hide his corpse?' mused Michael, looking away from the body and studying the faces of the Carmelite students who stood in an uncertain circle around him. The dull grey light made their expressions difficult to read.

'But why would anyone do that?' cried Lincolne. 'We Carmelites are not in the business of hiding the corpses of members of rival Orders in dirty holes in the ground!'

'Neither are most people,' said Michael. 'But you have not taken into account the possibility that whoever hid Kyrkeby's body might also have killed him.'

He gazed at the student-friars a second time, but could gauge nothing from their reactions. The younger lads seemed frightened by the sudden appearance of death in their midst, while the faces of the older students, like Horneby, were virtually expressionless, and the monk could not tell what they thought about the fact that the Dominican Precentor was dead in their graveyard.

'I cannot get him out,' muttered Bartholomew, as he knelt next to the tunnel. 'He is stuck.'

'No one killed him,' said Lincolne uncertainly, ignoring Bartholomew as, like Michael, he began looking around at his assembled scholars, as if not absolutely certain that he could make such a claim.

'Is that true?' demanded Michael of Bartholomew. 'Has Kyrkeby been murdered, or did he die in the tunnel by accident or from natural causes?'

Bartholomew pointed to the white leg that protruded

obscenely from the dirty hole. 'How can I tell that from a foot, Brother? I need to look at the whole body.'

'Hurry up, then,' ordered Michael, oblivious or uncaring of the weary look Bartholomew shot him. 'If Kyrkeby has been murdered, I want to know as soon as possible.' The expression on his face made it clear that he would start looking for suspects among the Carmelites.

'But why would any of *us* kill him?' asked Lincolne, in what Bartholomew imagined he thought were reasonable tones.

'Because someone murdered Faricius, and many of you believe that a Dominican was responsible,' replied Michael promptly. 'Or perhaps because one of you caught him trespassing on Carmelite property, and decided to kill him before he reported to his Prior all that he had learned from his illicit visit.'

'What could he report, Brother?' asked Lincolne in the same measured voice. 'You are assuming that we have something to hide. We do not.'

'But you do,' Michael pointed out. 'For a start, your students had very successfully hidden the fact that Faricius was writing an essay in defence of nominalism.'

'No!' objected Lincolne. 'That was different—'

'It was not,' interrupted Michael brusquely. 'And secondly, you have only just been told about this tunnel that is supposed to have been here for years. Perhaps Kyrkeby found it, and someone was afraid that if he told his brother Dominicans, you Carmelites would be vulnerable to attack.'

'None of my students would kill for such paltry reasons,' said Lincolne, although he continued to glance uneasily at his charges.

'No?' asked Michael. 'Then perhaps there are other reasons why someone here would want Kyrkeby dead. I have just seen two nasty secrets surface in the last few moments – three if we can count the presence of an extra corpse in the tomb of the illustrious Humphrey de Lecton – so perhaps there are yet more for me to uncover.'

Lincolne was finally silent.

'I really cannot move him,' said Bartholomew, in the brief lull in the accusations and counter-accusations. 'I cannot seem to get a good grip. His skin is too slippery.'

'We did not kill him,' said Horneby, taking up the defence of his Order where his Prior had left off. Neither he nor anyone else took any notice of Bartholomew, more interested in convincing Michael of their innocence than in retrieving the body that lay in the hole. 'We have no idea how he came to be here. I swear it.'

'And who do you mean by "we" exactly?' asked Michael archly. 'You Carmelites have at least thirty student-friars. Do you speak for them all? What about the masters? How can you know that no one has taken matters into his own hands and avenged Faricius by killing a Dominican?'

Horneby shook his head slowly. 'How can we have killed him? We have all been confined to the convent since Faricius was murdered. No one has left except to go to church, and then Prior Lincolne was watching us.'

'That is true,' said Lincolne.

'No,' said Timothy softly. 'That is not true. Horneby just told us that he and Simon Lynne went to look for Faricius's essay in the Church of St John Zachary on Monday. Obviously that was *after* Faricius had died, and so Horneby is lying when he says no one went out.'

'And we saw a whole pack of you lurking outside the Dominican Friary on Sunday intent on mischief,' Bartholomew pointed out. 'We followed you home, remember?'

Michael indicated the tunnel. 'Anyone could have slipped through this whenever he liked. You cannot prove otherwise.'

'However, no one would have been using it as long as Kyrkeby was here,' said Bartholomew, turning his attention back to the body. 'He is blocking it completely. And he will remain blocking it unless someone helps me. I cannot move him on my own.'

'A visit to St John Zachary counts as going to church,' said Horneby insolently. 'We just made a slight detour for a few moments to check Faricius's hiding place.'

'And what about your sally to the Dominican Friary?' asked Michael coolly. 'Does that count as going to church, too?'

Horneby sneered. 'We were only there for a short while. It was not worth mentioning.'

'I will help you, Matthew,' said Timothy, crouching next to Bartholomew and reaching into the hole to grab a handful of Kyrkeby's habit. His face was pale and his hands unsteady, and the physician saw yet again that dealing with corpses would not be part of a Junior Proctor's obligations that Timothy would enjoy.

'It is all right,' said Bartholomew, not wanting Timothy to do something that so obviously unsettled him. 'I can probably manage.'

Timothy gave a wan smile. 'You cannot. And no one else seems willing to assist.'

'When was the last time any of you used the tunnel?' asked Michael, glancing briefly at Bartholomew's struggle with Kyrkeby before returning to the more interesting matter of interrogating the Carmelites.

'Last Saturday,' replied Horneby immediately. 'It was used just before the riot in which those evil Dominicans murdered Faricius.'

'Horneby, Horneby,' said Lincolne, pretending to be shocked by his student's accusation, even though he had made the same ones several times himself. 'That attitude will get us nowhere. What will Brother Michael think when he hears words like that?'

'He will think that you decided to avenge Faricius's death and kill yourself a Dominican,' said Michael flatly. 'Even the most dull-witted of you must see that this is how it appears. And this sudden display of quiet reason does you no good, Prior Lincolne. Until a few moments ago, you, too, were claiming that Dominicans murdered Faricius.'

'That was then,' said Lincolne, unabashed. 'We were the wronged party. But now it will look as though we took justice into our own hands, and I can assure you we did not. If we are not careful, the Dominicans will march on us again, and more people might die.' He looked alarmed as a sudden thought crossed his mind. 'And they may even damage the friary!'

'Then we shall have to ensure that both Orders behave themselves,' said Michael. 'You are not the only one who does not want more bloodshed.'

'The Dominicans will not be so amenable,' said Lincolne bitterly. 'They will deny murdering Faricius and demand another death to pay for Kyrkeby. They may even secure the help of the Austin canons and the Benedictines, who seem to be on friendly terms with them at the moment.'

'But then we will call upon the Franciscans and the Gilbertines, who are not,' said Horneby defiantly. 'We can raise an army that will match the one any Dominicans can muster.'

Bartholomew glanced up in alarm as Horneby's friends began to voice their agreement in voices that were a combination of fearful and defensive. Michael watched the proceedings with his arms folded and an expression of distaste on his face. Timothy abandoned his attempts to help Bartholomew extract Kyrkeby, and stood, brushing the dirt from his hands.

'Have any of you heard of the Ten Commandments?' he asked, his quiet question cutting across the babble that was centred around Horneby.

Lincolne regarded him uncertainly. 'What have they to do with any of this?'

'Just the fact that one of them forbids killing,' said Timothy. 'You are men of God, and yet here you are discussing how to raise armies to attack your rival Orders. You should be ashamed of yourselves. You are supposed to be setting a good example to the townsfolk, not demonstrating how to form armies and instigate street fights.'

'The Dominicans started it,' began Horneby hotly.

'You do not know that for certain,' said Michael. 'And we will have no more of this talk of fighting. Is that clear?'

He glowered at each and every one of them until he was satisfied that they had acquiesced to his demand. Then he took a deep breath and resumed his questioning.

'Now, we were discussing Kyrkeby's death. I had just asked when the tunnel was last used. Horneby informed me with great conviction that no one has used the tunnel since Saturday. However, before that he admitted to using it with Lynne – on Monday – to see whether he could find Faricius's essay. So, I will have the truth, if you please. When did anyone last use the tunnel?'

Horneby flushed a deep red, and had the grace to appear sheepish. 'Lynne and I did use it on Monday night,' he said in a low whisper. 'But no one has used it since. I am sure of it.'

'Very well,' said Michael. 'The next question that springs to mind is why are you so sure?'

'Two very good reasons,' said Horneby. 'First, none of us wanted to be caught by the proctors, who we knew were keeping an eye on it. And second, none of us have had any desire to be out on streets teeming with hostile Dominicans.'

'How do you know that applies to everyone here?' pressed Michael. 'Can you account for the movements of thirty students every single moment of the last few days?'

No one could answer him, although Lincolne blustered that his students should be given the benefit of the doubt, conveniently forgetting that they had lied to him as well as to Michael.

'Damn!' muttered Bartholomew, as the habit he was tugging on ripped in his hands. 'This is impossible. We need a spade.'

'A spade?' asked Lincolne, horrified. 'Are you suggesting that we excavate poor Humphrey de Lecton's grave?'

'Do you have any other suggestions?' asked Bartholomew. 'Kyrkeby's body is wedged very firmly inside it. I cannot work

215

out whether someone rammed him down there with such force that he is stuck, or whether the tunnel has suffered some sort of collapse.'

'I do not see why it should have collapsed if it has been here since 1290,' said Michael. 'I think it would be a peculiar coincidence if it stood whole and safe for so long, and only fell the moment a Dominican set foot in it.'

'It is Humphrey de Lecton protecting us,' said Horneby suddenly, his voice low and awed. 'He saw that we were about to be invaded by a Dominican, and he caused the tunnel roof to collapse in order to save us!'

The Carmelites crossed themselves as Horneby made his pronouncement, and one or two of them dropped to their knees in a gesture of reverence. It was almost dark, and the curfew bells were beginning to toll, lending the graveyard an eerie atmosphere. Among the student-friars, a growing murmur that featured the word 'miracle' could be heard.

'Oh, Lord, Matt!' breathed Michael wearily. 'This situation is going from bad to worse. As soon as I prevent them from following one wild belief, they simply come up with another. I always knew friars were not of the same intellectual calibre as monks, but this is ridiculous!'

'We need to nip this one in the bud fairly quickly,' said Timothy urgently. 'The Dominicans will not sit by quietly while the Carmelites claim one of them was killed by divine intervention.'

'Let us not jump to rash conclusions,' said Michael loudly, silencing the reverent whispers that filled the dark graveyard. 'As my colleague said, the body is stuck. There is nothing mysterious about a body stuck in a hole.'

'Humphrey de Lecton saw this wicked man about to invade our sacred grounds and he struck him dead,' proclaimed Horneby, the light of religious fervour already burning in his eyes.

'No,' said Bartholomew firmly. 'That is not what happened. You can see for yourself that Kyrkeby's feet are pointing this way. That means that he was *leaving* here, not coming to attack.'

'He may have come feet first,' said Horneby stubbornly.

'The tunnel curves upwards,' said Bartholomew. 'No one goes up a tunnel feet first. It would be virtually impossible, not to mention uncomfortable. Where is that spade?'

One of the students handed him one of the heaviest and bluntest tools Bartholomew had ever seen. It possessed a wooden handle so worn that it was as smooth as new metal, and the rivets that held the iron blade were loose and wobbled disconcertingly when he leaned on it. He scratched away some of the muddy earth, then took hold of the cold, white foot to pull again.

'Have there been collapses of the tunnel before?' asked Michael of Horneby, watching Bartholomew strain and pant with the effort.

Horneby shook his head. 'Not that I know of. It is made of clay, and clay never collapses.'

'Do not speak nonsense,' snapped Michael irritably. 'Clay subsides just as readily as any other soil.' He saw Bartholomew lose his grip on the foot again, and the body slid back into its premature tomb. 'Oh, for heaven's sake! Let me do it.'

He elbowed Bartholomew aside, and began hauling and tugging on the foot for all he was worth. His sizeable girth gave the impression that he was flabby and weak, but Michael was actually a very strong man. Everyone winced when a loud crack indicated a broken bone, and Bartholomew stopped him before his impatience resulted in the removal of Kyrkeby's foot. He did not want claims of mutilation to accompany the accusations of murder that were sure to follow. He lay on his stomach and applied the spade with a little more vigour, digging while Timothy held the damaged leg. And then Bartholomew felt something give.

'He is coming out,' he gasped, digging harder. 'Pull!'

In a shower of pebbles and liquid mud, the Dominican Precentor shot from the earth, landing on Timothy, who was not quick enough to move out of the way. Revolted, the Junior Proctor scrambled away, leaving Kyrkeby lying in a dishevelled heap on the ground. Bartholomew knelt next to the corpse, wiping sweat from his eyes with the sleeve of his tabard, while Timothy hastily retreated behind Humphrey de Lecton's tomb, where Bartholomew was certain he was being sick.

The body was filthy, and the physician could barely make out the features of the face, even when one of the students obligingly held a lamp closer. Kyrkeby's head was loose, and rolled at an unnatural angle, while a brownish-red mess on the back of his skull indicated he had received a crushing blow there at some point.

'Well?' asked Michael, standing with his hands on his hips. 'You said we would know more when you had a whole body to inspect. You have a whole body, so what can you tell me?'

'Not here, Brother,' said Bartholomew quietly. 'I recommend we take Kyrkeby to St Michael's Church, where I can examine him properly. Then we can have him cleaned before returning him to the Dominicans.'

'Why?' demanded Horneby aggressively. 'Let them clean their own dead. They did not treat Faricius so kindly.'

'Because if you hand Kyrkeby back to his colleagues looking like this, you will have angry Dominicans massing outside your gates demanding vengeance,' said Bartholomew. 'We will break the news to them when we can show them a corpse that does not look as though it has been treated with disrespect.'

'Very sensible,' said Lincolne approvingly. 'I do not want a horde of nominalists yelling at me all night when I am trying to sleep.'

'Perhaps a prayer for this poor man's soul might not go amiss,' said Michael coldly. 'Whatever you might think of Dominicans, you might at least do that.'

'Very well,' said Lincolne with a sigh. He gestured to his students to kneel in a circle, and drew himself up to his full height to begin a mass that sounded impressive, even if it was probably not sincere. His flask of holy water emerged, and was splashed around with its customary vigour, splattering the students and the ground as well as Kyrkeby.

'Fetch Cynric,' said Michael in a low voice to Bartholomew. 'Ask him to summon my beadles to carry Kyrkeby to the church. I will remain here with the body, and ensure they do not tamper with the evidence.'

'Will you be all right alone?' asked Bartholomew, reluctant to leave the monk in a graveyard where the killer might be kneeling in the praying circle around his victim.

'Of course I will. Timothy will be with me, and anyway, even the most desperate of killers is unlikely to attack me in full view of the rest of his friary.'

'Do you think any of them will stop him?' asked Bartholomew nervously. 'They might decide it is better for you to die, rather than the killer be exposed.'

'They would find it difficult to explain my corpse and Timothy's, as well as Kyrkeby's, when you return with the beadles,' said Michael, smiling wanly. 'Go, Matt. Now that Cynric lives with his wife and not in Michaelhouse, he is not far away. You can be back within moments.'

Bartholomew glanced behind him as he left, and saw the lamplight gleaming around the edges of Lincolne's funnel of hair, like a halo. The Prior's prayers carried on the still air as the physician hurried out of the convent and into Milne Street, where his book-bearer occupied a pleasant room in Oswald Stanmore's business premises.

Cynric answered the urgent knocking almost immediately, and Bartholomew was surprised to see the small Welshman cloaked and fully armed, as though he had anticipated being summoned on University business.

'Have you been out?' asked Bartholomew, as Cynric closed the door behind him so that their voices would not disturb his wife.

Cynric shook his head. 'Not yet. Rachel and I have been going to the Holy Week vigils at St Mary's Church. There is no point undressing when you have to put it all back on again in a few hours, so we sleep in our clothes. Anyway, it is warmer. But what is the problem? It would not be another murder, would it?'

'How do you know that?' asked Bartholomew warily.

Cynric grinned, his teeth gleaming white in the dim light from the candle he held. 'What other business is there that brings you to me after dusk?'

'I occasionally need you to go with me to see a patient,' said Bartholomew.

'But not often,' said Cynric. 'And anyway, you tend to use your students for that. No, boy. When I hear your soft tap on the door after the curfew bell has sounded, I know it only means one thing: the University has itself another killing.'

'Well, that was an unpleasant day,' said Michael, flopping into a comfortable chair in Michaelhouse's kitchen much later that evening. He closed his eyes and willed himself to relax, aided by the large goblet of mulled ale that was pressed into his ready hand by Agatha the laundress.

It was very late, and most scholars were in bed, huddled under their blankets in an attempt to keep warm, even if they were not sleeping. It had been a long winter, and Michaelhouse had already spent the money allocated to firewood for the year. Langelee, juggling the College's finances with a skill that surprised everyone who knew him, had managed to provide funds for fuel to warm the hall during breakfast and dinner, but the remainder of the day was spent in chilly misery. At nine o'clock that evening, the hall was abandoned, and lay dark, icy and silent.

The kitchen was a different matter. It was not possible to cook without a fire, and so it was always the warmest place in the College. Also, Agatha the laundress, who unofficially supervised the domestic side of Michaelhouse, was not the kind of woman to freeze while there was kindling in the woods and all kinds of 'kinsfolk' to acquire it for her. There was a cosy fire blazing, even at that late hour, with a cauldron of spiced ale bubbling over it and fresh oatcakes heating on a griddle to one side.

Agatha was a formidable figure, whose personal opinions rivalled those of Father William for bigotry and ignorance. She had been laundress at Michaelhouse for years – how many years no one could remember – although she did not look any different to Bartholomew than she had done when he had arrived to take up his appointment as master of medicine some ten years before. She was a big woman, although Bartholomew would not have called her fat, and had a large, open face with a bristly chin that was the envy of some of Bartholomew's younger, beardless undergraduates.

'Terrible business about Walcote,' said Agatha, passing Michael the platter of oatcakes before settling herself in her large wicker throne near the fire. 'I was sorry to hear about him. He seemed a nice man.'

'He was,' agreed Michael. 'You have not heard any rumours about his death, have you? My beadles said you were in the King's Head the night he died, and that is often a good place to pick up snippets of information about such matters.'

'It was certainly discussed,' replied Agatha. 'Sergeant Orwelle from the Castle came into the King's Head for a drink to steady his nerves after he found poor Walcote hanging by the neck like some felon on a gibbet.'

'What did he say?' asked Michael, hastily suppressing the unpleasant image she had created in his mind. 'I spoke to Orwelle myself, but people often say more to their drinking companions than they do to the forces of law and order.'

'Only that Walcote was hanging from the drainage pipe outside the Dominican Friary,' said Agatha. 'And that someone had stolen his purse.'

'His purse?' asked Michael, startled. 'I did not know about that, and no one mentioned it at Barnwell Priory. How did Orwelle come to notice such a thing?'

'People do notice things like missing purses,' said Agatha,

surprised by the question. 'These are hard times, Brother, and no one is paid what he deserves. The dead have no use for earthly wealth, and so it is only fitting that whoever finds a corpse and raises the alarm should have what is left.'

'What are you saying?' asked Bartholomew, astonished by the assertion. 'That Tulyet's soldiers regularly engage in corpse-robbing?'

'You cannot rob a corpse,' stated Agatha authoritatively. 'A corpse cannot own anything, and so it stands to reason that you cannot steal from it.'

'Well argued,' said Michael. 'Although I am not sure I concur. A corpse might not own anything, but his next of kin are entitled to what he leaves. But never mind the ethics of all this. Tell me more about the purse.'

'Sergeant Orwelle noticed the purse was gone, because he was going to put it in a safe place for Walcote's next of kin,' said Agatha, unashamedly changing her story to protect Orwelle's reputation. 'We all asked him who might have killed poor Walcote, but he did not know. We all believe it was a scholar, though.'

'Really?' asked Michael, raising his eyebrows laconically. 'And why would that be, pray?'

'The proctors keep the scholars in order,' said Agatha. 'We townsfolk *like* proctors, but we do not always like the rest of you. You are always engaging in stupid squabbles. I heard in the King's Head that the latest argument is about whether things that do not have names are real. It is all a lot of nonsense, if you ask me.'

'Put like that, it sounds like a lot of nonsense to me, too,' said Michael, smiling at Agatha's terse summary of the nominalism–realism debate. 'Still, you show a better understanding of the issues at stake than Father William does.'

'Dear William,' said Agatha fondly. '*He* does not indulge in all this subtle plotting and cunning quarrelling.'

'I should say,' agreed Michael wholeheartedly. 'No one could ever accuse William of being subtle or cunning.'

'It is Thursday tomorrow,' said Agatha, easing her bulk

from her chair. 'Only three days left of Lent. I had better go to bed, because I have Easter supplies to buy, baking to supervise, and doubtless you will all want your albs washed for the celebrations; Matthew's will almost certainly need mending.'

'Why?' asked Bartholomew, puzzled. 'It is not torn.'

'Everything you give me to launder is torn,' Agatha admonished him. 'Just look at you now. The hem on your tabard is down, your shirt cuffs are frayed, and you have ripped the knee out of your hose.'

'That was from grovelling in the mud trying to pull Dominicans out of other men's graves,' muttered Bartholomew, noticing for the first time that thick, silty dirt still clung to him.

'Brother Michael was also pulling dead men from the ground, but he is not in such a state. You need to improve yourself,' instructed Agatha. 'I am a laundress, not a muck-collector, and I do not want to be up to my elbows in filth every time you give me a bundle of clothes to clean.'

Having said her piece and expecting no argument, Agatha banked the fire and made her way to her quarters above the service rooms behind the kitchens. As the only female member of the College, she had more space and a better room than Master Langelee. She was proud of the sway she held in the College, and expected to be treated with deference.

When she had gone, Bartholomew took her place, settling himself down among the cushions that still held her warmth and that smelled of wood-smoke and cooked food. In pride of place was one that was blue with a gold fringe. It had been used to smother Langelee's predecessor while the man had counted his money. Although Agatha swore it had been carefully cleaned, Bartholomew remained convinced that he could still detect a dark patch where the victim's saliva had stained it. Picking it up between thumb and forefinger, he flung it to the other side of the room, where it was gratefully received by the College cat.

'Pity about Kyrkeby,' said Michael, taking another oatcake for himself and throwing one to Bartholomew, so hard that the physician found himself with a lap full of crumbs. 'I confess I had not expected to find him dead when he was reported missing.'

'And I had not anticipated finding his body stuffed inside an old tomb,' said Bartholomew. 'As you saw, he was not easy to extricate.'

'He was not,' agreed Michael. 'How did he come to be thrust in it so tightly? I know it was growing dark, and that the Carmelites were fussing and flapping around us like bees at a honey pot, but what could you determine?'

'Not much,' said Bartholomew. 'The body was in such a mess that it was difficult to tell what had happened to it.'

'We will have a hard job cleaning it up,' said Michael. 'Will you do it? I will not.'

'I did not imagine you would,' said Bartholomew, sipping more of his ale, and relishing the warmth as it reached his stomach. 'But perhaps Agatha will help. She had a lot of experience laying out bodies during the plague.'

'You were right to suggest that we clean Kyrkeby before handing him to the Dominicans,' said Michael thoughtfully. 'I do not think I have ever seen a body in such a state. I know you said it was too dark to conduct a proper investigation until morning, but what are your first impressions?'

Bartholomew shrugged. 'There was enough light for me to see that there was a serious wound to the head that would have killed him had he been alive when it was inflicted. It was also light enough for me to tell that his neck had been broken.'

'So?' asked Michael. 'Are you saying that someone hit him on the head so hard that it broke his neck?'

'Lord, no!' said Bartholomew with a shudder. 'At least, I sincerely hope not. That kind of strength would mean that we have some kind of monster on the loose.'

'What then?' asked Michael impatiently. 'That someone

broke his neck and he damaged his head when he fell to the ground?'

'I cannot tell. And then, of course, there was his weak heart. I have been physicking him over several months for that complaint – and he was quite ill with it on Monday afternoon.'

'But you must be able to tell how he died,' pressed Michael, determined to have an answer. 'And what about the tunnel? Did it collapse naturally? Or did someone tamper with it?'

'I have no idea, although I cannot see that a body would be so firmly stuck just from someone pushing it inside.'

'The body was swollen,' suggested Michael. 'Maybe it just got bigger, as corpses are wont to do after death – gasses, you once told me.'

'It is possible, I suppose,' said Bartholomew. 'He has been missing for two days – since Monday evening – although the weather is cold, which tends to slow that sort of thing down. But if someone did use the tunnel as a hiding place, he did not do a very good job by leaving a foot sticking out. And if the tunnel were used fairly frequently, which was the impression I gained from Horneby and his friends, then it was not a very permanent hiding place, either.'

'Perhaps it was not intended to be permanent. Perhaps it was intended to hide the body long enough until somewhere better could be found.' Michael groaned suddenly. 'What a mess, Matt! We do not know whether Kyrkeby was hit over the head, his neck broken, rammed down a hole that collapsed on him, or died naturally. And we do not even know *when* it happened.'

Bartholomew nodded. 'But remember the position of the body? Kyrkeby appeared to be *leaving* the Carmelite Friary, not entering it.'

'Then perhaps he was meeting someone there. But he was taking a risk if he were. It would have been safer to arrange a meeting outside both friaries, on neutral ground – for him *and* for the Carmelite with whom he had business.'

'But that assumes that the person Kyrkeby was meeting knew Kyrkeby wanted to see him,' said Bartholomew. 'Perhaps he did not.'

Michael sighed and scrubbed hard at his temples with two forefingers that were flecked with oatcake crumbs. 'I do not understand any of this, Matt.'

'Nor me,' admitted Bartholomew. 'But I have the feeling that all the evidence we have gained so far has been very superficial and incidental, and that there is a lot more that we do not know.'

Michael agreed. 'But tomorrow we will find out. We will tell the Dominicans what has become of their Precentor first thing in the morning, and then I will ask whether any of them knows anything about a missing essay on nominalism.'

The following morning, just as the first glimmerings of dawn lightened the sky, Bartholomew dragged himself from a deep sleep, and washed and shaved in the dim light, muttering under his breath when he could not find a clean shirt. Michael tapped on the door and they walked into the courtyard together, ready to process to the church for the morning mass. The other scholars had barely started to assemble when Brother Timothy arrived, breathless and white-faced. Michael regarded his Junior Proctor uneasily, anticipating more bad news, but it was not Michael that Timothy wanted: he had been sent to fetch Bartholomew, because old Brother Adam was having trouble catching his breath. The physician grabbed his bag and set off at a run with Michael following at a rather more sedate pace.

It was raining steadily, and the High Street was little more than a river of thin, splashy mud. Those who were early risers looked cold and miserable as they trudged along, and seemed to be wearing clothes that had dulled to a shade of drab brown in the wet semi-darkness. Even the animals that were being herded to the Market Square were dirty and bedraggled. Roofs released thin trickles of filthy water into the streets below, and the plaster-fronted houses were grey with damp.

They reached Ely Hall, and Timothy shoved open the front door to precede them along the narrow corridor and up the stairs to the upper floor. What had once been a single large chamber had been divided into six small rooms to afford the Benedictines some privacy. Timothy had a chamber that overlooked a vile little yard at the back, while Janius and Adam had been allocated ones at the front with windows that boasted a view of the Market Square.

'Thank God you are here,' said Janius, crossing himself vigorously when he saw Bartholomew. 'We were beginning to fear that you would be too late. We have been praying hard, but God has not performed a miracle yet.'

Bartholomew pushed past him to where Brother Adam lay wheezing and gasping on his bed. The old man's face was grey, and his eyes indicated that he was very frightened. The room was stifling hot from the fire that blazed in the hearth, so the physician ordered the window opened. Then he helped Adam to sit and asked Timothy for a bowl of boiling water. While he waited, he gave Adam a small dose of poppy syrup to calm him, then a larger dose of lungwort in wine to ease the congestion. When the hot water arrived, he scattered myrrh into it and talked calmly while the old man inhaled the vapours with a cloth over his head.

After a while, Adam's breathlessness eased and colour began to creep back into his cheeks. The monks who had clustered around the door heaved a sigh of relief, and Janius began to recite a prayer of thanksgiving in a loud, braying voice. He glared at his brethren until they joined in.

'Thank you,' said Adam softly, leaning back against his cushions and smiling weakly at Bartholomew. 'This happens from time to time, especially when I go out.'

'Why did you go out?' asked Bartholomew. 'I recommended that you remain indoors, at least until the weather improves.'

'At dawn today I felt like a stroll in the Market Square,'

replied Adam. 'And in December I attended a meeting at St Radegund's Convent. Other than that, I have obeyed your instructions to the letter.'

'*You* were at the gatherings called by Walcote?' asked Michael in astonishment, crouching next to the bed so that he could hear Adam above the strident prayers emanating from the corridor.

Adam nodded. 'It was unpleasant walking there so late at night, and I was so ill afterwards that I told Walcote I would not attend any more. It was not a very interesting meeting, anyway.'

'Why did *you* go?' asked Michael. 'Why not one of the others?'

'Walcote invited me specifically, because I am Ely Hall's senior Benedictine,' said Adam. 'I was going to suggest that Janius or Timothy went in my place, but the meeting was a waste of time, as it happened. We did nothing but talk about how to repair the Great Bridge and how to suppress the ideas of the realists. I do not hold with realism personally, but I do not like the notion of censoring theories and thoughts. It is a dangerous path to tread.'

'Who else was there?' demanded Michael.

'Will Walcote and Prior Ralph represented the Austin canons, while Prior Morden put in an appearance for the Dominicans.'

'The Austins and the Dominicans,' said Michael in an undertone to Bartholomew. 'That is new information. Matilde and Eve Wasteneys told us about the Carmelites, Franciscans and Gilbertines. If Adam is right, then virtually every Order in Cambridge was represented at Walcote's nasty little covens.'

Bartholomew addressed Adam. 'What about the Franciscans, Carmelites and Gilbertines? Did you see any of those at these meetings?'

Adam shook his head. 'When Walcote told me that he was organising meetings for the leaders of the religious Orders, I told him I would be surprised if he could persuade the Dominicans to sit under one roof with Carmelites and Franciscans. I was right: he could not.'

'I see,' said Bartholomew in sudden understanding. 'Walcote probably divided his gatherings between those who follow nominalism and those who follow realism. That is why Matilde – whose information came from the Carmelite Lincolne – only knew about him, the Franciscans and the Gilbertines. And that is why only Benedictines, Dominicans and Austins were at the gathering attended by Adam.'

'It also explains why Eve Wasteneys said she was not sure whether the men she saw attended the same meetings,' said Timothy thoughtfully. 'She knew different people came on different occasions.'

Michael sighed heavily. 'But this still does not explain why no one told *me* about these wretched events. I am the Senior Proctor. It was not right for Walcote to have organised them without my knowledge.'

'It was not,' said Janius, who had finished his prayers and was apparently honing his talent for eavesdropping. 'But now Timothy is your Junior Proctor, such things will not happen again.'

'Did *you* know about all this?' Michael asked him.

Janius nodded slowly. 'Adam confided in me. He had been sworn to secrecy and so obviously I could not mention it to anyone else. However, I confess I had forgotten about it until Adam reminded me just now. It happened months ago – before Yuletide.'

'I remember it clearly, because it was the walk in the cold and the rain that caused my illness,' said Adam. 'I was stupid to have gone in the first place, and Janius recommended that I should attend no more of them.'

'And Walcote invited no one in your place?' asked Michael.

There were shaken heads all around. 'If he had, I would have suggested that we did not go,' said Janius. 'Who would want an assignation in a place like that, anyway?'

'The fact that the Benedictines did not attend after the

first time explains something else, too,' said Bartholomew thoughtfully. 'Matilde mentioned that the numbers of people at the meetings had been dwindling. Now we learn that Adam declined to go because he considered them a waste of time. I was worried that there might be a more sinister reason for the dropping attendance.'

'But someone still should have told me,' persisted Michael.

'There was very little to tell,' said Adam apologetically. 'As I said, we chatted about whether to donate money to repair the Great Bridge and the nominalism–realism debate.'

'But why did Walcote hold his gatherings in the middle of the night if you discussed such mundane matters?' asked Bartholomew.

'I suppose subsequent ones might have been more interesting,' admitted Adam. 'As I told you, I only went to one.'

'We will have that information from Prior Morden of the Dominicans,' determined Michael. 'We shall ask him about it when we deliver his dead colleague. Meanwhile, if you receive another invitation to one of these affairs, please tell me.'

'We can do better than that,' said Timothy with a grin. 'Janius or I will go in Adam's place and report everything that is said.'

Michael smiled his appreciation, then followed Bartholomew down the stairs and out into the Market Square, leaving Adam to rest. Timothy walked with them, then made his way to St Mary's Church, where the beadles were assembling to receive their daily orders. Michael watched him go.

'I made a wise decision when I chose a Benedictine as Junior Proctor. Timothy has held office for only two days, and yet I can trust him to direct my beadles already. I would have far less time to investigate these murders, if it were not for him.'

'There is Heytesbury,' said Bartholomew, pointing to a

small, neat figure who stood near one of the farmers' stalls in the Market Square.

'He is an early riser,' said Michael.

'It looks to me as though he has not yet gone to bed,' said Bartholomew, smiling at Heytesbury's display of whiskers and dishevelled appearance. 'He and Richard have probably been enjoying Cambridge's taverns. Look, there is Richard's horse.'

'Heytesbury is not the kind of man to indulge in all-night debauchery,' said Michael. 'I do not believe he has been carousing with your errant nephew.'

Heytesbury was watching with amusement the antics of the Black Bishop of Bedminster, which had managed to slip its tether and was browsing a stack of wizened apples. The outraged farmer was powerless to stop it: slaps on its gleaming rump resulted in flailing back hoofs that threatened to kill, while no one dared to grab the reins because they were too near its battery of strong yellow teeth. Black Bishop's eyes glistened evilly in its head, and its ears twitched back and forth as it listened for anyone rash enough to approach it while it gorged itself.

'I do not know what possessed Richard to buy that thing,' said Heytesbury, as Bartholomew and Michael strolled over to join him. Bartholomew detected the unmistakable odour of wine on his breath, and knew that Michael was wrong to think that Heytesbury was no carouser. 'He is quite unable to control it, and it is only a matter of time before it does someone a serious injury.'

'How much longer do you plan to stay in Cambridge?' asked Michael conversationally. 'Because if you intend to leave soon, I have the documents that will formalise our arrangements already drafted in my room at Michaelhouse. You can sign them any time you are ready.'

'I will bear that in mind,' said Heytesbury. He nodded to where Black Bishop still grazed the furious farmer's fruit. 'Is that the Fellow of Michaelhouse whom everyone claims is mad?'

Bartholomew started forward in alarm when he saw Clippesby – who had evidently managed to slip away from the Michaelhouse mass – stride up to the horse and take a firm hold of the reins. Black Bishop started to rear, angry eyes rolling white in its dark head. But Clippesby was talking in a low, intense voice, and the horse apparently had second thoughts. Its front hoofs thumped down on the ground, and its ears flicked, as if it were listening. When Clippesby's voice dropped to a whisper, Black Bishop's head craned forward, as if straining to catch everything that was said.

'I see what people mean about him,' said Heytesbury, regarding the scene in amusement. 'A Fellow who talks to animals is peculiar indeed.'

'You have seen nothing yet,' muttered Michael. 'In a few moments Clippesby will probably tell everyone in the Market Square what the Black Bishop of Bedminster said to him.'

Heytesbury laughed. 'How can I sign your document and leave Cambridge, Brother? There is simply too much here to entertain me.'

'Damn!' said Michael, as Heytesbury moved away from them and edged closer to Clippesby and the horse, aiming to gain a better view. 'I wish he would just make his mark on our agreement and go home. The future of our University lies in securing wealthy benefactors, and the longer he dallies, the less time I will have to coax Oxford's patrons over to Cambridge. I might have secured a couple this summer, but now I will not have sufficient time.'

'Why do we need to steal Oxford's patrons?' asked Bartholomew. 'Why can we not find some of our own?'

Michael gave him an incredulous glance. 'It is not so much that we need the patrons ourselves; it is more a case that we do not want *Oxford* to have them. They are already bigger than us, and I do not want to be in a position where they are capable of crushing us.'

'That will not happen. It was possible after the plague, when there was a shortage of scholars, but things seemed to have settled down since then. Oxford poses no danger to us now.'

'Do not be so sure. It is not impossible that the plague will return, and then there will be even fewer men willing to study. I do not want to see this University cease to exist for the want of a little forethought. Look what happened to the fledgling universities at Stamford and Northampton.'

'Scholars from Oxford and Cambridge joined forces and petitioned for them to be suppressed,' said Bartholomew. 'But it is a very different matter for two large universities to suppress a smaller third, than for one to suppress another.'

'You are wrong to be complacent, Matt.' Michael's mouth narrowed in a determined line. 'But if and when Oxford makes a move against us, I shall be ready.'

CHAPTER 7

I T WAS NO EASY TASK TO WASH KYRKEBY'S BODY CLEAN OF mud so that a glance at it would not send the Dominicans racing to the Carmelite Friary to demand vengeance. While his colleagues' voices echoed around the chancel of St Michael's as they completed the first mass of the day, Bartholomew went to the south aisle where Kyrkeby's body lay, and began his investigation as the early light filtered through the east window.

Kyrkeby looked even worse in daylight. His face was a mottled grey-white, partly from the filth that plastered it, and partly because his temporary tomb had been water-logged, and he had probably spent a good part of the previous two days buried in mud. Bartholomew had hoped to detect a slight blueness around the mouth and nose, which might indicate that the cause of death had been Kyrkeby's weak heart, but it was impossible to tell. Kyrkeby's eyes were slightly open in a head that lolled at a sickening angle, and there was also the wound to the back of the head. When the physician felt it, he could hear and see the broken skull bones grating under his fingers.

He stared down at the corpse. He knew that when a person died, the blood stopped moving in the veins. Thus, wounds inflicted after death tended not to bleed or to bleed very little. Bruises, however, were a different matter. These were injuries where a blow caused small blood vessels to rupture under the skin, rather than through it, and such ruptures did and could occur after death. Unlike with cuts, there-fore, Bartholomew knew of no way to tell when a bruise was inflicted. So he was unable to determine whether the damage to Kyrkeby was done while he had still been alive.

He inspected the man's hands, to see whether ripped or cracked nails indicated some kind of struggle with his attacker, as Walcote's had done. Kyrkeby's fingers were thick with dirt, but when Bartholomew wiped it off he saw nails that were gnawed to the quick and that would not have broken anyway. Next he checked for the kind of injuries he associated with someone trying to defend himself – wounds to the arms where the victim had tried to fend off an attacker, or where he had turned away to protect his head. There was nothing definitive, and the marks on Kyrkeby's arms did not tell him whether the Dominican had struggled against an attacker or not.

Dispirited, Bartholomew examined the rest of the body, but found nothing to give him any further clues as to what had happened. The soles of Kyrkeby's shoes were muddy, but with muck that seemed more like the dirt of the High Street than the clinging clay of the Carmelites' hole in the ground. Bartholomew rubbed his chin, wondering whether this implied that Kyrkeby had not entered the tomb of his own accord.

And that was all. Beneath his habit, the Dominican Precentor wore homespun hose of dark brown and a woollen vest, both of which were thick and warm and of a quality that indicated the friar had the means to purchase better clothes than the ones that were provided free of charge by his Order. Recalling the purses that had been stolen from Walcote and Faricius, Bartholomew rifled through Kyrkeby's clothes to see if he could find the leather scrip most friars carried at their waists, anticipating that the Dominican's would be large and well filled if his clothes were anything to go by. However, if Kyrkeby had possessed such an item, it was not with his body now.

Bartholomew was just finishing his examination when Agatha arrived. The church was silent, and he realised that the scholars had finished their prayers and had returned to Michaelhouse. She nodded a brusque greeting, and began her work, grunting and swearing as she scrubbed the dark

235

mud from the dead man's skin, her large hips swaying vigorously and her skirts swinging about her ankles. While Bartholomew fetched pail after pail of water from the well in the Market Square, she gradually turned Kyrkeby into something that resembled a human being. She sluiced the dirt from his hair and brushed it back from his face, and rinsed the muck from his eyes and ears.

At eight o'clock the bells began to toll for terce, the great bass boom of St Mary's drowning out the tinny clatters from St John Zachary and All Saints in the Jewry. Carts rattled along the High Street, and the shouts of the owners of the stalls in the market began to ring out as trade got under way. Feet splashed through puddles as students ran to lectures and apprentices hurried about their masters' business.

'That is better,' remarked Michael, walking into the porch a little later, and leaning over to inspect their handiwork. 'But he still looks rough. Can you do no better?'

'No,' said Bartholomew shortly, wiping his hands and arms on a piece of rag and rolling down his sleeves. 'I have spent a large part of the morning on this. We should tell the Dominicans what has happened soon, or they will be accusing us of withholding information from them – no matter how honourable our intentions.'

'True,' admitted Michael. 'Although I have been busy, too. I went to the Carmelite Friary to poke around that tunnel to see if we missed anything last night . . .'

'And did we?' asked Bartholomew hopefully.

'No. Then I walked to St Radegund's to see if Matilde had uncovered anything useful . . .'

'How is she?' asked Bartholomew anxiously.

'She sat in the solar with her hands cupped around her ears, so she had nothing to report. Tysilia informed me, somewhat out of the blue, that eating too many oatcakes would turn me into a horse . . .'

'That would not have been because you were eating the nuns' food, would it, Brother?' asked Bartholomew innocently.

'And I spoke to Sergeant Orwelle again,' continued

Michael, ignoring him. 'I asked whether there was anything more he could tell me about when he found Walcote's body.'

'And was there?'

'Of course not,' said Agatha dismissively. 'I told you all there was to know. I have already informed you that *I* was in the King's Head when he burst in and announced what had happened.'

'It is as well to be sure,' said Michael. 'You may have forgotten something, or thought something was unimportant when it was vital.'

'And had I forgotten anything?' demanded Agatha, hands on hips and eyes narrowed.

'No,' admitted Michael. 'However, I did learn one new thing from Orwelle.'

'I suppose you mean the fact that he found Walcote's purse at dawn this morning?' asked Agatha carelessly. 'He discovered it near Barnwell Priory.'

Michael stared at her. 'You already know about this?'

'Orwelle has been obsessed by that missing purse,' said Agatha smugly, gratified that her intelligence seemed to be better than Michael's. 'Walcote was a fairly wealthy man, you see, and Orwelle could not push the thought of a full purse out of his mind. He is always on the lookout for dropped pennies in the mud, and this morning he found Walcote's scrip.' She pointed to a sorry-looking item that Michael extracted from his own scrip and held distastefully between thumb and forefinger. 'That is it.'

'How do you know it is Walcote's?' asked Bartholomew, inspecting it carefully. 'It could be anyone's.'

'Because Walcote is the only man to have lost a purse recently,' said Agatha impatiently.

'Faricius lost one,' Bartholomew pointed out. 'How can you be sure this is not his?'

Agatha gave a heavy sigh. 'Because it is obvious that Walcote's killers stole it from his body, and then threw it away as they fled from the town, just as they passed Barnwell Priory.'

'That seems a strange coincidence,' mused Bartholomew. 'Walcote lived at Barnwell, and now Orwelle finds his purse nearby. Perhaps Walcote dropped it, and it was not stolen at all.'

'I think Agatha is right: the killer took the purse, then made off to the wasteland around Barnwell before removing its contents,' said Michael. 'Orwelle found it empty.'

'It is Walcote's purse,' declared Agatha firmly, seeing that Bartholomew remained uncertain. 'I have a feeling about it, and my feelings are never wrong.'

Bartholomew saw there was no point in arguing with her. She was convinced she was right, and that was that. He looked down at the sodden leather bag. It was filthy, consistent with lying in the mud and rain since Monday night, and was empty. Other than that, it was unremarkable. It was one of the ones sold by the dozen in the Market Square, and comprised a brown pouch with holes punched into the top, through which a string was threaded that sealed it when drawn tight. Bartholomew owned one just like it. He doubted whether anyone would be able to identify it as definitely Walcote's or Faricius's – or even Kyrkeby's.

'If Walcote was a man of means, why would he own a cheap purse like this?' he asked thoughtfully.

'He did, though,' said Michael tiredly. 'We proctors fine undergraduates in pennies, and a sturdy leather scrip like this is perfect for holding them. More expensive ones tend not to be strong enough to hold large quantities of base coins of the realm.'

'And what about Faricius?' asked Bartholomew. 'Did he own one of these, too?'

'We can ask,' said Michael.

'And Orwelle found this one empty?' pressed Bartholomew. 'He did not take its contents before passing it to you?'

'I confess that crossed my mind,' admitted Michael. 'But Orwelle was bitterly disappointed that there was nothing in it. I do not think he would have been able to lie quite so convincingly, had he taken its contents for himself.' He sighed. 'So, the motive for Walcote's murder looks to have been theft. It seems to fit the facts. And that means we are dealing with a random act of violence after all, not some clever conspiracy.'

'I am not so sure,' said Bartholomew. 'Theft is inconsistent with the manner of his death: why hang someone when it is easier, quicker and much safer to stab him? Walcote's death has the feel of an execution to me, not a simple robbery.'

Michael gestured to Kyrkeby's body. 'What can you tell us about him? You wanted more light so that you could see what you were doing, so what can you tell me now?'

'I am sorry, Brother,' said Bartholomew. 'I have learned nothing new. All the options I outlined last night – struck on the head, his neck snapped, crushed in the tunnel or his heart giving out – are still equally possible.'

'Not the latter, Matt,' said Michael. 'No one would need to hide a body that had died naturally. Oh, damn it all! Where did *he* come from?'

Bartholomew turned to see Richard Stanmore entering the church. His nephew's scented goose grease could be smelled the instant he pushed open the door, and Michael immediately sneezed. Behind Richard, and cruelly – although very accurately – mimicking his mincing walk, was Cynric, coming to see whether Bartholomew needed any help.

'God's blood, man!' Michael snuffled, removing a piece of linen from his scrip with which to dab at his nose. 'What have you done to yourself? You smell as though you have spent the night romping with whores.'

'And what would a monk know of such things?' asked Richard innocently. 'However, I can assure you that a man of my standing in society is hardly likely to "romp with whores", as you so delicately put it.'

Bartholomew was sceptical of this claim, recalling the presence of Richard's horse in the Market Square suspiciously early that morning.

Michael sneezed again, and looked Richard up and down disparagingly. Bartholomew could see why the monk was disapproving. Richard was wearing yet another set of exquisite clothes, this time in shades of red and gold. Around his waist was an ornate belt, from which dangled a dagger that was mostly handle and no blade. Bartholomew saw Cynric regarding it with amazement that turned to mirth. Despite his finery, however, Richard did not look well. There was a puffiness around his eyes, and his complexion was sallow and unhealthy, as if he were enjoying a lifestyle that was too hard on his body and required of him too many sleepless nights. With a flourish, Richard produced the bandage Bartholomew had lent him the morning after Walcote had died and wrapped it around the lower half of his face.

'That is better,' he declared in a muffled voice. 'The King's courtiers tie cloth around their noses to exclude foul smells from their nostrils. It stinks like a butcher's stall in here.'

'What do you want?' demanded Michael, irritated. 'Do not expect your uncle to waste time with you today. He is busy with University business.'

'Since when has that fat monk been your keeper?' asked Richard, addressing Bartholomew and deliberately turning his back on Michael. 'Does he decide when you see your family these days?'

'As it happens, he is right,' said Bartholomew shortly, not liking the way Richard and Michael bickered. Richard was arrogant and obnoxious, and Bartholomew understood exactly why Michael had taken a dislike to him. But when all was said and done, he was Bartholomew's nephew, and he felt Michael might have made some pretence at affability. 'I am busy today.'

'Very well,' said Richard, disappointed. 'I only wanted you to introduce me to Master Langelee. I suppose it can wait.'

'What do you want with Langelee?' demanded Michael immediately. 'He will have nothing to say to a young man who wears an ear-ring.'

'You should invest in one,' said Richard, treating the

monk to a knowing wink. 'They are very popular with the ladies.'

'Then maybe the ladies should wear them,' retorted Michael. 'Yours makes you look like a pirate, not a lawyer.'

'I thought they were the same thing,' muttered Cynric, regarding Richard, his ear-ring and his ornamental dagger with undisguised disdain.

Agatha stepped forward, and in one lightning-fast movement that caught Richard unawares, she seized the offending item between her thick fingers to inspect it minutely. Richard froze in alarm, while Bartholomew held his breath, half expecting her to rip the ear-ring from its lobe to underline her disapproval. But she merely released it and moved away, wrinkling her nose and pursing her lips to indicate that she did not like the scent of the goose grease that clogged the air around him.

'This particular fashion will not last long,' she announced, indicating the ear-ring with a jerk of her thumb. 'What sane person deliberately pierces himself with a piece of metal?'

'Everyone at court has one,' objected Richard, rubbing his ear ruefully. 'Those who do not are considered to be dowdy and not worth knowing.'

'It is comforting to know that our country is being governed by men with gold through their ears and buttons on their shirts,' said Michael coolly. 'No wonder we have been at war with France for so long: everyone spends his time thinking about ear-rings and clothes, while affairs of state are deemed unfashionable and unimportant.'

Disgusted, both by Richard and the courtiers he imagined were damaging his country, the monk began to stride towards the door. Richard hovered to talk to Bartholomew.

'Have you heard that Master Heytesbury is to give the University Lecture on Sunday in St Mary's Church?' he asked smugly. 'You have me to thank for that: I arranged it all.'

'You did what?' demanded Michael, storming back down the nave. 'It is not for the likes of you to organise who speaks in the University of Cambridge's public debates.'

'Because I am an Oxford man?' asked Richard insolently. 'I will tell Master Heytesbury you take that attitude. He will certainly rethink whether he wishes to do business with you, if you regard him and his colleagues in so poor a light.'

'You will mind your own affairs,' snapped Michael angrily. 'My arrangements with Heytesbury have nothing to do with you.'

'He asked me what I thought of you,' said Richard carelessly, relishing the fact that he had nettled the monk. 'He wanted to know whether you can be trusted.'

'My affairs have nothing to do with you,' repeated Michael in a venomous whisper.

'So, why are you prepared to give Oxford that property?' pressed Richard, unmoved by Michael's fury. 'As Heytesbury's lawyer, I have been over the deeds very carefully, but there is no trick. Since you are not a generous man, the only other explanation is that you are a fool.'

'That is for Heytesbury to decide,' said Michael, bringing his ire under control and turning away from the infuriating young man. 'Come on, Matt. We should go.'

'I do not think you are a fool,' Richard continued. 'I always remembered you as a cunning sort of fellow. Then I saw through your little game.'

Michael stopped walking and gazed at Richard, but his beady glare broke when he sneezed, suddenly and violently. Agatha coughed meaningfully, and flapped her hand back and forth in front of her face.

'Brother Michael is right,' she declared. 'You smell like a whore – although I do not know of any self-respecting women who would douse themselves in whatever stinking potion you have bathed yourself in.'

Richard looked her up and down with as much distaste as she had treated him. 'Better that than reeking of old onions and garlic,' he drawled.

Agatha advanced on him. 'Old onions and garlic—'

'Where is that sheet you had for Kyrkeby, Agatha?' asked Bartholomew quickly. 'The day is wearing on, and I am keen for the Dominicans to see the fine work you have done this morning. I imagine they will be very grateful to you.'

'It is in my basket,' said Agatha, easily diverted when told she could expect the praise of men like the Dominicans. 'I will fetch it.'

'Are you sure she is safe to be let loose in a small town like this?' asked Richard, watching her large figure sway importantly up the aisle to where she had left her belongings.

'She will rip you limb from limb if I ask her to,' said Michael nastily. 'So tell me what you meant when you said you had guessed my plan, or you shall see exactly how unsafe she can be.'

Richard glanced from Agatha to Michael and saw the cold fury in the monk's eyes. He decided it was not worth taking the risk to see whether Michael was bluffing.

'Heytesbury believes that you want to use the information he will give you to become the University's next Chancellor. He thinks you will use the names of the wealthy, but anonymous, Oxford patrons that he will divulge to you to make sure that you are elected.'

Michael did not reply.

'But I think there is another reason,' Richard went on. 'I think that you already know that one of the patrons is a man with large dairy farms, who is reputed to make the best cheese in the country. I think your motive lies entirely with your stomach!'

'I have never heard such nonsense in my life,' said Michael, shoving Richard out of the way as he started to walk towards the door. 'I can assure you that my stomach has nothing to do with my arrangements with Heytesbury.'

'It has!' crowed Richard triumphantly. 'You intend to dine on fine cheese, best butter and large brown eggs for the rest of your indulgent life.'

Bartholomew was thinking about something else Richard had said. 'What did you mean earlier, when you said Heytesbury was lecturing this Sunday?'

243

'Kyrkeby has not yet confirmed with the Chancellor that he still intends to speak,' said Richard. 'So, the Chancellor has been looking for a replacement.'

'If Kyrkeby does speak, it will cause some raised eyebrows,' muttered Agatha, walking towards them with a winding sheet clasped in one meaty hand. 'And it will not be his clean hair and scrubbed fingernails that people will notice.'

'Most scholars would be oblivious to the fact that they were receiving a lecture from a corpse,' Cynric replied in an undertone. 'I sometimes wonder whether half of them are dead anyway, but just do not know it.'

Agatha gave an inappropriate guffaw of laughter that echoed around the church and made everyone jump.

'The Chancellor was in a quandary,' Richard continued. 'University lectures are important events, and he had no distinguished speaker for Easter Sunday. I recommended Heytesbury.'

'You interfering little snake,' hissed Michael furiously. 'Heytesbury is England's leading nominalist. The mere presence of such a man in the University church will incite a riot.'

'Why?' asked Richard smugly. 'Is it because your scholars cannot trust their powers of reason and skills in rhetoric to win them the day?'

'It is because Cambridge is a tinderbox at the moment,' Michael almost shouted. 'It is on the verge of serious unrest, and something like this could tip the balance. Do you really want to see the streets of the town where you were a child run with blood?'

Richard blanched, but remained defiant. 'If they choose to use their fists rather than their wits, I cannot find it in my heart to mourn their fates.'

'I am sure you cannot,' said Michael coldly. 'But I care little for what is in your heart. I care about the innocent people this will affect.'

'I do not understand why you are in such a state about this,' said Richard defensively. 'Kyrkeby was going to speak on nominalism anyway, and the only difference is that your scholars will listen to a man whose logic is brilliant, instead of some bumbling old friar with bad teeth and no hair.'

'Kyrkeby did not have bad teeth,' said Bartholomew, startled. 'And he had plenty of hair.'

'Had?' asked Richard. 'What happened to it?'

Bartholomew gestured to the pale corpse, blotched and flaccid, that lay in the parish coffin. Agatha stepped past him and began to cover it with the sheet.

'It is Kyrkeby,' said Richard in horror, gazing down at the distorted features. 'And he is dead!'

'And you decided not to become a physician!' muttered Michael. 'With powers of observation like yours, the medical world should mourn such a dreadful loss.'

'He is a funny colour,' remarked Cynric, looking critically at Agatha's handiwork. 'What have you done to him?'

'That is what happens when you spend two days in a wet, muddy hole after you are dead,' said Bartholomew.

'I can do something about the colour of him,' said Agatha, treating Bartholomew to a conspiratorial wink. 'I can make him look good enough to eat.'

'What do you mean?' asked Bartholomew nervously, not certain what she intended to do, but very certain that she should not be permitted to proceed.

Agatha tapped the side of her nose and gave him a significant glance. 'Women know about these things. Just leave it to old Agatha.'

'Wait,' said Bartholomew, as her ponderous bulk began to move off down the aisle like a great ship leaving a harbour – stately and virtually unstoppable. 'Do not—'

'No wonder Kyrkeby did not contact the Chancellor,' said Richard, when Bartholomew's objections faltered away to silence. Agatha had decided she was going to act on whatever notion had sprung into her mind, and was underway.

'*When* did Chancellor Tynkell become concerned that Kyrkeby had not confirmed his intention to lecture?'

demanded Michael of Richard. 'He did not mention this to me.'

'He said he did not want to bother you with administration when you were busy with murders,' said Richard. 'But he was worried last night – Wednesday – when Prior Morden informed him that Kyrkeby had gone missing. I happened to be on hand to solve his dilemma.'

'What were you doing with Chancellor Tynkell?' demanded Michael. 'He is too busy to waste time on youths who believe that owning big black horses and an ear-ring make them respected members of the community.'

'Be that as it may, but I did him and your University a favour last night,' said Richard firmly. 'It would have been difficult to find a replacement, given that Kyrkeby's lecture is scheduled for three days' time.'

'It would not,' argued Michael. 'We have many skilled and distinguished speakers who are prepared to lecture at a moment's notice.'

'Name one,' challenged Richard.

'Your uncle,' replied Michael promptly. 'He is the University's most senior master of medicine. Will you claim he is one of these old friars with no hair and poor teeth?'

The young lawyer tossed the end of his capuchin over his shoulder in a deliberately casual gesture and gave a careless smile. 'I am sure he gives a fascinating account of lancing boils and examining urine. And he has fine hair and good teeth. But Heytesbury will talk about nominalism, not give some diatribe on pustules and amputation.'

Michael's smile was suddenly wicked. 'Perhaps you are right,' he said, so abruptly acquiescent that Richard's eyes narrowed in suspicion. 'Has Heytesbury actually agreed to speak?'

'Yes,' said Richard. 'It is all settled, so it is too late for you to interfere.'

'I would not dream of it,' said Michael, his grin widening. 'I shall look forward very much to Master Heytesbury's lecture on Sunday.'

'Good,' said Richard, giving a courtly bow before turning and strutting out of the church. The long points of his fashionable shoes flapped on the flagstones and his russet-red cloak billowed about his elegantly clad legs as he walked. One of the shoes caught in a crack and made him stumble, although his near fall did nothing to moderate his confident swagger.

'What did Oxford do to him?' asked Cynric. 'No one in the town likes him any more. I wonder whether a witch put a spell on him. Perhaps I will make enquiries at the Franciscan Friary.'

'Why there?' asked Bartholomew curiously. 'The friars will not know any witches.'

'But they know cures for curses,' said Cynric. 'They are very good with their remedies. Their rat poison is famous from here to Peterborough.'

'Perhaps so,' said Bartholomew. 'But killing rats and removing curses that make people unpleasant are scarcely the same thing.'

'You are wrong,' said Michael drolly. 'Both rid the world of something we would rather be without.'

Bartholomew glanced at him. 'Why were you suddenly so pleased to hear that Heytesbury's lecture is now an immovable feature?'

'The day that Faricius was stabbed – Saturday – Chancellor Tynkell told me he was worried that the subject of Kyrkeby's lecture might cause further problems,' began Michael.

'Is that why Kyrkeby was killed, do you think?' asked Bartholomew, glancing down at the grey body in the coffin. 'Because he was going to talk about nominalism? Lord help us, Brother! We had better keep our opinions to ourselves in future, if holding controversial theories might result in our being stuffed in someone else's tomb.'

'Your interpretation of nominalism involves accelerating units and stable velocities,' said Michael disparagingly. 'No one is likely to become too excited about that. Kyrkeby, however, was more interested in how nominalism relates to the nature of God – that the Father, Son and Holy Spirit are in fact three names – *nomen* – for the same being. That would make Him a universal, and universals do not exist in the real sense.'

'That would be contentious,' agreed Bartholomew. 'But not nearly as exciting as Heytesbury's ideas on uniformly accelerated motion.'

'Each to his own, Matt. But Chancellor Tynkell told me on Saturday that he was reconsidering whether to ask Kyrkeby to change the title of his lecture. Then, yesterday morning, Tynkell mentioned that he *had* made the decision to tell Kyrkeby that nominalism was banned. Tynkell, of course, did not know that Kyrkeby was missing, and so sent a note to the friary.'

'Then Kyrkeby never received that letter,' said Bartholomew. 'He has been dead for two days – probably since Monday night, when he was first missed from his friary.'

'So, he died still thinking that he was going to speak on nominalism,' said Michael. 'But I know that Tynkell was nervous about demanding a change in topics at such short notice, and his letter told Kyrkeby to confirm that he was happy with the new arrangements – hence Tynkell's concern last night when he still had not heard, I imagine.'

'A lecture takes a long time to prepare,' said Bartholomew. 'It was unfair of Tynkell to expect Kyrkeby to talk about something completely different just like that.'

'And that was exactly why he asked Kyrkeby to visit him, so that they could discuss it,' said Michael. 'But Tynkell thought he was doing Kyrkeby a favour, actually: everyone is so obsessed with the realism–nominalism debate at the moment, that Kyrkeby's lecture would have had to be very good – and he was an adequate scholar at best.'

'Why was he invited, then?' asked Cynric bluntly. 'I thought you had lots of brilliant scholars to choose from. At least, that is what you told Gold Ear.'

'We do,' said Michael. 'But we were obliged to invite a Dominican to speak, because it is their turn. The

Dominicans are short of brilliant scholars at the moment, and Kyrkeby was the best they could offer.'

'So what did Tynkell suggest Kyrkeby should speak about instead of nominalism?' asked Bartholomew curiously.

Michael's grin widened. 'The possibility of life on other planets. And that is the lecture Heytesbury will be obliged to give. Can you imagine a great man like Heytesbury discussing such a ridiculous topic? And it was Richard who arranged it – he told us so himself! Gold Ear will not be popular when Heytesbury learns that he is obliged to talk about civilisation on Mars!'

While Bartholomew, Michael and Cynric waited impatiently, Agatha gave her undivided attention to Kyrkeby's body, dipping frequently into a basket filled to the brim with mysterious phials and packages. When she finished, she covered the body with a sheet to protect it from the driving rain, but declined to allow them to inspect her handiwork, claiming that tampering with the sheet might spoil her efforts. Beadle Meadowman, who always seemed to be conveniently close when Michael needed him, took one corner of the coffin, while Cynric, Sergeant Orwelle from the Castle and Bartholomew took the other. Then Michael led the procession at a suitably sombre pace out of the church and towards the Dominican Friary on Hadstock Way.

'This is rough wood,' complained Orwelle, jiggling the coffin as he tried to find a better grip. 'Can St Michael's not afford a decent parish coffin? Lord knows, with you scholars murdering each other all the time, it would certainly get some use. I have a splinter already.'

'A splinter?' echoed Cynric in disbelief. 'I thought you were at the battle of Crécy, lad. What is a splinter compared to arrows, lances and broadswords?'

'I did not have to endure arrows, lances and broadswords,' replied Orwelle tartly. 'I was an archer. I shot at other people; they did not shoot at me. This splinter hurts!'

'Brother Timothy was at Crécy,' said Cynric admiringly.

'He was a captain under the Black Prince, and apparently fought very bravely. That is why it is good that the University made him Junior Proctor: a post like that needs a soldier, not just a cleric.'

'Not necessarily,' said Michael coolly, fixing Cynric with a look intended to remind him that some clerics made very good proctors.

'Damn this useless chunk of wood!' swore Cynric suddenly. 'Now *I* have a splinter!'

'Be quiet,' ordered Michael. 'The whole point of delaying the return of Kyrkeby's body to the Dominicans was so that our respectful treatment of it will mollify them and prevent them from marching on the Carmelites. Do not spoil it by chattering like magpies as we walk.'

'We were speaking softly,' said Orwelle, stung. 'And Kyrkeby would not have minded, anyway; he was a charming fellow. Not like that Richard Stanmore, who is too important to pass the time of day with the fathers of his old friends.'

'Richard has only been home a few days, yet half the town seems to dislike him already,' said Bartholomew, wishing his kinsman had made a more agreeable re-entry into Cambridge.

'We do not like his horse, either,' Orwelle went on. 'It kicked over a meat stall in the Market Square yesterday, and this morning it bit the Franciscan Warden.'

'Warden Pechem is back in Cambridge, is he?' mused Michael. 'Good. Now we can ask him why he attended Walcote's meetings.'

'Black Bishop bit Warden Pechem?' asked Bartholomew, appalled. 'What did Richard do?'

'He told Pechem that if he wanted medical attention, he should summon you,' replied Orwelle. 'He said you would treat him free of charge, whereas Robin of Grantchester and Father Lynton of Peterhouse would make him pay.'

'There is Master Kenyngham, free from his Easter vigil,' said Michael suddenly, stopping the procession and pointing.

'Speak to him about his role in these meetings now,' advised Bartholomew, watching the familiar figure of the former Master of Michaelhouse walk dreamily along the High Street. Such was Kenyngham's other-worldliness that Bartholomew noticed the hem of his pale habit was black with the mud through which he had unwittingly ploughed. 'He may start another vigil, and you could find you have to wait until Easter Day for your information.'

'Who is this?' asked Kenyngham, looking at the coffin as he walked towards them. His halo of white fluffy hair blew gently in the wind, like a dandelion clock.

'Kyrkeby of the Dominicans,' said Michael. 'Did you know him?'

Kenyngham nodded sadly. 'I suppose his weak heart must have failed him. But he now rests with God, in a better place than us.'

'He is in a cheap coffin covered with one of Agatha's old sheets,' said Orwelle, genuinely puzzled. 'How is that better than us?'

'I was referring to his soul,' said Kenyngham mildly. 'It is with God and His saints, which is where we will all be soon.'

'Not too soon, I hope,' muttered Cynric, indicating to the others that they should begin walking again and that Michael could catch them up when he had finished with Kenyngham.

But Kenyngham stood in front of them, inadvertently blocking their way so they were forced to stop, and then began a prayer that looked set to expand to a full requiem mass. Cynric and Meadowman shifted hands uncomfortably as the dead weight began to pull on their arms, and Bartholomew prodded Michael with his foot. Michael shrugged helplessly, not sure what to do in the face of such sincerity.

'I am going to drop this,' Orwelle said in a loud whisper. 'Tell him to hurry.'

'Prayers for the dead are our sacred duty,' said Kenyngham gently, admonishing the impatient soldier. 'We must never rush our time with God. But perhaps I should walk with you, and we can pray as we go.'

'Good idea,' said Michael quickly, taking his arm and pulling him forward. 'Having you with us will certainly add favourably to the kind of impression I intend to make on the Dominicans. But first I would like to ask you some questions. You can pray in a moment.'

'What sort of questions?' asked Kenyngham nervously. 'It is not about securing my vote for scouring the latrines twice a year instead of once, is it? That is for Matthew and Langelee to sort out between them.'

Michael raised an imperious finger to prevent Bartholomew from pursuing a matter that was very close to his heart – Michaelhouse's drains were cleaner than most in Cambridge, but they still did not reach the physician's exacting standards. 'Why did you meet my Junior Proctor and others at St Radegund's Convent?' he demanded of Kenyngham.

Kenyngham stared at him. 'How do you know about that?'

'How I know is not important. What were you discussing that warranted you walking all the way out there in the dark? And why to such a place?'

Kenyngham shuddered. 'It was like a foretaste of hell! I went perhaps five times, and on my last visit, that wicked woman tried to manhandle me.'

'I heard about that,' said Michael, and Bartholomew sensed he was struggling to maintain his sombre composure while his fertile imagination produced an image of Kenyngham wrestling with Tysilia. 'But why were you there in the first place?'

'I cannot tell you,' said Kenyngham.

'Why not?' demanded Michael, peeved that Kenyngham should refuse to reveal what he was sure had a bearing on the case he was struggling to solve.

'Because I promised I would not,' said Kenyngham simply. 'And now I must pray for—'

'Walcote was murdered, Master Kenyngham,' said Michael

harshly. 'Someone hanged him from a drainpipe. And in order to find out who did such a monstrous thing, and to prevent it from happening again, I need to know why you and various others met him at St Radegund's.'

'I took an oath,' said Kenyngham. 'I cannot reveal what I know, however much I may wish to.'

'But there is a killer at large,' protested Michael in frustration. 'What is more important – your promise or a life?'

'A promise before God is a sacred thing and cannot be broken,' replied Kenyngham with finality. 'And now, if you will forgive me, there is a soul that needs my attention.' He clasped his hands, bowed his head and gave himself entirely to praying for Kyrkeby.

'He is so annoying when he does that,' muttered Michael to Bartholomew irritably, casting a venomous glower at the saintly Gilbertine. 'How can he expect me to stand by and see my colleagues slaughtered by some maniac, just because *he* has sworn an oath?'

'We are here,' said Bartholomew, looking up at the great gates of the Dominican Friary. 'Perhaps now we shall have some answers. We can ask Morden about these meetings, since Kenyngham will not tell us.'

Michael rapped hard on the gate, until it was answered by a lay-brother, who immediately agreed to fetch his Prior when he saw what they had brought. They saw him intercept Morden on his way to the chapel, then watched the tiny Prior rush across the muddy yard towards them with Ringstead and Bulmer at his heels. Morden's face turned white when he saw the coffin; meanwhile Kenyngham prayed on, oblivious to the consternation and alarm that was ballooning around him.

'I am sorry,' said Michael gently to Morden. 'We discovered Kyrkeby late last night, and have had him at St Michael's Church to pray for his soul ever since. As you can see, Master Kenyngham has been active on this front.'

'But how did this happen?' asked Morden, his elfin face shocked and wan. 'Why?'

'I do not know how or why,' admitted Michael. 'I really am terribly sorry.'

Morden moved to the coffin and pulled back the sheet to look at his Precentor's face. 'My God!' he breathed in horror, dropping the cover quickly before his colleagues could see what was underneath. 'Did you find him like this?'

'Not quite,' said Bartholomew, who had also glimpsed what Agatha had done to Kyrkeby. He was not surprised she had declined to show them her handiwork in the church. The dead man's face was no longer grey and flat, but a lively assortment of colours. His cheeks had been carefully reddened with rouge, and his lips were verging on scarlet. His eyelids were blue, and even his nose had a curious orange glow to it.

'I think it would be best if we took him to the chapel immediately,' said Morden. He glanced anxiously at Bartholomew and the three pall-bearers. 'Does anyone else know about this?'

'Only us,' said Michael.

'Then perhaps we could keep it like that,' said Morden. 'He has done this before, you know.'

'Done what before?' asked Michael, bewildered. 'Died?'

'Put women's paint on his face,' said Morden in a whisper. 'It was many years ago, and I thought he had put an end to such peculiarities. But it seems he has not.'

'It was Agatha,' began Bartholomew, not wanting poor Kyrkeby's reputation sullied when he was not in a position to declare his innocence.

'Who is Agatha?' asked Morden. 'A whore?' He gave a sudden shudder. 'No! Please do not tell me. It is better that I do not know.'

'Very well,' said Michael. 'But Kyrkeby was found near the Carmelite Friary. Do you want to complain about that, or shall we keep it to ourselves for now?'

'Do not tell me that the Carmelites saw him like this?' whispered Morden in horror.

'They did not,' replied Michael truthfully. 'But you can

rest assured that I will do all in my power to discover how he died and why.'

'I am not sure that would be best for our Order,' said Morden nervously. 'What do you plan to do? Ask around the vendors in the Market Square to ascertain which of them sold him the paints? I really would rather you did not.'

'As you wish,' said Michael smoothly. 'I shall defer to you in that matter. But in return, I want certain questions answered.'

'Very well,' said Morden. He clasped Michael's hand gratefully. 'Thank you for what you have done, Brother – for tending Kyrkeby with such respect as well as for hiding him from prying eyes.'

'Well,' said Michael smiling in satisfaction as he watched Morden and his student-friars carry Kyrkeby to their chapel. 'It seems we have averted a riot, Matt. The Dominicans will not march on the Carmelites today at least.'

'Perhaps not, but word will soon spread that Kyrkeby was excavated from a tomb in the Carmelites' graveyard. And then where will we be?'

'That,' said Michael complacently, 'is a bridge we shall cross when we reach it.'

When Prior Morden had seen the body of his Precentor escorted to the chapel, Michael led the way to the small chamber that served as the Prior's sleeping quarters and office. The monk thrust open the door with such vigour that it crashed against the wall with a sound like a thunderclap. Morden sighed irritably.

'I wish you would not do that, Brother. Every time you visit my friary, I am obliged to repaint part of the wall.' He bent to inspect the damage, clicking his tongue over the flakes of plaster that fell to the ground.

'How long do you think Master Kenyngham will stay?' asked Ringstead worriedly. In the chapel below, Kenyngham's voice rose in an ecstasy of prayer. 'We appreciate his concern, but we have friars of our own to say masses for

Kyrkeby. I told him this, but he did not seem to hear.'

'Kenyngham hears very little once he is into the business of praying,' agreed Michael. 'But if he is still here when we leave, we will try to take him with us.'

'Good,' said Morden, leaving the door and clambering into the large chair behind the table, to sit with his short legs swinging in the air. 'He is a saintly man, but I do not want members of other Orders inside our grounds at the moment. The different sects have never been easy in each other's company, but I am sure you have noticed matters have been worse recently.'

'It is because it is Lent, and spring is a long time in coming,' supplied Ringstead helpfully. 'And because this realism–nominalism debate has everyone agitated.'

'It is the Carmelites who exacerbated that,' said Morden disapprovingly. 'We might have all agreed to differ if Lincolne had not been so aggressive and dogmatic.'

'He is a fanatic,' said Ringstead, just in case Bartholomew and Michael had not noticed. 'He gives the impression that he would defend realism to the death. I am not entirely convinced that nominalism provides all the answers, but his very attitude makes me want to oppose him.'

'Quite, quite,' said Michael impatiently. 'But we should not be discussing philosophy when your Precentor lies dead. I need to ask some questions. Did he own a purse or a scrip?'

'He had a leather scrip, as do we all,' said Morden, pulling a tiny one from his belt and showing it to Michael. It looked like something a child might carry. 'Why do you ask?'

'We did not find one with his body, and we need to know whether it was stolen,' said Michael. 'Is there anything distinctive about this scrip? Was it patterned in a particular way?'

'No,' said Morden immediately.

'Yes,' said Ringstead at the same time.

Michael raised his eyebrows, and treated Morden to the kind of glance that was intended to remind him that a favour had been granted, but could just as easily be withdrawn. The tiny Dominican swallowed hard, then gestured for Ringstead to speak.

'Kyrkeby's scrip was of a very delicate design,' said Ringstead. 'You can see that ours are plain, but his was patterned with flowers and butterflies.'

'Flowers and butterflies?' asked Michael, startled. He raised his eyebrows. 'Well, I imagine that will not be too difficult to identify!'

'It was more like something a woman would own than the scrip of a friar,' elaborated Ringstead. He saw Morden gesticulating not to give away more than was necessary, but went on angrily. 'They already know about the face paint, Father Prior, so it cannot matter if they know about the scrip, too. Besides, we all want to know why he died.'

Morden sighed. 'Then I hope you will be discreet with this knowledge, Brother Michael. Kyrkeby liked pretty things. He had jewellery, too.'

'I thought Dominicans were sworn to poverty,' said Bartholomew, thinking about the fine collection of crosses and rings that Ringstead had shown them when Kyrkeby was first reported missing. 'Why did your Order allow him to own such things?'

Morden spread his hands and gave a sickly smile. 'St Dominic did not intend us to live in poverty in a literal sense. He merely intended that we be aware of the dangers of earthly possessions, and that we eat bread and water from time to time.'

'I see,' said Michael wryly. 'That is the most conveniently liberal interpretation of St Dominic's Rule that I have ever heard. But let us return to Kyrkeby. Do you think he may have been wearing any of these rings when he died? It is important to know whether any are missing.'

'You have already looked at his possessions,' Ringstead pointed out. 'And I have already told you that I do not know whether anything has gone.'

'But I might,' said Morden tiredly. 'Fetch them, Ringstead, if you please.'

Ringstead left to do his bidding, while Bartholomew sat in a seat in the window and stared across the Dominicans' yard. The rain had stopped, but there were deep puddles everywhere, the surfaces of which wrinkled and shivered as the breeze played across them. He turned when he heard a soft tap at the door, and was surprised to see Clippesby ease himself through it.

The recent unrest had told on the Michaelhouse Fellow. His hair stood up in a wild halo around his tonsure, and Bartholomew suspected that he had been tearing at it. His eyes seemed unfocused, and he wore the serene smile that usually preceded some of his more peculiar antics. The scholars at Michaelhouse were growing used to Clippesby's eccentricities, and many of the students and masters barely noticed them any more. But the friary was less tolerant, and Bartholomew had the impression that they would have been happier if Clippesby did not pay them such regular visits.

'What are you doing here, Clippesby?' demanded Morden, none too pleasantly. 'Do not tell me that the pig has been giving you its philosophical opinions again?'

Clippesby smiled, his peculiar eyes shifty. 'The pig is convinced that nominalism is a more rational theory. She is a true Dominican in her beliefs.'

If Bartholomew had not known that Clippesby was verging on insanity, he would have suspected the man of playing a game with Morden. But Clippesby's face was a picture of earnest innocence and there was no humour there. Bartholomew heard Michael give a snort of laughter.

'What do you want, then?' snapped Morden, glaring at Michael as well as Clippesby. 'Can you not see that I am busy?'

'I came to tell you that someone has put paint all over poor Kyrkeby's face,' said Clippesby helpfully. 'Someone has made him look like a prostitute.'

'You can take *him* with you when you go, as well as Kenyngham,' said Morden nastily to Michael. 'I will not allow the Dominican Friary to become a venue for Michaelhouse eccentrics, who are probably here only because Michael-house is too poor to afford fires.'

'Michaelhouse is a cold place,' agreed Clippesby. 'But that will not matter soon.'

'Why?' asked Michael suspiciously. 'You are not thinking of setting it alight, are you? I know that would solve our heating problems, but it would also render us all homeless.'

Clippesby glared at him. 'Do you think I am mad; that I would do something to damage the place where I live? All I am saying is that this cold weather will break in three days, and that Easter will be sunny and warm.'

'Really,' said Morden flatly. 'And how do you know this?'

'My voices told me,' said Clippesby serenely. 'And the river ducks confirmed it this morning.'

'The man believes he is St Francis of Assisi,' muttered Morden, regarding Clippesby as he might something he had trodden in on the High Street. 'Can you not lock him away, Brother? I do not think he should be allowed to roam where he pleases. He may do himself some harm – and he is a danger to those on whom he foists his peculiar ideas.'

'I am not some dog to be tethered just because you are too insensitive to hear the sounds of nature,' said Clippesby angrily. 'You are so ensconced in your own troubles and your own comforts, that you cannot hear the Earth speaking to you.'

'Hello, Clippesby,' said Ringstead pleasantly, entering the chamber again with a huge armful of clothes and Kyrkeby's chest. 'You were wrong about the cow, by the way. She did not have twins.'

'But she told me she would,' said Clippesby, puzzled.

'Are these Kyrkeby's belongings?' asked Michael, changing the subject from one that promised to be increasingly bizarre, if Clippesby were to play a part in it. 'Can you tell if there is anything missing, Prior Morden?'

'His scrip is not here,' said Ringstead, watching Morden sift through Kyrkeby's jewellery with predatory eyes. 'I should have noticed it was missing when you last came.'

'Then we must assume it was stolen,' said Michael. 'Has anything else gone?'

Morden selected an emerald ring and held it up to the light. It was huge in his tiny hands. 'This is nice. It is a pity it is so large.'

'It is not too large for me,' said Ringstead, slipping it on to his middle finger and admiring it.

'It looks valuable,' said Michael, taking Ringstead's hand and inspecting the jewel minutely. 'Many people would commit murder in order to get something like this.'

'Murder?' echoed Ringstead, startled and pulling his arm away from Michael. 'Are you telling us that Kyrkeby was *murdered*?'

'The Carmelites!' exclaimed Morden, outrage mounting. 'They did it – not for a ring, but to avenge themselves for Faricius's death, despite the fact that we are totally innocent of it.'

'Our students will riot when they hear about this,' vowed Ringstead. 'They will tear down the Carmelite Friary stone by stone!'

Michael gave a heartfelt sigh of irritation. 'There is no evidence that anyone murdered Kyrkeby. And I thought you wanted to keep the details of his death to yourselves. Do you really want to accuse the Carmelites of murder, and have it revealed that your Precentor died decorated like a whore?'

Morden swallowed hard. 'Of course not. But at the same time, we cannot stand by and see one of our most beloved masters killed in cold blood and do nothing about it.'

'No one is asking you to do nothing,' said Bartholomew reasonably. 'You are helping the proctors to investigate, which is the best way to establish what really happened.'

'Kyrkeby was a dull man,' announced Clippesby bluntly. 'He was not the kind of person anyone would want to kill, even if he did paint his face. Are you sure he was murdered?'

'It is possible,' said Michael calmly, as though he were discussing the weather and not the brutal death of the Dominicans' second-in-command. 'As I said, I intend to discover how he died and why, which I can only do if you co-operate. Now, was Kyrkeby involved in anything we should know about?'

'No,' said Morden. He closed his eyes for a moment, deep in thought, and then shook his head. 'No. His main task was ensuring the proper liturgy was chanted in our offices, and he seldom left the friary, except to go to church.'

'And you say that nothing, other than his scrip, is missing from his belongings?' pressed Michael.

Morden sighed. 'I cannot be certain, but I thought he had more rings than this. One or two may be missing.'

'He must have been wearing them, then,' reasoned Michael.

'Oh, yes,' said Morden, bitterly. 'He was probably wearing them when he painted his face to make himself look like a woman.'

'When precisely did you last see him?' asked Bartholomew. 'You said he was supposed to supervise the students on Saturday when they marched on the Carmelites, but that he was avoiding his duties because he wanted to spend more time on his lecture. When was he first missed?'

'Monday evening,' said Ringstead. 'You had been tending him all that afternoon, and at dinnertime – after you had gone – I took him a bowl of soup. He was not in his room, and I could not find him anywhere in the friary. I was worried, because I could not understand why he had abandoned his lecture so suddenly – especially since it was going so well.'

'No one here recalls seeing him after dusk on Monday,' summarised Morden. 'I suppose he must have slipped out when no one was looking.'

'That makes him sound furtive,' pounced Michael. 'Why do you say he "slipped" out?'

Morden gave an expressive shrug. 'It seems he "slipped" out to indulge his inclination to daub himself with women's paints, Brother. How else would you have me put it?'

'The Chancellor was concerned about the subject matter

of Kyrkeby's lecture,' said Michael cautiously. 'Have you heard anything about this?'

'No,' replied Morden. 'But I can see why. Realists are narrow-minded bigots, who would have been unwilling to listen to what Kyrkeby had to say.'

'Very likely,' said Michael. 'And so Chancellor Tynkell decided to change the title of the lecture to that of life on other planets. You know nothing about this, you say?'

'That must be the letter waiting for Kyrkeby in the chapter house,' said Ringstead, looking at his Prior. 'It arrived yesterday, and we wondered what it was about.'

'None of you opened it?' asked Michael.

'Of course not,' said Morden, offended. 'That would have been most improper.'

'It is a pity no one will ever hear Kyrkeby talking about nominalism,' said Ringstead loyally. He paled suddenly as a thought occurred to him. 'But what shall we do about that? We Dominicans are supposed to give the University Lecture, and now that Kyrkeby is dead, we shall have to find a replacement!'

'Lord!' breathed Morden in alarm. 'We do not have anyone else who can give such a lecture – on nominalism, life on Venus or anything else! We need more time to prepare.'

'A replacement has already been appointed,' said Michael soothingly. 'Tynkell invited someone else to take Kyrkeby's place when he failed to acknowledge Tynkell's letter.'

'Do you know anything about an essay on nominalism?' asked Bartholomew, thinking about Faricius. 'We believe one of the Carmelites may have been writing one, but it has disappeared.'

'A Carmelite?' asked Morden in surprise. 'But they follow the heretical and outdated principles of realism.'

'Not all of them,' said Michael. 'Just as I imagine that not all Dominicans are nominalists. There are exceptions.'

'I doubt any Dominican would be foolish enough to believe in realism,' said Morden superiorly. He glanced covertly at Clippesby, as if expecting him to announce that he did, but the Michaelhouse man was silent, staring at the flames that burned in Morden's large hearth. 'But it is possible that the odd Carmelite may have seen the light, I suppose.'

'I know of no Carmelite essay, though,' said Ringstead. 'We use William Heytesbury's books for our lectures, not essays by unknown authors.'

'Thank you for your help,' said Michael, preparing to leave. He exchanged a glance with Bartholomew, who knew he wanted to quiz Morden about his nocturnal meetings at St Radegund's Convent but was reluctant to broach the subject and risk alerting Morden that he was investigating them. Bartholomew racked his brain for ways to introduce the topic, but Michael gave a small shake of his head, afraid that Morden would simply deny the accusation and promptly warn his associates that the Senior Proctor had wind of their dealings.

'Do not forget to collect Master Kenyngham on your way out,' said Morden, scrambling down from his chair to prevent Michael from opening the door. He was too late, and it crashed against the wall, so hard that he winced. 'And take Clippesby with you, too.'

'I am leaving now anyway,' said Clippesby, following Michael. 'It is kind of you to be concerned for my safety in these times of unrest, Father Prior, but you have no need to worry.'

'I am glad to hear it,' said Morden, clearly not at all interested in Clippesby's well-being.

'I often walk alone,' Clippesby went on. 'You and I are much alike in that respect.'

'What do you mean?' asked Morden uneasily. 'I do not wander the town unaccompanied. I always take a servant with me.'

'Not always,' corrected Clippesby, sounding surprised by the assertion. 'Sometimes you go alone. For example, I have seen you several times on the Barnwell Causeway at night.'

Michael closed his eyes in exasperation. He had decided that to interrogate Morden about the meetings might prove detrimental to the case, and the last thing he wanted was for the insane Clippesby to be conducting the interview.

But Clippesby was oblivious to the foul looks shot his way by both the Prior and Michael, although their disapproval was for very different reasons. 'You walked to St Radegund's Convent, where you met your friends,' he said.

'And which particular animal told you this?' asked Ringstead unpleasantly. 'An owl? Or do creatures who spy on men in the night tend towards slugs and bats and other unclean beasts?'

'No animal told me,' said Clippesby, offended. 'I saw him myself. He met Prior Ralph from Barnwell and old Adam from Ely Hall, and they went into St Radegund's Convent together.'

'Really?' asked Michael mildly, realising that it would look suspicious not to persist with the query now that Clippesby had raised the issue. 'And what were you doing there, Prior Morden?'

'If you must know, I had business with Walcote, your Junior Proctor.'

'And what business would that be?' pressed Michael.

'I cannot tell you,' said Morden, folding his small arms and looking away, signifying that he had said all he was going to on the matter.

Michael had other ideas. 'You *can* tell me. Or the Carmelites might discover what passed in the Dominican Friary involving certain face paints.'

'No!' exclaimed Morden in horror. He glowered at Clippesby, seeing in the Michaelhouse man the reason for his awkward situation. 'But this is blackmail!'

'My Junior Proctor was murdered, Prior Morden,' said Michael coldly. 'I will do whatever it takes to catch the person who did it, and if that includes telling the Carmelites that the Dominicans like to paint their faces, then so be it.'

Morden closed his eyes in resignation. 'Very well. But you will not like what I have to say.'

'Probably not,' said Michael. 'But you will tell me anyway.'

Morden sighed. 'I met three or four times with your Junior Proctor. Prior Ralph and some of his colleagues were there and once – in December – so was Brother Adam from Ely Hall.'

'Did Master Kenyngham of Michaelhouse ever go?' asked Bartholomew.

'No Gilbertines were invited. And no Franciscans or Carmelites, either. Doubtless Walcote only wanted civilised company.'

'And what did you talk about?' asked Michael.

'We discussed the validity of nominalism, among other things. We all believe it to be the superior philosophical theory.'

'Yes, yes,' said Michael impatiently. 'I know many Benedictines and Austin canons concur with you on that. But why did you go to St Radegund's in the middle of the night to discuss it? What was wrong with a lecture hall in the day?'

'We discussed other matters, too,' said Morden. He licked his lips, and glanced at the others. Ringstead, it seemed, was as curious as the others to learn what his Prior did at a place like St Radegund's Convent at the witching hour.

'Like what?' pressed Michael.

'Murder,' said Morden in a low voice. 'We discussed murder.'

'Now we are getting somewhere,' said Michael. 'Whose murder?'

'Yours, Brother,' replied Morden.

'I confess Morden's claim unsettled me at first,' said Michael, taking his place at the high table in Michaelhouse's hall for dinner that night. 'But on reflection, I think there is no need to worry.'

Bartholomew regarded him uneasily. 'And how did you reach that conclusion, Brother?'

'According to Morden, Walcote learned about the plan to kill me in December, but I am still here. Whoever it is must have given up the idea.'

'I am not so sure about that,' said Bartholomew, worried. 'Walcote is dead, and we cannot be sure that *he* was not murdered because he was close to exposing this plot.'

'It is also possible that he was murdered for the contents of his purse,' said Michael practically. 'I walked to Barnwell Priory this afternoon, and Nicholas identified the purse Orwelle found. He told me there was a small imperfection in its drawstrings, and when I looked I saw that he was right.'

'But Walcote carried that cheap purse because he collected penny fines,' Bartholomew pointed out. 'Why rob him?'

'For people with nothing, any purse is worth stealing.'

Bartholomew wavered, knowing that Michael was right on that score. But he still believed that hanging suggested a degree of premeditation, and imagined that most robbers would prefer the speed and silence of a blade.

'Did you see Matilde when you went to St Radegund's this afternoon?' asked Michael, breaking into his thoughts. 'Has she learned anything more about these secret meetings at which my murder was discussed?'

Bartholomew shook his head. 'But I told her what Morden had claimed, and she warned you to be careful. That is good advice, Brother.'

Michael waved a dismissive hand, indicating that he thought their fears groundless. 'Is she still convinced that there is more to Tysilia than the body of a goddess with no brains?'

'Apparently, she spent the whole morning trying to teach Tysilia how to hoe. It is not difficult: a child could do it. Tysilia could not, however, and repeatedly raked out seedlings instead of weeds. When Eve Wasteneys saw that Tysilia was incapable of hoeing, she was sent to work in the kitchens instead.'

'So?' asked Michael.

'So, the weather was cold and wet. Matilde believed Tysilia was only pretending to be inept, so that she would not have to be outside. It worked: Tysilia spent the rest of the morning in a warm kitchen, while everyone else was out in the rain. Matilde considered this evidence of Tysilia's cunning.'

'It could equally be evidence that Tysilia has an inability to learn,' said Michael. 'However, the Bishop is a clever man, and it is difficult to imagine him siring a child who is quite so dense.'

'Thomas de Lisle *sired* Tysilia?' asked Bartholomew, startled. 'You told me she is his niece.'

'Did I say sired?' asked Michael. He blew out his cheeks. 'Damn! I must be more careful in future. De Lisle certainly does not want *her* to know the identity of her father, and it is not good for bishops to have illegitimate children in tow.'

'I should think not,' said Bartholomew. 'But if Matilde and I are right about Tysilia, then she may very well know something about this plot to kill you. Perhaps *she* was the one who devised it in the first place.'

'I do not think so,' said Michael. 'Why would she do something like that? I am her father's best agent, and she has no reason to wish me harm.'

'If she is as clever as Matilde believes, then perhaps the plot is her way of striking at Bishop de Lisle. Or perhaps she wants to take your place, and become as indispensable to him as you are.'

'This is pure fantasy, Matt. You and Matilde seem to find it difficult to believe that some people – even women – are very stupid. You are quite wrong about Tysilia.' He sniffed the air suddenly, and groaned. 'Oh, Lord, Matt! Dinner is more of that stinking fish-giblet stew again! Not only is it freezing cold in this godforsaken place, but we are forced to eat stewed fish entrails and yesterday's bread.'

'Delicious,' boomed Father William, rubbing his hands together as he came to sit next to them. 'Lent is my favourite time of year. Sinful practices like over-indulgence and fornication are forbidden, there are none of those reeking flowers in the church to distract you from your prayers, and there are no frills and such nonsense adorning your altars. And yet we are still treated to tasty delicacies like fish-giblet stew.'

'And we think Clippesby is insane!' muttered Michael, eyeing the dirty friar doubtfully. 'Anyone who thinks boiled fish intestines in watery broth is the ultimate dining experience should be locked away.'

'Where is Langelee?' demanded the Franciscan, looking around him as if he imagined the Master would suddenly appear out of the rushes that were scattered across the floor. 'We cannot start the meal until he has said grace.'

'He is not a great lover of fish, and so probably feels no great compunction to hurry here,' said the Carmelite Suttone, scratching his short white hair with his large-knuckled fingers. 'He is talking to Clippesby, anyway.'

'Clippesby,' said William in disapproval. 'I caught him pulling the tail feathers from the porter's cockerel this afternoon. He said Cynric told him that burning them in a dish with a mixture of mint leaves and garlic has the power to remove curses. And he *claimed* that Cynric had this information from Prior Pechem.'

'The head of the Franciscans?' asked Michael gleefully. 'That sounds like heresy to me, William. Removing curses with feathers and garlic indeed!'

'Cynric misheard,' stated William immediately. 'Assuming that Clippesby even had half the story right, that is.'

'Clippesby puzzles me,' said Bartholomew. 'Sometimes he seems quite normal, and yet other times he indulges in these peculiarities of behaviour. I do not understand him at all.'

'That is because he is insane,' stated William uncompromisingly. 'The whole point about insane people is that their actions are incomprehensible by those of us who are normal.'

'But on occasions, what he says makes perfect sense, and his opinions are worth listening to.'

'Only if you are insane yourself,' said William firmly. He glanced at the door at the end of the hall, then at the painted screen near the spiral staircase that led to the kitchens. Behind it, the servants were waiting with the food in huge steaming cauldrons. 'I wish Langelee would hurry up. The soup is getting cold.'

'Good,' said Michael. 'The longer that abomination is kept from our tables, the better. And if we sit here long enough, it will be time for breakfast. Lukewarm oatmeal is not my favourite, either, but I would sooner eat that than rancid fish guts floating in greasy water.'

Bartholomew saw Suttone wince at the description. One or two students, sitting at the tables placed at right angles to the one where the fellows ate, also heard, and Bartholomew could see them reconsidering their options for dining that night. Since Langelee had been made Master, it had become much more difficult for the students to slip out of the College for a night in the town, but they were encouraged to lay in their own supplies of food, called 'smalls'. This had the advantage of saving Michaelhouse a certain amount of money and it prevented the students from wanting to eat in taverns.

'Have you caught your murderer, Michael?' asked William conversationally, picking at a lump of old food that adhered to the front of his habit. When it was off, yet another dark spot joined the multicoloured speckling on the Franciscan's chest. 'My offer of help is still open, you know.'

'Thank you,' said Michael politely. 'It is good to know who one's friends are these days.'

He raised his voice so that it would carry to Kenyngham, who was already muttering his own, much longer, version of grace, and who was oblivious of any meaningful comments or looks from the monk who sat to his right.

'I said, it is good to know who one's friends are these days,' said Michael, more loudly still. This time, even Kenyngham was among those who looked at him in surprise, startled by the sudden volume in the monk's voice.

'Are you addressing me, Brother?' asked Kenyngham, smiling in his absent-minded way. 'Are you in need of a friend? Join me after the meal, and we will pray together.'

'I certainly am in need of friends,' said Michael bitterly. 'And I do not count those who attend secret meetings at midnight, where plots to kill me are discussed.'

Kenyngham regarded him sympathetically. 'Who has done that? You should inform him that he will be bound for hell if he continues, and that to take the life of another is a deadly sin.'

Michael gaped in disbelief. 'You are a cool fellow, Father. I understand that *you* attended several such meetings. This plot was discussed at St Radegund's Convent, when men such as Morden, Pechem and Lincolne – and you, of course – were present.'

'Not Pechem,' said William immediately. 'We Franciscans do not do things like that.'

'And not me, either,' said Kenyngham. 'Really, Brother! Do you imagine that I would allow such a discussion to take place? You know how I abhor violence. I can assure you that the meetings I attended made no mention of any such topic.'

'Morden says Walcote had uncovered a plot to kill me, and that was on the agenda at these gatherings,' said Michael angrily.

'I attended no meeting with Morden,' said Kenyngham. 'The only people present, other than Walcote and me, were Pechem and Lincolne. And we certainly did not discuss murder.'

Michael sighed in exasperation. 'Then tell me what you *did* talk about.'

'I have already explained to you that I cannot. Please do not ask me to break my promise again. Come with me to the church after dinner, and we will pray together for God to give you patience.'

'I am going nowhere with you,' said Michael, giving the old friar a hostile glare. 'You are not to be trusted.'

At that moment, Langelee entered the hall, and everyone stood in silence with his hands clasped in front of him waiting for the Master to begin the grace. Clippesby was with

Langelee, and Bartholomew noticed that the mad Dominican's face was flushed and his eyes were bright, which were symptoms the physician associated with episodes of especially odd behaviour. His heart sank, knowing that it would not be long before Langelee would be forced to confine Clippesby to his room until the mood had passed.

Langelee reached the Master's chair, said a short prayer in his strong, steady voice, and had already seated himself before most of his scholars had completed their responses. He reached for the wine jug and filled his goblet. He then took a deep draught, as though the bitter, acidic drink was something to which he had been looking forward all day. The low hum of conversation restarted in the hall as he leaned back in his chair and closed his eyes in grateful appreciation.

'Master!' whispered William in a hoarse voice, loud enough to carry to the far end of the hall. 'The Bible Scholar!'

'What?' asked Langelee wearily. 'Oh, yes.' He gave a half-hearted nod to the student who received a free education in exchange for reading from the Bible at each meal. The practice was intended to give the scholars cause for contemplation while they were eating, and to dispense with the need for frivolous conversation. It was something of which the austere Father William very much approved, but which the rest of the Fellows preferred to do without, especially in the evenings when they were tired.

The student stood on the dais next to the high table, and began to read from the Book of Isaiah in a droning, bored voice. His phrasing was automatic, and Bartholomew suspected that his thoughts were as far away as those of most of his listeners. Michael turned his attention to the pale grey broth that was slopped into the bowl in front of him. He took a piece of bread, and dipped it in the mixture without much enthusiasm, chewing it as though it were wood chippings.

Bartholomew did not blame him. He did not like fishy

271

soup either, especially since his knowledge of anatomy allowed him to identify particular organs and their functions. The fact that the entrails had not been fresh when they were purchased, and tasted strong and slightly gamy, did not induce many scholars to finish what they had been given. Bartholomew took one mouthful and decided he would rather go without, wondering absently whether the seed cake his sister had given him was still in his room, or whether Michael had already found it.

'God's teeth! This is a vile concoction!' exclaimed Langelee, pushing away his bowl in disgust. He stood abruptly, and rattled off a closing grace, even though some of the students had still not been served. 'Goodnight, gentlemen. I hope your supper does not give you nightmares.'

'Well!' said William, as Langelee exited from the hall, leaving the Bible Scholar in open-mouthed confusion. 'There is a man who does not appreciate a good meal.'

'Then you can have mine, too,' said Michael, standing and emptying the grey liquid from his bowl into William's. Some of the resulting spillage shot across the table towards the friar's filthy sleeve. Bartholomew was fascinated to see that the deeply impregnated grease in the garment was easily able to repel the soup, and that it simply ran off like water from a duck's back. 'I would sooner starve than eat this.'

'It will be a long time before *you* starve,' said William, eyeing Michael up and down critically. 'You will be able to live off that fat for years.'

Michael glowered at him and stalked towards the door. Bartholomew followed, no more keen to sit in a cold hall that was full of the rank stench of rotten fish than was the monk. Other scholars were also taking advantage of the abrupt end to the meal, and the servants had even started to clear away bowls and goblets, anticipating with pleasure the treat of an early finish.

'What is it that makes everyone want to comment on my figure?' Michael demanded of Bartholomew. 'Do people not realise that it is rude? Even people I barely know talk about it – like your nephew, and that Ringstead at the Dominican Friary. I am growing heartily tired of it.'

'Eat less, then,' suggested Bartholomew. 'The reason people comment is because you are an imposing sight. There are not many people your size in Cambridge.'

'I am not that big,' objected Michael. 'And it is mostly muscle anyway. Just look at this. Grab it, go on.' He flexed an arm for Bartholomew to feel.

'Yes, I know,' said Bartholomew, declining the offer. He had witnessed the previous night that the monk was sufficiently strong to break the leg of a corpse, and knew that his bulk belied an impressive power.

'And if I am heavy, it is because I have big bones,' said Michael sulkily. 'I am not as fat as people believe.'

'It is partly your habit,' said Bartholomew, eyeing the black garment critically. 'It makes you look enormous.'

'That is an unkind thing to say,' said Michael huffily. 'What do you expect me to do? I can hardly go to my Bishop and tell him that I no longer intend to wear the Benedictine habit because it makes me look fat.'

'Do not take it so personally,' said Bartholomew. 'People are always criticising me because my clothes are soiled or torn. I just ignore them.'

'I shall punch the next person who calls me fat,' vowed Michael angrily, marching down the newel stair that led to the lower floor and heading for the door that opened into the yard. 'And that includes you, so just mind yourself.'

'We should probably visit Prior Pechem of the Franciscans tonight,' said Bartholomew, changing the subject, but not in the least intimidated by Michael's bluster. 'We need to ask him about his role at Walcote's meetings. Now that Morden – and Kenyngham – know we are aware of these gatherings, there is no need for us to worry about putting them on their guard. They will already have been warned, and our enquiries can do no harm.'

'I have already spoken to Pechem,' said Michael irritably.

'Since Clippesby introduced the subject so tactlessly with Morden, I decided there was nothing to lose by approaching Pechem directly.'

'And?' asked Bartholomew. 'What did he say?'

'He pretended he did not know what I was talking about, and said he had never been to St Radegund's in his life. More lies, Matt. Just when we force the Carmelites to be honest, the Franciscans start bombarding me with falsehoods.'

'Ah, Michael and Bartholomew. Just the men I wanted to see.' Langelee was approaching the door from the darkness outside. 'I would like to speak to you. Join me in my chamber, if you will.'

'Why?' demanded Michael irritably. 'It has been a long day and I am tired. All I want to do is go to bed and forget about that monstrosity that paraded itself as dinner.'

'Then that is even more reason why you should come to my chamber,' said Langelee, laying a meaty arm across Michael's shoulders. 'A beef and onion pie, a barrel of French wine, and a couple of loaves of fresh bread are waiting there.'

Michael eyed him suspiciously. 'Why? So you can laugh about the amount I eat and tell everyone that I have a stomach like a bottomless well?'

'Do you eat a lot?' asked Langelee, genuinely surprised. 'I cannot say I have noticed. But you and I are both large men, so healthy appetites are to be expected. Come and join me in my room, and we will do justice to this fine food. What do you say?'

Michael gazed at him. 'What kind of pie did you say it was?'

CHAPTER 8

ASMALL FIRE BURNED IN LANGELEE'S ROOM, AND TWO lamps placed on the windowsills filled the chamber with a warm yellow glow. Bartholomew looked around him appreciatively, noting the tasteful wall-hangings and the clean but functional rugs that lay on the floor. Here was no wasteful decadence, but a pleasant and simple room that managed to create an atmosphere of industry and efficiency. Bartholomew, who had known Langelee for two years before the philosopher had been elected Master of Michaelhouse, was impressed by the room and the changes that had occurred in the man.

'Where is this pie?' demanded Michael, sitting in the best chair and looking aggrieved. 'And what do you want to discuss? It is not those damned latrines again, is it? I have already told you that I do not care whether they are cleaned once a year, twice a year, ten times a year, or never again.'

'All the Fellows except Bartholomew concur,' said Langelee. 'So, we will have them cleaned once a year, and we will use the money we save to buy a new bench for the hall.'

'You will spend that money on medicines for intestinal disorders when summer comes,' warned Bartholomew. 'The latrines are not a problem now the weather is cold, but you remember how many flies they attracted last summer. The air was black with them.'

'Please, Matt!' said Michael with a shudder. 'I am about to eat. And there is a very simple solution to this fly problem: only use the latrines at night. There are not nearly as many then.'

'That is not the point,' began Bartholomew, exasperated by their refusal to acknowledge that dirty latrines were likely

275

to have serious repercussions on the health of Michael-house's scholars.

'I did not bring you here to talk about sewage,' said Langelee, cutting across Bartholomew's words as he sliced a decadently large piece of pie and handed it to Michael. 'I brought you here because Clippesby told me the disturbing news that Prior Morden plans to commit murder.'

Michael gave a small smile. 'That is not what transpired at the Dominican Friary. Trust that lunatic Clippesby to get it wrong! What Morden said was that Walcote discovered evidence that there was a plan afoot to harm me, and that meetings were organised between the religious Orders to discuss what should be done about it.'

'Why would anyone want to kill you?' asked Langelee, tearing the bread into pieces and passing it to his guests. 'I know that as Senior Proctor you cannot be popular with everyone, and that there are men who hate the power of the University that you embody. But it is another matter entirely to murder someone for it.'

'So far, there has only been a *plot* to murder me,' corrected Michael. 'I am still alive, remember?'

'But Walcote is not,' said Bartholomew. 'Do you think he was killed because he was trying to uncover the identity of the person who was planning to strike at you?'

Michael nodded slowly. 'As you pointed out earlier, the fact that he was hanged, rather than stabbed or hit over the head, smacks of execution rather than murder. It is obvious now that I think of it.'

'My experience of these matters, while I was an agent for the Archbishop of York, leads me to think that you are probably correct,' said Langelee, sitting opposite him and poking at the fire. 'Do you have any idea who this killer is?'

Michael shook his head. 'And according to Morden, Walcote did not know, either.'

'How did Walcote know about the plot?' asked Langelee. 'What evidence did he have?'

'Apparently, he found a letter in which details of a proposed attack were given,' said Michael. 'This letter was in the possession of one of my beadles – a man I did not like, as it happens – whose body was discovered in a ditch on Christmas Eve.'

'The beadle was called Rob Smyth, and he had been drinking in the King's Head,' elaborated Bartholomew. 'On his way home, he drowned in a puddle. Beadle Meadowman found the body.'

Michael eyed the pie until Langelee cut him a second piece. 'Matt inspected the corpse, and told me he was certain Smyth drowned accidentally – that no one else had done him any harm.'

Bartholomew agreed. 'It was obvious that he had slipped on some ice and tumbled face-down in a puddle. Being drunk, he was unable to move.'

'And this Smyth was the recipient of the letter?' asked Langelee doubtfully. 'I thought most of your beadles could not read.'

'Smyth was a courier,' replied Michael. 'The other patrons of the King's Head – including Agatha – claimed Smyth had been very generous that night: he bought ale for all his acquaintances, as well as for himself. Now I understand why: he was spending the money he had been paid to deliver the letter.'

'Only, fortunately for Michael, he never did,' said Bartholomew. 'Smyth died before he could deliver the message.'

'So, there are at least two people conspiring against you,' observed Langelee. 'The person who sent the letter, and the person to whom the letter was addressed.'

'Right,' said Michael. 'But, according to Morden, Walcote had failed to uncover the identity of either. Damn! I wish Walcote had told me about this!'

'Why did he keep it from you?' asked Langelee, politely sucking the pie knife clean before cutting Michael a piece of cheese. 'Had I found such a letter, you would have been the first to know, so that you could be on your guard against attack.'

'Apparently, he decided that Michael had enough to worry about, and thought he would be better not knowing,' replied Bartholomew. 'It was only a few weeks after that business with Runham and the stolen gold at Michaelhouse, and Walcote considered that more than enough anxiety for a while.'

Michael scraped the pie crumbs from the table into his hand and slapped them into his mouth. 'Matt is being politic,' he informed Langelee. 'It seems Walcote knew I was disappointed not to be elected Master of Michaelhouse, and thought I did not need to know that someone disliked me enough to end my life.'

'But this does not tally,' said Langelee, after a moment of thought. 'A few days ago you told me that Walcote's secret meetings started around or just after the time when Michaelhouse's stolen gold spilled across the Market Square. That was in late November. But Smyth died at Christmas. *Ergo*, Walcote's secret meetings had been taking place *before* he found the letter on the dead Smyth.'

'We had fathomed that, thank you,' said Michael testily. 'According to Morden, Walcote had been anticipating trouble between the religious Orders for months. The meetings were his attempt to understand the causes, so that he could try to minimise the effects. The subject of the intended murder was raised at a later gathering.'

'But I still do not understand why someone would want to kill you,' said Langelee, poking the fire again. 'Have you been involved in any especially dubious business recently that may have upset anyone? We all know about the arrangements with Oxford, of course.'

'Thanks to you,' said Michael, not without resentment. It had been Langelee's announcement regarding his liaison with Heytesbury that had ultimately deprived Michael of the Michaelhouse Mastership. 'But my Oxford business cannot be the reason. All I am doing is passing some property to

Heytesbury in exchange for a couple of names and one or two bits of information.'

'Controversial information?' pressed Langelee, keenly interested.

Michael could not suppress a gleeful grin. 'Not yet, but it will be. Heytesbury is almost ready to sign. He thinks I want to use the information to become Chancellor – which I might, as it happens – but I have other plans for it first. And Cambridge will emerge richer and stronger from it.'

'Good,' said Langelee, smiling warmly. 'It is gratifying to see Cambridge besting Oxford. But what about the other men whom Walcote met? You say one was Morden, and I know another was Kenyngham.'

'You do?' asked Michael, startled. 'How? He refused to speak to me.'

'He refused to speak to me, too,' said Langelee. 'So, I paid a visit to his Prior instead. Gretford admitted that he and Kenyngham had attended about four of these meetings, but told me that the main issues discussed were repairing the Great Bridge – anonymously, so that the town would not expect the University to pay in the future – and the relative merits of nominalism and realism.'

'Morden said much the same,' said Bartholomew.

'It seems to me that the person who wishes Michael dead may well be one of those powerful men who attended Walcote's meetings,' said Langelee thoughtfully. 'To kill a proctor is to strike at the heart of the University's authority – as I remarked when you first started to investigate this business. Thus, the would-be killer may be a high-ranking cleric.'

'I think you are right,' said Michael. 'He probably kept Walcote alive long enough to learn from him what was happening regarding the investigation of Smyth's letter, and then murdered him when he started to come too close to the truth.'

'Then all we have to do is find out precisely who attended these meetings,' said Bartholomew. 'That will at least give us a manageable list of suspects. Otherwise, we have to assume it could be anyone – not just in the University, but in the town, too.'

Langelee agreed. 'You have apprehended a lot of killers in your time, Brother. Many believed their crimes were justified and hated you for thwarting them, while others doubtless had families or friends who might want vengeance.'

'True,' said Michael. 'But luckily, most of them were either killed in the chase or were subjected to the justice of the King's courts – it was not I who hanged them; it was the Sheriff.'

'Then what about criminals' families?' asked Langelee. 'There are probably wives, children, parents and siblings who want you struck down for what you did to their loved ones.'

'That kind of person would not *plot* to kill Michael,' said Bartholomew. 'He – or she – would just strike, not devise elaborate plans and send details via disenchanted beadles.'

'I agree,' said Michael.

'So, let us consider your list of likely suspects, then,' said Langelee, passing Michael another hunk of yellow cheese and taking an equally large slice for himself. Bartholomew was not halfway through his pie. 'Who do you know for certain attended these meetings?'

'Dame Wasteneys and Matilde claim that Kenyngham, Lincolne and Pechem were regular attenders,' said Michael with his mouth full. 'Brother Adam added Ralph of the Austins and Morden of the Dominicans. However, Morden denies seeing Kenyngham, and Kenyngham denies seeing Morden and Pechem.'

'We have explained that, though,' said Bartholomew. 'Walcote simply arranged separate gatherings for the two factions of the realism–nominalism debate, because he knew they would squabble if he did not.'

Michael nodded. 'Eve Wasteneys told us Walcote held eight or nine meetings in total: Morden and Kenyngham both claimed to have attended four or five. Since they were not at the same ones, we can deduce that Eve was telling us the truth about the total number.'

'Can we be sure that Walcote's reason for separating the factions was honourable?' wondered Bartholomew thoughtfully. 'He may have been playing a game, pitting one group against another.'

'That would have been risky,' said Langelee, topping up his own goblet, then doing the same for Michael. Bartholomew had barely touched his, but the Master gave him more anyway, filling the goblet so that a trembling meniscus lay over the top. 'These are powerful men, who would not appreciate being pawns in the game of a mere Junior Proctor.'

'Then perhaps *that* is why he died,' said Michael soberly.

'Do you know a novice at St Radegund's Convent called Tysilia de Apsley?' asked Bartholomew, changing the subject slightly. 'She is tall with dark hair.'

'I know her,' said Langelee. He gave a salacious grin. 'And so does every other red-blooded man in the town, I should imagine. Why? Had she worked her charms on Walcote? I thought he had a long-standing affection with one of his Austin colleagues. Still, with a woman like that . . .'

'Matt thinks there is more to her than an evening of romping among the pews of the conventual church,' said Michael bluntly.

'Walcote's meetings took place at St Radegund's Convent,' Bartholomew pointed out. 'It is not the kind of place influential scholars should be seen frequenting, so they must have had good reason for choosing it over one of their own halls. I think the reason was that it suited Tysilia.'

Langelee rubbed his chin thoughtfully. 'I would dismiss any of our students foolish enough to be caught in that den of iniquity, and something far more important than philosophy would need to be on the agenda to attract the heads of the religious Orders there. However, it is an excellent place for clandestine meetings, because no one would ever think of using it for such purposes.'

'That is true,' said Michael bitterly. '*I* certainly had no inkling that they were taking place.'

'But Bartholomew is wrong about Tysilia,' Langelee went on. 'I have never met a person with fewer wits.'

'No one believes Tysilia is involved, because they say she is too dense,' said Bartholomew. 'But what if that is an act? She is related to the Bishop of Ely, who is as cunning a man as I have ever met. Why will no one accept that she may be clever enough to fool us all?'

'Because you only have to look at her face to see that there is nothing there,' said Langelee, tapping his temple as he spoke. 'It is like gazing into the eyes of a dead trout.'

'Is that something you do often?' asked Michael.

Langelee gave an irritable frown at Michael's flippancy. 'There is no earthly way Tysilia is involved, Bartholomew. I doubt the nuns even trusted her to open the convent doors on the nights these meetings took place. They would be afraid she would try to seduce their guests *en route*, or that she would forget they were supposed to be allowed in and see them out instead.'

'She did try to seduce Kenyngham,' said Michael, chuckling at the thought.

'The nuns need the money she brings, and Eve cannot afford to lose it,' said Langelee, ignoring him. 'Still, I suppose the Bishop is unlikely to find anywhere else that will take such a brazen whore, so perhaps he will turn a blind eye to the situation for a while longer yet.'

Bartholomew stared into the flames of the fire, thinking about what they had learned. 'If Walcote was killed because he came too close to discovering Michael's would-be killer, then we have a smaller list of suspects than ever. Morden claims the murder was discussed at the meetings he attended; Kenyngham claims it was not.'

'Kenyngham would never lie,' said Langelee, settling back in his chair with his wine. 'The poor man would not know how. I cannot imagine how he has managed to live to such a ripe old age by telling the truth, but there we are.'

282

'His ripe old age almost ended when he refused to tell me what passed during these gatherings,' said Michael resentfully. He raised Bartholomew's overfilled cup to his lips with a steady hand that did not spill a drop.

'We should return to the Carmelite Friary tomorrow,' said Bartholomew, taking his cup from Michael, much to the monk's annoyance. Langelee had provided a decent brew. 'I am not yet convinced that they are innocent of Kyrkeby's death. Perhaps they murdered him, and then killed Walcote because he heard or saw something on his patrols.'

'Why do you think that?' asked Langelee.

'The timing,' said Bartholomew. 'Kyrkeby was last seen on Monday evening, while we know that Walcote was killed just after dusk on the same day. Perhaps one witnessed the death of the other, and was murdered to ensure his silence.'

'That is possible,' said Michael, thoughtfully. 'And do not forget that Simon Lynne fled his friary on Monday night, too. We caught him in St Radegund's Convent the following morning, pretending to visit his "aunt".'

'It seems a lot happened on Monday night,' mused Langelee, voicing what Bartholomew had remarked upon at Faricius's funeral, when Lincolne had told them that Lynne had gone. 'Kyrkeby and Lynne disappeared and Walcote died.'

'Very true,' said Bartholomew. 'But I am more concerned with catching the person who may have designs on Michael's life than I am in looking for missing scholars.'

'Walcote found that note three months ago,' said Michael dismissively. 'So, why should the killer strike now? It is entirely possible that Smyth's death made him realise that murder is not an easy thing to do properly, and he decided to abandon the plan.'

'Or perhaps the plan is already in action, and Walcote was killed because he stumbled on it,' countered Bartholomew. 'I do not understand why you seem so unperturbed about it.'

'Because there is nothing I can do, so what is the point

in worrying?' replied Michael. 'This is an excellent brew, Langelee. Is there any more of it? Matt seems to have taken mine.'

Bartholomew excused himself from Langelee's room when the conversation degenerated into boastful accounts of Michael and Langelee's past lives. Bartholomew had heard the stories before, and did not want to spend the rest of the evening listening to wildly exaggerated adventures that painted Michael and Langelee in ever more flattering light, so he returned to his own room to work on his treatise on fevers.

He had not been writing for long, although his eyes were already beginning to close as the unsteady light of a candle made him drowsy, and he was considering beginning the unpleasant transition from a cold room to a colder bed, when there was a knock at the door and Cynric entered.

'I thought I would find you awake,' the Welshman said softly, so as not to wake Suttone and his students, who occupied the room opposite. 'I was just leaving home for the vigil in St Mary's Church, when I met blind Father Paul, who used to be a Fellow at Michaelhouse.'

'What was he doing out at this time of night?' asked Bartholomew in surprise, thinking about the kindly Franciscan who had been so popular with the students. 'He is too old to be roaming the streets so long after the curfew bell has sounded.'

'He claims his blindness means that he is better equipped for wandering around in the dark than the others, and that by delivering any night-time messages he can serve his community in a way that no one else can.'

'What did he want?' asked Bartholomew, knowing that the friar was proud of his blindness and the fact that he felt it gave him an advantage over other men. 'And where is he?'

'Waiting by the gate,' said Cynric. 'He says Warden Pechem needs a physician.'

'Why?' asked Bartholomew, reaching for his cloak and slinging his medicine bag over his shoulder. Then he recalled what Sergeant Orwelle had mentioned earlier that day. 'It is nothing to do with being bitten by Richard's horse, is it?'

Cynric grinned. 'Apparently, the wound is sore. He was urged to send for you earlier, but he declined because he was afraid that the Dominicans would hear about it and make fun of him.'

But Bartholomew knew the real reason why Pechem had dallied: he had lied to Michael about being at Walcote's meetings, and was now reluctant to talk to Bartholomew lest the physician also demanded some answers. That knowledge made Bartholomew even more determined to prise the truth from the Warden of the Franciscans.

He followed Cynric across the yard and out of the gate, where Father Paul was a pale grey shape in the darkness. The blind friar turned and smiled when he heard two sets of footsteps approaching him. Bartholomew took his arm and they began to walk towards the High Street, with Cynric slipping soundlessly in and out of the shadows behind them, watching over them like some dark guardian angel.

'Warden Pechem will be pleased to see you,' said Paul. 'He is in pain.'

'Bitten by a horse,' mused Cynric, fighting not to smile.

'It was not his fault,' said Paul defensively. 'He was lecturing to a group of novices in the Market Square, using his hands to illustrate the point, as is his wont . . .'

'He is like a windmill,' confirmed Cynric. 'Arms wheeling around like sails in the wind.'

'. . . and one of his hands came too near that horrible beast that Richard Stanmore uses to transport himself around a town where no distance is too great to walk.'

'I take it you disapprove of the Black Bishop of Bedminster?' asked Bartholomew mildly.

Paul nodded grimly. 'The name suits it – overly large and unmanageable. Richard did not even apologise. A group of

Dominicans witnessed the incident, and he merely joined in their mirth.'

'Oxford manners,' said Cynric disapprovingly. 'I remember how rude they were when I was there. People are far more gentle here.'

Bartholomew was sure he was wrong: he recalled very little difference between the rowdy, belligerent scholars he had known at Oxford and the rowdy, belligerent scholars he now knew at Cambridge.

They strode briskly up the High Street, where Paul proved that his memory of the larger potholes and ruts was better than Bartholomew's ability to peer into the gloom, and then turned right towards Bridge Street. The Church of All Saints in the Jewry loomed out of the darkness, and Bartholomew saw the glimmer of light from the candles that had been lit by the vigil-keepers within. Low voices murmured, some of them raised in a chant that rose and fell rhythmically. A pile of rubble lay to one side, where part of the tower had collapsed and its owners – the nuns of St Radegund's Convent – could not afford to have it repaired.

On the left was the dark mass of St John's Hospital, where lamps gleamed under the fastened shutters, and shadows moved back and forth as the friars tended their charges. Next to it was a noisy tavern called the Swan, and Sergeant Orwelle happened to reel out of it as they passed. As the soldier struggled to close the door, Bartholomew glimpsed the smelly cosiness within. He was surprised to see Richard and Heytesbury sitting at a table near the fire, raising slopping goblets in a drunken salute to the surgeon Robin of Grantchester. Heytesbury's face was flushed and he looked happy and healthy, although Richard seemed pale. Their effusive camaraderie with their companions indicated that they had been enjoying the tavern's ale for some time. Bartholomew thought his nephew looked seedy now that he was halfway through his second night of debauchery in a row, and he admired Heytesbury for his energy and dedication to his carousing.

Orwelle finally succeeded in closing the door, and the street was plunged into darkness again; the peace was then shattered by the sound of the soldier's slurred singing. Bartholomew, Cynric and Paul walked on, passing the Round Church, which stood short and sturdy with its little lantern tower perched on top. Suddenly, a figure darted out of the blackness surrounding the graveyard and snatched at Bartholomew's arm. The physician yelped in alarm, while a quick rasping sound indicated that Cynric had drawn his sword and was preparing to use it.

'The owls saw them,' hissed Clippesby wildly, gripping Bartholomew's wrist so tightly that it hurt. 'They told me to warn you.'

'Damned lunatic,' muttered Cynric testily, sheathing his weapon and glancing uneasily up and down the street. 'What is he doing out? I thought Langelee had locked him in his room.'

'I speak to the beasts of the night,' raved Clippesby. 'The owls and the bats and the unicorns.'

'Take him home, Cynric,' said Bartholomew, freeing his arm and feeling the fluttering panic in his stomach begin to subside. 'And make sure he cannot escape again – stay with him, if you have to. He may harm himself when he is like this.'

'He had better not try to harm me,' said Cynric sternly, grabbing Clippesby by the hood and beginning to march him away down the High Street. 'Or I shall see that his days with bats and unicorns are numbered.'

'The poor man,' said Paul with compassion, when the sound of Clippesby's deluded ranting had faded into the night. 'He is quite mad.'

Bartholomew took Paul's arm and guided him the short distance to the Franciscan Friary. 'You do not know anything about secret meetings held in St Radegund's Convent, do you?' he asked, as they waited for their knock to be answered, suspecting that Paul did not, but deciding he should question anyone who might have snippets of information, given that Michael's life might be at stake. The blind friar was disconcertingly perceptive, and it was possible he had heard something pertinent in his friary.

'No,' came the disappointing reply. 'Is it connected to the murders of Walcote and Faricius?'

'Possibly. Have you heard anything about those that may help us?'

Paul shook his head. 'But I knew Faricius. Were you aware that he was writing an essay defending nominalism? I think his room-mates knew, but they are unlikely to mention it, and his Prior was certainly not party to this information.'

'So how do you know?' asked Bartholomew. 'I thought you Franciscans, like Carmelites, were of the opinion that nominalism is heresy.'

'They are in general,' said Paul. 'But the Franciscan Order has not yet reached the point where it informs its members precisely which philosophical tenets they should embrace. Personally, I lean towards nominalism, although I do not feel it is wise to discuss it with my colleagues at the moment. This silly row will soon die down, and then we will all begin to see sense again.'

'And Faricius talked to you about nominalism?' asked Bartholomew. He closed his eyes, disgusted with himself as he realised the answer to that question was staring him in the face. When the dying Faricius had learned that his scrip was missing, he had asked Bartholomew to find it and hand it to Father Paul. And the Carmelite students had mentioned that Faricius had sought other nominalists in the University, including Paul.

Paul's opaque eyes were curiously glassy in the lamplight. 'Faricius attended a lecture on nominalism I gave last year, and he came to ask if we could discuss it. We discovered that we shared similar ideas, and he regularly read parts of his essay to me.'

'How long was it? His friends mentioned it, but I have no idea of its size.'

Paul turned his blind eyes on Bartholomew. 'Obviously, I

288

never saw it, but I imagine it ran to several large pieces of parchment. It was of a very high quality, too: well argued and concise. It would have become a standard text in time.'

'It was that good?' asked Bartholomew. 'I thought it was just an undergraduate analysis of the ideas proposed by Heytesbury.'

'Faricius's work was original and clever. He would have been a great scholar, had he lived.'

'Do you know where this essay is?' asked Bartholomew.

'Faricius kept it under a stone in the churchyard of St John Zachary. His friends Simon Lynne or Horneby will tell you where to look.'

'Lynne has fled,' said Bartholomew. 'But Horneby said the essay is missing.'

'How dreadful,' said Paul. 'I hope it comes to light. I can recall some of his arguments, but Faricius had a writing style that was beautifully concise. I could never hope to emulate it accurately.'

'When he was dying, he asked me to find his scrip and to bring it to you,' said Bartholomew. 'He wanted you to have his essay. What would you have done with it?'

Paul was moved by this, and tears spilled from his eyes and made their way down his leathery cheeks. 'I would have kept it safe until this latest bout of bickering is over and we all have regained our senses. And then I would have had it read at one of the University lectures, so that our greatest scholars would be able to appreciate the purity of his logic and the clarity of his writing.'

A lay-brother came to open the gate, and Bartholomew followed Paul across a courtyard and up some stairs to where Prior Pechem occupied a pleasant suite of rooms that were located above a barrel-vaulted storeroom. The physician looked around him as he entered the Warden's quarters. Like the leaders of the other Orders in Cambridge, the head of the Franciscans knew how to look after himself. Thick rugs spared him the unpleasantness of placing bare feet on the flagged floor, while tapestries adorned with exotic birds and plants meant that he was not obliged to stare at bare walls. There was a large bed heaped with furs near the window.

'Ah, Bartholomew! At last!' came a voice from under the bed-covers. Bartholomew jumped, because he had imagined the room was empty. 'That horse has done me some serious harm.'

'So I understand,' said Bartholomew, advancing on the mountain of furs and peering over them, to see if he could detect the owner of the voice.

'Young Stanmore promised you would not charge me for your services,' said Pechem, as Bartholomew continued to hunt for him. 'I plan to hold him to that – and you.'

'As you wish,' said Bartholomew, tentatively removing one fur, only to find another beneath it. 'Perhaps you will show me the damage, so that I might examine it.'

He started backward as an arm shot though the covers, although there was still no sign of its owner's face. He supposed that avoiding eye contact was the Warden's way of approaching what might prove to be an uncomfortable interview. He perched on the edge of the bed and began to unravel the crude bandage that someone had wrapped around the afflicted limb. After some moments, during which the chamber was still and the only sound was the distant hum of prayers coming from the tiny chapel across the courtyard, Bartholomew removed the bindings to reveal a hand in which the impression of a large set of equine teeth was clearly etched.

'This is not too bad,' he said, rinsing away dried blood with water from a bowl on the table. 'I have a salve of garlic and marsh-mallow that will ease the pain and encourage healing. You should have called me earlier, though. Bites have a nasty habit of festering unless treated quickly.'

'I have never been bitten by a horse before,' came the muffled voice. 'And our herbalist confessed he was uncertain about which of his potions to use.'

'Not his rat poison,' said Bartholomew, in a feeble attempt

at levity. 'Did you know that particular poison is famed from here to Peterborough?'

Pechem chuckled appreciatively. 'I am gratified. Rats can be a serious problem.'

He was silent while Bartholomew continued to clean the wound, and the only sign that the physician was tending a whole person and not merely an arm was when he touched a tender part, and the hand flinched.

'Your book-bearer, Cynric, came to us earlier today,' said Pechem, after a while, evidently deciding he needed something to take his mind away from the uncomfortable operation that was taking place outside his line of vision. 'He wanted to know how a curse might be lifted. I was inclined to dismiss him, because we are not in the habit of dabbling in that sort of thing, but then he told me who the cure was for.'

'Richard,' said Bartholomew.

'Richard,' agreed Pechem. 'I told him to burn the feathers of a pheasant with mint and garlic, say three Ave Marias and then give a groat to the church of his choice. That should see Richard restored to his former likeable disposition.'

'Do the feathers need to belong to a pheasant?' asked Bartholomew recalling Langelee's bemusement when Clippesby – evidently under Cynric's instructions – had caught the porter's bird. 'Or will a cockerel do?'

'I really have no idea,' said Pechem. 'It was something I saw written in one of our more secular books once. Let me know what happens, will you? If it is effective, there are others I would like to see rendered a little more agreeable.'

Personally, Bartholomew thought that a good part of Cambridge would benefit from being treated to such a potion, but he held his peace. He hoped the stench of burning feathers would not make his arrogant nephew ill.

'Kenyngham informed me today that you attended certain meetings in St Radegund's Convent,' he said, not entirely truthfully, as he worked. The fingers that had been wiggling in a tentative trial of movement, stopped abruptly.

'He should not have said that,' said Pechem sharply. 'I told Brother Michael when he questioned me earlier this evening that I did not know what he was talking about.'

'You lied to him,' said Bartholomew flatly.

'We all swore an oath. We vowed never to reveal the subjects that were discussed.'

'Did you make that vow to Walcote?' asked Bartholomew. 'Because if you did, then I suggest that the time has come for openness. Walcote is dead, and Michael is certain that whatever was discussed at the meetings has a bearing on the case.'

'Michael would think that,' said Pechem. 'But what we discussed had nothing to do with him.'

'You should let Michael be the judge of that,' said Bartholomew. 'And now it seems his life may be in danger. You should tell him what you know before more lives are lost – especially his. He is my friend, and I do not want to see him come to harm.'

Pechem's eyes appeared from beneath the bed-covers, small and black in a face that was flushed from the warmth of the furs. 'But we discussed nothing that will endanger Brother Michael.'

'Then what did you talk about?'

'The fact that the nominalism–realism debate seems to be gaining more importance than it warrants. Walcote, to give him his due, tried to suggest that both sides should meet and battle out the issue in the debating hall, but none of us thought that was a good idea.'

'Why not?'

'Well, because we realists might have lost the argument, for a start,' said Pechem. 'Some of those nominalists are clever men – especially the Benedictines and the Austin canons. The Dominicans would have presented us with no problem, since they have no good scholars to speak of.'

'Is that the only reason you did not want an open debate?' asked Bartholomew, thinking that it was a poor theory if its proponents declined to expound it in the lecture halls lest they lost.

'It was the biggest one. The other was that we did not want a riot on our hands. The Carmelites and the Dominicans, in particular, were on the verge of a fight, and we did not want a public occasion to provide the spark to set them on fire.'

'And what else was discussed?' asked Bartholomew.

Pechem sighed. 'I suppose now that Kenyngham has revealed what he knows it makes no difference whether I keep my silence or not. We had plans to donate money anonymously to the town for the Great Bridge to be repaired.'

'Why does that call for secrecy?' asked Bartholomew, who already knew from Adam that repairs to the bridge were discussed.

'Have you used the Great Bridge recently?' asked Pechem, answering with a question of his own.

There had been a bridge over the River Cam since at least the ninth century, and William the Conqueror had raised another to link his newly built castle with the rest of the town. Gradually, the Conqueror's bridge had fallen into disrepair, and in the 1270s a tax had been imposed on the town to build another. The money had promptly been pocketed by the Sheriff, who then declined to produce a new bridge and made superficial repairs to the old one instead. Since then, stone piers had been built, but the wooden planking was soft and rotten with age. The long wet winter had not helped, and the few remaining sound timbers had been stolen by soldiers from the Castle, who wanted to charge people for being rowed across the river in their boats. Anyone using the bridge therefore did so at considerable peril.

'Well?' demanded Pechem, still waiting for his reply. 'Have you crossed the Great Bridge of late? Most sane men have not.'

'I avoid it, if I can,' admitted Bartholomew. 'But the towns-folk would be deeply indebted to the religious Orders for repairing it. Why should you keep such charity secret?'

293

'Because we do not want the town thinking we have so much money that we can afford to scatter it in all directions,' snapped Pechem. 'If we did mend the thing, it would have to be funded discreetly.'

'Is that all you talked about at these meetings? Repairing the Great Bridge and how to avoid a proper debate with the nominalists?'

Pechem sighed and gnawed at his bottom lip. 'We discussed a theft from one of the University chests,' he said reluctantly.

'What theft?' asked Bartholomew, startled. 'What was stolen?'

'Deeds, books, all sorts of things,' said Pechem. 'The main University Chest is a large box stored in the tower of St Mary's Church. Since an attempt was made to steal it some years ago, a duplicate chest has been stored at the Carmelite Friary.'

'I know all this,' said Bartholomew. 'But when did this recent theft happen? I always understood that St Mary's tower was virtually impregnable these days, and that it was impossible to gain access to it without the right keys.'

'So it is,' said Pechem. 'It was the chest at the Carmelite Friary that was ransacked, not the one in St Mary's Church.'

'*When* was it attacked?' asked Bartholomew a second time.

'Christmas.'

'That was months ago. Why was it kept secret?'

'That is easy to answer,' said Pechem. 'When it was discovered that the chest had been breached, Prior Lincolne – who, as head of the Carmelite Order in Cambridge, is responsible for guarding it – immediately sent for the Junior Proctor to investigate.'

'Why Walcote? Why not Michael? Presumably, this theft was taken very seriously?'

'Very seriously,' agreed Pechem. 'But we could not have Brother Michael investigating the theft, could we?'

'Why not?' pressed Bartholomew. 'He is the Senior Proctor. It is his job.'

'Perhaps it is,' said Pechem. 'But not when there was plenty of evidence to suggest that it was Michael who committed the theft in the first place.'

Bartholomew returned to Michaelhouse, and was admitted by a student because the College was short of night porters. Martin Arbury had been reading by candlelight, and asked the physician for a summary of Heytesbury's position on accelerating motion. Bartholomew obliged, and the youngster listened intently before returning to his studies.

Bartholomew wanted to talk to Michael, but he discovered that the monk and Langelee had done some serious harm to Langelee's barrel of wine, and were still ensconced in comradely bonhomie next to the fire, toasting each other's health. Their carousing could be heard all over the courtyard, and was probably keeping more than one weary student from his sleep. The physician wondered how Langelee felt able to justify the heavy fines he imposed on the scholars he caught doing the same thing.

He declined to join them, and instead went to Kenyngham's room. He knocked softly on the door and slipped inside. Kenyngham was asleep, as were the three students who shared his room. They lay on straw mattresses that were stored under Kenyngham's bed during the day and were brought out to cover the whole floor at night. Their steady breathing indicated that Bartholomew's entry had not woken them, and he wondered whether they had been at the wine themselves, for the sounds of Langelee and Michael enjoying themselves in the room virtually above their heads were deafening. He sat on the edge of Kenyngham's bed and shook the elderly Gilbertine awake.

'I know what you discussed at these meetings,' he whispered when the friar sat up rubbing his eyes. 'The theft from the chest in the Carmelite Friary.'

He heard Kenyngham sigh softly. 'Come outside, Matthew. My students mark all seven offices at church during Holy Week, and it will not do if they fall asleep during them because you want to talk to me in the middle of the night.'

If Kenyngham's students were attending all the religious offices, as well as their morning lectures, no wonder they all slept so deeply, thought Bartholomew. He waited for Kenyngham to draw on a pair of shoes, then followed him into the courtyard.

'What is that?' asked Kenyngham, as his sleep-befuddled wits sharpened and he became aware of the row emanating from Langelee's room. 'I am surprised the Master permits such a racket at this time of night.'

'I visited Prior Pechem tonight,' said Bartholomew. 'He told me about the Carmelites' theft.'

'He should not have done that,' said Kenyngham, gazing up at the dark sky above. 'But now you know, I suppose there is no point in further secrecy. I wish you had not meddled: you are Michael's friend.'

'Michael is not a thief,' said Bartholomew. 'He skates on thin ice from time to time, but he would never steal.'

'The evidence suggests otherwise,' said Kenyngham. 'He was the only person with access to a key, other than Chancellor Tynkell.'

'That means nothing,' said Bartholomew. 'Someone could have used a knife to prise the chest open.'

'The master locksmith inspected it the morning after the theft. He told Walcote that it had been breached because someone had a key, not because it had been forced open.'

'But Tynkell – or even Michael himself – could have mislaid the key or left it unguarded, enabling someone else to make a copy,' Bartholomew pointed out. 'This so-called "evidence" of yours does not prove that Michael is a criminal.'

'I have not finished yet,' said Kenyngham. 'Michael was actually *seen* entering the friary by at least two people the evening the theft was committed. Walcote interviewed every Carmelite, and it was ascertained beyond the shadow of a doubt that he had visited no one there that night.'

'But a good deal of Michael's business is secret,' objected Bartholomew. 'Remember what happened when Langelee revealed his pending arrangements with Heytesbury last year? There was a perfectly honest explanation, but he could not tell anyone because of the delicacy of the negotiations.'

'There is yet more evidence against Michael,' Kenyngham went on. 'The same night, he was seen by his own beadles carrying a bulging bag from Milne Street – where the Carmelite Friary is located – to Michaelhouse. Michael told them it contained fresh bread as a gift to his Michaelhouse colleagues. But we had no fresh bread that morning.'

'How can you be sure of that?' demanded Bartholomew, becoming distressed as Kenyngham's accusations mounted. 'I doubt you remember what you had for breakfast this morning, let alone what you ate months ago, and Michael *does* occasionally buy bread for us.'

'But I do remember, Matthew,' Kenyngham insisted. 'It was Christmas Day. Traditionally, we give the parish children their breakfast then, but that morning we only had stale bread to offer.'

Bartholomew knew that was true, because he vividly recalled the expressions of abject disappointment in the faces of the children who had been waiting since dawn for their yearly treat. He also remembered that it had been Michael who had quietly suggested that they return that afternoon, when the children were given bread, apples, milk and cheese paid for from his own pocket. The fat monk had a soft spot for children.

'Walcote then visited the baker,' Kenyngham continued. 'The baker was unequivocal: there was some problem with the oven, which meant that no one had fresh bread that night – including Michael. Whatever he had been carrying was certainly not food.'

'And you think this proves Michael is guilty of theft?' asked Bartholomew.

'Well, yes,' said Kenyngham. 'And so would you, if Michael were someone other than your dearest friend.'

'There will be a rational explanation for all of it,' Bartholomew declared.

'I wish that were true,' said Kenyngham. 'But I do not see how there can be. Do you understand now why I declined to tell you what we discussed at St Radegund's Convent?'

Bartholomew nodded reluctantly. 'What else did you talk about? Was there any mention of a plot to kill Michael?'

'I have already told you there was not,' said Kenyngham. 'Who said there was?'

'Prior Morden.'

Kenyngham shook his head. 'Morden was at no meeting I ever attended.'

'Then what about the dead beadle and the letter?' asked Bartholomew. 'Surely that is good evidence that something was afoot?'

Kenyngham sighed tiredly. 'I know nothing of this. What beadle and what letter?'

'A beadle called Rob Smyth drowned in a puddle last winter. Walcote found a letter in his possession that gave details of a plot against Michael's life.'

'Was Michael with you when Morden spun this tale?'

'Of course,' said Bartholomew. 'We are investigating Walcote's murder and were trying to understand the nature of these secret meetings, so that we could work out who might have killed him.'

Kenyngham scrubbed at his halo of fluffy white hair. 'There is one explanation for why Morden chose to fabricate such lies, although I doubt you will appreciate the logic behind it.'

'What?' asked Bartholomew warily.

'Walcote was looking into the theft from the Carmelite Friary. He had collected enough evidence to incriminate Michael, and was waiting for an opportunity to confront him with it. Then he was murdered. Obviously, Morden was not going to say all this with Michael towering over him, and so he invented some silly story to distract Michael's attention from the real issue.'

Bartholomew gazed at Kenyngham in utter disbelief. 'Surely you are not suggesting that Michael is investigating

298

a murder he committed himself? How could you even begin to think such a thing?'

'Whoever hanged Walcote was strong, and probably had a couple of henchmen to help,' said Kenyngham heavily. 'Michael's beadles are loyal to him, especially Tom Meadowman. The killer was also able to stalk the streets at night; Michael regularly patrols the town, and few know it as well as he does.'

'This is insane,' said Bartholomew, beginning to back away from Kenyngham as though he was infected by a virulent contagion. 'It is all gross supposition. The rawest undergraduate could destroy your arguments like a house of straw.'

'Poor Walcote was horrified by his discoveries,' Kenyngham went on relentlessly. 'He told us he did not know what to do next, and said it was not pleasant for him to learn that a man he admired, and who is the embodiment of law and order in the University, is corrupt.'

'I do not believe I am hearing this,' said Bartholomew. He took another step away from Kenyngham, then turned his back on the Gilbertine and began to walk across the yard. 'I refuse to listen to any more of it.'

'God be with you, Matthew,' came Kenyngham's voice, drifting across the yard as he walked. 'And do not let friendship blind you to the truth.'

From the shadows near his staircase, Bartholomew watched Kenyngham return to his bed, then paced back and forth in Michaelhouse's dark yard, uncertain whether to join Michael and Langelee in the Master's quarters and tell them what he had learned from Kenyngham, or whether to go to his room and give himself time to identify more flaws in Kenyngham's story. The voices of Michael and Langelee, slurred from the wine, echoed around the stone buildings as they continued to carouse.

Bartholomew was unable to concentrate over their racket, and so he walked through the kitchens and opened a small back door, which led to a large garden that sloped towards the river. The grounds boasted vegetable plots that provided stringy cabbages and tough turnips, and a small orchard of apple and pear trees. Near the gate was Agatha's herb garden, a neat rectangle of thyme, mint, rosemary and parsley. Even on a cold winter night, their comfortingly familiar scents pervaded the air.

Next to one of the walls a tree had fallen many years before, and the trunk provided a comfortable seat for scholars who wanted to be alone with their thoughts. In the summer it was an attractive place shaded by leaves and carpeted with long green grass; at night in late winter, it was less appealing, with leafless branches clawing at the dark sky and a sprinkling of frost underfoot, but at least it was quiet. Bartholomew sat on the trunk and leaned back against the wall, marshalling his thoughts.

The physician knew perfectly well that Michael was not above breaking all kinds of rules in order to achieve his objectives. He was also sure that the monk treated his religious vows with a certain degree of laxness, that he owned property he should not have had, and that the Seven Deadly Sins – especially Gluttony and Lust – were what provided him with his greatest enjoyment in life. The monk was a conspirator, he was not averse to lying, and he regularly cheated the people with whom he dealt – as Heytesbury would discover if he ever signed Michael's contract. He played power games with the wealthy and influential, and was vindictive to people who tried to treat him in the same shabby way as he treated them. And despite the mutual back-slapping that was taking place, even as Bartholomew agonised over his quandary, Langelee had been responsible for Michael not being elected as Master, and Bartholomew knew Michael had not forgiven him. At some point in the future, Michael would have his revenge.

But to claim that Michael was a thief – and worse – was another matter entirely. Bartholomew's instinctive reaction was to dismiss what Kenyngham had told him, and to believe that Walcote had been mistaken. And yet the evidence for

Michael's guilt was compelling – especially the fact that he had been present in the Carmelite Friary without an excuse at the time of the theft, and that he had been seen carrying a bulky sack from the friary towards Michaelhouse. And then he had lied about the sack's contents.

There was something else, too. Bartholomew leaned forward and buried his head in his hands, reluctant to confront the mounting tide of evidence against Michael. When Bartholomew had first agreed to help the monk, they had sat together in Michael's room and Bartholomew had made notes on a scrap of used parchment. Walcote had written on it, and then someone – possibly Walcote but probably Michael – had scraped it and covered it in a thin layer of chalk so that it could be used again. But the scraper had done a poor job: Bartholomew had been able to read what had been written previously, and he recalled that one side had contained a list of items stolen from the chest at the Carmelite Friary.

So, what did that tell him? That Michael knew about Walcote's investigation, and he had even managed to purloin a list of the very items he himself had stolen? Or was the parchment just some scrap Michael had grabbed without looking at it, and its presence in his room purely coincidence? Bartholomew decided it had to be the latter. Michael was no burglar.

He sighed and leaned back against the orchard wall, gazing up at the dark sky above. He realised that he would have to prove Michael's innocence – that if he could show Michael had not committed the theft, then no one would have grounds on which to accuse him of murdering his Junior Proctor. But where was he to begin? How could he investigate a crime that had taken place months before? Any evidence that might have been left at the scene of the burglary would be long since gone.

He stood abruptly, and paced in front of the tree-trunk. Should he tell Michael what was being said about him, so that they could work together to clear the monk of the charges? Or would Michael be so outraged by the accusations that he would decline to respond to them at all, and forbid Bartholomew to give them credence by investigating on his behalf? He knew that the monk could be stubborn about such things. He also knew that Michael's position as Senior Proctor did not make him popular with everyone, and that many scholars would love to see him fall from grace, especially those who had fallen foul of his quick mind and sharp tongue. It would not be easy to exonerate him in some circles, no matter how much evidence Bartholomew might provide to the contrary.

The physician rubbed a hand through his hair, trying to decide upon the best course of action. Michael would know immediately if Bartholomew was concealing something important from him, and the physician thought that there had been more than enough lies already: he owed Michael his honesty. Then, if Michael reacted as Bartholomew feared, and treated the accusations with dismissive contempt, the physician would have to conduct his own investigation to clear his friend's name secretly, perhaps with Meadowman's help.

He was too tired to discuss the affair with the monk that night, and decided to wait until morning. Michael was also drunk, and drunkenness often led to belligerence. Bartholomew did not want to start some argument for the whole College to hear, or run the risk of the monk damaging his chances of proving his innocence by storming off into the night to inform the heads of the religious Orders that they were wrong.

He left the orchard and made his way back to his room. The bells started to chime as he walked past Agatha's neat rows of herbs, and he realised that it was time for the midnight vigil that many people kept in Easter Week. He was grateful that Michaelhouse did not insist that its scholars undertook such duties, as well as the other offices they were obliged to attend.

The kitchens were cold and empty as he walked through

302

them, and even the cat that usually slept there had gone to find a warmer spot to pass the night. The yard was also deserted, except for Walter the porter's cockerel, now minus several of its tail feathers. Michael and Langelee had moved on from noisy bonhomie, and were at the stage where they were sharing muttered confidences. Bartholomew knew Michael would learn a lot more about Langelee than Langelee would ever know about him, and as he passed under Langelee's window, he thought he heard the distinctive sound of Michael's chuckle.

He stood still for a moment, gazing up at the dark silhouettes of the buildings opposite. A soft groan invaded his thoughts. At first, he did not know where it had come from, but then he heard snoring coming from the chamber Suttone shared with three lively students from Lincolnshire: the sound had either been Suttone himself, or perhaps one of his students, caught in some restless dream. Then there was a blood-chilling howl followed by a babbling voice, which made him leap in alarm and silenced the soft sounds of merriment issuing from Langelee's chamber. Bartholomew heard Cynric sharply informing Clippesby that people were sleeping, and that he had best save his screeches for the daytime.

Bartholomew heaved a sigh of relief, and heard the muted conversation resume in Langelee's quarters. Nocturnal disturbances were commonplace when Clippesby was going through one of his episodes, and there was nothing anyone could do but try to calm him. Cynric seemed to have it under control, so, taking a final breath of sweet night air that was scented with a faint tang of salt from the marshes to the north, Bartholomew turned and entered his room.

It was dark inside his chamber without a candle, and Bartholomew groped around blindly, swearing under his breath when he stubbed his toe on the end of the bed. He ran his hands up the damp wall until his fingers encountered the wooden pegs that had been driven into it, and then hung up his cloak and tabard. He tugged off his boots, setting them near the window in the futile hope that the icy blasts that whistled under the shutters might serve to dry them out a little, and then washed in the jug of water left for him each night. The surface of the water cracked when he touched it, and tiny slivers of ice scratched him as he splashed handfuls of it over his face and neck. Finally, hopping on tiptoe on the freezing flagstones, with his hands aching and burning from the coldness of the water, he leapt into the bed.

The first few moments in bed during the winter were never pleasant, and on very cold nights, the unpleasantness sometimes lasted until dawn. The bed-covers were damp, and Bartholomew did not know which was worse: the chill wetness that forced him to curl into a tight ball until the warmth of his body began to drive the cold away, or the moistness that made him feel sticky and clammy once it had warmed up. He lay shivering in his night-shirt and hose, his hands tucked under his arms, rubbing his feet together in a futile attempt to warm them.

Gradually, the cold began to recede and he was able to uncoil himself bit by bit, until his feet were at the end of the bed. Once the misery of the icy blankets had been breached, his mind automatically returned to Michael and the accusations regarding the Carmelites' chest. He tried not to think about it, and to consider more pleasant matters, such as the treatment of the lepers at Stourbridge or the arguments he might use on Langelee regarding cleaning of the College latrines. But even these fascinating issues failed to distract him, and he found himself once again pondering how best to prove Michael's innocence.

He tossed and turned in an exhausting half-sleep, while his mind teemed with questions. He was restless enough to become quite hot, and the moist blankets stuck to him in a restricting kind of way that made him hotter still. At last he sat up, knowing that he would be unable to rest properly until he had spoken to Michael. He listened carefully, trying to hear whether the monk was still with Langelee, or whether he had returned to his room. A small creak from above indicated that he was at home, and was probably sitting at his table, working in the silence of the night.

Now grateful for the sensation of cool stone against his bare skin, Bartholomew walked across his room and opened the door, stepping into the small hallway beyond. Lamplight still gleamed under the window shutters in Langelee's quarters, and he imagined that Michael was not the only one to take the opportunity of the peace and quiet to do some work. He heard the bell of St Mary begin to toll, announcing the office of nocturns for those who were awake. It was three o'clock.

He turned, and began to grope his way forward until he encountered the wooden stairs that led to the upper floor, swearing under his breath when he stubbed his toe a second time that evening, this time on the metal scraper on which scholars were supposed to remove the worst of the mud from their shoes before entering their rooms. It was heavy and hard, and Bartholomew hopped around for several moments in mute agony as the pain shot through his foot. He hoped his inadvertent antics had not disturbed the scholars who were sleeping in the room opposite.

In Michaelhouse, each 'staircase' had four rooms: two on the ground floor and two on the upper floor. Suttone, the skeletal Carmelite, lived in the room opposite Bartholomew's, and the sounds of snoring that issued through the door suggested that he and his room-mates were doing what all decent people should be doing so late in the night – which was certainly not preparing to tell a friend that he was accused of murder and theft.

Bartholomew turned to the stairs and began to climb. They were rough and gritty under his bare feet, and at one point he trod on something soft. He did not even want to consider what it might be, and made a mental note to ask Agatha to see it cleaned up the following day.

The chamber opposite Michael's was occupied by three

elderly men whom Langelee had admitted to the College. They were priests who found the daily running of a parish too much and who wanted nothing more than to be provided with a bed at night, regular meals and a little teaching. The snores emanating from the old men's chamber were even louder than the ones issuing from Suttone's room, and Bartholomew wondered whether he would feel the door vibrating if he put his hand on it.

There was a ribbon of light under Michael's door, and another slight creak indicated that the monk was moving between the table and the shelves where he kept his pens and parchment, treading softly so that he would not disturb Bartholomew sleeping below. The physician was about to unlatch the door, when he heard the unmistakable sound of Michael laugh. But it had not come from his own chamber: it had come from Langelee's quarters across the courtyard, where, it seemed, he was still enjoying the Master's hospitality.

Then who was moving so carefully in the monk's room? Was it a Michaelhouse colleague looking for a book or a scroll that might have been borrowed from the College's library? But it was late to be ransacking the room of a friend for a book, and most people would have waited until the morning to ask for it. The only alternative was that it was an intruder from outside the College, and that whoever it was had no business to be there.

Bartholomew considered his options. He could run across the yard to fetch Michael and Langelee, both of whom were large men and a match for any would-be thief. But the intruder might escape while Bartholomew was rousing them, and then they would never know his identity. He supposed he could wake Suttone and his students, but Suttone was not a man noted for courage, and Bartholomew was afraid he would decline to help and forbid his students to become involved, too. There was only one real choice: he would have to approach the intruder himself. He had heard no voices, so he assumed the burglar was alone.

He took a deep breath to steady himself, and was reaching out to unclip the latch when the light disappeared as the candle was extinguished. Simultaneously, the door was jerked open. Bartholomew had a brief glimpse of a hooded outline in the doorway and heard a sharp intake of breath when, presumably, the intruder also saw Bartholomew. For a moment, neither of them did anything. Then the intruder struck.

Bartholomew found himself wrestled against the wall with one arm twisted behind his back. It happened so quickly that he had no time to react, and he was unable to move. Light footsteps tapped on the stairs as he was held still while someone else fled. So, there had been two people after all. He opened his mouth to yell, but the sound froze in his throat when he felt the prick of a knife against his throat. He tried to struggle, but the person who held him was strong and experienced, and he was barely able to breathe, let alone wriggle free.

He kicked backwards, but this only resulted in him being held even tighter. Then he became aware that his captor was bracing himself, and had the distinct impression the man was preparing to use the knife that lay in a cold line across his neck. Desperation gave Bartholomew the strength he needed. Gritting his teeth against the searing pain of his bent arm, he pushed away from the wall with all his might and succeeded in freeing himself.

Twisting around quickly, he kicked out as hard as he could, but his bare feet made little impression on the shadowy figure that now advanced with serious purpose. In the gloom of the hallway he saw the silhouette of a long, wicked-looking knife, and threw himself backwards as the blade began to descend. A metallic screech sounded as the knife blade met with plaster instead of flesh. He lunged at the intruder while the man was off-balance from the force of the blow, and succeeded in gripping the arm that wielded the knife. He opened his mouth to yell for help, but the intruder was an experienced fighter who knew that if

Bartholomew raised the alarm he would be caught. He reacted quickly, and the howl died in Bartholomew's throat as the intruder let himself fall backwards, pulling Bartholomew with him.

Still desperately trying to gain control of the knife, Bartholomew and his attacker crashed down the stairs in a confused tangle of arms and legs. The intruder landed on top, and used the advantage to struggle free of Bartholomew's grasp and head for the rectangle of faint light that marked the door. Bartholomew leapt to his feet to follow, but the shoe scraper was in the way, and he fell headlong. He glanced up in time to see a dark figure reach the wicket gate, tug it open and disappear into the lane outside.

Suttone's door flew open, and Bartholomew heard the scratch of tinder before the wavering halo of a candle illuminated the hallway. He climbed to his feet, but Suttone's students were milling around, and by the time he had extricated himself from them, it was too late to follow. The intruder would have reached the top of Foule Lane, and there was no way of telling whether he had turned towards the river, where he could hide among the wharfs, reeds and long grass that ran along the banks, or towards the High Street, where he could evade the night patrols by concealing himself in the overgrown churchyards of All Saints in the Jewry, St Clement's or St John Zachary. Bartholomew knew that pursuit was futile. He closed his eyes in mute frustration and allowed himself to slide down the wall until he was in a sitting position.

'My dear fellow,' cried Suttone in alarm, rushing to kneel next to him. 'What has happened?'

'He has been drinking with Brother Michael and Master Langelee all night,' said one of the students knowledgeably. 'It would not be difficult to fall down the stairs after a night of wine with those two. I certainly could not keep up with them.'

'I have not been drinking,' said Bartholomew tiredly. 'Someone broke into Michael's room and produced a knife

308

when I tried to stop him. Will someone fetch him and tell him what has happened?'

'Why would anyone want to burgle Michael?' asked Suttone, nodding to one of his students to do as Bartholomew asked. 'He owns nothing worth stealing. None of us do, otherwise we would all eat something other than fish-giblet soup for dinner.'

'Well, someone did,' said Bartholomew irritably. 'You can see from here that the wicket gate is open, where this man made his escape.'

Suttone screwed up his eyes as he squinted in the darkness. 'You are right. Go and secure it quickly, before we have marauding Dominicans in here.'

This last comment was directed at another of his students, who obligingly sped away to re-lock the door. Now that the skirmish was over and the attackers had fled, Bartholomew felt an unpleasant queasiness in his stomach. It was partly because he was cold, but it was also because he realised he had been foolish to try to take on the intruders alone, and that he should have fetched help. Not only had he rashly risked his life, but he had thrown away an opportunity to learn more about the case that had seen the University's Junior Proctor murdered and the Senior Proctor facing charges of theft.

'Martin Arbury is on duty this week, because Walter the porter is away,' said Suttone. 'I agreed to exempt him from a disputation, because Master Langelee thought he would be in no fit state for an examination if he had been awake all night. We discussed it at the last Fellows' meeting, if you recall.'

Bartholomew began to cross the yard, hobbling on the stones and grit that hurt his bare feet. 'Arbury is a reliable lad. What was he thinking of to let that pair of thieves in?'

As he drew closer to the gate, the answer to his question became clear. Arbury was half sitting and half lying against the wall of the porters' lodge, all but invisible as his black tabard blended into the darkness that surrounded him. His fair head lolled to one side, and there was a pitchy stain on the ground beneath him.

'Oh, no!' whispered Suttone in horror, his big hands fumbling to cross himself. 'What has happened? Is he dead?'

'Yes,' said Bartholomew, after a brief examination revealed that the lad was cool to the touch and that there was no life-beat in his neck. 'Someone has stabbed him.'

chapter 9

BARTHOLOMEW WAS COVERING ARBURY'S FACE WITH A sheet when Michael and Langelee arrived. The warm, sweet smell of wine preceded them, and Bartholomew questioned whether either was in a fit state to understand what had happened. Langelee's florid face was sweaty, and his eyes were puffy and red. Michael looked no different than usual, although he was slightly flushed. Cynric was among those who came hurrying to see what the fuss was about, with Clippesby's arm held firmly in one hand.

'My God!' breathed Langelee, looking at the body of the student in horror.

'Two people were ransacking your room,' Bartholomew explained to Michael. 'I tried to catch them, but they escaped.'

'I told you,' wailed Clippesby. 'I warned you tonight that there were bad men at large. You repaid me by locking me away.'

Bartholomew inspected him closely. 'Did you see them?'

Clippesby shook his head. 'The owls told me. But I saw them enter the College, when I was looking out of the window. I yelled to you, but Cynric told me to be quiet.'

'Who were they?' demanded Michael. 'Did you see their faces?'

Clippesby swallowed. 'Two men wearing dark clothes. They were just shadows in the dark.'

'And what about you?' asked Michael, turning to Bartholomew. 'Can you identify them?'

'No. One drew a knife, and we pushed and shoved at each other before he toppled us both down the stairs. As Clippesby says, it was dark.'

'What were you thinking of?' snapped Michael furiously. 'You are not a beadle, and you should not be challenging armed intruders to fights in the middle of the night.'

'I have no intention of making a habit of this,' replied Bartholomew testily, nettled by Michael's anger.

'And these intruders stabbed Arbury on their way out?' asked Langelee, kneeling unsteadily next to the dead scholar and pulling the sheet away so that he could inspect the young man's face. 'He is very cold. I must raise some funds so that the students on guard duty have a fire—'

'He is cold because he was stabbed hours ago,' interrupted Bartholomew impatiently. Langelee was often slow on the uptake, but large quantities of wine had made him worse. 'I imagine he opened the door to these men, and they knifed him so that they could enter without him raising the alarm.'

'And then they went to my room?' asked Michael, his eyes huge in his flabby face.

Bartholomew sighed irritably. 'I have no idea what they did next. All I can tell you is that I caught them leaving your chamber.'

'All right, Matt,' said Michael gently. 'I know you are distressed by yet another unnecessary death – as am I – but that is no reason to snap at me. I am only trying to learn what happened.'

Bartholomew rubbed his hand through his hair and stared away into the darkness of the night. Michael was right: the incident had left him badly shaken. But it was his own stupidity that made him angry. He should not have tried to take on the intruders without summoning help, and he now wished he had listened to Clippesby when he had met him earlier that evening. For all his ravings, the Dominican occasionally made very astute observations, and the physician realised he should not have dismissed him so readily.

Langelee stood, grabbing Michael's arm to steady himself. 'Arbury is clearly beyond anything Bartholomew can do, so I commit him to your hands, Suttone. You can mount a vigil for him. Take him to the hall, though, not to the church. I do not want you leaving Michaelhouse at this hour of the night when there are killers at large.' He turned to Bartholomew. 'But before Suttone removes Arbury, is there anything you need to do? I know your examination of bodies in the past has helped you to identify killers.'

Bartholomew shook his head. 'All I can tell you is that he died from a single wound to the chest, and that he bled to death.'

'And you think this happened some time ago, because he is cold?' clarified Langelee.

Bartholomew nodded. 'But I cannot tell you exactly when.'

'I see,' said Langelee. He turned to Michael. 'We should go to your room, to see whether anything is missing.'

'Nothing will be missing,' replied Michael. 'I have very little to steal.'

'What about your collection of gold crosses?' asked Langelee immediately. 'And your fine array of habits and expensive cloaks? And since your office at St Mary's is not particularly secure, I expect you store certain documents here, too.'

Michael shook his head. 'I keep my crosses behind a stone in the hearth – and I defy even Cynric to identify which one. Meanwhile, there is not exactly a thriving market for used Benedictine garments. Mine are distinctively large, and a thief would be caught immediately if he tried to sell any of those at Ely Hall.'

'And the documents?' asked Bartholomew.

The monk shrugged. 'Anything important is locked in the chests at St Mary's or the Carmelite Friary. There is nothing in my room worth taking.'

'We should check anyway,' said Langelee, beginning to walk across the courtyard towards Michael's room.

Bartholomew and Michael followed him, leaving Suttone and his students to carry Arbury to the hall and begin their prayers for a soul that had died without the benefit of final

313

absolution. As he climbed the stairs, Bartholomew saw the deep groove where the knife had raked the plaster in the wall. He shivered, not wanting to think of the force behind a blow that had left such a mark. Michael reached out to touch it, then turned to scowl at the physician, making it clear that he was unimpressed by the foolish risk his friend had taken.

The shock of the brief encounter with the intruders and finding Arbury dead was beginning to take its toll. Bartholomew felt exhausted, while his bare feet were so cold that he could barely feel them. The chill reached right through his bones to settle in the pit of his stomach, and he wondered whether he would ever be warm again.

Langelee pushed open the door to Michael's room and the three scholars looked around them. Michael's possessions had been dragged from their shelves and chests and scattered, so that the chamber looked as if a violent wind had torn through it. Michael took a sharp intake of breath when he saw the mess, and Langelee whistled, holding up the lamp so that it illuminated every corner.

'The thief was certainly thorough. I wonder if he found what he wanted.'

'They,' corrected Bartholomew. 'There were two of them. I heard the feet of one running down the stairs, while the other fought with me.'

'So, the first intruder did battle with you to allow the other to escape,' summarised Langelee. 'Was the first bigger than the second?'

'I did not see the one who ran,' said Bartholomew tiredly. 'I only heard his footsteps. I suppose he did sound small and light, though. Or perhaps he was on tiptoe because he was in the middle of a burglary. I really do not know.'

'And the first?' pressed Langelee. 'Is there anything you can tell us about him? Was he taller than you? Fatter? Was he wearing a cloak, or just hose and shirt? Was there anything at all that you remember about him – perhaps a distinctive smell or a peculiar physical feature.'

314

'It was dark,' said Bartholomew wearily. 'And he was waving a knife at me. I noticed very little about him, other than that. He knew what he was doing, though; he was a competent fighter.'

'And you took him on,' muttered Michael. He slumped down on his bed and surveyed the mess with round eyes. 'I do not know whether I am more angry with you for risking your life, or with whoever had the audacity to enter the Senior Proctor's College and go through his personal effects.'

'Have you been keeping a record of your murder investigation?' asked Langelee, sitting next to him and scratching his head as he tried to think of reasons why Michael's room should have been subjected to such treatment. 'Perhaps that is what they were looking for, so that they could see how close you are to catching them.'

'I am not close at all,' said Michael gloomily. He picked up a linen shirt that had been tossed carelessly on the floor, flinging it just as carelessly on to the chest that stood under the window. As he did so, something fell out. Bartholomew leaned down to retrieve it. It was a tiny glove, like something that had been made for a child.

'A boy was one of the intruders?' asked Langelee, taking it from him and turning it over in his hands. 'I suppose it makes sense. A small child could search places that an adult could not reach. I have heard of monkeys being used for such purposes.'

'You said the footsteps of the second intruder sounded light,' said Michael to Bartholomew. 'Could they have belonged to a child?'

'It is possible,' said Bartholomew, snatching the glove from Langelee and inspecting it in the candlelight. 'But I do not think this belongs to a child. I think it belongs to Prior Morden, the leader of the Dominicans.'

It was nearing dawn, and the dense black of the sky was just beginning to show signs of brightening, although it would be another hour before it was light enough to see. Even at that early hour the town was stirring, and a lone cart could be heard rattling up the High Street on its way to the Market Square. A dog barked, and somewhere two people were greeting each other cheerfully. A dampness was in the faint wind that rustled the few dead leaves remaining on the winter branches, threatening more rain that day, and the sky was its usual leaden grey.

Bartholomew sat with Michael in Langelee's room, sipping near-boiling ale that he knew nevertheless would not drive out the chilly sensation that still sat in the pit of his stomach.

'And you say young Arbury was alive when you returned from tending Pechem at the Franciscan Friary?' asked Langelee of Bartholomew again. 'He opened the gate for you?'

Bartholomew nodded. 'He had been reading Heytesbury's *Regulae Solvendi Sophismata*, and he asked me a question about it.'

'Then you went to the kitchens, and on the way back the bells were chiming for the midnight vigil and you heard him groan,' Langelee went on.

'Not quite,' said Bartholomew. He did not want to tell Michael about Kenyngham's accusation in front of Langelee, who had demonstrated in the past that he was not averse to using such information to suit his own ends. He would speak to the monk later, when they were alone. 'I heard a groan, but I thought it was Suttone or his students making noises in their sleep. I realise now that it may have been Arbury. I wish I had checked.'

'But Clippesby knew what was happening,' said Michael. 'Damn the man! If he was not so habitually strange, you would have known to take him seriously.'

'Arbury's injury was serious; you would not have been able to save him anyway,' said Langelee kindly. 'I am no physician, but I have seen my share of knife wounds. I think it would have made no difference whether you had found him three hours earlier or not.'

316

'We could have asked who attacked him, though,' said Michael. 'And we might have caught his murderers, who then spent half the night rummaging in my room.'

'But more important yet, I might have been able to make his last moments more comfortable,' snapped Bartholomew, nettled by Michael's pragmatic approach to the student's death. 'He would not have bled to death all alone and in the bitter chill of a March night.'

Michael's large face became gentle. 'I am sorry, Matt. I did not mean to sound callous. It is just that I now have four murders to investigate – Faricius, Kyrkeby, Walcote and Arbury – and I have no idea what to do about any of them.'

'At least you know the motive for Arbury's death,' said Langelee. 'He was killed because someone wanted to search your room. Either they stabbed him as soon as he opened the gate, or they killed him when he would not let them in.'

'The former, probably,' said Michael thoughtfully. 'And if Matt is right, then they spent at least three hours searching my room – from the beginning of the midnight vigil, by which time Arbury had been stabbed, until he heard the bells chime for nocturns, when they were just leaving.'

'What do you possess – or what do they think you possess – that would warrant such an exhaustive search?' asked Langelee. He gestured around his own quarters. 'It would not take anyone long to rifle through my belongings, even including all the College muniments.'

'I really cannot imagine what they wanted,' said Michael. 'As I told you, I leave the most sensitive documents in the University chests.'

'All of them?' asked Bartholomew. 'Are you sure there is nothing that you might have brought home? And Langelee has a good point – perhaps we should consider what they may have *thought* you had, rather than what you actually do have.'

'What about the deed signing the two farms and the church to Oxford?' asked Langelee. 'Where do you keep that? Presumably there is only one copy, because Heytesbury has not signed it yet – there would be no point in copying it until he has agreed to its contents.'

Michael dropped his hand to his scrip. 'I have that in here. I do not know when Heytesbury will agree to sign, and so I have been carrying it about with me recently, so I can be ready the moment he relents. But why would anyone want to steal that?'

'Because they do not want you to pass this property to Oxford?' suggested Bartholomew. 'Thanks to Langelee, a lot of people know you have some kind of arrangement in progress, and not everyone is sufficiently far sighted to see that you have the ultimate good of Cambridge in mind.'

'I have apologised for that *ad nauseam*,' protested Langelee wearily. 'How much longer will you hold it against me?'

'I suppose someone may think that the best way to prevent Oxford from getting what is perceived to be valuable property is to steal the deed of transfer,' said Michael, ignoring Langelee's objections and addressing Bartholomew. 'But we are forgetting that one of the culprits seems to have been Prior Morden. I did not know he felt so strongly about it.'

'We have never discussed it with him,' said Bartholomew. 'Perhaps he does. He is certainly the kind of man to latch on to an idea like a limpet and follow it doggedly. He seems to have done exactly that by championing the cause of nominalism.'

Langelee sighed. 'I am a philosopher by training, but I find this nominalism–realism debate immensely dull. Am I alone in this? Is there not another living soul who would rather talk about something else?'

'Not among the religious Orders at the moment,' said Michael. 'They are using it as an excuse to rekindle ancient hatreds of each other. But I did not know that Morden was against passing property to Oxford. After all, Heytesbury is a nominalist, so Morden should approve.'

'That is not logical,' said Bartholomew. 'Just because

Morden is a nominalist does not mean that he is willing to share his worldly goods – or those of his University – with other nominalists.'

'You have not explained how you happened to be outside Michael's room at that hour of the night, Bartholomew,' said Langelee, moving on to other questions. 'Did you hear a sound that roused you from your sleep?'

'The only sounds I heard were you and Michael finishing that barrel of wine,' said Bartholomew evasively, so that Langelee would not ask him what it was that he had considered so pressing that it could not wait until the morning. 'Doubtless the killers heard it, too, and they knew that they were safe from discovery as long as Michael was enjoying your wine.'

'Damn!' swore Michael softly. 'If ever there were a moral to a tale condemning the sin of gluttony, it is this. And poor Arbury paid the price.'

'Arbury would have died anyway,' said Langelee. 'And so might you, had you been asleep in your room and not here with me.'

With a shock, Bartholomew realised that was true, and that Michael's escape might have been as narrow as his own. He considered Arbury, and how the intruders – determined to search Michael's room whether the monk was in it or not – might have gained access to Michaelhouse. It was obvious, once he thought about it.

'I have a bad feeling that the killers watched me when I returned from the Franciscan Friary, and then did the same,' he said.

'Meaning?' asked Michael.

'Meaning that I did what we all do: hammered on the door and demanded to be let in. Arbury opened the wicket gate, I stepped inside and then pushed back my hood so that he could see who I was. If the killers were watching from the bushes opposite, it would have been easy to do the same, and then stab the lad before he saw that he should have been more careful.'

319

'But the only people who have leave to be outside the College after curfew are you two,' said Langelee. 'Arbury *should* have been more careful – especially since he had already admitted Bartholomew, and he probably could hear Michael with me.'

'That may be true generally, but not this week,' said Michael. 'It is Lent, and a number of our scholars have been attending midnight vigils and nocturns, especially those in the religious Orders. Arbury probably did not know who was out and who was in.'

Langelee sighed. 'Catch these killers, Michael. I want to see them hang for this.'

'I will do my best,' vowed Michael.

'Well, the day is beginning,' said Langelee, going to the window shutters and throwing them open. A blast of cold air flooded into the room, which rustled the documents and scrolls that lay in untidy piles on the table. 'We all have work to do.'

'You seem out of sorts this morning,' said Michael, as he followed Bartholomew from Langelee's chamber and across the courtyard. By unspoken consent, they made their way to the fallen apple tree in the orchard, where they could talk without fear of being overheard. Their rooms were usually sufficient for that, but neither felt much like being in the chaos of Michael's chamber, while Bartholomew's tended to be plagued by students with questions in the mornings.

It was no warmer in the garden that dawn than it had been during the night, and a thin layer of frost glazed the scrubby grass and the leaves of Agatha's herbs. Michael settled himself on the trunk of the fallen apple tree and watched Bartholomew pace back and forth in front of him.

'What is the matter?'

'These murders,' said Bartholomew. 'And the fact that I feel as though I am in a river where the current is dragging me relentlessly somewhere, but I do not know where.'

'That sounds familiar,' agreed Michael. 'I have worked

hard to try to discover what plot is under way that makes necessary the deaths of a talented philosopher called Faricius of the Carmelites, a very untalented philosopher called Kyrkeby of the Dominicans and my Junior Proctor. I have interviewed at least fifty people who live near the places where these men were killed or found, and you have examined their bodies. But neither of us has come up with anything.'

'What about the cases Walcote was working on before he died?' asked Bartholomew. 'Have you discovered anything from them?'

Michael shook his head. 'He was busy, but there was nothing to suggest he was working on something that would result in murder.'

'What about the plot to kill you?' asked Bartholomew. 'That sounds as though it might lead to murder to me.'

'But I can find out nothing about that,' said Michael plaintively. 'I have questioned my beadles again and again, but none seems to know anything unusual about Walcote or secret meetings in St Radegund's Convent. Certainly none of them accompanied him to any.'

'Not even the ones who work closest with him?' pressed Bartholomew. 'Tom Meadowman follows you around like a shadow. Did Walcote have a beadle like that?'

'If he did, then it would have been Rob Smyth, who drowned at Christmas. He latched himself on to Walcote, although I neither liked nor trusted the man.'

'The fact that no one is honest with us does not help,' said Bartholomew. 'I did not want to mention it in front of Langelee, but I persuaded Kenyngham to break his vow of secrecy last night.'

'You did?' asked Michael, pleasantly surprised. 'I will not ask how; I do not want my innocent mind stained by knowledge of your unscrupulous methods.'

'There was a theft from the Carmelite Friary,' said Bartholomew. 'He thinks you are responsible for it, and so does Warden Pechem.'

'What theft?' asked Michael, puzzled. 'Do you mean Faricius's essay? I thought we had reasoned that it had been stolen from him after he was stabbed on Milne Street. Why do they think I had anything to do with that?'

'I mean the theft of documents that occurred at Christmas,' said Bartholomew.

'What are you talking about?' demanded Michael. 'What documents?'

Bartholomew edged away from the monk, slightly alarmed by the anger in his voice. 'According to Pechem and Kenyngham, Lincolne reported a theft from his friary to Walcote—'

'Did he now?' asked Michael softly. 'And how is it that I have been told nothing about it?'

'Kenyngham said it was discussed at Walcote's secret meetings,' said Bartholomew, regarding the monk uneasily. He had predicted outrage and indignation when he informed Michael about the rumours that were circulating about him, but not cold fury.

'And they accuse me of this crime?' demanded Michael.

Half wishing he had not broached the subject, Bartholomew continued: 'They said you were seen in the Carmelite Friary the night the documents went missing; you were spotted carrying a loaded bag away from the friary towards Michaelhouse the same night; and they told me you claimed it contained bread for your colleagues, when it did not.'

'I see,' said Michael. He gazed into Bartholomew's face. 'And what do you make of this story? Do you imagine me to be the kind of man to steal from a friary in the middle of the night?'

Bartholomew shook his head. 'Of course not, Brother. And I told both Kenyngham and Pechem that they were wrong. But what is worse than this accusation of theft is that they have reasoned that whoever stole the documents also had a good reason for killing Walcote.'

Michael gazed up at the bare branches of the trees above

him. 'They think I murdered Walcote because he was about to expose me as a common thief. Damn Walcote for his suspicious mind!'

Bartholomew shot him a sidelong glance. 'I have no doubts about your innocence. We will have to work to prove it to those who do.'

Michael gave a tired grin. 'You are a good friend, Matt. I do not deserve such unquestioning loyalty. It makes me feel guilty.'

Bartholomew gazed at him in alarm. 'What are you saying, Brother?'

Michael shrugged. 'I see I have disappointed you.'

'No!' said Bartholomew, still staring. 'Are you telling me that Kenyngham and Pechem are right? That you really did break into the friary and make off with some of the University's most valuable documents?'

'Yes and no,' said Michael. 'I removed documents, but I was hardly "breaking in". I had arranged for doors and gates to be left unlocked and the porter to be drinking ale in the kitchens with a servant who owed me a favour. It was a pity I did not know about the baker's problematic oven sooner, because obviously I would not have used buying bread as my excuse for being caught red-handed on my way home. That was poor planning on my part.'

Bartholomew rubbed a hand through his hair, his thoughts tumbling in confusion. 'But why did you not tell me this sooner? It may be important.'

'It is not,' said Michael dismissively. 'However, I understand why Walcote thought so. He must have wondered why the Senior Proctor was raiding friaries in the middle of the night.'

'He was not the only one,' said Bartholomew, horrified. 'So do the heads of half the religious Orders in Cambridge.'

'It is unfortunate Walcote did not confront me about it, though,' continued Michael pensively. 'Then I could have taken him into my confidence, and he would not have felt the need to chatter about it at his secret meetings with people who had no right to know my business.'

323

'And what was this business?' asked Bartholomew warily.

Michael glanced at him. 'I can assure you it was nothing sinister. The truth is that Prior Lincolne had become somewhat fanatical in his beliefs by Christmas, and I did not like the idea of storing sensitive information at his friary. Because he is radically opposed to nominalism, I did not want him to see any of the documents pertaining to the arrangements I am making with Heytesbury – who is a nominalist.'

'You took the deeds relating to the Oxford proposal?' asked Bartholomew in sudden understanding.

Michael nodded. 'I took the property deeds of the church and farms I propose to pass to Heytesbury, along with the information telling us how profitable they are. Plus, I took priceless books written by other great nominalists, like John Dumbleton and Richard Swineshead. Lincolne is the kind of man to consign that sort of text to the flames, and I do not approve of book-burning.'

Bartholomew knew Michael was right on that score. When Heytesbury's *Regulae Solvendi Sophismata* had been found among Faricius's belongings, Lincolne had ordered it burned without a moment's hesitation.

'That was all?' he asked. 'You committed the theft only to remove sensitive items from the Carmelite Friary?'

'Yes,' Michael confirmed. 'But I wish you would not insist on calling it a theft. It was nothing of the kind. It was merely me taking documents from one place and securing them in another. If I were a serious thief, I would have had the gold that was stored in the chest, too, not just the texts.'

'True,' acknowledged Bartholomew, recalling the scrap of parchment he had found in Michael's room when he had been writing an account of Faricius's murder. Walcote's list of stolen items had mentioned no missing gold.

'I could hardly be open about what I was doing, could I?' Michael continued. 'How do you think Lincolne would have reacted if I had told him he was no longer to be trusted with some of the University's business?'

'He would have been offended,' said Bartholomew. 'And he might even have been vindictive.'

'Quite,' agreed Michael. 'This arrangement with Oxford is important, and, after losing the Mastership of Michaelhouse to it, I did not want all my work to come to nothing because an old bigot like Lincolne got wind of it by rummaging through the documents stored in his friary.'

'Where did you put these books and deeds?' asked Bartholomew. 'You could not store duplicate copies in St Mary's tower – what would be the point of keeping two sets in the same place? – and you always claim that you never keep anything valuable in your office or in your room at Michaelhouse.'

'Right,' said Michael. 'But I *do* keep them in a damp little corner of Michaelhouse's wine cellars. But only Chancellor Tynkell, Agatha and now you know about that.'

'So you had good reason to assume that last night's intruders did not find what they wanted: you knew that whatever it was would have been in the cellar?'

Michael rubbed his chin, the bristles rasping under his fingernails. 'I have already considered the possibility that last night's raid was related to the documents I "stole", and discounted it. I suppose it is remotely possible that someone was desperate to get his hands on an annotated copy of Dumbleton's *Summa Logicae et Philosophiae Naturalis*, but I sincerely doubt it. I do not know what these intruders thought they might find, but I cannot believe it was anything to do with my arrangements with Oxford or the nominalist texts I have safeguarded.'

'How can you be sure?' asked Bartholomew. 'I imagine Heytesbury would love to see the finances of the properties he plans to take from you. Has it occurred to you that he has a very good reason to search your room?'

'Heytesbury?' asked Michael, startled. 'I do not think so, Matt! The man is a scholar, for God's sake, not a burglar!'

'He is also a cunning negotiator who is determined to do his best for Oxford,' argued Bartholomew, declining to mention that Michael himself was also a scholar, but that did not stop him from removing what he wanted from the Carmelite Friary. 'You cannot be sure that he was not one of the intruders.'

'Heytesbury and Morden?' asked Michael, amused. 'They would make odd bedfellows.'

'Heytesbury might have hired someone else to commit the burglary,' pressed Bartholomew. 'He is not stupid, and would not risk being caught stealing from the Senior Proctor's room himself.'

'We will put these questions to Morden later today,' said Michael. 'But I think you are wrong. And anyway, the person in Cambridge whom Heytesbury seems to like best is your nephew Richard. The lad has taken to carrying ornate daggers and riding black war-horses around the town. Perhaps he has also taken to burglary.'

'No!' said Bartholomew firmly. 'Not Richard. He may be a fool, but he is not a criminal.'

Michael shrugged. 'As I said, we will ask Morden.'

'Several important issues were discussed at Walcote's meetings,' said Bartholomew, dragging his thoughts away from the unpleasant possibility that Richard might have been the man who attacked him on the darkened stairwell. 'Besides repairing the Great Bridge and discussing philosophy, they talked about the plot to murder you and the theft from the friary. I wonder whether Walcote thought the two subjects were connected.'

'You think he believed that someone wanted me dead, because I am seen as a thief?' asked Michael. He blew out his cheeks in a sigh. 'It is possible, I suppose.'

'Some people believe that Walcote's investigation of the theft led him too close to the culprit,' Bartholomew pointed out. 'Pechem and Kenyngham saw an association between his death and the theft you committed.'

Michael's face was sombre. 'I can accept that people see me as the kind of man to steal, but I cannot imagine how they could see me – *me* – as the kind of man to take the life of my deputy.'

'What shall we do about it?' asked Bartholomew. 'It was my original intention to prove you innocent of the theft, so that you would be absolved of the murder. Your confession just now has put paid to that plan.'

'Then we shall just have to go one step further, and find Walcote's killer instead. That will prove me innocent beyond any shadow of a doubt.'

They were silent for a while, each wrapped in his own thoughts.

'Did you know that Walcote made a list of the documents you took from the Carmelite Friary?' asked Bartholomew eventually.

Michael nodded. 'He jotted down his initial report in rough, then scribed it more neatly for the Chancellor – who knows exactly why I removed those particular items, before you ask. Carelessly, Walcote discarded his first copy in the box where we keep used parchment. I found it later.'

'It was among the scraps in your room.'

'I meant to burn it, but I forgot. It must have sat there undisturbed and forgotten for three months, until you discovered it by chance.'

'Why did the Chancellor not tell Walcote that the theft from the Carmelite Friary was not what it seemed?' asked Bartholomew. 'Did Tynkell distrust Walcote?'

'He considered him too gentle and too easily led. Tynkell decided not to tell Walcote the truth about the "theft", although he was obliged to ask him to investigate. It would have looked odd had he instructed him to forget about it.'

Bartholomew was feeling exhausted by the twists and turns the plot had taken. He was also hungry, and was grateful when the bell chimed to announce that breakfast was ready.

'And there are other things I do not understand,' Michael went on as they walked slowly towards the hall, 'such as what is Simon Lynne's role in all this? I am sure he is connected in some way, because I am positive he is lying.'

'And Tysilia and the meetings at St Radegund's,' said Bartholomew. 'There is a link between her and Walcote, I am sure.'

'Perhaps,' said Michael noncommittally, 'although I am less convinced of that than you. We shall visit Matilde again today, to see if she has learned anything new.'

Matilde. Bartholomew sighed at yet another aspect of the case that was worrying him, and he wished with all his heart that she was anywhere but at St Radegund's with Tysilia for company.

Michael nudged him in the ribs, and gave a weak grin. 'Do not look so sombre, Matt. I know this has not been a pleasant night, but we will solve this mystery. And we will have Arbury's killers brought to justice.'

'But not by Easter Day,' said Bartholomew. 'You claimed we would have this mess cleaned up before Sunday, and it is Friday already.'

'That was when I had only two deaths to investigate, and when the case seemed less complex. I had not anticipated that more people would die. The wager we had, giving the winner an evening of indulgence at the Brazen George, is now invalid. What are your plans today? Will you help me?'

'I have patients to see,' said Bartholomew.

'Then I will accompany you, and you can assist me when you have finished,' suggested Michael. 'Now that the only decent student you ever had – Tom Bulbeck – has gone to make his fortune in Norwich, you are in need of a good assistant.'

'I have other students,' said Bartholomew, not wanting Michael with him while he did his rounds. Although he often did take his students with him, he preferred to work alone. Most people did not take kindly to spotty youths poking at them and asking impertinent questions, and he knew that the sick were more likely to be honest about embarrassing symptoms if there was not a crowd of undergraduates listening with mawkish fascination. And Michael would be worse. He would not like hearing descriptions of bowel movements and phlegm production, and was likely to intimidate any nervous patients with his impatience and distaste.

'None of your students will compare with me,' bragged Michael. 'You will see. Once you have seen me in action, you will never want a student with you again.'

'Very well,' said Bartholomew reluctantly, seeing that the monk was not to be deterred and that he would have company that morning, whether he wanted it or not.

'We shall see your patients as soon as we have eaten breakfast, and when we have done that, we will return this glove to Prior Morden and ask him how he came to lose it. And then I think it is time we paid another visit to St Radegund's Convent. The time for lies and deceit is over, Matt. We shall put the fear of God into all these people who have been lying to us – Lincolne, Morden, Simon Lynne, Horneby and those disgraceful women at St Radegund's Convent – and then we shall have some answers.'

'My God, Matt!' breathed Michael, as they emerged from the single-roomed shack near the river where Dunstan, one of Bartholomew's oldest patients, lived. 'How can you stand to do things like that day after day?'

'The same way you are happy dealing with the crimes of the University, I imagine,' replied Bartholomew. 'Although I do not see what you are making a fuss about. None of the cases this morning have been particularly difficult.'

'Not for you, perhaps,' said Michael fervently. 'I have a new-found admiration for you, Matt. You have nerves of steel and nothing revolts you – not the phlegm that old man had been saving for your inspection, not that festering wound that smelled as though its owner was three days dead, and not prodding about in that screeching child's infected ear. No wonder you do not object to examining bodies for me. It is a pleasure for you after what your living patients require you to do.'

'Do you plan to help me in the future?' asked Bartholomew mildly, smiling at the monk's vehemence. 'You promised that I would never want a student after I had been assisted by you.'

'You probably will not,' said Michael haughtily. 'I have no doubts that I dealt with your patients better than would any of your would-be physicians. But I am not for hire. You will have to manage without me.'

'How will I cope?' asked Bartholomew, amused.

'Now you have finished, we should begin the real business of the day,' said Michael, taking Bartholomew's arm and steering him up one of the lanes that ran between the river and the High Street. 'We must talk seriously to Morden about his glove, then I want to question Eve Wasteneys again: I want to know whether Dame Martyn's "nephew" – Lynne – still lingers with his "aunt".'

'Not if he has any sense,' said Bartholomew. 'He was frightened of something, and abandoned the Carmelite Friary very promptly. He may be at Barnwell, though. Perhaps we should look for him there, as well as St Radegund's.'

As they walked along the High Street, they met Brother Timothy outside St Mary's Church. He had been giving the beadles their daily instructions, and was just dispatching the last of them to go about their business. He was grimly satisfied to hear they finally had a solid clue regarding the mystery, and willingly agreed to accompany them to arrest Morden. Together, the three of them made their way to the Dominican Friary, where Timothy knocked politely at the gate.

While they waited for an answer, Timothy nodded down at his cloak. 'Look at this. What a mess, eh?'

Bartholomew had already noticed that instead of the black prescribed by the Benedictine Order, Timothy's cloak was a uniform and rather tatty grey.

'You should invest in another garment,' advised Michael, regarding it doubtfully. 'No self-respecting Benedictine wants to be mistaken for a Franciscan – and you will be, if you wear that.'

Timothy grimaced. 'It was filthy from wandering around Cambridge's muddy streets, and so I took it to Yolande de Blaston to be cleaned.'

'Yolande de Blaston?' asked Michael. 'The whore?'

'She also takes in laundry,' said Timothy. 'She is expecting her tenth child, and her whoring days are limited now. She needs all the money she can lay her hands on for her first nine brats, so all us Benedictines send her our laundry; we feel sorry for her.'

'She is not as good a laundress as Agatha,' said Michael, studying the cloak critically. 'Yolande used water that was too hot, and it has taken the colour out.'

Timothy nodded. 'I shall have to take it to Oswald Stanmore to be re-dyed. Do not mention this to Yolande, will you? I do not want her to worry that the Benedictines will take their trade elsewhere when she is about to give birth. She has more than enough to concern her already.'

Bartholomew was impressed that Timothy should consider the feelings of a lowly prostitute when he must have been angry that his fine cloak had been so badly misused. It was true that Stanmore could re-dye the damaged fabric, but it was unlikely to be as good as it had been. Bartholomew felt new admiration for a man who was not only prepared to overlook the damage to his property and the inconvenience of looking like a Franciscan, but was also keen that the perpetrator should not suffer for it. Timothy was right: Yolande de Blaston was desperately poor, and would need any work provided by the Benedictines.

Eventually, the door was answered by Ringstead, who admitted them to the yard. He told them to wait while he informed Morden that he had visitors, but Michael was having none of that. Shoving his way past the startled friar, he thundered up the stairs to Morden's room and flung open the door so hard that it rattled the candle-holders on the table. An inkwell rolled on to its side, then dropped to the floor, where a spreading black stain began to inch towards one of Morden's fine rugs, and something dark dropped from the rafters to the floor. At first, Bartholomew thought it was a dead bat. Timothy shot him a nervous glance, uneasy with an approach so violent that it shook dead animals from the roof.

'I want a word with you,' snapped Michael, addressing the diminutive Dominican, who perched on a chair piled with cushions so that he would be able to reach his table. Small legs clad in fine wool hose swung in the air below.

'What do you mean by bursting into my room like this?' demanded Morden, outraged. 'It is customary to knock. And will you *please* refrain from slamming that door? Next time, I shall send you the bill for the damage you cause.'

'Does this belong to you?' demanded Michael, ignoring the Prior's ire as he removed the small glove from his scrip and tossed it on to the table.

Morden picked it up, turning it over in his hands in surprise. 'Where did you find this?'

'In my room,' said Michael coldly. 'It was dropped very late last night, after its owner had stabbed a Michaelhouse student to death in order to gain access. And not only did this villain kill our student, but he attacked Matt with a knife. I do not take kindly to people who threaten my friends with weapons.'

Morden's face turned white as the implications of Michael's words sunk in. 'What are you saying, Brother? I can assure you—'

Michael cut through his words. 'Is this your glove?' he shouted. 'Yes or no?'

Morden agreed reluctantly. 'But it was not I who dropped it at Michaelhouse. It has been missing—'

'How convenient,' snapped Michael, his tone of voice making it obvious that he did not believe a word the Prior was saying. 'And for how long has it been missing?'

Morden shrugged helplessly. 'I do not know. I seldom go out these days, because of the cold weather. I first noticed it had gone a couple of days ago, because I had to go to St Mary's Church to tell the Chancellor that Kyrkeby would not be able to give the University Lecture. But I have no idea whether it went missing then or whether it has been gone a lot longer.'

'And where do you think it might have been?' asked Timothy. The incredulous expression on his face suggested that he was of the same mind as Michael. 'Are you suggesting that someone stole it?'

'Of course someone took it,' stated Ringstead firmly, leaping to the defence of his superior. 'How else could it have ended up in your room, Brother? I can assure you that Prior Morden did not put it there.'

Michael and Timothy did not reply; they simply gazed at Morden, as if they considered him to be the lowest form of life. Bartholomew began to feel sorry for the little man – until he looked more closely at what had fallen from the rafters when Michael had flung open the door.

'And who do you think may have taken your gloves and left them in Brother Michael's chamber, Father?' asked Timothy softly.

'Glove,' corrected Bartholomew, stooping to retrieve the object that lay on the floor. 'Here is the twin of the one that we found at Michaelhouse. It seems that someone thought the ceiling a good place to hide it.'

'I certainly did not put it there,' said Morden, white-faced with worry. 'I could not reach.'

'You do not need to reach,' Bartholomew pointed out. 'You could have thrown it.'

'Well, I did not,' said Morden, shooting wary glances at his interrogators. 'Someone else must have put it there – and placed the other one at Michaelhouse.'

'Really,' said Timothy flatly. 'This is all very curious. You are claiming that someone took *one* of your gloves – which coincidentally just happened to reappear in Michael's quarters shortly after the murder at Michaelhouse – and then hurled the other into the rafters to conceal the fact that the first glove was missing?'

'I do not understand this,' said Morden miserably. 'I

cannot imagine how one ended up in Michaelhouse or the other on the ceiling, but I do know it has nothing to do with me. I certainly did not stab any student to gain access to his College. Why would I do such a thing?'

'Is there someone who can verify your whereabouts between midnight and the office of nocturns last night?' asked Michael, declining to speculate on answers to the Prior's question.

'The entire friary,' replied Morden immediately. 'Everyone knows I retire to bed immediately after compline, and that I do not rise until it is time for matins.'

'That is true,' concurred Ringstead loyally. 'Prior Morden likes a good night's sleep.'

'That is not the same as people actually *seeing* him here,' Timothy pointed out. 'He could have retired to bed, then slipped out when everyone else was asleep. Do you share your chamber with anyone, Prior Morden?'

'I shared it with Kyrkeby,' said Morden bitterly. 'But he is scarcely in a position to vouch for me. But how could I have slipped out at night, anyway?'

'By walking down the stairs and across the yard,' said Michael promptly. 'Like every other night porter in Cambridge, yours dozes when he should be on watch. It would be an easy matter to tiptoe past him and leave the friary through the wicket door.'

'Well, I did not,' said Morden in an unsteady voice. 'I am a Dominican Prior, and I have no need to sneak out of the friary in the middle of the night. And I ask you again, why would I want to go to your room anyway?'

'That is what I should like to know,' said Michael. 'For your information, and for that of anyone else who may be interested, I never keep notes of the cases I am investigating in my room. I would not put Michaelhouse at risk like that. I keep them elsewhere.'

'Where?' asked Morden automatically.

'Why?' pounced Michael. 'Because you did not find what you were looking for last night?'

Morden rubbed his eyes with his tiny fingers. 'This is a nightmare! I do not know why I asked that. Even you must admit that your statement was a little provocative.'

'Enough of this,' said Michael, turning away from him. 'I am too busy to waste any more time with you. You are under arrest for the murder of Martin Arbury. Brother Timothy will escort you to the proctors' cells.'

'What?' cried Morden in horror, darting around to the other side of the table when Timothy took a step towards him. 'But you cannot arrest me! I have done nothing wrong!'

'Whoever broke into my room last night murdered the student on gate duty and attacked my friend,' said Michael harshly. 'Your glove was found at the scene of the crime, dropped when the culprit fled the College. That is evidence enough for me.'

Timothy grabbed the protesting Morden and led him from the room, easily encompassing the scholar's small arm in one of his hands. Michael returned the glove to his scrip to use as evidence in the trial that would come later, then followed them down the stairs. Bartholomew brought up the rear, fending off the horrified Ringstead, who was trying to shove past him to reach Timothy and his prisoner.

'This is an outrage!' Ringstead shouted, his agitated voice ringing across the courtyard. Several student-friars heard it, and began hurrying to where their Prior struggled ineffectually against Timothy's strong hand. 'What will the Bishop of Ely say when he hears you have arrested the head of an important Order in the town?'

'He will congratulate me for removing a ruthless killer from the streets,' replied Michael. He glanced coolly at the assembling friars, who muttered and shuffled menacingly. 'And unless you want more of your Dominican brethren to join Prior Morden in his cell, you will instruct your students to return to their rooms and behave themselves.'

'Do not worry, Father,' Ringstead called to Morden. 'I will find the best law clerk in Cambridge, and he will have you back here in a trice.'

'Hire that young man Heytesbury recommended,' Morden shouted back. 'He is said to be clever and crafty.'

'But he is also Doctor Bartholomew's nephew,' said Ringstead, glowering at the physician. 'We will have someone else.'

Meanwhile, the student-friars had been edging closer to where Timothy hauled his reluctant prisoner to the gates. Michael eyed them coldly.

'Tell them to disperse, Ringstead,' he ordered. 'Or Morden will not be the only Dominican requiring the legal services of a "clever and crafty" lawyer.'

For a few uncomfortable moments, Bartholomew thought Ringstead would refuse, and that the sullen, resentful crowd would attack the proctors and prevent them from taking Morden into custody. But Ringstead was not a stupid man. He knew that Morden would end up in the proctors' cells eventually, and that all that would happen if he fought against it would be a delay of the inevitable. He hung his head as Timothy opened the gate, still holding Morden by the arm.

'Very wise of you,' said Michael, as Ringstead reluctantly told the students to return to their rooms. 'Nothing would have been gained from a display of violent behaviour, and it would have looked bad for when you try to prove your Prior's innocence in the courts.'

'But he *is* innocent,' protested Ringstead, following them to the gate. He watched Morden precede Timothy on to Hadstock Way and head in the direction of the cells that were located near St Mary's Church. Timothy was not an unkind man, and Bartholomew saw him bend to say something to which the small Prior nodded agreement. Timothy released Morden's arm, and although he stayed close and was clearly alert for tricks, he did not submit Morden to the indignity of being marched through the busiest part of the town in the grip of a proctor. To anyone who did not know what had just transpired in the Dominican Friary, Morden and Timothy were simply walking side by side.

While Bartholomew approved of Timothy's sensitivity, Michael muttered venomously that Morden deserved no such consideration, and started to compare his new junior unfavourably with Walcote, who was similarly kind to malefactors. Ringstead broke into his mumbled tirade.

'How can you think Morden could stab students? He is not big enough.'

'Arbury was knifed in the chest,' said Michael. 'Morden could easily have done it.'

'That is no kind of evidence,' objected Ringstead, almost in tears that he was so powerless. 'And neither is that wretched glove. Lots of things seem to have gone missing from our friary recently – the glove was just one of a number of items we seem to have mislaid.'

'What else?' asked Michael, uninterested.

'Perhaps the most important thing is Kyrkeby's lecture,' replied Ringstead. 'When we learned about his death, we decided his work should not have been in vain, and we were going to publish it posthumously. But we cannot find it.'

'Perhaps he hid it,' suggested Bartholomew. 'Some people do not like their work known before their public lectures, and he may have put it away from prying eyes.'

'Never,' said Ringstead firmly. 'We have no need to hide things from each other here, and anyway, he read parts of the lecture to several of us to test his performance. He did not hide his notes. I went to collect them from his cell, and they simply were not there.'

'Then are you suggesting that someone took them?' asked Bartholomew. 'Or that Kyrkeby merely mislaid them?'

'A few moments ago, I would have said the latter,' said Ringstead. 'But given that poor Morden is now under arrest because a missing glove has appeared somewhere I am sure he did not leave it, then I suggest that they must have been stolen.'

'So, you wish to report a theft,' said Michael heavily.

'Yes I do,' snapped Ringstead, resentful that Michael clearly did not believe him.

'You have no evidence the lecture has been stolen,' said Michael, exasperated by Ringstead's heavy-handed attempts to exonerate his leader. 'You only know that it is not in Kyrkeby's cell. Perhaps he gave it to someone else to read; perhaps he put it in a different place.'

'But he did not have another place!' insisted Ringstead. 'His life was here, at the friary.' He sighed and relented a little. 'But I suppose he may have given it to someone else to read. I know he discussed it with Father Paul at the Franciscan Friary. Perhaps he passed it to Paul.'

'Why would he do that?' asked Michael doubtfully. 'Paul is blind. He cannot read anything.'

Ringstead flushed with embarrassment. 'Well, in that case, my first supposition must be right: Kyrkeby's lecture has been stolen.'

'What a mess,' said Michael tiredly. 'Still, at least we have the killer of poor Arbury under lock and key. And who knows? Perhaps Morden may confess to other crimes once he has had time to reflect on his evil deeds through the bars on his cell window. We shall see.'

Bartholomew hoped he was right and gave Ringstead a wide berth as he left the friary. It was certainly not the tiny Morden with whom he had struggled at Michaelhouse, and he realised that the young secretary could well be Morden's accomplice.

While Timothy locked Morden in a cell, Bartholomew and Michael walked slowly along the High Street, thinking about Morden's claims of innocence and Ringstead's assertion that someone had been in the Dominican Friary stealing gloves and lectures on nominalism. The day was wet and dull, and clouds hung in a solid canopy over the Fen-edge town. There was no wind, and the bare branches of trees and bushes were static and skeletal, while the leaves that had fallen the previous autumn lay in brown-black soggy piles filled with worms. The market was in full swing, and the hoarse voices of competing traders rang out in the still air, accompanied by the mournful bellow of a cow that was being led towards the butchers' stalls. Bartholomew saw its rolling eyes and quivering flanks, and wondered if it knew what was in store for it, or whether it was simply the stench of rotting blood and the sound of metal against bone as the butchers dealt with a sheep that it did not like.

Michael led the physician towards an insalubrious establishment at the edge of the Market Square called the Cardinal's Cap. A joyous red sign hung outside, and from within came the contented murmur of men enjoying their ale. Michael did not use the front entrance, but slipped down a filthy runnel that cut along the side of the building, and entered a much smaller room via an almost invisible rear door.

Inside, a number of scholars were sitting at rough wooden tables; some were gathered around a fire that roared in the hearth, listening to a dialogue by a man Bartholomew knew to be Father Aidan of Maude's Hostel. None seemed in the slightest disconcerted by the sudden presence of the Senior Proctor in their midst, and one or two even nodded friendly greetings in Michael's direction.

'I need a pot of warm ale inside me before we walk to St Radegund's in this rain,' said Michael. 'And perhaps a bowl of beef stew.'

'Not beef,' said Bartholomew, thinking about the cow he had just seen led to slaughter. He thought he could still hear its baleful lows echoing across the Market Square. 'It is Lent, remember. But what is this place? A room in a tavern devoted exclusively to serving scholars?'

'Have you never been here before?' asked Michael, raising his eyebrows in astonishment. 'I thought every University master knew that the Cardinal's Cap was a good place for a quiet drink. Students are not welcome here, of course. They would be rowdy, and then we would all be in trouble.'

'Scholars are not supposed to drink in the town's taverns,' said Bartholomew. 'It is what leads to fighting between us and the townsfolk.'

Michael gestured to the conversations that were taking place around him. In one corner, a number of Gilbertines were discussing the sermons of St Augustine, while Father Aidan's audience appeared to be listening to an explanation of how to deal with the problem of dry rot. At other tables, single scholars read or wrote with their cups at their elbows, enjoying the comfort of hot ale and a warm fire while they worked.

'These men are unlikely to challenge the apprentices to a fight,' said Michael. 'They are all respectable people, who like a little intelligent conversation away from their own Colleges and hostels. Where lies the harm in that?'

Michael had arranged for Timothy to meet them in the Cardinal's Cap when he had finished locking up Morden. The Benedictine arrived and sat opposite them, ordering bread and cheese, and if he noticed that Michael was breaking the rules of Lent by eating meat, then he said nothing about it.

'What do you think about these killings, Brother?' asked Michael, when Timothy's food had arrived. 'You know everything we have learned. How do you interpret the information?'

'Theft,' said Timothy promptly. 'Kyrkeby's scrip was missing; Walcote's purse was stolen; and Faricius's scrip was cut from his belt. These men were killed purely and simply for the contents of their purses.'

'But they were all friars who are not supposed to be wealthy,' said Bartholomew, not convinced. 'Why attack them?'

Timothy shrugged. 'First, many friars in this town are extremely rich – you have only to look at Morden or in Kyrkeby's jewel box to see that they own a good deal. And second, Walcote and probably Kyrkeby were killed in the dark. Perhaps their killers did not know they were clerics.'

'But it was obvious *Faricius* was a cleric,' argued Bartholomew. 'And *he* was killed in broad daylight. I am sure his death was connected to the essay that is missing.'

340

'I think you are attributing too much importance to this essay,' said Timothy. 'Just because you cannot locate a few scribbled notes does not mean Faricius died for them. You know how poor many people are these days: some would kill for a loaf of bread – and Faricius's purse almost certainly contained enough for that.'

'I thought you admired Faricius and his work,' said Bartholomew.

'I did,' said Timothy. 'But that does not mean to say that I believe his writing was the cause of his death. He did not mention the essay specifically to you on his deathbed, so how do you know there was not something else in his scrip that he was concerned over? He had a ruby ring at the friary, so perhaps there were more riches in his purse that he was worried about.'

Bartholomew could think of no arguments to refute what Timothy said, although he remained convinced that the monk was wrong to dismiss the essay so completely. Michael was halfway through his second bowl of beef stew, and Bartholomew had just finished a dish of buttered turnips, when the door opened and more people entered the cosy tavern. Bartholomew saw Michael's eyes narrow when he recognised Richard Stanmore, then watched the monk's face assume an expression of innocent friendliness when Heytesbury followed the young lawyer in.

'How does your nephew know about this place?' asked Michael of Bartholomew, maintaining his pleasant expression, although his voice was petulantly angry. 'It is not open to just anyone.'

'Good afternoon, Brother,' said Richard cheerfully, taking a seat next to Michael and peering into his bowl. 'What is this? An additional meal to see you through to suppertime? And meat, too! Do you not know it is Lent?'

Michael glowered at him, suddenly not caring that Heytesbury saw his murderous expression. 'I missed my midday meal, because I was engaged with important University business.'

341

'A missed meal would do you no harm,' said Richard rudely. 'To be grossly fat—'

'Show some manners, Richard,' said Heytesbury sharply. 'It is not polite to comment on another man's personal appearance.'

'He is not fat, anyway,' said Timothy loyally. 'These habits make us look larger than we are.'

'Quite,' muttered Michael, casting a venomous glower at Richard, whose clothes that day were green and whose earring glittered tantalisingly close to the monk's fingers.

'I thought you said you would punch the next man who commented on your girth,' said Bartholomew, thinking that a good thump might do Richard some good. Timothy regarded Bartholomew in alarm, and the physician had the feeling that the Junior Proctor wondered whether to arrest him for inciting a scholar to fight with a townsman.

'Next time,' vowed Michael. 'I do not fight men who are unwell. What have you been doing to make you so wan and pale, Richard? You look worse than Kyrkeby's corpse.'

Bartholomew saw what Michael meant. Richard's green clothes did nothing to improve the unhealthy pallor of his face, and even the powerfully scented goose grease that was plastered on his hair was not quite able to disguise the fact that he had recently been sick. Evidently, Richard and Heytesbury had indulged themselves in yet another night of merrymaking in some tavern or another. Michael sneezed, then yelped suddenly.

'Sorry,' said Richard, giving the monk a grin that was far from apologetic. He held his decorative dagger in his hand. 'Your sneeze made you wobble into this.'

'What is it?' asked Timothy disparagingly. 'I would confiscate it as a dangerous weapon, but it looks like a toy – all handle and no blade.'

'And what would a monk know about such things?' sneered Richard.

'I was a soldier once,' said Timothy. 'I fought at Crécy with the Black Prince. He is a man well acquainted with court fashions, but he would never carry a thing like that.'

'What is wrong with it?' asked Richard, offended. 'I can defend myself with it well enough.'

'Put it away,' said Michael, seeing that the other occupants of the tavern were beginning to wonder why a townsman was brandishing a knife at the University's proctors. Father Aidan had already left, unwilling to be caught in a place where trouble might be brewing. 'And tell us how you come to be looking so peaky this morning.'

'I had a meeting with Mayor Horwoode last night,' began Richard by way of explanation, slipping the silly weapon into an equally impractical scabbard. 'He wanted to ask my opinion about who is legally responsible for maintaining the Great Bridge.'

'He wanted you to find a loophole in the law that will make someone other than the town liable,' surmised Timothy tartly. 'He is loath to levy a tax on the townsfolk to pay for it, and is hoping that you could put the onus on the Castle or the University.'

'How did a meeting with Horwoode make you ill?' asked Bartholomew. 'Did he give you bad food?'

Richard shook his head. 'He gave me a good deal of wine, although that stopped flowing as soon as I told him that the bridge was the town's responsibility and he had better raise some funds before someone was killed on it and he was held accountable. On my way to collect Black Bishop from the stables, I met Heytesbury, and we adjourned to the Swan for a drink.'

'It sounds to me as if you had had more than enough to drink already,' muttered Michael.

'I have given Richard some of my gum mastic,' said Heytesbury, withdrawing the packet of yellow resin from his scrip. 'Mixed with alehoof, it is an infallible remedy for over-indulgence.'

Bartholomew saw that Heytesbury's fingers were coloured a deep yellow, rather like the stains the physician had noted on the bodies of Walcote and Faricius. Had they

343

also used gum mastic as a cure for too much drink? Neither had seemed the kind of man who drank a lot, although neither did Heytesbury, and Bartholomew guessed the Oxford scholar was actually very partial to his ales and wines. That morning, there was an amber sheen to the whites of Heytesbury's eyes, and his hands were unsteady, as if they required a jug of something fermented to settle them.

'And what would Oxford men know of over-indulgence?' asked Michael archly. 'Surely the noble men of that fine institution do not need such remedies?'

'We use them on rare occasions,' said Heytesbury, unruffled by Michael's sarcasm. 'But by the time we left the Swan it was rather late to return to Trumpington, so we spent the night at Oswald Stanmore's business premises on Milne Street, instead.'

'However, when I woke this morning, someone had been in my room during the night,' Richard went on. 'There was a bowl of burnt feathers and garlic next to my bed, and the stench was unbelievable.'

Bartholomew smiled, knowing exactly who had been responsible for placing the foul-smelling substance near Richard, and why. The superstitious Cynric was following the Franciscans' instructions for removing the curse of an unpleasant personality. The physician recalled that William had caught the mad Clippesby taking feathers from the College cockerel, doubtless at Cynric's request.

'I had a rotten night,' complained Richard churlishly. He fiddled restlessly with something he had pulled from his pocket. Bartholomew saw it was a gold pendant, and wondered whether his nephew's excesses now ran to jewellery.

'It looked to me as if someone had been practising witchcraft,' said Heytesbury, amused. 'We all know that burned feathers are a common ingredient in spells.'

'Cynric, probably,' grumbled Richard. 'He is Welsh, and so believes in that kind of thing. I expect he imagined he was protecting me from evil spirits. But, what with the stink of burning feathers, the bad wine in the Swan, and the Carmelites carousing across the road, I slept badly.'

'The Carmelites?' asked Timothy, startled. 'Lent is not over and they have recently buried a colleague. They have no cause for carousing.'

'I hope it was not because they found Kyrkeby dead on their property,' groaned Michael. 'I thought we had averted a fight over that particular issue.'

'Actually, I think they were just pleased that Kyrkeby is not to give the University Lecture,' said Heytesbury wryly. 'They were angry that he planned to talk in defence of nominalism, and were delighted to hear that the lecture will now revolve around life on Venus.'

'Perhaps there are nominalists on Venus,' suggested Richard. 'Have you considered talking about what Venusian nominalists might believe? It would be a clever way to give a lecture on nominalism while still complying with the unreasonable demands imposed by Chancellor Tynkell.'

'It would not,' said Heytesbury sternly. 'Such a tactic would be ungentlemanly, not to mention painfully transparent. And anyway, it would make a mockery of my beliefs. The realists would laugh at me if I claimed nominalism was followed on Venus.'

'I still have that document ready,' said Michael to Heytesbury, patting his scrip. 'It seems to me that you do not like Cambridge, and I would hate to think that you felt obliged to linger here for my benefit.'

'It has been quite an experience,' said Heytesbury, leaning back in his chair and smiling enigmatically. 'But I shall decide whether to sign this deed by the time I give my lecture. You are right: I do not like Cambridge, and I am beginning to miss the hallowed halls of Oxford with their atmosphere of learning and scholarship, and the stimulating presence of great minds.'

'I see,' said Michael icily. He opened his scrip and passed Heytesbury the document. 'This is ready whenever you are.

I can even provide you with a decent horse to speed you on your way.'

'Just as long as it is not a large black one,' said Heytesbury, taking the document as if he expected it to bite. 'I would not want to be thrown off and break my neck.'

'No,' said Michael ambiguously.

Heytesbury folded the deed and placed it in his own scrip. 'I shall read it myself, then ask Richard to assess it for loopholes. I must be sure that it does not harm Oxford.'

Michael pretended to be offended, although Bartholomew thought Heytesbury was acting with commendable common sense in securing the services of a lawyer. The monk stood and indicated that Timothy and Bartholomew should leave with him. 'We must go to visit the good nuns of St Radegund's Convent. There are questions to ask.'

'Do not go there, Brother,' advised Richard weakly. 'Those are no nuns; they are sirens, who entice innocent men inside their walls. A chaste and inexperienced man like you will be easy prey.'

'How do you know?' demanded Bartholomew. 'Are you one of those men who visits the nuns when decent folk are sleeping?'

'I know the occupants of St Radegund's Convent,' replied Richard evasively. 'There have been rumours about the place ever since I was a boy.'

'Do these rumours bear any resemblance to the truth?' asked Heytesbury, raising his eyebrows in amusement.

'Oh, yes,' said Richard weakly. 'Beyond your wildest imaginings.'

chapter 10

BARTHOLOMEW, MICHAEL AND TIMOTHY LEFT THE Cardinal's Cap and set off in a dull drizzle of early afternoon towards St Radegund's Convent. When Michael tapped on the door there was a sound of running footsteps, the grille on the gate was snapped open and Tysilia peered out.

'Oh, it is you,' she said to Michael, sounding pleased. 'We always like visits from Dominicans and Franciscans.'

'I am a Benedictine, not a Dominican,' said Michael, offended. 'You should be able to tell the difference; you wear the habit of a Benedictine novice yourself.'

Tysilia shook her head in evident impatience with herself. 'Dame Martyn told me that I could always tell a Benedictine from a Dominican because Benedictines are fat. I must remember that!'

Bartholomew glanced at Michael and smiled.

'I said I would punch the next *man* who called me fat,' muttered Michael in reply. 'And Tysilia is no man.'

'She is not,' agreed Timothy, not bothering to mask his distaste.

'I keep forgetting that Black Monks and Black Friars are different,' Tysilia went on cheerfully. 'It is like White Friars are Carmelites and White Monks are cisterns. And Grey Friars, like him, are Franciscans.' She beamed at Timothy in his damaged cloak.

'Cistercians,' corrected Michael. 'And Timothy is no Franciscan; he is a Benedictine, like me.'

'But he wears grey,' Tysilia pointed out. 'And grey equals Franciscans.'

It was clear to Bartholomew that Timothy had no time

for the owner of the sultry eyes that peered through the grille, although he had plenty of compassion for the struggling Yolande de Blaston. 'Enough!' Timothy snapped. 'We did not come here to bandy words with you, woman. Inform your Prioress that we are here to see her.'

'Then I suppose you had better come in,' said Tysilia with a pout. 'I may be a while, because she is asleep and I will have to wake her up.'

'It is cold out here,' said Michael, rubbing his hands to warm them as a bitter wind laden with misty droplets of rain cut in from across the Fens. He did not comment that early afternoon was no time for a Prioress with a convent to run to be asleep. 'I do not know why the founders of this convent chose to locate it in so wild a place.'

'They put it here so that we would be removed from men,' explained Tysilia brightly, opening the door to admit them. 'Of course, that just means that men have a bit of a walk to get here . . .' Her hands flew to her mouth in agitation. 'Damn it all! I forgot. Eve Wasteneys told me I am not to admit anyone into Prioress Martyn's presence without first telling her who it is. Would you mind leaving?'

'You mean you want us to wait outside?' asked Michael, startled.

'Yes,' said Tysilia.

'But why can we not wait here?' asked Michael, unwilling to leave the relative shelter of the convent walls to stand in the rain while Tysilia woke the Prioress from her slumbers.

'Because Dame Martyn may not want to see you,' said Tysilia with an impatient sigh at his stupidity. 'And if she does not, I shall have to tell you that she is not here and refuse you permission to come in.'

'I see you have a clear understanding of the duties of gatekeeper,' mumbled Michael, reluctantly stepping out. He shivered in the wind as she closed the door again, and gave Timothy a sudden grin. 'Matt thinks Tysilia is behind these meetings of Walcote's, and that she is a criminal mastermind who is capable of manipulating some of the most important men in the University.'

Timothy shook his head, laughing. 'I do not think so!'

'It is just not possible for someone to be that stupid,' said Bartholomew, defensive of his theory. 'It must be an act.'

'If her stupidity is contrived, then she has taken it too far,' said Timothy, still smiling. 'She needs to moderate herself.'

'Here she comes,' said Michael, as footsteps clattered across the yard. 'Now we will see whether the Prioress is prepared to see us, or whether she is pretending to be out.'

The door opened a second time, and Tysilia waved them in. 'Eve Wasteneys told me to tell you that Dame Martyn is in the stellar,' she said breezily.

'Solar,' corrected Michael. 'And we know she is in, or you would not have gone to ask her whether she was prepared to grant us an audience.'

'You what?' asked Tysilia blankly.

'Never mind,' said Michael wearily. 'Lead on.'

She led the way across the yard to the building in which the solar was located. Michael kept his hands firmly inside his sleeves this time, so that the Bishop's 'niece' ascended the stairs unmolested, despite hips that swung more vigorously at every step. She shot him a look of bewilderment when they reached the top, as though she could not understand how the monk could have resisted her.

'How is your murder instigation coming along?' she asked.

'Investigation,' corrected Michael. 'And it is not coming along at all.'

'That is because you think Will Walcote was killed by a single person,' said Tysilia. 'And he was actually murdered by three.'

Bartholomew stared at her. Was she simply giving voice to whatever came into her head, or was she passing Michael a clue? 'What makes you say that?' he asked curiously.

'It is obvious,' said Tysilia with a careless shrug. 'I heard his hands were tied and he was robbed of his purse before he was hung.'

349

'Hanged,' corrected Michael. '"Hung" is what you do to game. But how does this prove there were three killers?'

Tysilia sighed, to indicate her impatience at his slow wits. 'Because it would need one person to tie his hands, another to steal his purse, and another to put the rope around his neck. One person could not have done all that, could he?'

Bartholomew had reasoned much the same, although he was disconcerted to hear such rational thinking emanating from the lips of Tysilia. He shot Michael a triumphant glance to show that this proved he had been correct all along, and that she was deeply involved. Michael declined to look at him.

'We are wasting time,' said Timothy distastefully, indicating with a curt nod of his head that she was to open the door to the solar. His cool disdain made it clear exactly what he thought of the novice's comments. 'We have a killer to catch, and we will not do it listening to this nonsense.'

Or would they? Bartholomew gazed uncertainly at Tysilia, trying to gauge yet again whether she was a cunning manipulator who was enjoying the spectacle of their floundering progress through the case, or the dull-minded harlot she seemed to be. But his intense scrutiny of her face told him nothing, and her eyes seemed empty behind their superficial sparkle. Pouting at Timothy's brusque dismissal of her suggestion, she opened the door to admit them to the solar.

'Brother Michael,' said Eve Wasteneys, rising to greet her visitors. 'Do come in.'

Bartholomew glanced around him. The few nuns present were industriously engaged in darning, and all of them were fully clothed. Dame Martyn slumbered quietly in a corner, and there was not a wine cup in sight. Matilde, still playing the part of Mistress Horner, was with them. Her eyes were bright and interested, and even with all the make-up that covered her smooth white skin, Bartholomew could see she was enjoying herself.

'These are *not* the nuns from Ely who want to spy on us,' stated Tysilia, inadvertently revealing why the day-room was not in its usual state of comfortable debauchery. 'These are Brother Michael and his two friends, who are not as fat as him and who therefore do not look like Benedictines.'

'Nicely announced, Tysilia,' said Eve dryly.

'Nuns from Ely?' asked Michael, raising questioning eyebrows.

'We are to be inspected by high-ranking abbesses,' replied Eve. 'What do you think they will say when they find us mending shirts for beggars and everyone wearing the prescribed habits with no personal deviations?'

'They will think that you had wind of their visit and that you have prepared accordingly,' said Michael. 'But if you really want to fool them, you should appoint a new gate-keeper for the day, or you will find all your efforts have been in vain.'

Eve looked thoughtful. 'You are right. Tysilia should spend the duration of the visit in the kitchen.'

'A cellar might be a better choice,' muttered Bartholomew. 'She can still speak in a kitchen.'

'I can sew, too,' announced Tysilia. She threw herself on to a cushion, careful to treat the visitors to a flash of her legs as she did so, then held up a scrap of linen that was covered in clumsy stitches.

'Very nice,' said Michael ambiguously. 'But what is your sewing supposed to be?'

'Be?' asked Tysilia, frowning in puzzlement. 'Why should it "be" anything?'

'She sounds like a realist,' muttered Timothy. 'Questioning the existence of things.'

'Hardly,' said Eve, waving a hand to indicate that Tysilia should retire to a window-seat, where she would not be able to interrupt every few moments with her peculiar announcements. 'We are still learning basic table manners, and have a long way to go before we graduate to philosophy.'

'Is she really as dense as she seems?' asked Timothy baldly. Bartholomew winced and cast an anxious glance at Matilde, afraid that Timothy's question might put her in danger if

Tysilia suspected that her disguise was being questioned.

'No,' said Eve shortly. 'She is trying very hard to be intelligent at the moment.'

'She is not playing games with you?' pressed Timothy.

Eve shook her head. 'I thought the same when I first met her: no one could be as dim-witted as Tysilia and survive to adulthood. But I have spent a long time watching her, mostly when she thought she was alone, and I am certain her gross stupidity is genuine. Why do you ask?'

'No reason,' said Michael, unable to resist a victorious glance at Bartholomew. The physician remained sceptical, still thinking about Tysilia's notion that they should be looking for more than one killer. He happened to think that she was right: it would be difficult to overpower a man, tie him up and hang him singled-handed.

'Is there word from my kinsman?' asked Matilde in the croaking voice she reserved for Mistress Horner's use, fiddling with the ring on her finger to indicate that she wanted to talk to them alone. She levered her bulk from her cushions and made her way unsteadily towards Bartholomew. 'Did you give him the message I dictated to you?'

'I did,' said Bartholomew. 'And Robin of Grantchester sends greetings in return.'

'Good,' said Matilde, steering him towards an alcove where they could at least speak without being overheard, even if everyone could still see them. 'Here is a penny for your trouble.'

'Thank you,' said Bartholomew, gazing at the brown coin she pressed into his palm.

'My standing here dropped dramatically when they thought I was related to Robin,' said Matilde, her eyes bright with mischief. 'You deserve to be paid only a penny.'

'Have you learned anything?' asked Bartholomew urgently. 'We do not have much time.'

'Nothing. Tysilia rises late, has the manners of a peasant and is the most active member of the convent during the night. Sometimes she says things that are so stupid they are actually quite clever.'

Bartholomew nodded. 'Michael and Timothy believe she is exactly what she appears to be.'

'So I gathered. And they may yet be right.'

'What have you learned about the other members of the convent? Tysilia is not the only one who might be involved in something sinister.'

'Eve Wasteneys is a clever and astute woman; Dame Martyn is a drunkard who barely knows what day of the week it is. I have been trying to watch Eve, but it is difficult, because she spends a good deal of time alone.'

'Why?'

'Dame Martyn is incapable of running the convent, and so Eve does most of the work. I imagine a good portion of her time is spent juggling the finances, but I cannot be certain. She may well be organising meetings where Walcote left off.'

'I want you to leave here,' said Bartholomew. 'Today. Tell them Robin has summoned you.'

'But I have not yet done what I came to do,' objected Matilde.

'I do not care,' said Bartholomew. 'A student was murdered at Michaelhouse last night, and Michael's room was ransacked. I have the feeling the killer knows we are closing in on him, and I want you well away from here.'

'I will just stay until tomorrow,' said Matilde. 'It will be Saturday, and—'

'No,' said Bartholomew. 'Leave today. I will call on you this evening at home. If you are not there, I shall come here to fetch you.'

Matilde, seeing the determination in his face, reluctantly agreed, and Bartholomew left her to rejoin the others. Eve waved a gracious hand to indicate that her guests were to be seated near the fire. 'How might I help you gentlemen? I would offer you wine, but you will understand that I would sooner you were gone before these nuns arrive. I do not want them jumping to the wrong conclusions.'

'Then I will be brief,' said Michael. 'I want to know about Dame Martyn's nephew.'

'Which one?' asked Eve uncertainly.

'How many does she have?' asked Bartholomew.

Eve shot him a playful grin. 'It depends on how much trouble they are in for wandering along the Barnwell Causeway after dark.'

Michael sighed impatiently. 'Lynne. He was here when we first visited you.'

'Oh, him,' said Tysilia, bored with her sewing and coming to join them. She knelt down and began to pet a cat that lay in front of the fire. Her attentions were rough, and the animal's fur was vigorously combed the wrong way. It was not long before it fled to the sanctuary of Matilde's lap. 'Lynne is a dull youth. He lives with the Carmelites on Milne Street.'

'What was he doing here the first time we came?' asked Michael.

Eve's expression was unreadable. 'He came to visit his aunt.'

'You mean he came to avail himself of your services?' asked Timothy bluntly.

Eve smiled enigmatically. 'He came to visit his aunt,' she repeated.

'I want to know more about these meetings that Walcote arranged,' said Michael, seeing that Eve was not prepared to be more forthcoming about Lynne. 'I want to know *exactly* how many of them there were, and I want to know *exactly* when they occurred.'

'But I have told you all I know,' said Eve with a sigh. 'How many more times do you want me to say the same thing? Walcote hired our chamber eight or nine times. I observed several men whom I thought I recognised and whose names I have already told you. I do not know what they discussed, and I cannot recall specific dates.'

'Dame Martyn did not tell the King's Commissioners about the money Walcote gave her,' supplied Tysilia helpfully. 'She did not want to give them any of it for tax, so she never wrote anything down in case they saw it.'

'Thank you, Tysilia,' said Eve coldly. 'Now be quiet, and do your sewing.'

'Can you recall just one date?' pressed Michael, turning his attention back to Eve.

Eve shook her head. 'Although I would not have mentioned it myself, Tysilia is right. We did not record the money Walcote paid us, because we did not want to be penalised for it when the tax collectors come. Therefore we have no way to check dates and times. All I know is that the second one was around late November, because we had been able to mend the roof – using gold coins I grabbed from Master Runham's icon. It was still leaking when he first came.'

'And times?' urged Michael. 'How late?'

'Well after dark, but not before matins. I suppose they were all some time between nine o'clock and midnight.'

'And you never eavesdropped, to try to learn why the Junior Proctor and the heads of the religious Orders met here in the middle of the night?'

Eve shook her head firmly. 'What if I had been caught with my ear to the door? Walcote would not have used our room again, and that money was very useful. Too much was at stake for me to risk it for mere curiosity.'

'I listened,' said Tysilia, beaming at them. She ignored Eve's heavy sigh of exasperation at her orders for silence being disobeyed. 'I wanted to know when they would be finished, so that I could be ready for them when they came out.'

Bartholomew saw Matilde hiding her laughter by pretending to inspect her sewing at close range, so that it covered her face.

'They chattered endlessly about whether things have names, and they talked about mending the Great Bridge, because Prior Lincolne once fell through it,' Tysilia went on. 'He is a fat man, like you, Brother, and I expect he was too heavy for it.'

'This is becoming intolerable,' muttered Michael. 'I am *not* fat.'

'What else did you hear?' asked Timothy, addressing her reluctantly.

'Nothing. I was bored and went to bed,' said Tysilia carelessly. 'They were a lot of gasbags, repeating themselves and muttering about tedious things. The only interesting one was that young man with the nice fingernails. But he only came to the last meeting – the one that was held a day or two before Walcote died.'

'And who might he be?' asked Michael, trying to imagine which of the religious heads paid attention to his manicure. Neither he nor Bartholomew recalled any of them as notably clean.

'He has good calves and a handsome face,' offered Tysilia.

'That is not very helpful,' said Michael. 'How are we supposed to guess who came to these meetings based on the fact that you found him attractive?'

'Well, I suppose I could tell you his name,' suggested Tysilia. 'Would that help?'

'For God's sake, woman,' snapped Michael, exasperated. 'Tell us!'

'His name is Richard Stanmore,' said Tysilia, smiling her vacant smile.

'What do you think, Matthew?' asked Timothy as they left St Radegund's Convent and started to walk along the causeway towards Barnwell Priory, where Michael suggested they might find Lynne. 'Is your nephew the kind of man to embroil himself in a plot to kill Brother Michael the instant he arrives home?'

'I have no idea,' said Bartholomew bitterly. 'I no longer know him. But when all is said and done, he loves his parents dearly, and I cannot see him becoming involved in something that might hurt them – as his being implicated in a murder certainly would. But I know that Tysilia is telling the truth when she says she knows him.'

356

'She is?' asked Michael, surprised. 'How do you know?'

'Because Richard had Matilde's pendant,' replied Bartholomew. 'She mentioned last time that Tysilia had stolen it, and then I recognised it when Richard pulled it from his pocket in the Cardinal's Cap this morning. Tysilia must have given it to him.'

Michael nodded slowly. 'You are doubtless right.'

Bartholomew sighed as a few more pieces of the puzzle came together. 'I should have seen this before. Eve said she took Tysilia to Bedford, to keep her occupied for a few days, and Bedford is between Oxford and Cambridge. We all know that travellers gather in large parties when they take to the roads. It is obvious that Richard joined Tysilia's group, and that is how they met.'

'Are you sure about this?' asked Timothy uncertainly.

'No,' admitted Bartholomew. 'But Eve told us Tysilia misbehaved on the homeward journey, which was about two weeks ago. Richard arrived in Cambridge at about the same time.'

Michael thought for a moment, then said, 'This means that Tysilia met Richard at least twice – once in Bedford and once when he attended Walcote's last meeting here. However, you treated Dame Martyn for drunkenness the morning after Walcote was killed, and Tysilia was there. Surely you would have noticed had they recognised each other?'

'Then there are two possibilities,' said Bartholomew, after a moment of thought. 'First, it may suggest that Tysilia and Richard did not acknowledge their prior acquaintance for sinister reasons. Or, second, it may be because Richard wore a scarf over his nose to mask the smell of pigs; Tysilia did not see his face and so did not recognise him.'

Timothy raised his eyebrows. 'The first theory suggests she is your cunning demon; the second that she is even more lacking in wits than I imagined.'

Michael frowned. 'If Richard *had* tampered with her on their Bedford journey, he would not want Tysilia squealing a delighted greeting in front of all those disapproving nuns. It would be in his interest to keep himself hidden.'

'It sounded to me as though Richard had considerable knowledge of St Radegund's,' said Timothy thoughtfully. 'This morning he referred to the nuns as sirens, about whom he had heard rumours. I deduce that Tysilia is telling the truth, and that Richard is more familiar with the convent than he wants us to know.'

'But why would Richard be involved in these meetings?' asked Bartholomew, not liking the notion of his nephew being involved in the plot. 'Everyone else was the head of a religious Order. Richard is certainly no cleric.'

'No,' said Michael. 'But it seems he was involved in these meetings some way or another. We shall just have to leave it to him to tell us why. And there is something else I want to know, too. Ever since he arrived, he has been showing off his new clothes and his new horse. I want to know how he pays for all these things.'

'The proceeds of crime,' said Timothy darkly. 'But I do not think his offences are related to Walcote's murder. I remain certain that the motive for *his* death was theft. Someone stole his purse, which was later recovered empty. What more evidence do you need?'

'What about the meetings?' asked Bartholomew.

'A group of religious heads chatting about the Great Bridge and philosophy?' countered Timothy dismissively. 'How can such things result in murder?'

'But Morden said they also discussed the plot to kill Michael,' said Bartholomew. 'And what about this alleged theft from the Carmelite Friary? That was mooted, too. Perhaps Walcote was using it to discredit Michael so that *he* could be Senior Proctor instead.'

'I do not believe that,' said Michael immediately. 'Walcote did not have sufficient presence to take on a man of my standing in the University. Who do you think people would follow: a weak Austin, who is pleasant but ineffectual; or me, who has been Senior Proctor for years and whom everyone likes and respects?'

'I am not sure everyone would see the alternatives quite in those terms,' said Timothy diplomatically. 'They may have seen it as a choice between a weak man, who could be manipulated to their advantage, or a man with known connections to Oxford, who is planning to give away our property to further his own career.'

'That is *not* why I am dealing with Heytesbury—' began Michael angrily.

Timothy patted his arm reassuringly. 'I am merely voicing an opinion that may be expressed by others. Your years as Senior Proctor have not made you popular with everyone. You have made enemies as well as friends.'

Michael knocked at the gate of Barnwell Priory, and the three men were admitted by Nicholas, who was still ravaged by grief for Walcote. His red-rimmed eyes indicated that he had been crying, and the dirt that was deeply impregnated in his skin and under his fingernails showed that he had been engaged in manual labour in the gardens, perhaps to secure himself some privacy and be alone with his unhappiness.

'Just the person I wanted to see,' said Michael, taking the man by his arm and leading him to a quiet corner. 'I am no further forward in catching Walcote's killer. I know you two were close, and I want you to tell me anything – no matter how small or insignificant it may seem – that may help us.'

'I have told you all I know,' said Nicholas miserably. 'I have no idea what business Walcote was involved in, which is just as well, given what happened last night.'

'Why?' demanded Michael. 'What happened?'

'Someone gained access to our grounds,' explained Nicholas. 'It must have been nearer to dawn than midnight, because our cockerel had already started to stir. But it was still an hour or two before we were due to rise.'

Michael exchanged a significant glance with Bartholomew. Their own intruders had been busy during the first part of the night, and now it seemed others had been in the Austin Priory near dawn. Were they the same people?

'And?' pressed Michael. 'What did this intruder do?'

'A lay-brother was stabbed,' said Nicholas. 'He is in the infirmary being cared for by Father Urban from the leper hospital.'

'We will speak with this lay-brother,' declared Michael, still holding Nicholas's arm as he began to walk. 'Take us to him.'

'I am not sure whether you will be allowed into the infirmary,' said Nicholas, alarmed by the way he was being steered in a direction he did not want to go. 'It is full of sick people.'

'I will be admitted,' said Michael confidently, dragging the unhappy Nicholas along with him as he made his way through the church. 'Now, tell me what this intruder did.'

'He entered Prior Ralph's solar, and ransacked the chest where we keep all our valuable documents,' said Nicholas. 'And then he left.'

'Was anything stolen?' asked Bartholomew.

Nicholas shrugged. 'Prior Ralph says not. But although we own land, we are not really wealthy and we do not have much gold and silver for thieves to take.'

'What about documents?' asked Bartholomew. 'Were any scrolls or parchments stolen?'

Nicholas shrugged again. 'You must address that sort of question to the Prior. I am only a lowly canon, and I have no idea what documents were stored in the chest.'

'Have you learned anything more about the meetings Walcote organised?' asked Timothy.

Nicholas took a deep breath, and cast a nervous glance over his shoulder. 'I know he dealt with powerful men, like the heads of priories and convents. That in itself was sufficient to make me feel that I do not want to know about his business. In my opinion, life as Junior Proctor was dangerous.'

360

'Hardly,' said Michael, surprised by the man's unease. 'Powerful men do not always have evil in their hearts, and dealing with them is not always sinister.'

'It killed Walcote,' said Nicholas bitterly. 'Tell *him* that.'

He had a point. Someone had executed Walcote in a most grisly manner, and whatever Timothy might believe about the purse they found, Bartholomew remained convinced that there was more to Walcote's death than a simple case of robbery. Nicholas might well be right, and that one of the powerful men with whom Walcote dealt was responsible.

'Is there anything more you can tell us?' pressed Michael. 'Any cases he was working on that he may have told you about?'

'Nothing that you do not already know,' replied Nicholas unhappily. 'This Oxford business was the most risky, but he said you were dealing with that.'

'And what about his spare time?' asked Michael, ignoring the fact that persuading another academic to sign a piece of parchment was scarcely life-threatening. 'What did he do when he was not working for me or fulfilling his duties here at Barnwell?'

'He liked to read,' said Nicholas. 'We were studying the writings of William of Occam together, and next week we had planned to move on to the works of Heytesbury.'

'But reading about nominalism is not dangerous, either,' said Michael, frustrated by the lack of relevant information.

'I am not so sure,' said Bartholomew thoughtfully. 'Walcote would not be the first to die because of an interest in philosophy.'

'There is Lynne,' said Michael suddenly, grabbing Bartholomew's arm. 'I want a word with him. The lay-brother in the infirmary can wait.'

Lynne watched them warily as they approached, but made no attempt to flee, as Bartholomew suspected he might at the sudden arrival of the University's Senior Proctor.

'I have some questions I want to put to you,' said Michael

peremptorily. 'Why did you run away from the Carmelite Friary?'

'I have never been to the Carmelite Friary,' said Lynne. 'You are confusing me with my brother. We are very alike.'

'Really,' said Michael flatly. His hand shot out to seize a handful of Lynne's habit at throat height; then he lifted, so that the student-friar's feet barely touched the ground. The lad's sullen arrogance was quickly replaced by alarm.

'I know nothing about anything,' he squeaked. 'I am an Austin novice. I am not a Carmelite.'

'My cells will be full tonight,' said Michael softly. 'First Morden and now Simon Lynne.'

'This is *John* Lynne,' said Nicholas, surprised by Michael's statement. 'We have no Simon Lynne here.'

'Simon is my brother,' gasped John Lynne. 'I told you.' He struggled out of Michael's failing grasp and brushed himself down. 'And I know nothing about what Simon may have done.'

'How do we know you are not lying?' demanded Michael unconvinced. 'You look like Simon Lynne to me.'

'He is my younger brother. He ran away from the Carmelite Friary on Monday night because he was afraid. He went to hide with our Aunt Mabel at St Radegund's Convent, but you found him on Tuesday, so he was forced to go elsewhere.'

'Where?' demanded Michael angrily. 'Are you hiding him? If you are, you had better tell me, because if I later discover that you knew of his whereabouts and that you concealed them from me, I shall arrest you and charge you with conspiracy to murder. And that is a hanging offence.'

John Lynne paled. 'I do not know where he is; I doubt anyone does, even Horneby. Simon fled because he was terrified.'

'Terrified of what?' asked Michael.

'Of what happened to Kyrkeby.'

'Kyrkeby? You mean Faricius, surely? Faricius was Simon's friend; Kyrkeby was the Dominican Precentor.'

362

'I know who Kyrkeby was. And it was Kyrkeby's death that frightened Simon.'

'But Simon was reported missing *before* we discovered Kyrkeby's body,' said Michael thoughtfully. 'He fled on Monday night, and we found Kyrkeby on Wednesday. Are you saying that he knew what had happened to Kyrkeby?'

John Lynne nodded slowly. 'Simon knew Kyrkeby was dead. And he did not want the same thing to happen to him.'

'Where is he?' asked Michael. 'If he knows who killed Kyrkeby, then he must speak out. As long as the killer is free, then Simon will never be safe.'

'I keep telling you that I do not know,' insisted John Lynne, and the fear in his eyes that he would be dragged into the mess created by his brother indicated to Bartholomew that he was telling the truth. 'But if I see him, I will tell him to contact you. It is the best I can do.'

'Then make sure you do,' said Michael, apparently deciding to accept the young man's story. He gave a hearty sigh and turned to Nicholas. 'And now we will talk to this stabbed gatekeeper in the infirmary.'

'There are sick men in there,' said Nicholas again. 'I do not know whether Prior Ralph will agree to an invasion by the Senior Proctor.'

'Let me go,' said Bartholomew to Michael. 'I am a physician: Prior Ralph can scarcely object to me visiting the sick.'

Michael seemed reluctant. 'Very well. But if you take too long, I shall assume this man has something worthwhile to say, and I shall come to hear it for myself.'

The patient lay on a cot piled high with blankets in the large and airy room that served as the priory's infirmary. Two other Austins were also there, one with a thick bloodstained bandage around his hand, indicating an accident that had probably seen the removal of some fingers, while another had the sallow, yellow look of some undefined and persistent problem with his liver. All three looked up as Bartholomew entered the room, hopeful of something that would break the monotony of a day in bed.

'How is he, Father?' asked Bartholomew of the small man in the stained habit. Urban was the canon who cared for the inmates of the nearby leper hospital, as well as tending the sick at Barnwell Priory. 'Is his wound serious?'

Urban shook his head. 'The cut is little more than a scratch. He claims it aches and burns, but so might I if the alternative was a day mucking out the pigs. Nigel is malingering, Doctor.'

'Would you like me to examine him?'

'He would not, because you would expose him as a fraud,' said Urban with a smile. 'I shall allow him his day or two of ease, but if he continues to complain after Easter, you can come and tell him he is fitter than most of the rest of us.'

'Are you here to ask about the men who almost killed me last night?' called Nigel, energetically plumping one of his pillows in a way that indicated Urban's diagnosis was correct. On a small table next to him was a jug of wine, which, judging from his flushed face and confident manner, Nigel had been making the most of.

'Men?' asked Bartholomew. 'How many of them were there?'

'Two,' said Nigel. When he had first started speaking, his voice had been a hoarse whisper, but this was soon forgotten as he began to tell his story. Bartholomew smiled, suspecting that the man's spell of ease was likely to end a lot sooner than Easter unless he worked on his malingering skills. 'They were big brutes, all swathed in black and meaning business.'

'What business would that be?' asked Bartholomew.

'Stealing,' replied Nigel promptly. 'Prior Ralph says they were unsuccessful, although they broke into the documents chest and made a terrible mess of his room. He does not keep any gold there. That is all in the church, and no one would dare to steal from a church.'

'How do you know the thieves wanted riches?' asked Bartholomew, aware that many people had no such scruples but declining to argue the point. 'Perhaps they came for something else.'

'Such as what?' asked Nigel, giving Bartholomew a baffled look. 'They came for gold and they stabbed me to get it.'

'Then tell me exactly what happened,' said Bartholomew.

'I was on duty at the gatehouse,' began Nigel, fortifying himself from the jug. 'It was very late, and the canons were preparing themselves for matins, which takes place before dawn.'

'Yes,' said Bartholomew. 'I attend matins myself.'

Nigel looked Bartholomew up and down, taking in his scholar's tabard. 'Anyway, I heard a knock on the gate, so I answered it. I was obviously slow in the wits – I had spent all day with the pigs, and then passed the night on gate duty, you see.'

'You mean you had fallen asleep, and you opened the gate in a drowsy haze?' interpreted Bartholomew.

Nigel's pursed lips told him that he was right. 'I had only opened it the merest crack, when they were in. It happened so fast that one moment I was standing at the door, and the next I was lying on the ground pumping my life blood on to the floor.'

'Your injury was not that serious,' said Urban mildly.

'They locked me inside the gatehouse,' Nigel went on, treating Urban to an unpleasant look. 'I was able to shout, but only weakly.'

'It was loud enough,' said Urban. 'The gatehouse is a long way from the infirmary, but I still heard it. The truth is that you only started to yell when you were sure the intruders had gone.'

Bartholomew did not blame Nigel; it must have been a harrowing experience to be stabbed and then be in fear that the attackers might return to complete what they had started. But, at the same time, Bartholomew could see that Nigel's wound was not debilitating, and the man should have raised the alarm, not cowered in a dark corner until it was safe to come out.

'By the time anyone heeded my cries, the two intruders had left,' concluded Nigel. 'And that was that. I was carried here, and now lie in great pain waiting to recover.'

He took another gulp of wine and gazed at Urban with challenging eyes, daring him to contradict him further. Urban raised his eyes heavenward, then busied himself with his other patients, declining to waste his time listening to Nigel's exaggerations.

'Was there anything about either of them that was familiar?' asked Bartholomew. 'Did you see a face or a distinctive mark?'

'I saw big men,' said Nigel promptly. 'I may recognise them again; I may not. It was dark and, as I said, it all happened very fast.'

'How big?' asked Bartholomew. 'As big as me?'

'Bigger,' said Nigel immediately, barely glancing at the physician as he poured himself more wine. 'They were both huge.'

Bartholomew gazed down at him thoughtfully. Was he telling the truth, or did he feel that being overpowered by large men gave more credence to his story? If he were being honest, his evidence would certainly vindicate Morden. Even the cowardly Nigel would have to concede that Morden was not a large man. Bartholomew wondered whether Michael would be obliged to release the Dominican Prior on the basis of Nigel's report.

'Why do you ask about their appearance?' queried Nigel, looking up at Bartholomew with sudden fear in his eyes. 'Do you have a suspect you want me to identify? I will not be able to do it. I did not see a thing before they struck me and I do not want to see them. They may try to kill me again.'

Bartholomew regarded him dispassionately, unimpressed by the man's cowardice. 'You were lucky. Our gatekeeper was killed when these intruders invaded Michaelhouse.'

For the first time, it seemed to occur to Nigel that he really had had a narrow escape, and that the danger he had

366

faced had been genuine. Swallowing hard, he glanced around fearfully before subsiding under his blankets and was silent.

At Urban's request, Bartholomew examined the man with jaundice, discussing possible medicines and treatments and forgetting that Michael was waiting outside, now that he was confronted with the far more interesting and immediate question of a malfunctioning liver.

'How are the lepers?' asked Bartholomew, as he jotted down a recipe for tincture of hellebore on a scrap of parchment for Urban. 'I have not had time to visit them lately.'

'Not good,' replied Urban. 'It has been a long winter and supplies are scarce for everyone. Lent has not helped, either.'

'Why not?'

'No meat,' explained Urban. 'And the Benedictines used to give us all their eggs and butter during Lent, but they have needed them this year for Brother Adam. My poor lepers cannot expect good health on stale bread and cloudy ale alone.'

'Spring cannot be far away,' said Bartholomew.

'It may be too late by then,' said Urban. 'Mistress Matilde often helps us when we are in need, but she is not at home and no one knows where she has gone. I have been to her house three times now with no success.'

'I know where she is,' said Bartholomew, pleased to have another reason to entice Matilde out of St Radegund's Convent, if she had not already left. 'I will tell her.'

Urban gave a relieved smile, while the physician turned his attention back to his writing. Everyone in the infirmary jumped when the door was thrown open violently, and Michael stepped across the threshold to glare around him. Timothy was behind him, his face apologetic, as though he had tried his best to stop the monk from bursting in, but had failed. Bartholomew started guiltily, knowing he should not have spent so long discussing the other patients with Urban while the monk was waiting for him.

'Well?' Michael demanded of Bartholomew. 'What have you learned?'

Nigel gave a sudden cry of horror, and Bartholomew saw the colour drain from his wine-reddened face.

'It is him!' he shrieked, pointing at Michael. 'There is the man who tried to kill me last night!'

'I know where Simon Lynne is hiding,' said Michael smugly, as he walked with Bartholomew and Timothy back to the town.

'Really?' asked Bartholomew. 'I thought his brother said he had no idea.'

'He probably does not,' replied Michael, pleased with himself. 'I have worked this out for myself.'

'How?' demanded Timothy. 'We have no clues.'

'We have enough,' said Michael, a self-satisfied smile creasing his fat features. 'We have been told – by Ringstead of the Dominicans, by the Carmelite student-friars and by Father Paul – that two people went to one man for intellectual discussion and understanding: Faricius and Kyrkeby both spoke to Paul at the Franciscan Friary.'

'They wanted a debate, Brother,' said Bartholomew. 'Simon Lynne does not want to talk: he wants somewhere to hide.'

'And that is why he has gone to Paul,' persisted Michael. 'Paul is a gentle man, who is popular with students. He would never turn away a soul in need.'

'We can try speaking to Paul, I suppose,' said Bartholomew, unimpressed with Michael's reasoning. 'Although I cannot see why a Carmelite would seek sanctuary with a Franciscan.'

'Why not?' asked Michael. 'He first sought sanctuary with a convent of Benedictine nuns, and probably even considered hiding with his brother at the Austin Priory. Desperate situations call for desperate measures.'

'How do you explain Nigel's accusation?' asked Timothy of Michael, when Bartholomew could think of no further arguments to refute Michael's claim. 'He thought you were one of the men who stabbed him last night.'

'I have no need to explain his ravings,' said Michael haughtily. 'While that incident was under way, I was at Michaelhouse, trying to work out what had happened to Arbury. Of course it was not me he saw.'

'It seems he did not see enough of these intruders to identify them anyway,' mused Timothy. 'He remembered large men in dark clothes, then howled his head off at the first big black-robed person he set eyes on.'

'But all the Austin canons wear dark robes,' said Bartholomew. 'So why did he not howl at them?'

'All right, Nigel yelled at the first *unfamiliar* black-robed person he saw, then,' said Michael impatiently. 'Do not quibble, Matt. Nigel's information is worthless anyway: most men wear dark cloaks in winter, and he only claimed his attacker was large because he did not want to admit to being bested by someone small.'

'Will you let Morden go?' asked Timothy. 'Even the exaggerating Nigel would have noticed if one of the intruders had been Morden's size. He is very distinctive.'

'I will keep Morden for a while yet,' said Michael. 'I refuse to allow him to go free on the word of such an unreliable witness. And do not forget that his glove implicates him in the burglary of my room, even if he did not later travel to Barnwell and stab Nigel.'

'What do you think these intruders wanted from Ralph?' asked Timothy. 'Was it the same thing that they wanted from you?'

Michael shrugged. 'I cannot imagine what, although I think we are right to assume that these two burglaries were committed by the same people.'

'Ralph and you are not the only ones to be burgled,' said Bartholomew thoughtfully. 'If Morden is telling the truth, then items have been stolen from him, too.' He snapped his fingers suddenly. 'And I think I may know exactly what those raiders were looking for.'

369

'Well?' asked Michael, when his friend was lost in thought.

'Of course,' said Bartholomew, as one assumption led to another and another, and gradually pieces of the puzzle began to fit together.

'What?' snapped Michael irritably. 'I am in no mood for games, Matt. If you know, tell me; if it is some wild guess, then you can keep it to yourself. I am already confused, and I do not want more untenable theories muddying the water.'

'This is not a guess,' said Bartholomew excitedly, as parts of the mystery became crystal clear. 'It was your mention of Father Paul that made me think of the solution. All this trouble has been over Faricius's essay.'

'How?' asked Timothy doubtfully. 'And why should Paul make you think of it?'

'The essay defends nominalism,' said Bartholomew. 'There is our first clue.'

Michael sighed. 'I fail to see how.'

'Horneby and Simon Lynne went to Faricius's hiding place in St John Zachary after Faricius's murder; the evidence, however, suggests that Faricius had already collected his essay and was returning to the friary with it when he was attacked.'

'It was not on his body, and his last words were spent asking you to find it,' agreed Michael, impatiently. 'And?'

'Meanwhile, Kyrkeby was struggling to write a lecture defending nominalism, to be presented at the most auspicious event of the University year. He was unwell anyway – I treated him for an irregular heartbeat – and the pressure was beginning to mount. Morden thought Kyrkeby's first attempts at the lecture were poor. But the day *after* Faricius's death, Ringstead said that Kyrkeby's lecture had improved.'

'You think Kyrkeby killed Faricius for his essay?' exploded Michael in disbelief, exchanging a glance with Timothy that was half-amusement and half-annoyance that they had wasted time listening to the physician. 'Matt, you are out of your wits! I have heard you suggest some peculiar motives for murder in the past, but never one as bizarre as this.'

'Because it is bizarre does not mean it is inaccurate,' said Bartholomew defensively. 'Perhaps racked by remorse, Kyrkeby may have tried to return the essay to the Carmelites by using the tunnel—'

'Your theory fails here, Matt,' interrupted Michael. 'Kyrkeby did not know about the tunnel. How could he have done? Even Prior Lincolne was unaware of it and *he* is a Carmelite who lives in that friary, not a Dominican who has probably never set foot in it.'

'Well, there is another possibility,' said Bartholomew. 'But you will not like it.'

Michael sighed. 'I do not like this one. But go ahead. We have heard one insane idea today. Another cannot harm us.'

'Walcote was also a nominalist, who knew Faricius and admired his work. Walcote may even have known about the essay. He was with us when we interviewed the Dominicans the day after Faricius's murder, when Ringstead told us about the sudden improvement in Kyrkeby's lecture. Walcote also knew about Faricius's stolen scrip. He may have deduced that the essay was in it, and therefore reasoned that the missing essay and Kyrkeby's sudden improvement were more than coincidence.'

'Why should he have reasoned that?' demanded Michael. 'We did not.'

'Because at the time we did not know that Faricius's missing scrip probably contained his essay – we did not know the essay even existed.'

'Are you suggesting that Walcote killed Kyrkeby for stealing Faricius's essay?' asked Timothy, exchanging another uncertain glance with Michael.

'Walcote killed Kyrkeby for stabbing a man he knew and admired. Horneby told us that Walcote knew about the tunnel, because he had caught him using it and had ordered it to be sealed. What a perfect hiding place for a corpse! Even if the Carmelite students did find Kyrkeby's body, they would never be able to report it without admitting that they knew secret ways in and out of their friary.'

371

'I do not know about this, Matt,' warned Michael. 'I can see a lot of holes in your arguments.'

'Such as what?' asked Bartholomew.

'Such as the fact that Walcote was not the kind of man to kill, for a start,' said Michael. 'I complained to you many times about his gentleness and his annoying habit of looking for the good in people. Such men do not murder others.'

'That is not true,' said Bartholomew. 'We have seen gentler men than Walcote commit all manner of crimes.'

Michael disagreed. 'Your reasoning has a Dominican Precentor killing a Carmelite student-friar, and my Austin Junior Proctor murdering the Dominican. Such men do not go around slaughtering each other, Matt. And anyway, Faricius, Kyrkeby and Walcote himself were dead long before Arbury was murdered and Nigel was stabbed. How many killers do you imagine there are stalking the streets of Cambridge?'

Bartholomew regarded him sombrely. 'I have no idea, Brother. But I suggest we should find out before anyone else dies.'

Michael wanted to go straight to the Franciscan Friary, to ask Father Paul whether he had Simon Lynne secreted away, and then question the lad about the mysterious death of Kyrkeby. They were approaching the Barnwell Gate when they became aware of a commotion taking place just outside it. A small crowd had gathered, and was standing around a prostrate body on the ground. Thinking it was probably someone in need of a physician, Bartholomew hurried forward to see if he could help. Sighing irritably at the delay, Michael followed.

Bartholomew pushed through the ring of spectators, then stopped in horror when he saw that the person lying flat on his back in the town's filth was his nephew.

'I want a word with him,' muttered Michael, eyeing Richard dispassionately. 'I want to know why he conspired against me at St Radegund's Convent with the leaders of the religious Orders.'

'Not now, Brother,' said Bartholomew, unlooping the medicine bag from around his shoulder and kneeling in the mud next to his stricken relative.

'I can do nothing here,' said Timothy to Michael. 'You and Matthew can visit Paul when you have carried Richard home to his mother. Meanwhile, I am worried about the plight of the lepers Matthew told us about. With your leave, I would like to tell Matilde about them, so that she can arrange for supplies to be sent today.'

Michael knew that his Junior Proctor regularly distributed alms to the poor and sick, and that he had a good deal of compassion for the unfortunates who lived in the leper hospital. 'Go ahead. I do not like to think of them starving either, and Matilde can be relied upon to help,' he told him.

'I will not be long,' said Timothy, beginning to stride away. 'As soon as I have spoken to Matilde, I shall return to help you at the Franciscan Friary.'

Bartholomew was pleased Timothy would urge Matilde to leave the convent; he knew she would not linger if there were people who had need of her charity. She would return home immediately, and then she would be safe. He turned his attention to Richard, whose white face and bruised temple suggested that he had swooned and toppled from his monstrous black horse.

'I was here first,' came a petulant voice. Bartholomew glanced up to see Robin of Grantchester. The town's surgeon held a fearsome array of rusty, bloodstained knives, and was busily deciding which one he would use to slice through the veins in Richard's arms.

'Leave him, Robin,' warned Bartholomew. 'This is my nephew and I do not want you shoving your filthy instruments into him.'

'He needs to be bled,' protested Robin. 'I will do it now, and he can pay me sixpence when he revives. He will not mind paying above the odds for an operation performed in the street.'

Bartholomew ignored him. 'What happened?' he asked, addressing the watching crowd.

'I found him first,' repeated Robin angrily. 'With those expensive clothes and that fine black horse, he can afford to pay me what I ask. I will not stand by why you take the bread from my mouth. Go away.'

'What happened?' Bartholomew asked again, while the crowd, anticipating a fight between the surgeon and the physician, looked on expectantly.

'Robin did find him first,' offered Bosel the beggar, who had been relieved of a hand for persistent stealing and who now worked on the High Street, demanding money on the fraudulent claim that he had lost an arm fighting in France. He was not a man Bartholomew liked.

'But Doctor Bartholomew has a right to him,' replied Isnard the bargeman, who sang bass in Michael's choir, and who was in debt to Bartholomew for once setting his broken leg, free of charge. 'He is kin.'

'Did anyone see what happened to Richard?' pressed Bartholomew loudly, before the argument could escalate and everyone started to take sides.

'He fell off his horse,' said Bosel, gloating. 'One moment he was riding along, trampling us under his hoofs and pretending to be a great man, and the next he was on the ground in the muck.'

'He just fell?' asked Bartholomew, pushing Robin's hands away as the surgeon made a grab for Richard's arm. 'No one threw anything at him or pushed him off?'

There was a chorus of denials, although several of the crowd muttered that they wished they had.

'The horse was prancing and waving its front feet around,' explained Isnard. 'But it always does that. It is the most badly behaved animal in the town.'

'Let me bleed him,' pleaded Robin, trying again to lay hold of one of Richard's wrists. 'If you wait until he regains his senses, he will refuse my services and I will have lost sixpence.'

'I will give you sixpence if you leave him alone,' said Bartholomew, covering his nephew with his tabard. He tapped the young man's cheeks until Richard opened his eyes, squinting against the white brightness of the sky.

A grubby hand was thrust under Bartholomew's nose. 'All right, then,' said Robin ungraciously. 'Give.'

Seeing that the hand was likely to remain where it was until he paid, Bartholomew rummaged in his scrip for six pennies. He could find only three, even with the one Matilde had given him, and Michael was obliged to provide the rest.

'What is wrong with him?' asked the monk, crouching next to Bartholomew and peering at Richard's pale face. 'Has he swooned?'

Bartholomew nodded. 'And then the horse threw him. That thing is far too powerful for a man of his meagre riding abilities.'

With Michael's help, Bartholomew raised the dazed Richard from the ground, put a supporting arm around the young man, and walked him towards Milne Street, where he could be deposited at his father's business premises. Michael paid Isnard a penny to find the escaped Black Bishop of Bedminster and bring it back before it ate someone, and then followed them.

Oswald Stanmore stared expressionlessly when he saw Richard helped across the courtyard, but did not offer to assist when the physician lowered the invalid gently on to a bench.

'Has he been drinking with that Heytesbury again?' Stanmore asked folding his arms and regarding his son with disapproval. 'The man is leading him to a life of debauchery and lust.'

'Heytesbury is leading Richard astray?' asked Michael. He watched Bartholomew help Richard sip some water. 'Why do you think that?'

'Because Heytesbury is in an inn at every opportunity,' said Stanmore crossly. 'And when there is no tavern available, he insists on being provided with wine.'

'Really,' said Michael, interested. 'Would you say that this affinity with wine is more marked than in most men?'

'I certainly would,' said Stanmore firmly. 'He has already drunk the best of my cellars, and is inveigling invitations to friaries and Colleges all over Cambridge, so that he can have a go at theirs. He is one of those cunning imbibers – not the kind who becomes roaring drunk so that the whole town knows what he has been doing, but the kind who indulges himself steadily and heavily and shakes like a leaf when there is too long an interval between tipples.'

'Like Dame Martyn,' said Bartholomew. Stanmore nodded.

'Well, now,' said Michael, his eyes gleaming. 'Perhaps Heytesbury will sign my deed sooner than he anticipates.'

'Yes, blackmail him,' said Stanmore harshly. 'Then he will remove himself from my house and return to that den of iniquity he calls Oxford. I do not want to order him to leave, because he is Richard's friend, but he cannot depart soon enough for me or Edith.'

Michael draped an arm over Stanmore's shoulders with a grin of immense satisfaction. 'Just leave it to me.'

'I do not know why you needed Oswald to tell you this,' said Bartholomew. 'It has been apparent from the start that Heytesbury likes his wine. I have seen him in the Swan *and* the Cardinal's Cap, and he carries gum mastic – a breath freshener – with him at all times to disguise the scent of wine on his breath.'

'Then why did you not point this out to me sooner?' asked Michael coolly. 'Had I known, it would have made a big difference to the way I dealt with him.'

'It was so obvious I did not think it necessary to mention it. You do not need to be a physician to detect the symptoms of a committed drinker. However, Richard has not been drinking – not today, at least.'

'What is wrong with him, then?' said Stanmore, finally becoming worried. 'It is not the Great Pestilence again, is it? Oxford is exactly the kind of place it would come from a second time.'

'It is not the plague,' said Bartholomew, taking Richard's wrist and measuring the pace of his life-beat. It was within the normal range for a man of his age and size, and Bartholomew did not think there was anything seriously wrong with his nephew. Richard's eyes flickered and he began to show signs of awareness.

'What happened?' he asked. 'Where am I? Where is my horse?'

'You fell off it,' said Michael unsympathetically. 'It is too spirited for you; you would do better with a palfrey.'

'I cannot be seen on a palfrey,' said Richard, not too unwell to be indignant. 'What would people think?'

'They would think that you are a man who is sensible, modest and steady,' replied Michael. 'They would not snigger behind your back because you have purchased a mount over which you have no control, and they would not think you are an ambitious toady, who is so aware of outward appearances that there is no substance to him.'

Richard's eyes were wide. 'Is that what you think?'

'It is what *you* tell people to think with your Black Bishop of Bedminster and your dangling ear-ring and your glittering buttons,' scolded Michael.

Richard turned on his father. 'I told you that horse was too ostentatious and that we should have bought the brown one instead!'

Stanmore's features hardened. 'You told me you wanted to make an impact on the town. The brown nag would not have achieved the same effect.'

Bartholomew gaped at his brother-in-law. '*You* bought him that thing, Oswald? It was *your* idea?'

Stanmore sighed heavily. 'Damn it all, Richard! The only condition I imposed on you for my generosity was that no one should ever know who paid for the Black Bishop.'

'What were you thinking of?' asked Bartholomew, appalled. 'You must have seen that the impression your son was making was not a good one.'

'On the contrary, Richard has secured a good deal of

work since he arrived here,' snapped Stanmore. 'Several wealthy merchants have hired him. The black horse did *exactly* what we hoped. But you had better not tell Edith about this. She will be furious with me.'

'Since we are on the subject of money, how do you afford all your fine clothes and your handsome saddle?' asked Bartholomew of his ailing nephew. 'I am sure Oswald did not give you funds to squander on those.'

'The saddle came with the horse,' admitted Stanmore reluctantly. 'A splendid horse would be no good without a matching saddle, would it?'

'The clothes are paid for with my own funds,' said Richard sullenly, 'although I cannot see it is any affair of yours. I worked hard in Oxford, and I have secured several lucrative customers here in Cambridge. I have no family to care for, so why should I not spend my earnings on clothes?'

'Well, at least this tells us that not all your young nephew's flaunted wealth was ill-gotten,' whispered Michael to Bartholomew. 'The most expensive item was a gift from his loving and very misguided father.' He turned to Richard. 'Never mind all this for now. I have a question to ask. What were you doing at St Radegund's with Walcote?'

'When?' asked Richard, a trace of his old insolence insinuating itself into his voice.

Michael's eyebrows drew together in annoyance. 'Do not play games, boy. One of the items on the agenda of these gatherings was my murder. Why would you implicate yourself in that?'

'Oh, no!' breathed Stanmore, as he slumped into a chair with one hand pressed over his heart. 'Not again! Do not tell me that another member of my family is involved in something criminal! I thought my brother's fate five years ago would have warned you against that sort of thing, Richard.'

Richard hung his head, and Michael eyed him with distaste. 'You came to Cambridge to make your fortune, and immediately set about wooing the richest and most

378

influential men in the town. These included Junior Proctor Walcote, who invited you to one of his nocturnal meetings, probably not realising that you were the nephew of my closest friend.'

'Walcote did not know that,' acknowledged Richard in a low voice. 'He was horrified when he discovered I am Matt's kinsman. He was afraid I would tell you about his business.'

'And why didn't you?' demanded Michael.

Richard rubbed his eyes wearily. 'I only went to one meeting; then Walcote died and there were no more. The discussion included raising funds for mending the Great Bridge, and then went on at length about nominalism and realism. There was mention that you had been seen stealing from the University Chest in the Carmelite Friary, Brother, but I told them that they were insane if they believed you would do such a thing.'

'Quite,' said Michael, a little mollified by Richard's belief in his innocence, regardless of the fact that it was wholly unjustified. 'What else did you talk about?'

'That was all. I doubt the whole thing took more than an hour. Nothing was decided and nothing was resolved, because Walcote was not forceful enough to allow any item to be concluded.'

'Explain,' ordered Michael.

Richard gave a wan smile. 'He meant well, but he wanted to please everyone. No one will ever be happy with everything, and there comes a point where you just have to go along with the majority. But Walcote did not want to offend the dissenters. We made no decisions, and everything was postponed until later. Pechem told me it had been like that from the start.'

'Walcote was weak,' agreed Stanmore. 'He was a nice man, who was a pleasure to have at the dinner table, but was far too conciliatory to make unpopular decisions. I cannot imagine him ever taking a stand on anything.'

'He was a follower of nominalism, yet he readily agreed with you that realism was just as valid,' said Bartholomew, recalling the discussion with Michael that had taken place after Faricius's death. 'He also thought you should have gone to interview the Dominicans the day that Faricius died, but was too diffident to press his point when you declared otherwise.'

'He always did as he was told,' said Michael thoughtfully. 'And I can see he would have been poor at leading discussions. Very well, Richard. I accept that you are telling the truth about that. But why did anyone bother with these meetings, when nothing was ever achieved?'

'I think the attenders enjoyed the opportunity to rant and rave to people who were of the same philosophical persuasion. Everyone loved the slander and lies that were hurled at the other side. The only things they did *not* agree on were those that really mattered – spending money on the Great Bridge and useful things like that.'

'Why were *you* invited?' asked Bartholomew. 'Everyone else was a cleric.'

'Walcote needed a lawyer to read various documents. Heytesbury recommended me to him.'

'And who else was at these nasty little covens?' asked Michael.

Richard rubbed his eyes again. 'Kenyngham and Gretford of the Gilbertines, Pechem of the Franciscans, and a few of their minions. It was a waste of time. What we did afterwards was fun, though.'

'And what was that?' asked Bartholomew.

Richard winked. 'The nuns entertained us in ways that were quite extraordinary.'

Stanmore regarded his son in disgust. 'I thought you would have known better than to engage in that sort of activity. And in a convent, too! What would your mother say if she knew?'

'Did Heytesbury join you?' asked Michael innocently. 'If the answer is yes, then I could have my deed signed this very afternoon.'

'No,' said Richard sullenly.

'Do not lie,' warned Michael. 'You are already in a good deal of trouble for attending these illegal gatherings. If you are honest now, I may be prepared to overlook your role in them.'

It was an empty bluster, given that there was nothing illegal in a group of scholars meeting each other in a convent, and, although it was hardly respectable behaviour, there was nothing unlawful in the frolics they had allegedly engaged in afterwards, either. But Richard's mind was evidently not working as quickly as it might, and he gave way in the face of Michael's belligerence.

'Heytesbury was not invited to the meeting itself, because the business discussed was private to Cambridge, but he waited for me in the church and joined us for the fun afterwards.'

'He would,' said Stanmore in disapproval. 'Mayor Horwoode told me that he was after Yolande de Blaston the instant he set foot in the town. I have never seen a man locate his prostitutes with such speed.'

Bartholomew nodded. 'Matilde told us days ago that Heytesbury had employed Yolande.'

Michael rubbed his hands. 'Excellent! I could not have hoped for a better way to persuade that sly Oxford rat to sign my deed.'

'Really, Brother,' said Bartholomew mildly. 'I did not expect you to stoop so low. I thought you were anticipating a battle of wits with one of Oxford's greatest thinkers, not that you would resort to blackmail because he is fond of a barrel of wine and enjoys the company of women.'

'If I were not investigating four murders, I would concur,' said Michael pompously. 'But blackmail will be a good deal quicker, and I shall be assured of a favourable result. It may not be necessary anyway. If Heytesbury agrees to sign my deed on Sunday, I will not need to mention dalliances with nuns or frequent visits to taverns. But there is something else I want to know, since you are in a mood to talk, Richard: what is Tysilia's role in all this?'

381

Richard's eyes widened in surprise. 'Tysilia? None. Why do you ask?'

'But you know her,' said Bartholomew. 'You met her in Bedford, and you travelled in the same party to Cambridge.'

Richard shook his head in disbelief. 'Nothing escapes the notice of you two, does it? But what of it? I cannot see that my brief dalliance with Tysilia is any of your affair.'

'You allowed that whore to seduce you?' asked Stanmore in horror. 'You could not resist her vile charms? I expected more of you, Richard. I credited you with good taste.'

'I saw no reason to resist her,' said Richard sullenly. 'I only took what was freely offered.'

'Like that pendant she stole from Mistress Horner?' asked Bartholomew. 'I saw you with it this morning.'

'This?' asked Richard, pulling the gold locket and its chain from his scrip. 'This is not stolen.'

'It belonged to a convent guest, and Tysilia took it,' said Bartholomew. He snatched it from his nephew and put it in his own scrip, determined that Matilde should have it back.

'But it was given to me,' said Richard indignantly.

'By whom?' demanded Bartholomew. 'And why?'

'Tell him, Richard,' said Stanmore wearily. 'I am sure there is a good reason why you happen to have this thing.'

Richard said irritably, 'I did not know it was stolen. Tysilia told me her uncle had passed it to her.'

'Why did she give it to you?' asked Michael. 'I thought *she* would have demanded payment from *you*, not the other way around.'

Richard swallowed. 'Because I was going to help her escape. She does not like St Radegund's; she finds it too restrictive.'

'Lord help us!' muttered Stanmore, regarding his son in disgust. 'You are a foolish boy, although not, I think, a dishonest one. How could you even think of embroiling yourself in a plan to free that whore? What do you think Bishop de Lisle would say when he learned that you helped spirit his niece away from her protectors?'

'He might be grateful to be rid of her,' muttered Michael. 'She is more trouble than she is worth.'

Stanmore stood and loomed over his son. 'I have been tolerant of your idiosyncrasies since you returned, Richard, but I am rapidly losing patience. You will abandon this life of debauchery, and you will remove Heytesbury from my household by Sunday – as soon as his lecture is over. And then perhaps we can begin to forgive and forget.'

Richard stared at the floor, and Bartholomew could not tell whether he intended to follow his father's orders or whether he would revert to his old ways as soon as Stanmore's back was turned.

'And that ear-ring will go, too,' added Stanmore as an afterthought.

Without looking up, Richard slowly removed the offending jewellery from his lobe. He drank more water, then claimed he was tired and asked that he be allowed to rest. He closed his eyes, and Bartholomew imagined he could already see a hardening of the youthful features, indicating he was unwilling to give up his pleasantly debauched lifestyle in Heytesbury's company. Perhaps both of them would return to Oxford together.

Bartholomew stayed with Richard a little longer, then followed a chuckling Michael down the stairs and across the courtyard to the road outside. Michael sniggered all the way up the High Street, although Bartholomew was not sure whether his amusement derived from the fact that Richard had been cut down to size or that he now had two very powerful weapons with which to bully Heytesbury into signing his document.

'Here we are at the Franciscan Friary,' said Bartholomew. 'Now we will find out whether Paul is hiding Simon Lynne, as you believe.'

'And, if he is, we shall have some answers at long last,' said Michael, rubbing his hands together in gleeful anticipation.

CHAPTER 11

BARTHOLOMEW AND MICHAEL REACHED THE FRANCISCAN Friary just as the first gloom of dusk was approaching, and were startled to find its normally sedate atmosphere shattered, with grey-robed friars running here and there in panic. Warden Pechem stood in the middle of it, his hand swathed in the bandage Bartholomew had tied, as he answered questions put by Brother Timothy. Pechem was shivering, and Bartholomew noticed he was not wearing his cloak, as though he had been dragged from his warm quarters too suddenly to allow him to grab it.

Standing to one side was Clippesby, his eyes so wild that the white parts gleamed peculiarly against the black of his Dominican habit. His hair jutted in all directions, so that he looked even more eccentric than usual. Bartholomew saw that his robe was dirty, as if he had been rolling in mud.

'What is the matter?' asked Bartholomew, watching Clippesby twist one of his sleeves so hard that he threatened to do it permanent damage. 'All this has nothing to do with you, does it?'

'No!' wailed Clippesby, his voice loud enough to draw the hostile attention of several Franciscans. 'If they had listened to me, this would not have happened.'

'I warned you to stay away from the Franciscans,' said Michael angrily. 'You know they do not like Dominicans on their property.'

'But I wanted to see Father Paul,' howled Clippesby. 'He is the only person in this town who is not short of a few wits. I have a right to sane conversation if I want it.'

'Lord save us,' muttered Michael. 'If the likes of *him* are demanding sane discussions, what does that say about the rest of the University?'

'What is going on?' asked Bartholomew of Clippesby a second time. 'What has caused this disturbance?'

'You will get no sense out of him,' said Michael, giving Clippesby a disparaging glance as he took Bartholomew's arm and pulled him away. 'Timothy will tell us what is happening.'

'Another robbery,' explained Timothy as they approached. 'And it happened just moments ago.'

'We were lucky Brother Timothy happened to be passing when it occurred,' said Pechem unsteadily. 'He and Brother Janius gave chase, but the culprits disappeared into the scrub-land that leads to the Barnwell Causeway.'

'We did our best,' said Timothy apologetically to Michael. 'But they were too fast for us.'

'Was anyone able to identify the thieves?' asked Michael. 'Who were they?'

'We do not know,' said Pechem. 'But they were brazen. Two men just joined the end of our procession as we walked home from the church after vespers. Everyone assumed they were the guests of someone else, and no one questioned their right to be inside.'

'*I* did,' shouted Clippesby, coming to join them. 'I *told* you they were not Franciscans, but no one took any notice of me.'

'They did worse than not listen to him,' explained Timothy to Michael. 'They ejected him from their premises, because they thought his warnings were the ramblings of a madman.'

'Whatever gave them that idea?' asked Michael.

'They threw me in the mud,' cried Clippesby, looking down at the front of his habit as though he had only just noticed that it was splattered with the grime of the road. 'They picked me up and hurled me into the street.'

'What would *you* have done if some lunatic from a rival Order thrust his way into your premises and started making

385

wild accusations?' asked Pechem, appealing to Michael. 'It is not the first occasion he has made a nuisance of himself here, and there was no reason to assume that this time was any different.'

'Did *anyone* recognise these robbers?' asked Michael, exasperated that everyone seemed to be more willing to discuss Clippesby and his antics than the real culprits. 'It is only just growing dark, so there must have been sufficient light to see their faces when they were here.'

With Michael's appearance, the Franciscans had calmed down, and now stood in a quiet circle around the monk and their Warden, listening. They shook their heads when Michael glanced around at them: it seemed no one had recognised the intruders. Pechem began to shiver more violently than ever in the frigid breeze of early evening, and Clippesby, in a rare moment of sensitivity, removed his own cloak to drape around the man's shoulders.

'You should not be out here,' Bartholomew reprimanded Pechem gently. 'That horse bite may have unbalanced your humours and rendered you more susceptible to chills.'

'Those thieves stole my cloak!' cried Pechem, agitated again. He realised with a start that he was wearing a Dominican's robe, and almost flung it away. But it was a warm garment, and he was very cold. He clutched it more closely around him.

'So, what happened is that two strangers calmly joined the end of your procession and entered your friary,' said Michael. 'And not one of you asked who they were. Is that what you are telling me?'

'We could not see their faces because their hoods were up,' said a short, obese friar called John de Daventre, whom Bartholomew regularly treated for trapped wind. 'All of us had our cowls drawn, because it is windy and there is rain in the air. It did not seem odd that these two men were also protecting themselves against the weather.'

'And what happened when these two were inside?'

386

Michael demanded. 'Did they dine with you, too, before they decided to commit their crimes?'

Daventre treated him to an unpleasant look. 'We all went about our own business, and no one noticed where this pair went. But it seems they followed Father Paul to his cell and forced their attentions on him.'

Bartholomew's stomach churned. 'What do you mean? Did they hurt him?'

'No,' came Paul's familiar voice as he elbowed his way through the watching friars. 'They only questioned me. They did me no harm.'

'What did they want?' asked Michael.

'Faricius's essay on nominalism,' replied Paul. 'I am afraid I was obliged to give it to them.'

'But you do not have it,' said Michael. 'You told Matt that you were distressed it had gone missing, and that you hoped it would reappear one day, so Faricius's name would be remembered.'

'I never told Matthew I did not have it,' said Paul. 'He did not ask me that specific question, and so I did not feel obliged to answer it and tell him it was in my room.'

Michael gave a heavy sigh. 'That is hardly acting in the spirit of the truth, Father. How did it come into your possession? And why did you decline to tell Matt?'

'I thought he would be safer knowing nothing about it, and anyway, I swore to tell no one. Oaths are sacred things.'

Angrily, Michael said, 'You sound like Kenyngham. Has it never occurred to you that it is sometimes better to be honest with the forces of law and order? We are hunting someone who has taken the lives of four people, Father. Surely that transcends any promises you made?'

Paul's usually expressive face was unreadable. 'I am a novice in the world of killers and thieves, and I find it hard to see what is right and wrong in such circumstances. But suffice to say that Faricius's essay was brought to me for safe keeping.'

'By whom?' asked Michael. 'And where is Simon Lynne of the Carmelites? He seems to be missing, too.'

'Here I am.' Simon Lynne, wearing a Franciscan novice's habit that was far too large for him, pushed his way past Daventre and stood next to Paul. He and his brother had been telling the truth, Bartholomew thought: they were indeed peas in a pod. He saw Pechem's jaw drop in astonishment.

'But you told us this boy was your kinsman,' cried the Warden, regarding Paul accusingly. 'You said he wanted to stay here until he decided whether or not to take the cowl.'

'That is true,' said Paul, smiling benignly in Pechem's direction. 'I just did not specify which cowl he would be taking – it will be that of a Carmelite, not a Franciscan. And as for him being my kinsman, well, we are all brothers in the eyes of God.'

'That is a rather liberal interpretation,' said Pechem sternly. 'We Franciscans are not in the habit of taking waifs and strays from other Orders.'

'We Franciscans also never close our doors to those in need,' retorted Paul sharply. 'Here is a young man who came to me because he was in fear of his life. I did what I thought was right; I would do the same again in similar circumstances.'

'But I was not safe here,' said Lynne unsteadily, on the verge of tears. He pressed more closely against Paul, who put a comforting arm around his shoulders. 'I thought no one would find me in a friary of Franciscans, but I was wrong. It took those devils less than four days to hunt me down.' He scrubbed at his nose and sniffed loudly.

'Who are these "devils"?' asked Michael gently. He saw the lad was frightened, and realised that now was not the time to give vent to his irritation that Lynne had eluded him for days and probably had been withholding information that might have allowed him to solve the case far sooner.

'The men who murdered your Junior Proctor,' said Lynne miserably. He glanced around him fearfully. 'You must see

388

how dangerous these men are, Brother Michael. If I, a Carmelite, feel driven to seek refuge in a convent of Franciscans – with whom we have been at loggerheads for years – you will understand how deeply I am afraid.'

'It is clear to me that the men who have terrified Lynne are the same ones who marched in here and demanded Faricius's essay,' added Paul.

'How do you know that?' asked Bartholomew, a little bewildered by the sudden flow of information.

'It is complex,' said Paul. 'And I do not want to discuss it here. It is cold and there is rain in the air. It is fine for you youngsters, but not for an old man who has just had a dagger at his throat.'

'But you said they did not harm you,' said Bartholomew, alarmed. 'Now you say they held you at knife point?'

Pechem gave a hearty sigh. 'I understand none of this. My friary is robbed, I learn that Carmelites have invaded the sanctity of our walls, and now you are talking about the murder of the Junior Proctor and stolen essays on nominalism. I think you all have some explaining to do.'

Paul agreed. 'It is time the unpleasantness regarding Faricius's essay was laid to rest. He was a gentle man, and would have been appalled to think that his scholarly opinions should be the cause of so much bloodshed and anguish.'

'He should have considered that before he put pen to parchment, then,' said Timothy, rather bitterly. 'Faricius should have used his common sense to see that writing an essay on a subject that is currently so contentious would do nothing to improve the unity and peacefulness of the town.'

'We should discuss this inside,' said Bartholomew, taking Paul's arm and leading him towards the steps to Warden Pechem's office. 'Father Paul is cold.'

'Come with us, Lynne,' instructed Michael. 'The rest of you should be about your business. Timothy, would you mind informing the beadles what has happened, and instruct them to be on the alert for these two robbers on their patrols tonight?'

Timothy nodded dutifully, and walked briskly across the courtyard. Bartholomew saw him offer to escort Clippesby back to Michaelhouse, although it was scarcely on his way. Bartholomew was again impressed by the man: it was not safe for Clippesby to linger inside the Franciscan Friary, and now that it was growing dark, it was not safe for the Dominican to be out at all. Timothy was kind to think of him, when virtually everyone else in Cambridge wished the crazed Dominican would just disappear. Clippesby allowed himself to be led away like a tame dog.

'Good,' said Paul, as they reached Pechem's office where there was a fire blazing in the hearth. He turned his sightless eyes on Bartholomew and gave a mischievous grin, speaking in a low voice so that Pechem would not hear. 'Actually, I am not particularly cold, but this will warm me nicely before I retire to bed tonight.'

Bartholomew looked around at the men who had gathered in Pechem's small room, making it feel cramped and stuffy. Paul huddled close to the flames, holding towards them translucent, knobbly hands that were streaked with lumpy blue veins. Lynne hovered near the door, as if he imagined he might be able to escape if Michael's questions became too uncomfortable. Pechem had retired to his bed, piling himself high with blankets in an attempt to warm himself.

'Right,' said Michael, gazing coolly at Lynne. 'I am not pleased that you ran away, thus withholding valuable information from me. But I might be prepared to overlook that if you are honest with me now, and tell me what I need to know.'

Lynne nodded miserably.

'So,' began Michael. 'Let us start with Faricius's death. He was stabbed and, as we have done, you reasoned that he had been killed *after* he had retrieved his essay from its hiding place – that someone killed him because they wanted to steal it.'

'Kyrkeby,' said Lynne unhappily. 'He killed Faricius for

the essay. He was due to give the University Lecture, and he needed something more inspiring than the dull tract he had compiled. Faricius told me that Kyrkeby had given him a ruby ring in exchange for the essay.'

'So that is where that ring came from,' said Michael, carefully not looking in Bartholomew's direction so he would not have to acknowledge that the physician's speculations about Kyrkeby had been correct. 'We discovered it in Faricius's spare scrip when we went through his belongings.'

Lynne nodded. 'I was not there, but Horneby told me you had found it. Faricius took the ring from Kyrkeby, and promised to give him the essay later.'

'Why would Faricius want a ruby ring?' asked Pechem curiously. 'He was a friar who had taken vows of poverty.'

'Many friars forget that vow,' said Paul from the fireside. 'And Kyrkeby had a fine collection of jewels. He offered me some, too, if I would agree to write his lecture. I declined, because I do not consider it ethical for one man to pen work for another.'

Bartholomew recalled the jewellery among Kyrkeby's personal possessions. Morden had thought some of the rings were missing, although he had been unable to specify which ones, and had assumed Kyrkeby had been wearing them when he had died, linking them with Kyrkeby's penchant for women's attire. He was wrong: one ring at least had been given to Faricius.

'Why did Faricius agree to sell his work?' asked Michael of Lynne. 'Paul is right: it is wrong for one scholar to try to pass off the work of another as his own.'

'Faricius wanted to go to Oxford,' said Lynne. 'Heytesbury had encouraged him to go to a place where a Carmelite could speak freely without fear of suppression by his Order, and Faricius planned to use Kyrkeby's ring to pay for his education.'

'Heytesbury!' muttered Michael, his eyes narrowing in anger. 'I might have known *he* was involved.'

'He told us about it,' said Bartholomew, recalling the

evening they had spent at Edith's house, when Heytesbury had claimed his 'other business' in Cambridge was poaching students. 'He said the man he had seen was unsuitable – doubtless because by the time we asked him, Faricius was dead. He was also at Faricius's funeral, claiming that he had admired him.'

Lynne took a deep breath and continued. 'Faricius took the ring, and promised to give the essay to Kyrkeby. But then Lincolne nailed his proclamation to the church door, and the Dominicans marched on the Carmelites.'

'And Faricius, being a prudent man, decided he could not risk leaving his essay in its hiding place at St John Zachary, and so he left the Carmelite Friary – via the tunnel – to retrieve it,' concluded Michael.

Lynne nodded. 'He had taken Kyrkeby's payment, you see, and he felt that the essay was no longer his to stuff behind stones in graveyards. We tried to stop him, but he was adamant that he should make certain the essay was safe. When we saw his body, we realised that someone had cut the strap that attached his scrip to his belt, and that the essay had gone. I went with Horneby to check the churchyard at St John Zachary two days later – on Monday night – but it was not there.'

'And the stone had been replaced and the bushes arranged in a way that implied Faricius had collected the thing, and had covered up his secret hole as he liked,' said Michael.

Lynne nodded again.

'So Kyrkeby stabbed Faricius and made off with the essay,' said Michael. 'But who murdered Kyrkeby? It was not the Carmelites, anxious to avenge the wholly unnecessary death of their most brilliant thinker, was it?'

'It was not,' said Lynne tearfully. 'Walcote did that.'

'Walcote?' echoed Michael, again not looking at Bartholomew. 'I do not believe you!'

'Horneby and I had just climbed through the tunnel after searching St John Zachary's churchyard for Faricius's essay on Monday night when we heard an altercation taking place in the lane outside. Horneby said it was none of our affair and left, but I lingered. I wish to God I had not.'

'Why?' demanded Michael. 'And who was involved in this "altercation"?'

'I heard Walcote and his beadles ordering Kyrkeby to give them the stolen essay. Kyrkeby refused, because he said he had paid a good price for it. Then I heard Kyrkeby make a vile, strangled sound, as if he were trying to be sick, and Walcote urging him to stand up. At that point, I could stand no more, and I ran away.'

'A strangled sound?' asked Bartholomew. 'Then it was Kyrkeby's weak heart that killed him.'

'How do you know that?' asked Michael sceptically.

'Because he would not have been making strangled sounds if Walcote had hit him on the head – there would probably have been a thump and then nothing at all. And there would have been no strangled sounds if Walcote had broken Kyrkeby's neck. All that damage must have been caused when the body was pushed inside the tunnel.'

'So, Walcote did not kill Kyrkeby?' asked Michael. 'It was an accident?'

'Yes and no,' said Bartholomew. 'If Walcote frightened or agitated Kirkby to the point where his heart gave out, it may well be deemed that the death was not natural. But the real evidence is that Lynne says Walcote talked to Kyrkeby *after* he made this strangled sound, urging him to stand. It sounds to me as though Walcote was alarmed by the sudden seizure, and that he had not intended to harry the man so.'

'Harrying was not Walcote's style,' agreed Michael. He turned to Lynne. 'You say you were inside the Carmelite Friary when all this was taking place. The walls are high, so I know you could not have seen over them. How do you know it was Walcote demanding this essay from Kyrkeby?'

'I recognised his voice,' said Lynne. 'He caught me using the tunnel the week before, so I was familiar with it.'

'You said Walcote's beadles were there, too,' said

Bartholomew. 'Are you sure it was Walcote who was badgering Kyrkeby, and not them?'

'I do not recall who said what exactly,' admitted Lynne. 'But Walcote did a lot of the talking, because he was the Junior Proctor. That is what his beadles kept saying.'

'What are you talking about?' demanded Michael. 'You say the beadles kept telling Walcote he was Junior Proctor? I can assure you that he knew.'

'They kept reminding him,' insisted Lynne. 'Everyone knows he was weak. They told him that he was the Junior Proctor, and that it was up to him to locate the essay.'

'How curious,' said Michael, puzzled. 'Still, I suppose someone like Meadowman might have reminded him of his responsibilities, perhaps sensing that Kyrkeby knew more than Walcote's gentle questions would reveal. But then who killed Walcote?'

'I imagine the pair who have been busy searching half of Cambridge for this damned essay was responsible for that,' said Bartholomew.

'Yes,' agreed Lynne nervously. 'That is why I ran away. When I heard that Walcote had been murdered, I decided that the power of men able to kill a proctor was more than I wanted to challenge. I fled to Father Paul, because I knew he would tell me what to do.'

'But how did *you* come by the essay?' asked Michael of Paul. 'We know that it was stolen from Faricius by Kyrkeby. But how did it get from Kyrkeby's possession to yours?'

'Walcote brought it to me the night he died,' replied Paul. 'I thought at the time he was acting strangely; he was nervous and vague.'

'Did he look as though he had been in a fatal struggle with someone?' asked Michael.

Paul raised his eyebrows and pointed to his sightless eyes. 'How can I answer that, Brother? He approached me as I was walking back to the friary after the evening vigil. I was alone, and I doubt anyone else saw him. He pressed the

394

essay into my hands, made me swear to tell no one about it, and then left.'

'Why you?' asked Michael.

'I suppose he knew I am sympathetic to the views of the nominalists, and he decided it would be safer with me than with anyone else. Who would think to look for a written essay with a blind friar?'

'Those two intruders,' said Michael promptly. 'They knew where to look, because they made straight for you once they had insinuated themselves on to Franciscan property. They did not hunt around or ask questions of anyone else: they came directly to you.'

'They certainly came to the point when they questioned me,' said Paul ruefully. 'They said they knew I had the essay and that no harm would come to me if I handed it over.'

'Did they say anything else?'

Paul closed his eyes and leaned back in his chair. Suddenly he seemed like the old man he was, and for all his confidence and poise, Bartholomew suspected that being attacked in his own cell and having a knife pressed to his throat had been a great shock. He would never admit to such weakness but Bartholomew knew he was not as unperturbed as he wanted everyone to believe.

'They asked whether I had read the essay,' said Paul. 'I told them that I was blind, and that I had read nothing for many years. They seemed to accept my statement and left – with the essay.'

'And have you read it?' asked Michael.

Paul smiled wanly. 'Of course not. But I know what was in it. However, I suspect the killers allowed me to live because they believe I do not know the contents of the essay. Do not tell anyone that is not so, or I may go the same way as others who have dealt with it in various ways – Faricius, Kyrkeby and Walcote.'

'I disagree,' said Michael. 'I think they allowed you to live because you could not see them. Young Arbury of

Michaelhouse was murdered so that he would not reveal their identities, and I suspect the gatekeeper at Barnwell Priory was stabbed for the same reason. I wonder why they did not finish *him* off?'

'Perhaps because they saw no light of recognition in his face when they attacked him,' suggested Bartholomew. 'Arbury must have been different, and may even have addressed them by name.'

'That implies that he knew the killers,' said Michael doubtfully.

'Yes,' said Bartholomew, his mind whirling as he considered the possibilities.

'Perhaps you are right,' said Paul. 'But in my case, I think they were more interested in whether I knew the contents of the essay than whether I knew who they were.'

'Why do you think the contents of this essay are so important?' asked Michael. 'I thought it was just an essay on nominalism. It is hardly a list of scholars who regularly visit St Radegund's Convent, or a document outlining my negotiations with Oxford. I do not see why the intruders want to ensure that no one knows its contents.'

'You are underestimating the power of this work,' said Paul. 'You dismiss it as the ramblings of some vague-minded undergraduate. It is not. It will be an important document for many years to come, and I imagine it will be discussed in universities all over the world, not just in Cambridge.'

Michael shrugged. 'That still does not explain why the intruders did not want you to have read any of it.'

'Because they plan to publish it and steal the glory for themselves,' said Bartholomew in sudden understanding. 'The fact that they have gone to so much trouble to get it speaks for itself. They searched the Dominican Friary and Barnwell Priory, because the Dominicans and the Austin canons are professed nominalists. They looked in Michaelhouse because they thought the Senior Proctor might have seized it as evidence. And then they came here.'

'I suppose so,' said Michael, unconvinced.

'These intruders were desperate to get at Lynne, because they thought he would be able to tell them the whereabouts of the essay,' said Paul, putting into words what Bartholomew had already reasoned. 'Their way to Lynne was through me, so they came to me first.'

'They did not actually expect you to know where the essay was,' said Bartholomew slowly. 'They demanded that you divulge its location simply to terrify you.'

'I do not understand,' said Michael, confused. 'Why bother asking him, if they thought he did not know the answer?'

'Because they intended to ask him a whole series of questions that they knew he could not answer,' said Bartholomew. 'Every time he did not know, he would become more frightened. Eventually, he would be so relieved to be asked a question he could answer, that he would tell them immediately. It is a standard interrogation technique. Father William told me it is used by the Inquisition.'

'I thought the robbers seemed surprised when I handed them the essay,' said Paul. 'Now I know why. And because they have the essay, you are now irrelevant, Simon. You can go back to your own friary without fear.'

Bartholomew was thoughtful. 'If whoever stole the essay intends to publish it under his own name, then the Carmelites, Franciscans and Gilbertines are not to blame. They despise nominalism.'

'Excellent,' said Michael gloomily. 'That only leaves all the Dominicans, all the Austin canons and most of the Benedictines.'

'Right,' said Bartholomew. 'But when we deduced that a good place to hunt for Lynne was with Father Paul, there was only one Benedictine present other than you: Timothy.'

'You think Brother Timothy is the killer?' asked Michael, aghast at the notion. 'But he is my Junior Proctor! Junior Proctors uphold the law, not break it.'

'So?' asked Bartholomew. 'Being a Junior Proctor does

not seem to mean much. Walcote frightened Kyrkeby to death, and Timothy probably stabbed Arbury and the Barnwell gatekeeper.'

'No,' said Michael firmly. 'This is nonsense.'

'Why?' asked Bartholomew. 'Because he is a Benedictine? Because you like him, and because he seems like a nice, respectable sort of fellow? We have met that kind of person before, Brother, and it means nothing.'

'Timothy would not commit murder, Matthew,' said Father Paul with quiet reason. 'He is a good man who gives alms to the poor. Also, I would have recognised his voice if he had been the intruder who demanded the essay: I did not.'

'But everyone agrees that *two* men joined the end of the procession and strolled on to Franciscan property,' said Bartholomew. 'Did you hear both of them speak?'

'No,' admitted Paul. 'But I am sure I would have known if one of them had been Timothy.'

'How?' asked Bartholomew. 'Does he have a distinctive smell, or a particular way of moving his feet when he walks that you might have noticed?'

'No,' said Paul again. 'He does not. But I would have recognised his voice.'

Bartholomew sighed. He understood that Paul was unwilling to admit that his blindness might have been a disadvantage, when he liked everyone to believe it was a boon, but the old man's obstinacy might lead them astray. 'Think carefully, Father. Did *both* these intruders speak or did just one of them do the talking?'

'One,' said Paul, rather reluctantly. 'But it was not Timothy. He has a distinctive voice, pleasant and rich. The person who spoke had a thin voice, which had a disagreeable smugness to it.'

'Have you ever heard Brother Janius of the Benedictines speak?'

'Now wait a moment—' began Michael angrily. Bartholomew raised a hand to silence him.

'I do not know Janius,' admitted Paul. 'So I do not know whether I have heard him speak or not. Does he have a thin, reedy voice that sounds as if he could do with a good meal?'

'Yes,' said Bartholomew immediately.

'A good meal? I thought you said he was a Benedictine,' muttered Pechem.

'Janius does have a high voice,' said Michael begrudgingly. 'But that does not identify him as one of these killers.'

'Would you recognise the voice if you heard it again?' asked Bartholomew of Paul. 'Was it sufficiently distinctive for that?'

'I am not sure,' said Paul. He flushed, embarrassed. 'Normally, I am observant, as you know. But I was flustered by the knife at my throat, and I did not think much about voices and their timbres.'

'Of course you did not,' said Michael, favouring Bartholomew with a scornful look. 'And no one would expect you to, under the circumstances.'

Bartholomew was persistent. 'Paul would have recognised Timothy's voice; Timothy knows that, because we have made no secret of the fact that we admire Paul's powers of observation. So, Janius did the talking.' He shrugged. 'And it does not sound as though Paul enjoyed a lengthy conversation with these intruders, anyway. The dialogue seems to have comprised a few direct and aggressive questions.'

'That is true,' said Paul. 'The whole incident lasted only a few moments. The essay was on my table, and I knew they would have it whether I told them where it was or not. There was little point in dying over it, so I told them.'

'We have no strong reasons to rule Timothy and Janius out as possible suspects,' pressed Bartholomew, seeing that Michael remained sceptical.

'Another Junior Proctor,' said Lynne bitterly. 'It is as well I fled here, or one of them would have arrested me, and I would have died in his cells. You should be more careful who you choose as deputies, Brother.'

'There is no evidence that Timothy is the culprit,' said Michael impatiently. 'Matt's logic is faulty as usual.'

'There is evidence,' insisted Bartholomew. 'You just do not want to see it, because you do not want Timothy to be guilty. First, there is the fact that as soon as we had identified Father Paul as someone who might help us, the killer came here.'

'Coincidence,' said Michael.

'Not coincidence,' said Bartholomew. 'It was a perfect opportunity. Timothy slipped away from us as soon as he could, by pretending to go to speak to Matilde about the lepers. He doubtless went immediately to collect Janius, so that they could act before it was too late.'

'Too late?' asked Michael.

'You were coming here. Timothy knew that he had to get to Lynne – and then to the essay – before you laid hands on either and secreted them away. Once you had them in Michaelhouse, where security has been tightened since the murder of Arbury, reaching either would have been impossible.'

'But I do not keep valuable documents in my room at Michaelhouse,' protested Michael, carefully making no mention of the secret chest in the cellars. 'I would not have taken the essay or Lynne there.'

'Does Timothy know that? Have you told him where you keep your secret scrolls and parchments?'

Michael shook his head, and Bartholomew pressed on.

'Timothy knows he cannot mount a second successful attack on Michaelhouse. The student on gate duty tonight will be cautious and watchful, given that the last person to do his job was murdered. Timothy knew that if he wanted the essay he would have to come to Paul before you did.'

'I am not sure about this,' said Michael uncertainly. 'It is very circumstantial.'

'Then think about the raid on Michaelhouse that I discovered in progress: two men, one with light footsteps who ran away first, and one who was strong enough to best me in a hand-to-hand contest.'

'I thought you were convinced that the nuns at St Radegund's were involved,' said Michael disparagingly. 'Perhaps one of the intruders was a woman. Tysilia, for example.'

'The person I fought was no woman,' said Bartholomew. 'He was an experienced fighter. And Timothy told us only today that he was at Crécy. That is partly why you wanted him for your deputy – you knew that his fighting skills would come in useful for skirmishes with restless students.'

'This is not evidence,' said Michael impatiently. 'This is pure conjecture.'

'All right,' said Bartholomew, trying a different tactic. 'What about the fact that it was terribly convenient that Timothy just happened to be walking past when these two intruders fled the Franciscan Friary? Why was he there at such an opportune moment?'

'On patrol, I imagine,' said Michael, exasperated. 'Of all the people in Cambridge, Timothy is probably the one who has more reason to be out on the streets than anyone else. It is his job; he is paid to walk around preventing trouble.'

'And he did give chase to the intruders,' added Lynne. 'He followed them until he lost them among the reeds that lie between here and the Barnwell Causeway.'

'How do you know that?' demanded Bartholomew.

'He told us,' said Lynne. 'He returned breathless and sweating to say that they had escaped.'

'*He* told you,' said Bartholomew. 'That means nothing. He probably did run to the wasteland, with his accomplice Janius. But as soon as he reached the cover of the reeds, he left the cloak he had used as a disguise, along with the essay, and returned to tell you that the two intruders had eluded him. And that is another thing. The cloak.'

'What cloak?' asked Michael wearily.

'The men who stabbed Nigel at Barnwell Priory wore dark cloaks,' said Bartholomew. 'Timothy did not wear a dark

401

cloak today; he wore a pale one that he claims was ruined in the laundry. Cloaks are expensive, and I do not accept that Timothy would be so stoical if Yolande really had turned his fine Benedictine garment into one that looked like a Franciscan's.'

'Mine is missing,' said Pechem, rubbing his temples, as if the accusations and counter-accusations had given him a headache. 'He must have taken it when he came to check that all was well with us earlier today. I wondered what had happened to it.'

'Why did he feel the need to check on you?' demanded Bartholomew.

'I do not know,' admitted Pechem. 'He told me he wanted to make sure my hand was healing.'

Bartholomew shot Michael a triumphant look. 'Timothy paid an unexpected visit to the Franciscans with the specific intention of stealing a cloak, because he was afraid he might be recognised by Nigel if he wore a dark one. But Nigel *did* recognise him. It was not you Nigel was howling at, Brother: it was Timothy, grey cloak or no. He entered the infirmary just behind you.'

'He yelled at *me* because I was a stranger in a dark cloak,' said Michael tiredly. 'And anyway, Nigel did not see enough of the intruders to identify Timothy or anyone else.'

'Nevertheless, Timothy was not prepared to take that chance. He donned the grey gown, and would have claimed that he no longer possessed a black one if challenged about the stabbing at Barnwell the previous night.'

'Then it is his word against yours,' said Michael. 'And there is no compelling evidence why we should believe you.'

'At the precise moment when the men who attacked Paul were fleeing, you and I were on the causeway near the Barnwell Gate with Richard,' said Bartholomew. 'The Causeway stands proud of the land around it, and you can see for a long away. I saw no chase across the wasteland, did you?'

'I was not looking for one,' said Michael. 'But I did not

see Timothy double back on himself to come here when he said he was going to St Radegund's Convent, either.'

'I am sure he made certain you did not,' said Bartholomew. 'It is easy to stay hidden among all that scrub, if you do not want to be seen. But we should go back to the convent now, to ask whether he returned there as he says.'

'No,' said Michael. 'It will be a waste of time. Timothy is innocent of these charges.'

Bartholomew did not think so, although he also knew for certain that Timothy had not returned to the convent: he would not have had time to walk all the way to St Radgund's and then be back in Cambridge in time to chase the 'intruders' across the marshes. Timothy had done exactly as Bartholomew had surmised: he had grabbed Janius, invaded the Franciscan Friary and then escaped into the marshes while pretending to 'give chase' to the culprits.

Michael glared at Pechem, Paul and Lynne. 'You three will say nothing about this to anyone. Matt has no evidence to support his accusations, and I do not want to lose a good Junior Proctor on the basis of a few wild guesses on his part.'

'Then there is only one way to resolve this,' said Bartholomew, undeterred. 'We must pay Timothy and Janius a visit, and see whether they have an essay, two dark cloaks and a bloodied knife in their possession.'

'No, Matt,' said Michael yet again, stretching bare feet towards the flames that blazed in the kitchen hearth later that evening. The College cat jumped into his lap, and began to purr loudly as he scratched it under the chin. He sneezed, almost tipping it on to the floor, but it declined to abandon the comfortable haven it had located. 'I will not allow you to invade the privacy of my Junior Proctor on the basis of the flimsy evidence you have presented.'

'It will not be flimsy evidence when we find what we are looking for,' persisted Bartholomew. 'Within a few moments, your investigation will be over.'

'I like Timothy,' said Michael. 'He has proved himself an

403

excellent Junior Proctor over the last few days – better than Walcote could ever have been. I do not want him to resign just because you think he is a murderer.'

'But he *is* a murderer,' said Bartholomew, becoming exasperated. 'He killed your last Junior Proctor so that he could step into his shoes and steal Faricius's essay.'

'Make up your mind, Matt. Timothy cannot have turned murderer for both reasons.'

'Does it matter?' asked Bartholomew. 'He and his henchman Janius have committed terrible crimes. Are they really the kind of men you want representing law and order in the University you love?'

'You are on the wrong track entirely,' said Michael impatiently. 'Walcote was murdered because of these nocturnal meetings he arranged. He was trying to discredit me, so that *he* would be appointed Senior Proctor and assume the power that I have accrued over the past five years. And it would have been disastrous for the University: he scraped by as Junior Proctor, because I was there to help him. He could never have managed what I do alone.'

'But you were thinking of moving on anyway,' said Bartholomew, seeing all kinds of problems with Michael's assumptions. 'You were prepared to become Master of Michaelhouse last year, and it is only a matter of time before a suitably prestigious position comes and you take it. Then Walcote would have been appointed Senior Proctor automatically. Why should he feel the need to organise secret meetings to oust you when his promotion was inevitable?'

'Perhaps he wanted the appointment now, not at some unspecified point in the future,' said Michael. 'He accused me of stealing from the Carmelites—'

'But you did steal from the Carmelites,' Bartholomew pointed out.

Michael ignored him. '—so I suppose it is possible that he was murdered by someone loyal to me. Everyone knows that I keep the University stable and prosperous, and it is not inconceivable that someone decided to rid me – and the University – of a potential problem.'

'Then why did this well-wisher not simply tell you about these meetings of Walcote's?' pressed Bartholomew. 'You are a man who knows how to look after himself, and you would not need to murder your Junior Proctor to stop him from spreading lies about you.'

Michael sighed. 'You are tired, Matt. You did not sleep much last night, because of that business with Arbury. Things will look different in the morning, when you have rested.'

He settled himself more comfortably in Agatha's chair, and within a few moments, both he and the cat were snoring comfortably. It was a cosy scene, and Bartholomew might have been amused had he not been so frustrated. He poked viciously at the fire, and then made for the door.

'Wait, lad,' came a voice from the shadows.

Bartholomew nearly leapt out of his skin at the close proximity of Cynric's voice. 'What are you doing here at this time of night?' he asked, a little irritably. 'You should be at home with Rachel.'

'She has a chill from attending all the midnight vigils this week,' said Cynric. 'She has gone to bed with possets and blankets, and is snoring almost as loudly as Brother Michael. I came here for some peace; instead I find you two arguing.'

'How long have you been here?' asked Bartholomew. 'Did you hear what we were saying?'

'I heard,' said Cynric. 'And I agree with Brother Michael. You only have nasty accusations, not evidence. If you accuse a man of murder, you may see him hang. Is that what you want, based on the information you have?'

'That is why I want to search Timothy's room,' whispered Bartholomew, glancing back across at the sleeping Michael. 'I am sure the essay will be there.'

'So will Timothy, most likely,' said Cynric. 'It would be a risky thing to do.'

'He will not be in his room all evening,' said Bartholomew. 'I will wait until he leaves.'

'Then do it tomorrow,' suggested Cynric. 'It will be Saturday, and many people – especially monks – will be keeping the Easter Eve vigil. He will almost certainly be out then.'

Reluctantly, Bartholomew conceded that Cynric was right. He was restless and his head ached from tension and lack of sleep, but he felt he had to do something. He certainly did not feel like going to bed.

'I am going to see Matilde,' he said, reaching for his cloak. 'I want to make sure she arrived home safe from St Radegund's.'

'She did,' said Cynric. 'I saw her at sunset. But if you feel like visiting her anyway, old Cynric will escort you to make sure you do not disregard his advice and make a detour to places you have no right to be.'

Bartholomew smiled, touched by his book-bearer's concern, and headed towards the front gate. He told the student on guard duty that he was going to visit a patient, grateful that it was dark and that the boy would not see from the sudden flush in his cheeks that he was lying, then he and Cynric strode briskly along the High Street to the area called the Jewry where Matilde lived. It was a silent night, although rain pattered on the cobbled streets and on to roofs that were so sodden that they looked as though they would not take much more miserable weather.

'Have you noticed any change in Richard yet?' asked Cynric conversationally, as they walked. 'Because he gets drunk with Heytesbury most nights, neither of them is in any condition to return to Trumpington, so they sleep at Oswald Stanmore's business premises. As you know, Rachel and I have a chamber there, so it allows me to apply the Franciscans' charm.'

'I thought the dish of burning feathers he mentioned was something to do with you,' said Bartholomew, smiling.

Cynric nodded. 'Clippesby has a way with animals, and I persuaded him to grab me a handful of tail from the College cockerel. We were supposed to use a pheasant, but you do not see many of those around.'

'Richard fell off his horse today,' said Bartholomew. 'I hope this charm is not harming him.'

'It would be worth it,' said Cynric, unrelenting. 'His foul manners are upsetting his mother, and I will not see that good lady distressed if I can prevent it. A few bad mornings might do him good.'

'It cannot make him any worse,' said Bartholomew. 'He is an arrogant—'

Cynric grabbed Bartholomew's arm suddenly, and tried to pull him into the shadows of a doorway to hide. But Bartholomew did not move quickly enough, and he heard Cynric's tut of annoyance. It was too late, anyway. He had already been seen by the two people who reeled towards them, much the worse for drink. They were William Heytesbury and Yolande de Blaston. Bartholomew saw the philosopher's jaw drop when his wine-befuddled mind registered that it was Brother Michael's friend who was looming out of the darkness to catch him intoxicated and in the company of one of the town's prostitutes.

'Damn!' Bartholomew heard him mutter. Rather too late, he covered his face with the hood of his cloak.

'Good evening, Master Heytesbury,' said Bartholomew wickedly. 'What are you doing here at this time of the night?'

'I was lost,' said Heytesbury, feebly floundering for a plausible excuse. 'This kind lady offered to escort me to Stanmore's house.'

'Are you going to visit Matilde, Doctor?' asked Yolande, evidently understanding that Bartholomew had just won some kind of victory over Heytesbury and deciding to even the score by making it clear that Heytesbury was not the only scholar visiting women after the curfew.

Bartholomew smiled at her cleverness. 'I hear you take in laundry these days,' he said, seeing an opportunity to discover whether she really had been responsible for damaging Brother Timothy's cloak.

Yolande nodded, her hand on the bulge beneath her dress where her tenth child was forming. 'Agatha is teaching me.

She said I should learn a different profession, because every time I work on the streets I produce another baby. Of course, I have been making exceptions for my regulars, like Mayor Horwoode and Prior Lincolne, and for high-paying customers like Master Heytesbury, here.'

Heytesbury sighed heavily at this blunt revelation of his intentions, wafting in Bartholomew's face a powerful scent of something nutty that only thinly disguised the wine underneath. The physician supposed it was the gum mastic he used for removing incriminating smells, although even the new import from the Mediterranean was not up to the task of hiding the fact that Heytesbury had imbibed a good deal more than was good for him that evening.

'Please do not tell Brother Michael that I was foolish enough to lose my way tonight,' said Heytesbury in a reasonable tone of voice. 'He was rather cool towards me earlier, and I am concerned that he is having second thoughts about our agreement.'

'Very well,' said Bartholomew, suspecting that Michael no longer felt obliged to charm Heytesbury now that he possessed knowledge that rendered Heytesbury's signing a virtual certainty. As far as Michael was concerned, the deal had been concluded, and his clever mind had doubtless already forgotten the Oxford man and had moved on to more stimulating problems.

Heytesbury blew out his cheeks in another scented sigh. 'Something must have happened to make him act so. Perhaps those two farms and the church have suddenly become profitable, and he no longer wishes to part with them.'

'Possibly,' said Bartholomew. 'Or perhaps he learned that you lied to him about Faricius.'

Heytesbury regarded him uneasily. 'What do you mean?'

'When we first met you claimed the "other business" you had in Cambridge was seeing one of our scholars with a view to enticing him to Oxford. That scholar was Faricius.'

Heytesbury raised his eyebrows. 'True. But I never lied

about it. I said he was "unsuitable", if I recall correctly. He *was* unsuitable: he was dead.'

'But he was obviously not dead when you first met him.'

'No,' said Heytesbury. He rummaged in his scrip and tore a piece of gum mastic from his ever-ready packet; even in the darkness Bartholomew saw the pale stain it left on his fingers. 'I had heard of his excellent mind, and I sought him out because it would have been an honour to teach him.'

'Then why did you not tell us this straight away?'

'Why should I?' asked Heytesbury. 'What would you have thought if I had revealed that the one person I had spoken to in Cambridge had been murdered within a couple of days? It might have put my arrangements with Michael at risk.'

'You may have done that simply by keeping quiet about it,' said Bartholomew maliciously, gratified to see the Oxford man blanch. Heytesbury seemed about to protest his innocence again, but Bartholomew turned his attention to Yolande. 'Did you wash Brother Timothy's cloak recently?'

Yolande nodded. 'It was filthy with muck from walking along the High Street. Why do you ask?'

'Did the dye come out?' asked Bartholomew.

Yolande's world-weary face became ugly with anger. 'It certainly did not, and you can keep that sort of tale to yourself! I will not have the likes of you accusing me of damaging the clothes I wash.'

'I was only asking,' protested Bartholomew. 'It may have been made of inferior cloth or coloured with cheap dye that did not stay.'

'Well, it was not,' said Yolande firmly. 'That cloak was returned to Brother Timothy just as black as when he gave it to me, and a whole lot cleaner. Agatha taught me not to use hot water on black garments for exactly that reason.'

She grabbed the agitated Heytesbury and flounced off with him down the High Street, leaving Bartholomew frowning after her thoughtfully. So, Timothy *had* lied about the cloak. He wondered whether he should tell Michael immediately, so that they could act on the information that night. But Bartholomew suspected that the monk would be unwilling to listen to any more accusations regarding Timothy. Reluctantly, because he wanted the whole business done with as soon as possible, he conceded that it would still be best to follow Cynric's advice, and launch a raid on Timothy's room during the Easter vigil the following night.

'I have that document,' said Heytesbury, pulling away from Yolande and calling back up the High Street to Bartholomew. 'My lawyer has read it with care, and I am ready to sign it now.'

Bartholomew waved a hand in acknowledgement, and looked around for Cynric, who was still hidden in the dense shadows at the side of the road.

'I will sign it tomorrow,' Heytesbury shouted again, as he was hauled away by a huffy Yolande. 'Tell Brother Michael I will sign whatever he likes first thing in the morning.'

Cynric, who emerged from the shadows as soon as Heytesbury and Yolande had gone, chuckled to himself. 'This will please the good Brother. Michael tried all manner of tricks to make Heytesbury sign, but the one that worked was when he acted as though he no longer cared whether the business was concluded or not.'

Bartholomew tapped gently on Matilde's door, then backed away hastily when he heard voices murmuring within. Appalled that he had been so thoughtless as to assume she would be alone and that he might be about to intrude on something he preferred not to think about, he began to move away. The door was opened, and Matilde peered out.

'Matthew?' she called, peering around her into the darkness. 'Is that you? I have been waiting for you all evening. You said you would come.'

Reluctantly, Bartholomew stepped out of the shadows and Cynric followed him into the neat, pleasant room where Matilde entertained her guests. It was a lovely chamber, and always smelled of clean woollen rugs and the herbs that she added to the logs that burned on the fire. A golden light filled every corner, softened by the subdued colours of the wall hangings. Down-filled cushions were scattered artistically on the benches and chairs, while a large bowl of nuts and fruit stood in the centre of a polished oak table.

Bartholomew stopped dead in his tracks when he saw that Matilde's visitors, who sat side by side on a bench with goblets of wine in their hands, were none other than Tysilia and Eve Wasteneys of St Radegund's Convent. Bartholomew's stomach lurched. Had they learned that the portly Mistress Horner and the slender prostitute were one and the same? Had they come to do Matilde harm for attempting to spy on them?

'What are you doing here?' he demanded, quite rudely.

'I might ask you the same question,' retorted Eve, surprised by his hostility. 'We are women visiting a woman for sensible advice. You are a man visiting a woman at a time that is not seemly.'

'It is hardly seemly for a pair of nuns to be out so late, either,' retorted Bartholomew. 'But I am a physician, and I am often called out at night.'

'Has Mistress Matilde summoned you, then?' asked Eve archly. 'She does not look in dire need of a physician to me.'

'Why visit Matilde at night, when you could come in the day?' countered Bartholomew.

'Dame Martyn said we had to come in the dark because we could not be seen visiting a whore in broad daylight,' supplied Tysilia helpfully. 'She also said—'

'Our business with Mistress Matilde is nothing to do with you,' interrupted Eve, giving Tysilia a none too subtle dig in the ribs with her elbow to silence her. She stood up and made a gracious curtsy to Matilde, casting a sour glance at Bartholomew as she did so. 'We should go. I would not wish our presence to deprive you of company this evening.'

She headed towards the door, although Tysilia clearly had

no intention of leaving. She remained seated, so that Eve was obliged to walk back again and grab her by the hand.

'No!' Tysilia cried, trying to free herself. 'I like it here.'

'I am sure you do,' muttered Eve, tugging harder. 'But we must return to the convent.'

'Matilde is the leader of the town's whores,' Tysilia announced to Bartholomew, resisting the older woman and attempting to sit again. 'She knows everything about them. Mistress Horner, that fat woman who was staying with us, told Eve all about Matilde, and said we should come to see her with our problem.'

'What problem?' asked Bartholomew.

'I am sure Mistress Horner did not mean you to come to see me in the dark, though,' said Matilde reasonably. 'It is not safe for women to be unaccompanied at night.'

'Whores wander the streets alone,' said Tysilia brightly. 'In the dark, too.'

'No,' said Matilde quietly. 'They do not. They used to, but it was dangerous. These days, most of them gather their clients from taverns or more public places.'

'Really?' asked Tysilia, fascinated. She turned to Eve with pleading eyes. 'Can we go to a tavern? Tonight?'

Even Eve's composure began to slip at this brazen request, while Matilde was startled into a laugh. Bartholomew studied Tysilia carefully. Her eyes were bright and shiny, but he still could not read the emptiness behind them. Most of her conversation was vacuous, but she had asked directly about the progress of the murder enquiry on two separate occasions, and had pointed out that Walcote was likely to have been killed by more than one person. He realised he was as unable to fathom her now as he had been on their first meeting.

'No, we cannot tarry at an inn,' said Eve sharply, reclaiming Tysilia's wrist and dragging her towards the door. 'It is time for us to go home.'

'Perhaps Cynric would accompany you,' suggested Matilde. 'As I said, it is not wise for women to be out alone

412

so late, especially once you leave the town. The Barnwell Causeway is a lonely and desolate place.'

Eve looked grateful, and Bartholomew had the impression that the nocturnal mission had not been her idea, and that something had happened that had called for desperate measures. Once they had left, and Tysilia's demands to be taken to an inn immediately had faded into the night, Matilde closed the door with a grin.

'Tysilia is pregnant again,' she said. 'Eve wanted me to tell her the name of a midwife who would end it, but I told her that was not the sort of thing the sisters know.'

Bartholomew was horrified and unconvinced. 'That is just an excuse! Do you not think it odd that they just happen to visit you the moment you leave the convent? They know what you have been doing.'

Matilde shook her head. 'I do not see how. However, I can assure you that it was not Mistress Horner who told them I was "the leader of the town's whores", as Tysilia put it. Mistress Horner never once mentioned Matilde.'

Bartholomew rubbed a hand through his hair, wishing that Matilde had never agreed to try to obtain information for Michael. 'Then how did they know?'

Matilde shrugged. 'It is no secret that I run an unofficial guild for the sisters, and that I help them to organise themselves in a way that minimises the danger inherent in their profession. Perhaps Eve Wasteneys claimed Mistress Horner as a source of information to Tysilia, because she did not care to explain how else she knew. Mistress Horner has gone, and will never know what she is supposed to have said.'

Bartholomew nodded. 'You may be right. But if Tysilia is as clever as we think, then she may simply be telling you that she knows Mistress Horner is a fake. I do not like this at all, Matilde. I want you to go and stay with Edith tomorrow. You will be safe in Trumpington.'

'With lecherous old Heytesbury prowling the house?' exclaimed Matilde, laughing. 'I do not think so, Matthew! I will be quite safe here. You ordered me out of the convent

413

and I complied, but I will not be ordered anywhere else by you.'

'Very well,' said Bartholomew reluctantly. He felt in his bag and gave her the pendant he had reclaimed from Richard. 'Here is the locket Tysilia stole from you.'

'How did you find it? Did she give it to you?'

'She gave it to Richard in return for helping her to escape from St Radegund's.'

Matilde chuckled. 'So that is where all the nuns' trinkets go. She gives them to various men in exchange for some undetermined help in the future. I actually heard her bargaining with William Heytesbury one night. He is her lover of the week. She seldom keeps them for longer than that; I think she is afraid they might do something dreadful, like try to hold a conversation with her, if they come to know her too well.'

Bartholomew recalled that Tysilia had once said much the same to him herself. 'Did Brother Timothy tell you about the lepers wanting your charity?' he asked, wishing that the Junior Proctor did not know that Matilde had been helping Michael.

She shook her head. 'When was he supposed to come? I left the convent just before sunset.'

'This afternoon,' said Bartholomew. 'He said he would tell you that the lepers desperately need the food that you sometimes send them.'

Matilde nodded. 'The Benedictines have been giving all their eggs and butter to the ailing Brother Adam this year. Janius has taken the lepers nothing for weeks now.'

'Really,' said Bartholomew thoughtfully, recalling that Janius had walked with them to Barnwell the day Timothy had been appointed Junior Proctor. He had carried a basket that he said contained food for the lepers, which he had covered with a cloth, ostensibly to protect it from the rain. Why had he taken a long walk in the drizzle, when it had not been an errand of mercy that had called him? Had it been to drop Walcote's purse near the Barnwell Priory for

414

the eagle-eyed Sergeant Orwelle to find? Was that why he had placed the cloth over the basket, so that Bartholomew and Michael would not see that it was empty of provisions for the lepers?

Bartholomew turned to Matilde. 'I wish you would go to Trumpington, away from all this. I would feel happier knowing that you are safe.'

She reached up and touched him gently on the cheek. 'I know. And I appreciate your concern. You cannot know what a comforting thing it is to have a good friend in a place like this, where nothing is ever what it seems.'

'What do you mean? Are you referring to Tysilia again?'

Matilde shook her head slowly. 'I do not know, Matthew. Perhaps we were wrong, and there is nothing more to that woman than an empty-headed wanton. She was certainly not feigning her pregnancy. I was surprised I had not noticed it before, given that it is so well advanced.'

'It is true, then?' asked Bartholomew. 'I thought it was an excuse to come to threaten you.'

'She really is with child,' Matilde repeated. 'Her habit disguises the signs to a certain extent, but there is no question about it. Poor Eve. The convent will miss the money the Bishop pays to have Tysilia looked after.'

'They have not looked after her very well if they have allowed her to become pregnant. It would serve them right if the Bishop took her away.'

'I defy anyone else to have done better,' said Matilde. 'The woman is virtually uncontrollable and I wonder whether she is not so much cunning as deranged.'

Bartholomew did not know what to think. He stayed for a while, drinking wine and listening to her stories about convent life until he felt himself begin to fall asleep. Cynric's sudden appearance at the door as he was about to walk home almost made him jump out of his skin, and he was not sure whether to be relieved or more confused to learn that the two nuns had gone directly back to St Radegund's and had not stopped at taverns or to meet any accomplices.

When he reached Michaelhouse, he washed quickly and dived between his cold, damp bed-covers, his mind still whirling with questions as an exhausted sleep finally claimed him.

chapter 12

THE FOLLOWING DAY WAS EASTER SATURDAY, AND Bartholomew attended the obligatory services in the church, ate his meals and worked on his treatise on fevers, trying not to dwell on what he planned to do that night. As evening approached, the clouds thinned, so that flashes of golden sun started to break through them. By dusk, they had fragmented to the point where there were only a few banks left, each one tinged salmon pink as the sun began to set. Cheered by the sight of a clear sky after so many overcast days, Bartholomew wandered into the orchard, and watched the bright orange globe sink behind the trees at the bottom of the garden. The clouds seemed more vividly painted than he had ever seen them before; they glowed amber and scarlet, before fading to the shade of dull embers and then to a misty purple as darkness fell.

He walked back to his room, lit a candle and worked a little longer. The bell rang for the evening meal, and he picked at the unwholesome mess of over-boiled cabbage and under-cooked beans without much appetite. The students were in a state of barely suppressed excitement, because it was the last day of Lent and the following morning would see all the miserable restrictions lifted. When he found part of a dead worm in the shredded cabbage that was heaped on his trencher, Bartholomew began to long for the end of Lent, too.

Michael sat next to him, crowing triumphantly over the fact that Heytesbury had finally signed his document, somewhat unexpectedly, and that the nominalist would leave Cambridge the following day. Father William was of the opinion that Heytesbury should leave *before* he had given his

417

lecture, because he did not believe that the Oxford man would be able to resist talking about nominalism. Bartholomew hoped William was wrong, certain that if one philosophical tenet passed Heytesbury's lips, the man was likely to be lynched by rabid realists waiting for just such an opportunity.

While Michael tried to inveigle himself an invitation to consume another barrel of Langelee's excellent wine, Bartholomew returned to his room and dressed for his pending raid on Brother Timothy's quarters. He donned thick black leggings, a dark woollen jerkin, and shoes that were easier to climb in than his winter boots. He was reaching for one of his surgical knives, in case he needed to use force to prise open a window, when Cynric slipped into his chamber.

'Are you ready?' the Welshman asked. 'If we can have this finished in less than two hours, I will still be able to go to the Easter vigil. Ely Hall is only a stone's throw from St Mary's Church.'

'You plan to come with me?' asked Bartholomew, pleased. 'You believe that Timothy and Janius are the killers?'

'Not really,' said Cynric bluntly. 'But I do not want you to do this alone. I was hoping that the delay I recommended yesterday would make you see sense, but I can tell from the expression on your face that you intend to go ahead with this foolery.'

'It is not foolery,' said Bartholomew. 'Tonight we will see a pair of murderers revealed.'

'If you say so,' said Cynric. 'Well, come on, then. I do not want to be breaking into other people's property all night. It is too cold.'

It felt odd to be gliding through the darkness with Cynric moving like a ghost in front of him. Bartholomew and Cynric had shared many such nocturnal adventures, which Bartholomew was sure the Welshman had enjoyed a lot more than he had, but the physician's life had been blissfully free of them for several months. A familiar uneasiness settled in his stomach, and he found his hands were shaking, although whether it was as a result of the cold of the starlit night or from anticipation, he could not say.

He followed Cynric along the High Street, where everything was in complete darkness, except for one house where the cries of a baby indicated a sleepless night for the hapless parents. A dog howled in the distance, like a wolf, and the sound sent shivers down Bartholomew's spine. He glanced up at the sky: the stars glittered and twinkled so brightly that he could make out the outlines of the road and the ditches below, even though the moon was temporarily hidden behind a lone cloud.

'Here we are, lad,' said Cynric, gazing up at the dark mass in front of him that was Ely Hall. 'What now? Shall I pick the lock on the door, or were you planning on entering through a window?'

Bartholomew had not been planning anything. He had thought little beyond the fact that he needed to enter Timothy's room at a time when the Junior Proctor was out. He gazed helplessly at Cynric, and the Welshman sighed.

'Come with me around the back. The last time I was here, I noticed that the kitchen is a lean-to shack in the yard. You may be able to climb on top of it and force a window upstairs.'

Bartholomew was having serious misgivings about the wisdom of what he planned to do. Suddenly, it seemed madness to break into the private chamber of the Junior Proctor, especially given that the Senior Proctor had told him that he had no right to do so. But Bartholomew could see no other way forward; the thought of a murderer patrolling the streets and dispensing his own justice to scholars who flouted the University's rules was not an attractive proposition.

Forcing his uneasiness to the back of his mind, Bartholomew followed Cynric down a stinking alley that led to the rear of Ely Hall. The stench was eye-watering, since the Benedictines had apparently been using it as a latrine

419

instead of going to the public ones in the Market Square. Lazy cooks, who could not be bothered to take their waste to the river, had left their mark on the yard, too, and rotting cabbage stalks, unusable parts from joints of meat and old trenchers sodden with grease all festered together in a slimy mass that was as slick as ice under Bartholomew's shoes.

'Timothy's room is that one,' said Bartholomew, pointing to the tiny window, little more than a slit, that was above and to one side of the shack that acted as a kitchen. He frowned as he tried to recall details of Ely Hall from his visits to tend Brother Adam. 'That larger window to the right is a small landing. I think I should be able to squeeze through it.'

He felt Cynric gazing at him witheringly in the darkness. 'Why do you think I suggested we enter this way? I know where Timothy's room is, and I know the landing window is large enough for you to enter. How many more times must I tell you that if you intend to break into someone else's property, you should have a feel for the layout first?'

'Right,' said Bartholomew, hoping it was not something he would have to do again.

'Here,' said Cynric, moving an abandoned crate carefully, so as not to make a noise. 'Climb on this, and see whether you can prise open the window. It will be dark inside, do not forget. How do you plan to see what you are doing?'

'There was a candle on the table when I was last here,' Bartholomew whispered back. 'I think it is better to risk a light and search quickly, than to fumble around in the dark for longer.'

'Did you bring a tinder to light the candle?' asked Cynric.

It was Bartholomew's turn to treat Cynric to a withering look. 'I am not that incompetent. And before you feel the need to suggest it, I know I should lay a blanket across the bottom of the door to hide the light from any restless Benedictines who happen to be passing, too.'

'Good thinking,' said Cynric, impressed. 'I can see I taught you well after all.'

420

Bartholomew scrambled inelegantly on to the crate, wincing when his hands touched something soft that stank, and then heaved himself on to the kitchen roof. Using his knife, he then prised open the hall window. Cynric indicated that he should enter, and made a sign that he would keep watch by the entrance of the alleyway. Bartholomew was horrified.

'Are you not coming with me?'

'It is you who wants to raid a Benedictine's chamber, lad,' whispered Cynric hoarsely. 'Not me. I will hoot like an owl if I hear anything. Good luck and do not be long.'

He had slipped soundlessly down the runnel before Bartholomew could suggest that Cynric did the burgling while Bartholomew kept watch. The Welshman was far better at such things, and the physician felt sure he would have the document in a trice and then they could both go back to Michaelhouse to tell Michael what they had done. Bartholomew gazed at the open window with trepidation, took a deep breath to steady his pounding heart, and started to climb through it. Feeling as though the Benedictines who were asleep in the adjoining chambers would have to be deaf not to hear the racket he was making, he clambered on to the landing, then stood still for a few moments, straining his ears for any sound that might indicate he had been heard. Opposite, Janius's room was still and silent.

Bartholomew groped his way along the darkened corridor. He located the door to Timothy's chamber with his outstretched hands, and listened for a few moments before carefully lifting the latch and stepping inside.

He recalled that a candle had been set on the table near the window, and reached out cautiously until he encountered wood. He located the candle and withdrew the tinder he carried tucked in his shirt, blinking as a dim light filled the room. Before he forgot, he took a blanket from the bed and dropped it against the door. And then he looked around.

For a moment, when he saw the neat room with its plain

421

wooden cross nailed to the wall, he thought he had been gravely mistaken and that his invasion of Timothy's privacy had been unwarranted, but then he saw that the blanket he had used to block the door was no blanket at all; it was a heavy black cloak. He poked at it, noting that it had been freshly laundered. Yolande had been telling the truth, and the grey cloak that Timothy had worn had nothing to do with her washing of it. Bartholomew glanced at the row of hooks on one of the walls. A grey cloak hung there. He inspected the inside of the collar, where the tailor had sewn a small mark that indicated it had been made for the Franciscan Order. It was Pechem's.

He took a deep breath. Finding the cloak was good, but it was not conclusive evidence of Timothy's guilt. What he needed to find was the essay that seemed to have been the cause of so many deaths. He began to search, resisting the temptation to ransack blindly, and forcing himself to be methodical. Timothy had gone to considerable trouble to gain possession of the text, and would hardly leave it lying around somewhere obvious.

Wax dripped as he began to inspect the floorboards, knowing such places were popular as hiding places. Sure enough, there was a loose plank, and Bartholomew prised it up quickly. In the small cavity below was a dirty scrip, stained with blood. Bartholomew was in no doubt that it had belonged to Faricius. He dug deeper, and emerged with a second purse, this one in immaculate condition and decorated with flowers and butterflies, consistent with the one of Kyrkeby's that Ringstead had described.

A noise from the hall made him freeze in alarm. Brother Adam began to cough, loudly and desperately, and it sounded as though he could not catch his breath. Thumping footsteps on the stairs and on the landing outside suggested that the brothers were panicking, not knowing how to help the old man, despite the fact that they had watched Bartholomew prepare soothing balsams for him at least twice and he had even written the instructions down for them.

The coughing grew worse, and Bartholomew was in an agony of indecision. The physician in him longed to throw open the door and go to the old monk's aid, knowing that he could ease the problem within moments. But then he would have revealed himself, and he would never have another opportunity to search the room of the man he was certain was a killer.

'Brother Timothy has it, I believe,' came the voice of one of the monks, edged with fear. 'Shall I see if I can find it?'

Bartholomew's heart leapt into his mouth as the latch on Timothy's door began to rise. Quickly, he pinched out the candle, and was only just under the table when Brother Janius burst in holding a lamp. Bartholomew held his breath when the skirts of Janius's habit swung so close to his face that he could make out the individual fibres in the cloth. The monk then rummaged among documents on the very table under which Bartholomew crouched.

'Here we are,' Janius said suddenly, and Bartholomew heard the rustle of parchment. 'I knew it was Timothy who had taken Bartholomew's instructions.'

He left as abruptly as he had entered, leaving the room in darkness. Bartholomew released a shuddering breath, and tried to quell the fluttering in his stomach. He heard more footsteps pounding on the stairs as hot water was fetched, and there was a clank as someone produced a metal bowl in which to mix the herbs and water so that Adam could inhale the steam. The frightened rasp of Adam's laboured breathing began to ease.

Bartholomew began to relax, too, and was considering resuming his search when he realised that Janius must have noticed the cloak that lay across the bottom of the door. Would he assume it had fallen there? But it was fairly obvious that the garment had been placed in position by someone inside the room, and that it had not coincidentally fallen in such a way as to block light. With a surge of panic, Bartholomew scrambled out from under the table, half expecting Janius to burst into the chamber and catch him red-handed.

He glanced at the ambry in the far corner, not knowing whether to risk a few more moments to complete his search, or whether to count his blessings and leave while he still could. Instincts of self-preservation urged him to go, but he knew he would never have such a chance again – Timothy would know someone had been in his room because there was candle wax all over the floor, and Bartholomew intended to take the two purses he had recovered to Michael. If Bartholomew did not find the essay first, Timothy would move it elsewhere, and it would never be found. Reluctantly, he made his decision and turned towards the ambry, fumbling with the latch. It was entirely the wrong thing to have done. The door burst open and a sudden light flooded the room.

'Is this what you were hoping to find, Matthew?' asked Janius pleasantly, holding aloft a sheaf of parchment. 'Here is Faricius's essay. I assume that is what you were looking for?'

Timothy closed the door behind them, a hefty broadsword in one hand. 'Do not even think of howling for help, Doctor. If you so much as try, I will kill you.'

For several moments, Bartholomew was too shocked to speak. He looked from the pile of parchments that Janius held, to Timothy's amiable face with its ready smile. Behind Timothy, Janius's blue eyes, which usually gleamed with the light of religious fervour, now seemed cold and sinister.

'How did you know I was here?' asked Bartholomew, trying to keep his voice steady and not to look at the monstrous sword that Timothy brandished with practised ease.

Janius continued to grin. 'We expected you yesterday, but we knew you would come sooner or later. We have been waiting.'

'But how did you know?' asked Bartholomew again.

424

'We met Simon Lynne strolling along the High Street last night,' said Janius. 'He was under the impression that he was safe, but he told us all about your suspicions before we killed him and hid him in the tunnel so conveniently vacated by Kyrkeby. It was a squeeze, given that the thing has collapsed, but it will do for now.'

Bartholomew gazed at him. The intense blue gaze was just as sincere when he talked about murder, as it had been when he had talked about his God. The physician tried to suppress a shudder.

'I see you found my well-laundered black cloak,' said Timothy, nodding at the garment that lay on the floor.

'I found the grey one you stole from Pechem, too,' said Bartholomew.

'And the scrips that belonged to Kyrkeby and Faricius,' said Janius, looking at the two purses that lay on the table. 'Timothy took them, so that Michael would believe that some passing outlaw was at work, murdering men for the contents of their purses. It would have worked, if you had not insisted on looking for other motives.'

'You took Walcote's scrip and left it near Barnwell Priory for Sergeant Orwelle to find,' said Bartholomew, looking hard at Janius. 'You had it in the basket you claimed was filled with food for the lepers. But the lepers received no food from you that day – or any other day this Lent.'

'We have been feeding the riverfolk,' said Janius, offended that his good works were being questioned. 'We cannot provide for the whole town, and it has been a hard winter, even for us.'

'You took Faricius's essay from Paul yesterday,' said Bartholomew, more bravely than he felt. 'But only after you raided the Dominicans, Michaelhouse and the Barnwell Priory to look for it. You stole a glove when you burgled the Dominican Friary, and left it at Michaelhouse, so that we would accuse Morden of the crime.'

'I was surprised you fell for that,' said Janius, exchanging an amused glance with Timothy. 'You must have seen that neither of us was small enough to be Morden when you tussled with us. Why did you allow Michael to believe it?'

'He believed it because of the way the other glove dropped from the rafter when Michael slammed open Morden's door,' said Timothy gloatingly. 'I flung it up there in the hope that Michael would see it "hidden", but when it fell to the ground so conveniently – as if God Himself wanted you to see it – it made Morden appear more guilty than ever.'

'Janius spoke to Father Paul,' said Bartholomew, more interested in the raid on the Franciscan Friary than in how Timothy had laid false evidence against Morden. He watched Timothy test the blade of his sword with his thumb. It came away smeared with blood, indicating that it was very sharp. 'Timothy kept silent, because he knew Paul would recognise his voice, while Janius demanded the essay.'

Janius inclined his head to indicate that Bartholomew had guessed correctly. 'Obviously Paul could not see us, but we know his powers of observation are greater than those of many sighted men. We acted accordingly. As long as I never have cause to speak to him, he will never know our paths have crossed.'

'If you spared Paul, why did you kill Arbury?' asked Bartholomew, wondering whether he could shout and still evade the wicked blade Timothy wielded. He realised it would be hopeless. Timothy had been a soldier, and it had probably not been an empty boast when he promised to run Bartholomew through if he called for help. 'There was no need to murder the lad.'

'He recognised me,' explained Timothy. 'He addressed me by name, and politely offered to extract Michael from Langelee's chamber, even though I had my hood pulled well over my eyes. We had a choice: we could abandon the notion of searching Michael's room and fabricate some excuse as to why we were there, or we could continue with what we had planned.'

'So, you chose the second option,' said Bartholomew. 'And you left Arbury to die.'

426

'It was a pity,' said Timothy. 'But there is more at stake here than the life of a student.'

'Such as what?' demanded Bartholomew, realising that even if he did manage to shout for help before he died, the other monks would merely applaud Timothy for protecting them against someone who had just forced a window to gain entry to their hostel. 'What is more important than human lives?'

'The University,' said Timothy immediately. 'It transcends all of us. We will be dead within a few years – sooner in your case – but the University will still be here for centuries to come.'

'Not if it has people like you in it,' said Bartholomew, startled by the monk's claim. 'The King will not want a University that is in the control of murderers and thieves.'

'You are wrong,' said Janius smoothly. 'He needs the University to produce educated men to be his lawyers, secretaries and spies. He will not care what we do as long as we continue to provide him with what he wants. But we had a Senior Proctor who gave away University property to promote his personal ambition, and a Junior Proctor who was weak and ineffectual.'

'Had?' asked Bartholomew uneasily. 'Michael has not gone anywhere.'

'Not yet,' said Timothy. 'But his days as Senior Proctor are numbered. I will take that position soon, and I shall appoint Janius as my deputy.'

'Is that why you murdered Walcote?' asked Bartholomew. 'Because you want to be proctors?'

'Why do *you* think we killed Walcote?' asked Janius, giving the impression that he was merely amusing himself at Bartholomew's expense. Bartholomew wondered how he ever could have imagined that the monk was a good man, when the glint in his eyes was so patently cruel and cold.

Bartholomew spoke quickly, seeing that the longer he could engage their interest, the longer he would live, although a nagging fear at the back of his mind told him

427

that he was merely delaying the inevitable. 'Lynne said he heard Walcote shouting at Kyrkeby until he had a fatal seizure and died. Lynne also heard "beadles" reminding Walcote of his appointment as Junior Proctor, and urging him to force the truth about the stolen essay from Kyrkeby. No beadles would have done such a thing. The "beadles" were you.'

'Quite right,' said Janius patronisingly. 'Walcote was going to let that murdering Kyrkeby go, and was quite willing to believe the lying scoundrel when he said he did not have the essay.'

'And did he have it?' asked Bartholomew.

'Of course he did,' replied Janius scornfully. 'When we pressed him, he admitted that he had been loitering around the Carmelite Friary, hoping to find one of Faricius's friends, so that he could return it. He claimed he should not have stolen it, and wanted to give it back. Foolish man!'

'This happened on Monday night,' said Bartholomew. 'By then, Chancellor Tynkell had decided to change the topic of Kyrkeby's lecture, so Kyrkeby would not have needed Faricius's essay anyway. He did not know it, but he killed Faricius for nothing.'

'Walcote's interrogation was pathetic,' said Timothy in disgust. 'Kyrkeby expected us to believe that he found Faricius already stabbed, and all he did was take his scrip.'

'So, Kyrkeby handed Walcote the essay, but then his weak heart killed him,' said Bartholomew. 'What happened next?'

'Walcote offered to distract patrolling beadles, so that Timothy and I could hide Kyrkeby's corpse without being seen,' said Janius resentfully. 'We should never have trusted him. We were furious when we realised that he had taken the essay.'

'So furious, that you broke Kyrkeby's neck and smashed his skull when you hid the body?'

'No,' said Timothy. 'That was not our fault. The tunnel collapsed on him.'

428

'But why was Walcote prepared to hide Kyrkeby's body in the first place?' asked Bartholomew, puzzled. 'Why not just say that Kyrkeby's heart had failed?'

'We told Walcote that he would hang for murder if he tried that,' said Janius smugly. 'We said we should dispose of the body, so he recommended using the tunnel he had discovered earlier. Timothy climbed through it, pulling the body behind him.'

'I reached the other side, and was in the process of dragging Kyrkeby after me when the tunnel caved in,' explained Timothy. 'I suppose a combination of exceptionally wet weather and having a heavy object dragged through it caused it to collapse. Unfortunately, I then found myself on the wrong side of the Carmelite Friary walls.'

'How did you escape?' asked Bartholomew, glancing at the small window to assess whether he could hurl himself through it before Timothy reached him. He could not: it was too small and he knew Timothy would get him before he even turned.

'Walcote obligingly fetched a rope from St Mary's Church,' said Timothy. 'He always did what he was told. He threw it to me, and I was able to climb out.'

'And, of course, it came in useful to hang him with,' said Janius, chillingly cold.

'I am confused,' said Bartholomew, glancing at the door and realising that his chances of reaching it before Timothy acted were even less than an escape through the window. 'You killed once to gain possession of the essay, and you killed again because you wanted rid of Walcote. Which was more important – obtaining the essay or being appointed as proctors?'

'One led nicely to the other,' said Timothy. 'Faricius's essay is a brilliant piece of logic that no one has yet seen, because his narrow-minded Order forced him to keep his ideas hidden. But now he is dead, there is no reason why Janius and I cannot take credit for them. Blind Paul obviously has not read the essay and Lynne is dead, so no one will ever be able to prove that Faricius wrote what we will claim as our work.'

'It will make us rich,' said Janius smugly, 'and we will be able to use the wealth that will accrue to spread the word of God among disbelievers. If the world does not mend its wicked ways, the plague will come again. It is my intention to prevent that.'

'And is that why you want to become proctors?' asked Bartholomew. 'Because such positions of power will enable you to force your own rigid religious views on people?'

Janius's blue eyes were hard. 'It will be for their own good. If we do not want God to send another Great Pestilence, we must act now. Walcote was too weak, and Michael is a debauched glutton who is more interested in making suspect deals with Oxford than in safeguarding the spiritual well-being of the University. Neither was fit to be a proctor.'

Bartholomew gazed at him. 'Walcote uncovered a plot to kill Michael at Christmas: your plot.'

'Unrealised plot, unfortunately,' said Janius. 'That stupid beadle drank so much with the money we paid him to deliver our message to a hired assassin, that he fell into a puddle and drowned. Walcote found the document, and started to investigate. It was me who suggested that it would be kinder not to tell Michael about it.'

'And, as everyone knows, Walcote could be made to agree to anything,' added Timothy. 'When Janius said sharing such information would only upset Michael, he immediately agreed to keep it from him.'

'Walcote told the men who attended his nocturnal meetings, though,' said Janius, peeved. 'I have no idea who told him to hold those gatherings, but I am sure they were not his own idea.'

'They were,' said Bartholomew. 'He paid for St Radegund's room with money he had seized from Master Wilson's broken effigy. He believed he was acting in the best interests of the University.'

'And look what he did,' said Janius in disgust. 'He encouraged the two factions in the realism–nominalism debate to argue with each other more fiercely than ever. The issue would never have become so violent if he had not provided a forum for like-minded men to whip each other into a frenzy. Stupid man!'

'It did work in our favour, though,' said Timothy thoughtfully. 'It showed all those scholars that Walcote was acting behind Michael's back, and that Michael was too incompetent to prevent it.'

'Then why *kill* Walcote?' asked Bartholomew, rubbing a hand through his hair. He was finding the discussion exhausting, and was not sure how much longer he could keep it up. And why should he try anyway? Help would not be coming. Even if Cynric thought he was taking too long, there would be little the book-bearer could do. 'Why not wait until someone complained that Walcote was not the man for the job? Michael said his days as Junior Proctor were numbered.'

'This business with Oxford forced us to act sooner,' said Janius. 'We do not approve of it.'

'Why?' asked Bartholomew. 'Michael plans to use the information from Heytesbury to Cambridge's advantage.'

'No,' said Janius. 'He wants to use the information to ensure he will dine on good cheese and fresh butter for the rest of his days. Imagine how it will look when word spreads that the Benedictine Order dispenses with University property for the good of its stomach.'

'Michael may have allowed people to believe that personal greed is his motive, but I can assure you it is not,' said Bartholomew. 'He was simply trying to fool Heytesbury into thinking he had the better end of the bargain. And it worked. Heytesbury signed the deed today.'

'No!' exclaimed Timothy, shocked. 'We are too late?'

'Then we should bring an end to this futile chatter,' said Janius, indicating with a nod of his head that Timothy was to kill Bartholomew. 'We must ensure that Heytesbury does not leave the town alive, and that Michael is blamed for his death.'

'How did you kill Walcote?' asked Bartholomew quickly, realising that he had made a mistake in mentioning the signed deed. While he found the company of the two monks distasteful, and disliked hearing their sanctimonious, gloating voices bragging about their cleverness, he was certainly not ready to die. 'You hanged him the same night that Kyrkeby died.'

'Enough questions,' said Janius.

Timothy took a step towards Bartholomew, who quickly moved behind the table, and continued to speak in the same patronising, gloating tone. 'While we were struggling to hide Kyrkeby, Walcote gave the essay to Father Paul. Walcote lied: he told us he was going to keep nosy beadles away, while all the time his intention was to hide the essay from us.'

'We threatened to hang him unless he handed it over,' said Janius. 'He refused, and so he died. And that is what you are about to do.'

'And how will you explain my corpse in your hostel?' asked Bartholomew, desperate to keep them talking.

'Your nephew,' replied Timothy, coolly assessing which side of the table to approach. 'He will be the perfect scape-goat for the murder of his uncle and his uncle's friend.'

'No one will believe that Richard would kill me or Michael,' said Bartholomew, so defiantly that Timothy paused in his relentless advance. 'He may be a fool, but he is no killer.'

'You are wrong,' said Janius. 'First, lots of people heard you scolding him for his reprehensible treatment of Sergeant Orwelle the other day. Second, we all know how disgusted you are that he allowed the Black Bishop of Bedminster to try to eat Pechem. And third, no one likes Richard anyway. They will be only too pleased to see him accused of a crime.'

That was probably true, Bartholomew thought. Richard's behaviour had won him no friends. 'So, what is your plan?' he asked, trying to keep the unsteadiness from his voice as he eased away from Timothy. 'Whatever it is, there will be a flaw that will warn Michael before you harm him. You should know by now that he is not an easy man to fool.'

'God will see that our plan works,' said Janius confidently. 'He has chosen us to do His bidding, and He will not let us fail.'

Bartholomew gazed at him. He had been afraid from the moment he had been caught, but Janius's calm and serene conviction that what he was doing was good had just sent a new chill of fear through him. Bartholomew had learned from Father William that there was no arguing with a zealot, but Janius's moral fanaticism was far more invidious than William's crude dogmatism, because it was disguised by a coating of sugary goodness.

'What are you going to do?' he asked again, in another desperate attempt to delay the inevitable.

'Brother Adam is unwell, and it is time he made a will,' said Janius. 'The best lawyer in Cambridge is Richard Stanmore – he told us so himself – and so we have sent for him. When he arrives, the pair of you will fight and he will kill you.'

Bartholomew was startled enough to laugh. 'No one will believe that happened.'

'But we will witness it,' said Janius simply. 'Who will disbelieve two Benedictine monks with a reputation for honesty and compassion?'

'And I suppose Michael will then see what Richard has done, and they will kill each other in the ensuing struggle,' said Bartholomew. 'But Michael does not carry weapons; you should know that.'

'He snatched up yours to parry Richard's first blow,' said Janius, unperturbed by the inconsistencies in his plot. 'As the son of a nobleman, Michael had some knightly training before he joined the Church. His riding skills are legendary, and so there is no reason to assume that his Benedictine habit does not conceal a little-used talent for swordplay, too.'

'And now,' said Timothy, raising the sword and advancing

on the physician again, 'the time for chatter is over. Richard will be here soon, and I do not want to tackle two of you at the same time. Would you like to be absolved before you die?'

Bartholomew looked from the wicked edge of the sword to Timothy's determined face, and knew that it was an offer he should consider very carefully.

'The only person dispensing absolution tonight will be me,' said Michael, opening the door and stepping into Timothy's room. 'You were right, Timothy. I am a practised swordsman, and even though my habit – and yours – forbids us to carry steel, I will fight you unless you put up your weapon immediately.'

Cynric was behind him, with his sharp sword, and a sudden clatter of voices, both in the building and in the street outside, indicated that they were not alone. The beadles had arrived, and so had Richard, pale and shocked, and holding his ornate dagger ineptly in one hand. The other Benedictines, seeming as appalled by the turn of events as was Richard, stood in the corridor and regarded their two brethren with a mixture of disbelief and unease.

'It is over, Timothy,' said Brother Adam, his face sickly white in the pale light of the lamp that he held. 'We heard everything you said, including your admission that you killed Walcote and the lad at Michaelhouse. Put down your sword and surrender, before anyone else is hurt.'

'Give ourselves to Satan?' cried Janius, as he backed against a wall. 'Never! What we did was good and right. We will not be put on trial by men who cannot see the truth through the veil of lies Michael and his associates have created.'

'You confessed to murder,' said Adam softly. 'Nothing else is relevant. But we will have no more bloodshed. Put up your sword, Timothy.'

'But we were so careful!' whispered Timothy, aghast at the intrusion of armed men in his domain. 'We watched

Bartholomew grope his way along the corridor, and *saw* he was alone. We even left the front door open, so that he would be able to gain access more easily.'

Cynric gave a soft laugh. 'I discovered that open door when I was keeping watch. At that point, I realised that he was expected. I chanced to meet Richard, who had been summoned by you, and I dispatched him to fetch Brother Michael instead.'

'Cynric was all for rescuing Matt straight away,' said Michael. 'But I wanted to hear what you had to say first. We entered Ely Hall by the door you so obligingly left open, and have been royally entertained ever since.'

'You were safe enough, lad,' said Cynric kindly, seeing Bartholomew's shock when he realised that Michael and Cynric could have rescued him much earlier. 'I would not have let them harm you.'

Janius sneered at Michael. His quick mind had assessed his predicament, and he had reasoned that all was not lost. 'Do you really think the people of Cambridge will believe you rather than us? Respectable men like Kenyngham and Pechem know that you stole from the Carmelite Friary *and* that you are in league with Heytesbury of Oxford.'

Michael shrugged. 'The entire Benedictine community of Ely Hall just heard your confession. No one will doubt them.'

For the first time, Bartholomew saw Timothy's mask of saintliness begin to slip; underneath was the face of a frightened man. 'It was not us,' he said, a note of desperation in his voice. 'None of this was our idea.'

'Give me your sword, and we will talk about it,' said Michael, unmoved.

'We were only obeying instructions,' Timothy whined, a sheen of sweat appearing on his forehead and speckling the skin above his lips. 'Do you really think we could have done this alone? Us? Two lowly men of God?'

'Shut up,' snapped Janius furiously. 'They can prove nothing. The only evidence they have is an alleged confession overheard by a crowd of bumbling monks in ill health.'

Timothy was not convinced. 'Perhaps we can come to some arrangement,' he said, smiling nervously at Michael. 'I will put up my sword and reveal to you the name of our associate; you will let me go free.'

'I do not think so,' said Michael icily. 'You will hand me your sword, then you will come with me to the proctors' cells, where you will await your trial.'

'No gaggle of sinners will try us,' said Janius viciously. Suddenly, there was a flash of metal, and Bartholomew saw that he held a dagger. He threw himself to one side as it whipped through the air towards him, then struggled to regain his footing as pandemonium erupted in the small room.

Timothy was wielding his sword in a series of savage arcs that threatened to decapitate anyone who went too close, while Janius was engaged in a deadly circling game with Cynric. With a howl of rage, Timothy turned on Bartholomew.

'This is *your* fault! If you had not started questioning that grey cloak and telling Michael that the motive for the deaths of Kyrkeby, Walcote and Faricius was not the theft of their purses, then none of this would have happened. You deserve to die.'

Bartholomew ducked backwards as one of the blows whistled past his face, so close that he felt the wind of it on his skin. Timothy staggered with the force of the swing, but then recovered and prepared to make a swift end of the man he saw as the author of all his troubles. Michael tried to force his way into the room, but was blocked by Cynric and Janius, engaged in their own life or death struggle. Bartholomew came up hard against the wall, and knew he had nowhere else to go. Timothy raised the sword above his head in both hands and prepared to strike.

All at once, the expression on the monk's face turned from fury to mild surprise. He dropped to his knees, and the sword clattered from his hands. Then he pitched forward, and Bartholomew saw the hilt of Richard's decorative dagger protruding from his back. Richard gazed down at it, then looked up at Bartholomew, tears brimming in his eyes.

'He laughed at my dagger yesterday,' he said unsteadily. 'He said it was all handle and no blade.'

'There was blade enough to kill him,' remarked Michael, still trying to insinuate himself through the door to put an end to the continuing skirmish between Janius and Cynric. 'You did well, lad.'

'Then it is the first thing I have done well since arriving in Cambridge,' said Richard in a voice thick with self-pity. 'I was looking forward to doing business with this pair, and now I discover they are killers. It is Heytesbury's fault for befuddling my wits with wine. I have never felt so ill in my life as I have the last few days. I swear to you I shall never drink again. I will be a new man.'

Cynric's eyes left Janius just long enough to wink at Bartholomew, to indicate his belief that the change in character was due to the charm he had applied. It was a mistake: Janius took advantage of his wandering attention to knock the Welshman from his feet. Bartholomew tensed, ready to spring at Janius and take him on with his bare hands if he threatened to harm Cynric. But Janius was not interested in the prostrate book-bearer; he had his sights fixed on larger prey.

'You are no Benedictine,' he hissed furiously, turning on Michael. 'You are a fat, gluttonous pig who has no right to wear the sacred habit of a monk.'

Michael said nothing, but there was a blur of white followed by a sharp crack, and Janius staggered backwards holding his broken nose. Blood spurted from under his fingers and his dagger clattered to the floor.

'I told you I would punch the next person who called me fat,' said Michael mildly, rubbing the knuckles of one hand with the palm of the other. 'Take him away, Cynric.'

Cynric leapt to his feet and pinned Janius against the wall, ignoring the monk's cries of pain.

437

'We were doing God's will!' shouted Janius, as Cynric began to haul him away. 'It is you who are evil, and it is because of men like you that the Great Pestilence came in the first place. It will return if you are permitted to continue in positions of power.'

'I thought the plague had come because some Cambridge scholars were nominalists,' said Michael, raising his eyebrows in amusement. 'That is what Lincolne told us.'

Janius glowered at him. 'Lincolne is obsessed with the notion that nominalism is heresy. He is a fanatic.'

'Unlike you, I suppose,' said Michael wearily. 'Take him away, Cynric. I want to hear no more of his raving.'

'God will punish you for this!' Janius howled, as he was wrestled out of the room and down the corridor. 'He will not stand by and see evil men the victors. You will see.'

'I hope he is wrong,' said Richard nervously. 'I thought his capture and Timothy's death signified an end to all this vileness.'

'They do,' said Michael firmly. 'He is just ranting to unsettle us. He and Timothy were behind all this murder and mayhem, and neither of them is in a position to do anything more now.'

'I hope you are right,' said Bartholomew.

The following day was Easter Sunday. Clippesby's predictions about the weather had been correct, and the rain clouds that had been dogging the town for the past few weeks were blown away by a cool, fresh wind from the south. The morning dawned with a blaze of gold when the sun made a rare appearance, and the sky was a clear and perfect blue.

Later than usual, because it was a Sunday, the Michaelhouse scholars gathered in their yard to process to St Michael's Church for the high mass. There was an atmosphere of happy anticipation for the festival itself, the debate that was to follow in the afternoon and the feast that had been arranged for the evening. Every scholar seemed to have made an effort with his appearance to celebrate the end of Lent, and even Langelee's exacting standards were surpassed by most of the students. Bartholomew had never seen so many polished shoes and brushed tabards.

In honour of the occasion, the Stanton silver had been brought out of the strong-room, and stood in a gleaming line along the altar. Patens, chalices and thuribles had been buffed until they shone like mirrors, and a new festive altar cloth, sewn by Agatha, was so brightly white that it hurt the eyes. The sun blazed through the east window, casting pools of coloured light into the chancel, and the parishioners had decorated the church with flowers of cream and yellow, so that the whole building was infused with the sweet scent of them.

Michael's choir excelled themselves with an anthem they had been practising since Christmas, and the church rang with the joyous sound of their singing, making up in volume what they lacked in talent. Afterwards, the scholars spilled out into the sunlit churchyard, and Bartholomew saw that snowdrops were beginning to bloom among the grassy mounds. Langelee raised one lordly arm to indicate that his scholars were to fall in behind him, and began to lead the way back to Michaelhouse, where a special breakfast of oatmeal, eggs, boiled pork and fresh bread awaited them.

'What a glorious day!' exclaimed Michael, turning to the sun and closing his eyes, relishing its warmth on his flabby face. 'Blue skies, a bright sun, the scent of spring in the air, and no murderers walking free on the streets of Cambridge.'

'For now,' said Bartholomew.

Michael jabbed him with his elbow. 'It is a beautiful day and I am happy. Do not dispel my good temper by speculating any more on the unsavoury business of last night.'

'But I still have questions,' said Bartholomew. 'And so does Richard.'

'Richard!' spat Michael in some disgust. 'That silly boy! Last night's events will teach him not to play politics with men he does not know. Had that plan of Timothy and Janius's worked, not only would he have been dead, but he would have forced his parents to live in the knowledge that he had killed you, too. It would have broken Edith's heart.'

'She would not have believed it,' said Bartholomew. 'That was what I kept telling Timothy and Janius. They were basing their plan on actions that people would just not have taken: Richard would not have killed me in a fit of pique and you would not have killed him in retaliation.'

'But they did not succeed,' said Michael comfortably. 'So it does not matter.'

They reached the College, and walked to the fallen apple tree in the orchard; they sat on its ancient trunk and rested their backs against the sun-warmed wall and waited for the breakfast bell to ring. The light danced across the thick green grass in tiny pools of brightness as it filtered through branches that were beginning to show signs of new leaves, and the town was unusually peaceful.

'We have done well,' said Michael, pleased with himself. 'We have exposed two vicious killers and thwarted a plot that would have seen my beloved University in the hands of the excessively religious.'

'So,' said Bartholomew, trying to marshal his thoughts and summarise what had happened in chronological order. 'In November last year, Timothy and Janius grew concerned by rumours – put about by Langelee – that you were involved in a scheme to pass Cambridge property to Oxford. They decided to act.'

Michael nodded. 'At roughly the same time, weak Walcote started to arrange meetings at St Radegund's Convent that would discuss important issues without my knowledge. These were paid for with coins he had grabbed when Wilson's effigy spilled gold in the Market Square in November. He had been away in Ely while I was wrestling with that particular problem, but arrived back in Cambridge just in time to snatch himself a small fortune.'

'He was also concerned by your Oxford connections, and was thinking about the time when he would be Senior

440

Proctor. He wanted to impress the leaders of the religious Orders, who hold a good deal of power in the University. However, his gatherings merely aggravated the growing realism–nominalism debate and caused the conflict to escalate.'

'Janius and Timothy hired a mercenary to kill me. Their messenger drowned in a drunken stupor, and Walcote came into possession of the letter to the assassin. Walcote was convinced by my Benedictine fellows that I should not be told about the plot. Meanwhile, I removed property for safe keeping from the Carmelite Friary and brought it here. Walcote assumed I was stealing, and said as much to everyone who attended his nasty meetings.'

'Three months passed, and then two things happened at once,' said Bartholomew. 'First, Kyrkeby murdered Faricius for his essay on nominalism and Walcote caught Kyrkeby, racked by guilt, trying to give it back. And second, Heytesbury appeared in Cambridge intending to find out more about the man with whom he proposed to do business.'

'They were unrelated events,' said Michael. 'But they provided a perfect opportunity for Timothy and Janius to use a tragedy to further their own ends. Two days after Faricius's death – on the Monday – Walcote discovered Kyrkeby lurking near the Carmelite Friary, probably while checking to see whether Lynne had sealed up the tunnel.'

'I spent that afternoon with Kyrkeby,' said Bartholomew. 'He was agitated and uncharacteristically uncommunicative. I thought it was because he was worried about his lecture, but I see now that it was a guilty conscience that was making him irritable and ill.'

'Bullied by Timothy and Janius, Walcote badgered the guilt-ridden Precentor until he died,' Michael continued. 'Walcote then agreed to hide the body in the Carmelites' tunnel.'

'No one would have blamed Walcote for Kyrkeby's death under the circumstances,' mused Bartholomew. 'But Timothy and Janius preyed on his insecurities. And at this point, Walcote revealed a grain of strength they had not anticipated.'

Michael nodded slowly. 'The fact that he escaped them for a few moments to hide the essay with Father Paul indicates that he was already worried by their motives. And he refused to tell them where he had put it, so they did as they threatened and hanged him.'

'Then you played right into their hands by appointing Timothy as Junior Proctor the next day,' said Bartholomew. 'Your record of selecting good juniors is not impressive, Brother.'

Michael ignored him. 'Janius allowed Walcote's purse to be found, so that we would assume he had been killed by desperate outlaws, and he took Kyrkeby's scrip for the same reason. You declined to accept that the three murders were committed for theft alone, and then they learned from Simon Lynne that you wanted to search Timothy's room for the essay. Therefore, they were waiting for you when you effected that daring but ill-advised assault on their hostel.'

'You refused to help,' said Bartholomew. 'What was I supposed to do?'

'If their plan had been successful, you and Richard would have been murdered, with me "proved" to be the killer,' continued Michael, ignoring the question. 'Timothy would have appointed Janius as his Junior Proctor; the arrangements with Heytesbury would have fallen to pieces; and the University would have been under the power of two men who would have made additional fortunes by publishing Faricius's essay under their own names.'

'I still have three questions, though,' said Bartholomew. 'First, why did Walcote hold his meetings at a place like St Radegund's Convent? Second, why did he agree to hide Kyrkeby's body in the Carmelite Friary tunnel? And third, what was that yellow sticky stuff on his and Faricius's bodies?'

'I doubt you will ever know the answer to the first question, Matt, but I can tell you the answer to the second. They were right outside the tunnel, and no one wants to traipse around the town with a corpse. It was simply a convenient hiding place.'

'And the third?'

'Lord knows,' said Michael, sighing and stretching his feet in front of him, revealing a pair of monstrous white calves. 'Frankly, I do not care.'

At that moment, the bell began to clang, summoning the Michaelhouse scholars for their Easter breakfast.

'Good,' said Michael, rubbing his hands happily. 'All this thinking has given me an appetite. We will have breakfast, then go to the University debate. I would not want to miss hearing the great Heytesbury discussing life on other planets.' He gave a malicious snigger.

'He is still going to speak?' asked Bartholomew, as they picked their way through the long grass towards the path that led to the kitchen door. 'I thought he would have left with his deed as soon as he could hire a horse.'

Michael grinned wickedly. 'He thinks he has bested me, and so feels no need to rush away. Heytesbury is now the proud owner of a church and a couple of farms that will cost him more to run than they will make. Meanwhile, I have several important bits of information secreted in one or two places.'

'You cheated him,' said Bartholomew, not particularly surprised. 'You made him think he was gaining something valuable.'

'Not cheated, Matt: outwitted. He should not have wasted his time coming to Cambridge to assess *me*. He should have gone to these properties and asked to inspect their records. I certainly would have done. But that is why Cambridge will always be superior to Oxford in all respects. We think with our minds, not our pockets. And speaking of pockets, you owe me an evening of fine wine and good food at the Brazen George.'

'I do?' asked Bartholomew, startled. 'Why is that?'

'I told you we would resolve this by Easter Day, and we have.'

'But you said the wager was invalid when you discovered you had more than one murder to solve,' objected Bartholomew. 'And you failed to mention it was back on again.'

'Well, I am mentioning it now,' said Michael with a grin. 'We will go after the debate.'

The recently rebuilt Church of St Mary was packed to overflowing with scholars from the University, as well as a few hardy souls from the town. The black robes of Benedictine monks, Austin canons and Dominican friars formed stark blocks among the pale grey of the Franciscans and the white of the occasional Cluniac monk. Between them were the blue tabards of Bene't College, the black of Michaelhouse, and the various uniforms of Peterhouse, Clare Hall, King's Hall and the other Colleges and hostels.

The church was a beautiful building, and its new chancel was made of bright sandstone and adorned with delicate pinnacles that reached towards the sky. As befitted a University church, it was the largest building in the town, raised to accommodate as many scholars as possible within its walls. The air rang with the sound of voices, some raised in cheerful greetings, some in laughter, and others in argument. Michael nodded to Meadowman, who inserted a group of elderly commoners from the Hall of Valence Marie between some Carmelites and Dominicans who were already eyeing each other challengingly, in the hope that they would keep the two factions apart.

'This is a nightmare,' remarked Michael to Bartholomew. 'Usually, it is not necessary to keep rivals apart at debates, because even if people hold strong opinions, they are not usually committed to proving them with their fists. But this is different; everyone seems ready for a good fight today.'

'Good morning, Brother,' came Heytesbury's smooth voice from behind him. The Oxford man looked pleased with himself in his ceremonial red gown, and Bartholomew wondered how long it would be before he discovered he had not done as well out of Cambridge as he had anticipated. Heytesbury nodded to the assembled hordes. 'I am honoured. It seems almost every scholar in your University has come to bid me farewell.'

'Michael tells me you are leaving today,' said Bartholomew, politely making conversation.

Heytesbury smiled. 'A clever man always knows the right time to make an exit. It is time now: Cambridge no longer holds any attraction for me.'

'How unfortunate,' said Michael ambiguously.

Heytesbury allowed his gaze to rove over the gathering crowd again. 'I am astonished that Cambridge scholars are so keen to learn about life in other universes. Such a topic would not intrigue Oxford men. They are concerned with greater issues.'

'Really,' said Michael, bristling at the criticism. 'Such as what, pray?'

'The irrefutable premises of nominalism, for a start,' replied Heytesbury immediately. 'I am one of the foremost thinkers on the subject. I cannot imagine why you will not allow me to lecture on it here. Some of that rabble might even learn something from it.'

'I have already explained that,' snapped Michael, made irritable by the worry of keeping the students from each others' throats that day. 'Nominalism is too contentious a subject at the moment. Return next year, and I shall be happy to oblige you, but today we will hear about whether you think there is life on Mars.'

Heytesbury sighed. 'As you wish, Brother. I warrant I shall clear this church within moments once I start to speak on such a tedious subject, but you shall have it, if that is what you want.'

'It is,' said Michael firmly. He glanced at the door as more people began to elbow their way into the church, headed by a flock of white-robed scholars, the size of which had every head turning in astonishment. 'Look at that! It is

Lincolne, with virtually every Carmelite friar in the county! Where did they all come from?'

'He summoned them from their parishes,' said Beadle Meadowman, breathless from his exertions. 'His gatekeeper told me that he wants to prove the superiority of the realist argument by sheer dint of numbers.'

'But the debate is not about realism,' said Michael, exasperated. 'Damn your nephew, Matt! It is his fault that all these friars are here. He should never have suggested that Heytesbury speak here.'

'There is Chancellor Tynkell,' said Bartholomew, watching as the head of the University climbed unsteadily on to a wooden platform that had been erected in the middle of the nave. Immediately, there was a hush, as scholars waited to hear what he had to say. Heytesbury left Michael and went to stand next to him. From a distance the scholar looked small and unassuming, even in his handsome robes, and Bartholomew thought it was not surprising that the likes of Lincolne imagined they could best him in an argument. The Carmelite Prior would be in for a shock if he tried, Bartholomew thought, recalling the short work Heytesbury had made of such men in Oxford.

As the assembled masses in the church waited for the Chancellor to begin, Lincolne elbowed his way to the front with his gaggle of friars in tow, and Bartholomew saw the scholars behind him trying to see around the large expanse of his person and his peculiar turret of hair. On the other side of the church, his mortal enemy, Morden of the Dominicans, recently freed from the proctors' cells, gave him an unpleasant glower. Morden had taken the precaution of bringing his own box to stand on, so that he would be able to look over the shoulders of the scholars in front. Meanwhile, the Franciscan Prior Pechem looked uneasily from one to the other, clearly anticipating trouble, while the student-friars from all Orders were alert and aggressive.

'This Easter Sunday, we have gathered in St Mary's Church to hear Master William Heytesbury of Merton College in

Oxford,' began Tynkell in a grand voice. 'Although an esteemed proponent of nominalism, Heytesbury will speak on a different matter to us. The question we shall ponder is: Let us debate whether life exists in other universes.'

Bartholomew saw Heytesbury grimace, and one or two supporters of realism begin to grin at each other, gloating over the fact that the greatest nominalist in the country had been forbidden to speak his mind. Lincolne, looked as black as thunder.

'Does he think God will strike him down?' he boomed, the sudden loudness of his voice making several scholars jump in alarm. 'Is he afraid to declare his heretical theories in a church?'

Heytesbury gave a long-suffering sigh. 'I am willing to explain my theories anywhere, but I have not been invited to talk about them. I have been asked to speak about whether hairstyles like yours exist in parallel universes.'

The Dominicans began to cheer, drowning Chancellor Tynkell's attempt to silence them and to bring the debate back to the subject in hand. The Carmelites objected to Heytesbury's remark, and began to yell insults at him.

'Perhaps it was not such a good idea to try to censor the debate,' Bartholomew shouted to Michael, trying to make himself heard over the din. 'You might cause more trouble by declining to discuss the problem than if it had been aired in the open.'

'Our mistake was trying to hold the debate at all,' yelled Michael. 'We should have waited until matters calmed down.'

'Look at Lincolne,' said Bartholomew, pointing to the distinctive topknot making its way towards Heytesbury and Tynkell. 'I have a feeling he intends more than a quiet chat about nominalist principles, Brother. Unless you want Heytesbury riding home with a blackened eye and tales of Cambridge's violent debates, you should stop him.'

'Come with me,' instructed Michael. 'I will never restrain Lincolne and fend off his students alone, and my beadles are struggling with the Dominicans.'

Bartholomew followed the monk as he elbowed his way through the surging mass. Any control Tynkell might have commanded had been lost, and the church was filled with ringing shouts and threats. Michael reached Lincolne and grabbed him by the arm.

'Let me go!' howled the Carmelite Prior furiously, trying to free himself. 'I will not stand here and be forced to listen to the lies of that wicked man.'

'Leave,' suggested Michael breathlessly. 'Then you will not have to.'

'Our Prior will not be forced from his University church by a nominalist,' declared Horneby hotly, trying to push his way past Bartholomew. 'It is unthinkable!'

'I will kill him where he stands,' vowed Lincolne, white-faced with anger.

With a shock, Bartholomew saw that Lincolne had a knife in his hand, and the expression on his face indicated that he fully intended to use it. Even loyal Horneby's jaw dropped in shock at the sight of his Prior armed and murderous in a church.

'Wait!' Horneby yelled, catching Lincolne's sleeve and trying to pull him back. 'This is no place for a fight, Father.'

'It is the perfect place,' snarled Lincolne, trying to free his arm from Horneby and the rest of him from Michael. It was easier said than done, and he started to lose his balance, threatening to drag his restrainers down with him.

Lincolne was not the only one who had decided it was a good time for a debate with fists rather than wits. Here and there, small skirmishes had broken out in the nave, and Bartholomew found himself hemmed in tightly by a throng of struggling, shoving scholars. Lincolne began to topple and snatched at Bartholomew to try to retain his balance. But Bartholomew was being pushed, too, and he grabbed at Lincolne at about the same time. They both fell, surrounded by churning boots and shoes that threatened to trample them.

A heavy foot planted on his hand convinced Bartholomew

that the floor was no place to linger, but the press of bodies around him was such that he could not stand. Through the milling legs and swirling habits that surrounded him, he glimpsed the wooden platform that had been erected for Heytesbury to stand on. He made his way towards it on all fours.

When he arrived, bruised and rather breathless, he eased himself into its sanctuary only to discover that he was not the only one determined to use it as a refuge. Lincolne was already there, filling most of it with his bulk.

Michael saw that Bartholomew was still on the ground, and surged forward to try to pull him upright before he was injured. He snatched at a handful of the physician's gown, and pulled as hard as he could. The rip was audible even over the frenzied yelling that filled the church, and the sudden removal of Bartholomew's sleeve caused Michael to lose his balance. He staggered, crashing into Bartholomew, who was knocked forward into Lincolne. The physician reached out with both hands, instinctively grabbing at anything he could reach to save himself.

Unfortunately, his flailing hands encountered Lincolne's topknot. He was horrified, embarrassed and slightly revolted when it came off. He glanced up. Without it, Lincolne was just an ordinary-looking man with a bald, yellowish forehead.

'Give that back,' snapped Lincolne, snatching it from the physician and replacing it. He glowered furiously at Bartholomew, who felt he had committed a most frightful indiscretion.

Mortified, the physician looked away, gazing at the hand that had deprived Lincolne of his hairpiece. He was confused to see that it was marked with a yellowish, sticky residue. He had seen a stain just like it on Walcote, and on Faricius before that. Bewildered, he stared at Lincolne.

'I use gum mastic to keep my hair in place,' explained Lincolne. 'It is a better glue than anything else I have discovered, but it still has a habit of coming off in situations like this.'

449

'"Situations like this"?' echoed Bartholomew. 'You mean situations in which you are trying to kill someone?' He flinched as a Dominican, punched hard by a Carmelite, reeled into the platform, and scrambled further inside.

'It has come off in public twice before today,' confided Lincolne. 'Is it on straight? I do not like to be seen without it. It is nice, do you not agree?'

'Is it real?' asked Bartholomew, ghoulishly curious, despite the fact that he knew he should be asking Lincolne about his role in the deaths of Faricius and Walcote, not discussing fashions.

Lincolne nodded. 'I had it made from my own hair, when I still had some.'

'I have seen this glue before,' said Bartholomew, glancing down at the vivid stain on his hand. 'It was on the bodies of Faricius and Walcote.'

'Yes,' said Lincolne. 'As I just said, it has a habit of coming off when I am trying to rid the world of people who should not be in it.'

'*You* killed Faricius?' asked Bartholomew, bewildered.

Lincolne pursed his lips. 'The boy was writing the most scurrilous nonsense I have ever read. When he went out during the riot to retrieve it, I saw too good an opportunity to miss.'

'*You* stabbed him and left him to die?' asked Bartholomew in a sickened whisper.

'I thought I had killed him, and I was going to bury that vile essay with him. But the Dominican Precentor must have stolen it from his body. You understand, do you not? I could not have the Carmelites' reputation sullied by the filth of nominalism.'

'It is only a philosophical theory,' said Bartholomew, his shocked voice only just audible over the deafening racket of the fight that surged above him. 'An idea. It is nothing to kill for. But you urged Michael to investigate the Dominicans, while all the time the killer was you?'

'Of course I encouraged him to look at the Black Friars,'

said Lincolne testily. 'I did not want him discovering it was I who killed Faricius, or even worse, him learning about the existence of the essay.'

'But why did you not just confiscate Faricius's work?' asked Bartholomew, ducking as someone in a grey habit tried to kick him.

'I tried, but Faricius would not be silenced,' replied Lincolne, striking out at the grey habit with his knife. There was an agonised howl and blood dribbled on to the creamy yellow tiles of the floor. 'When I confronted him on Milne Street, he told me he intended to go to Oxford with Heytesbury, so that he could become a better nominalist than ever.'

'And you killed Walcote, too?' asked Bartholomew. 'I thought Timothy and Janius did that, but the gum mastic stain on Walcote's hand indicates otherwise.'

'He declined to hand over the essay. We offered him a chance to live, but he refused to take it. We hanged him, and Michael generously furthered our plan by appointing Timothy in his place.'

'But why should that matter to you?' asked Bartholomew. 'I thought you were only interested in retrieving the essay.'

'Then you are wrong,' said Lincolne. 'I am concerned with wider issues, too, such as Michael's cavorting with Oxford men and threatening the welfare of the entire University. I had to stop him, and Timothy and Janius were helping me.'

'So Timothy was telling the truth after all,' said Bartholomew. 'He said someone else was in control, but we did not believe him, especially when Janius denied it. But I did not imagine it was you. To be honest, I suspected Heytesbury, given that he is always chewing gum mastic.'

Lincolne snarled his disgust. 'I am a decent man, who is prepared to act to see our University saved from men like Michael and Walcote. But that evil nominalist chews gum mastic to hide the fact that he is a heavy drinker.'

'But what were *you* doing there when Walcote, Timothy

451

and Janius caught Kyrkeby outside your friary?' asked Bartholomew, confused. 'Did Timothy summon you?'

'I was watching Kyrkeby,' said Lincolne, stabbing at another pair of legs that came too close. He grimaced in annoyance when they moved before he could pierce them. 'He was hovering outside our friary, as if he meant us harm. The other three frightened him to death and Walcote suggested we should hide him in the tunnel. It was time it was sealed anyway.'

'But you said you did not know about it,' said Bartholomew. Then he recalled what Lincolne had said the first time they had met, when the Carmelite had been ranting about the death of Faricius: that he had been at the friary since he was a child. And if that were the case, then he would certainly have known about the tunnel. Masters were never told, but Lincolne had been a student.

Lincolne saw the understanding in his face and sneered. 'Did you imagine I was the only student ever to pass through the friary who was not party to the secret of the tunnel?'

'Did you attend any of those meetings Walcote arranged at St Radegund's Convent?' asked Bartholomew. 'And did you know that Timothy and Janius were going to kill Michael?'

'Of course I attended Walcote's meetings,' snapped Lincolne impatiently. 'I am the leader of the Carmelites, and an important man. It was I who recommended that he hold them at St Radegund's.'

'Why?' asked Bartholomew. 'It is no place for decent men.'

'Walcote did not invite decent men,' said Lincolne reasonably. 'He invited Pechem and Morden and Ralph. Holding the meetings there ensured they all came – they were all very sanctimonious about the venue, but I knew they would not attend if he held them anywhere less interesting. It was also the last place Michael would think to look for us.'

'You are wrong about the others,' said Bartholomew. 'You are the only one to cavort regularly with prostitutes.'

'Lies!' spat Lincolne. 'I do no such thing.'

'You have a long-standing arrangement with Yolande de Blaston,' said Bartholomew, recalling what Matilde had told him. 'None of the others break their vows with such regularity. But I want to know more about St Radegund's. Did Eve Wasteneys, Mabel Martyn or Tysilia help you?'

'Tysilia?' exclaimed Lincolne in genuine horror. 'The woman is a half-wit in a pretty body. She killed my poor novice – Brother Andrew – by breaking his impressionable heart. She is vermin, who will not survive the Death when God sends it a second time to rid the world of evil.'

'What about the other nuns, then?' pressed Bartholomew, wincing as Michael tumbled against the platform, threatening to demolish it with him and Lincolne still underneath. 'How much did they know about what was discussed?'

Lincolne pulled his thoughts away from Tysilia. 'Eve Wasteneys was too busy to be interested, while it was Dame Martyn's task to arrange for services to be provided for those who required them. And I do not mean services of a religious nature, so do not tell me the likes of Pechem, Morden and Ralph are saints where women are concerned.'

'Did you know that Timothy and Janius retrieved Faricius's essay because they intended to have it published under their own names?' asked Bartholomew, knowing that would shock the friar.

'Liar!' snapped Lincolne.

'They stole it from Father Paul. Janius is in the proctors' cells, and doubtless will confirm it when you join him there.'

'Not me,' said Lincolne, lunging at Bartholomew with the knife. 'I am going to no such place.'

Bartholomew twisted to one side, and the gleaming blade made a long groove in one of St Mary's beautiful decorated tiles. Lincolne stabbed again, and Bartholomew hurled himself against the Prior, aiming to crush the man against the side of the platform. Michael, however, intervened. Determined to haul the physician to his feet before he was trampled, he took a firm hold of Bartholomew's arm and pulled with considerable force. Bartholomew found himself pinned against the platform himself, unable to move. With a grin of triumph as he saw his quarry rendered immobile, Lincolne began to move towards him.

Just when Bartholomew thought that Michael would unwittingly bring about his death, Lincolne's determined advance was brought to a halt by a group of skirmishing Dominicans and Carmelites, who collided with the platform, causing it to topple. Bartholomew struggled free of Michael as it fell with an almighty crash that hurt his ears. Lincolne suddenly found himself deprived of the relative safety of his refuge, and Bartholomew took advantage of the Prior's moment of confusion by diving at him. One of the brawling Dominicans blundered into the physician at exactly the wrong moment, so that he fell awkwardly, and managed to end up underneath Lincolne rather than on top, as he had intended.

There was a sudden shriek and a yell of 'fire!' The milling mass of bodies was still for an instant, and then there was a concerted dash for the door. Feet pounded and trampled as people rushed forward. Some tripped over the prostrate Lincolne, and Bartholomew's attempts to struggle free and make his own way to the door were futile. He winced as someone kicked his leg in the frantic dash from the burning building, and then curled into a ball to protect his head to wait until the stampede was over. Fortunately, his position under Lincolne saved him from most of the bruising footsteps that pounded across the floor.

Finally, the church was empty. Bartholomew pushed Lincolne away from him and sat up to see the last of the scholars disappearing through the great west door. One or two were limping and others were being helped by their friends, but at least everyone was walking. Recalling the reason for the panic, the physician gazed around him wildly, but could see no flames. He could not even smell smoke.

'Where is the fire?' he demanded, scrambling to his feet.

'There is no fire,' said Michael. 'That was someone's idea

of a practical joke. Still, at least it put an end to all that fighting.'

'Everyone is going home peacefully,' reported Beadle Meadowman, running breathlessly back into the church to Michael. 'I thought they would continue to fight outside, but too many of them have bruises already, and they are dispersing quite quietly.'

'Lincolne!' exclaimed Michael, staring down at the Carmelite friar when he became aware that the man was lying unnaturally still amid a spreading stain of blood. Horneby was next to him, kneeling and muttering the words of the final absolution.

'Prior Lincolne killed Faricius,' said Horneby, gazing up at them with a face that was pale with shock. 'I heard what he told you, Doctor. We thought the Dominicans killed Faricius, but all the time it was him. Our own Prior.'

'What is this?' asked Michael in confusion. 'And what is wrong with Lincolne?'

'He fell on his knife,' said Horneby quietly. He fixed Bartholomew with a calm, steady gaze that was impossible to interpret. Had Horneby killed the Prior, to avenge the death of his friend? Or had the murderous Lincolne been pushed on to his own dagger when so many feet had thundered across him?

Bartholomew knelt next to Lincolne, and saw the knife protruding from his stomach. He stared at Horneby, noting his bloodstained hands, and wondered whether the fact that Lincolne had died in the same way as Faricius was significant. Horneby said nothing, but continued with his absolution. As he touched the body to anoint it, yet more blood darkened his fingers, and Bartholomew knew it would be impossible to tell whether Horneby had taken his own vengeance. Horneby knew it, too, and gave Bartholomew a small, bitter smile as he straightened the curious topknot that had provided Bartholomew with his final clue.

'I told you I would clear the church within moments, if

I spoke about life on other planets,' said Heytesbury, coming to stand next to them. He was amused by the whole incident, and did not seem too concerned by the fact that a scholar lay dead at their feet. 'I was right.'

'It was you who shouted that there was a fire?' asked Michael in sudden understanding.

Heytesbury grinned at him in a way that made it clear he had been the one responsible. 'But, although I may have been correct about emptying the church, I was wrong about one thing, Brother.'

'And what was that?' asked Michael suspiciously.

'I thought today would be a dull experience. It was not. You Cambridge men certainly know how to organise a memorable debate!'

EPILOGUE

BARTHOLOMEW LEANED BACK AMONG THE SCENTED cushions in the chair nearest to Matilde's fire and watched her bring mulled wine for him and Michael from the small parlour at the back of the house. It smelled rich and sweet, and the aroma of cloves and cinnamon mingled pleasantly with the pine needles that crackled and popped in the hearth.

'So,' said Michael with great satisfaction, leaning forward to see which of the three goblets was the fullest and then taking it. 'We emerge victorious once more. You would think criminals and murderers would have learned by now that Cambridge is not the place to be if they want their nasty plans to succeed. They would do better going to Oxford.'

'Speaking of Oxford, did Heytesbury leave on Sunday afternoon?' asked Matilde, drawing a stool near the fire and perching on it as she cupped her goblet between both hands. Clippesby's prediction of a spell of sunshine had proved uncannily accurate, but clear skies meant cold nights, and it was chilly once the sun had set, even in Matilde's cosy home.

Michael nodded. 'He is now the proud owner of the Black Bishop of Bedminster, and he set off on it at noon, shortly after his unexpectedly brief lecture.'

'Heytesbury *bought* that thing?' asked Bartholomew in astonishment. 'I thought he was as wary of it as everyone else.'

Michael chuckled happily. 'Stanmore – ever the salesman – caught him in a tavern late one night when he was not at his most alert, and persuaded him to buy it. It was, after all, his to sell, not Richard's. Meanwhile, all our suspicions that

457

Richard was involved in something sinister were essentially unfounded. His father bought him the horse and the saddle, while his fine new clothes and fancy ear-ring came either from his own savings or from the money Heytesbury paid him.'

'Why did Heytesbury pay him?' asked Matilde curiously.

'Because he did not trust any Cambridge-based lawyers to read the deeds relating to his arrangements with me,' replied Michael. 'And because he was strapped for choice, Richard could name any price he liked.'

'I imagine a good deal of haggling took place over the fee, though,' added Bartholomew. 'They certainly spent a lot of time in taverns, trying to take advantage of each other by indulging in drinking games. But Richard has been a changed man this week. He even visited some of my patients with me, and claims he may yet become a physician.'

'He helped me take food to the lepers, too,' said Matilde. 'And I hear that the Franciscans are making a good deal of money by selling the cure that lifted the curse from him.'

Bartholomew laughed. 'Richard is a young man who is rarely ill, and the combination of too much ale with Heytesbury and the burning feathers that Cynric left for him made him sick. He was frightened, and there is the essence of the Franciscans' cure.'

'What do you mean?' asked Matilde incredulously. 'Are you telling us that it did not actually work?'

'Of course not,' said Bartholomew. 'How can burning feathers change a person's character? They made him ill, and convinced him to turn over a new leaf – that and the knowledge that he killed a monk and does not want to be damned for it.'

'So, he may revert to his former charming self?' asked Matilde, disappointed.

Bartholomew nodded. 'But he was a nice enough lad before he left home. Perhaps living with Edith will keep him pleasant.'

'The Franciscans are making a lot of money by selling gum mastic, too,' said Michael. 'When the news spread that

Lincolne's impressive topknot was held in place so perfectly by a glue made from a new import from the Mediterranean—'

'It only stayed in place when he was not killing people,' corrected Bartholomew. 'It tended to come off in the hands of his victims – Walcote, Faricius and almost me.'

'— a good many people asked the Franciscans if they had any,' finished Michael. 'It is fine stuff – virtually invisible and fat-based so it does not rinse off in water.'

'It leaves yellow stains, however,' said Bartholomew. 'Lincolne's scalp was deeply impregnated with it, and so were Heytesbury's fingers. He uses gum mastic resin as a breath-freshener to disguise the fact that he likes wine. It is quite a useful plant.'

'So, it was Lincolne who killed Faricius and Walcote,' mused Matilde. 'He was a cool customer, ordering you to investigate his student's stabbing among the Dominicans and then watching you excavate Kyrkeby from the secret tunnel.'

Bartholomew agreed. 'So was Timothy, although he at least had the grace to go white when we found Kyrkeby, and he did not like being in the conventual church at Barnwell, where the body of another of his victims lay. I recall feeling sorry for him, because I assumed that it was simply the sight of corpses he did not like.'

'He probably just did not like to see the corpses of the men he had murdered,' said Michael. 'But Lincolne was good. It never occurred to me that *he* knew about the tunnel and Kyrkeby's body in it.'

'He had been a student at the Carmelite Friary,' Bartholomew explained to Matilde. 'Therefore, he was aware of the tunnel, although it is a Carmelite tradition to keep the secret from the masters. I suppose people simply forgot that Lincolne had been a student here as time passed.'

'He saw Faricius slip out through it while the Dominicans were storming the Carmelite Friary,' continued Michael. 'He followed him, watched him collect the essay, then confronted him in Milne Street. Feeling betrayed by his best student, Lincolne stabbed Faricius in a fit of rabid fury.'

'Lincolne was lucky the Dominicans did not catch *him* in Milne Street,' said Matilde. 'It was his proclamation that started the riot in the first place.'

'That was why he abandoned Faricius's body before he had the chance to grab the essay,' said Bartholomew. 'He heard the Dominicans coming and was forced to flee.'

'Meanwhile, Kyrkeby had also been dogging Faricius,' Michael went on. 'Time was passing, and he needed the essay on which to base his lecture. He must have been desperate, to dash over to the dying Faricius and cut the strings to his scrip while his own students were closing in.'

'He *was* desperate,' confirmed Bartholomew. 'The lecture was in a week, and his own work was mediocre. He needed the essay urgently, if he were not to disgrace himself and his Order at the most auspicious event in the University's calendar.'

'And by the Monday – two days later – Ringstead observed a marked improvement in the lecture's quality,' said Michael. 'But meanwhile, Lincolne became obsessed with hunting down the essay and destroying it.'

'He knew he was not in a position to look for it himself,' said Bartholomew, 'so he turned to Timothy and Janius, who were already working with him in the plot to overthrow Michael and Walcote and thus save the University from what they considered to be evil influences. The Benedictines eagerly obliged Lincolne, but did so because they intended to publish it themselves, not because they wanted to destroy it.'

'It would have brought them fame and fortune,' said Matilde. 'But why would the fanatical Lincolne join forces with monks like Timothy and Janius? They seem odd bedfellows.'

'They were not so different,' said Michael. 'They all used religion as a means to force their own views on people who begged to differ. And they were all afraid that my arrangement with Heytesbury would harm Cambridge. It just shows that they were poor judges of character, and that they did not know me at all.'

'And poor Walcote, who we all chastised for being so meek and mild, showed considerable strength in the end,' said Matilde. 'He died because he refused to tell that wicked trio where he had hidden Faricius's essay.'

Michael nodded. 'He knew if he told them they would probably kill Paul, and he did not want that on his conscience. He died to protect Paul and to keep Faricius's essay from men like Timothy and Janius, who would seek to profit from it, and from Lincolne, who would have burned it.'

'Where is it now?' asked Matilde.

'Where Faricius wanted it to be,' said Michael. 'In the care of Father Paul.'

'They must have killed Walcote very quickly,' said Bartholomew, his mind still dwelling on the grisly details of the Junior Proctor's death. 'Lynne heard the commotion with Kyrkeby shortly after sunset, and both Kyrkeby and Walcote were dead before compline, because that is when Sergeant Orwelle found Walcote's body and it was already cold.'

'Why did Walcote not tell *you* about the tunnel?' asked Matilde of Michael. 'It seems the sort of detail proctors should share.'

'I quite agree,' said Michael. 'But Walcote was a man of his word, and he had promised the Carmelite student-friars he would say nothing if they blocked the tunnel within a week. Also, you must remember that he was not present when the question about Faricius's escape from the friary came up: he was making sure the Dominicans had all gone home at that point. He never knew that we were pondering the question of how Faricius could have left the friary without using the main gate, or I imagine he would have told us.'

'You and he did not seem to work well together,' remarked Bartholomew. 'You may have liked each other, but you did not trust him – or he you.'

'No,' admitted Michael. 'I thought him too weak, and he did not understand me at all. We did not talk as much as we should. I realised this was a mistake, and I determined such a lack of communication should not sully my working relationship with his successor. I told Timothy everything – which was also a mistake, as it happened.'

'My role in this was rather worthless,' said Matilde ruefully. 'I thought I was helping you solve two murders, but despite the fact that I had a thoroughly enjoyable time at St Radegund's Convent and I learned a good deal that might benefit the sisters, my spying was a waste of time as far as you are concerned.'

'Not true,' said Michael. 'Matt was sure the nuns had a role in those deaths. And he was right in a way: Walcote's meetings at St Radegund's caused a good deal of trouble.'

'Matt and I were mistaken about Tysilia, though,' admitted Matilde. 'We thought she was a highly intelligent manipulator, who masterminded the meetings and the murders. We could not have been more wrong. She is exactly what she appears to be: a pretty woman with a completely empty head. She thinks she will have a better life if she escapes from the convent, and regularly gives the men she meets small baubles in return for a promise of help.'

'But she only keeps her lovers for a week, and so is obliged to buy off rather a large number of them,' said Bartholomew, smiling. 'She offered Richard trinkets to help her – which certainly accounts for how he paid for some of his new clothes.'

'She gave him my locket,' said Matilde, taking it from around her neck and gazing down at it. 'She really is foolish: she has not realised that she needs to keep her lovers for longer than a few days if she ever wants to capitalise on the favours she has purchased.'

'Richard was bitter about the nuns of St Radegund's when we discussed them in the Cardinal's Cap,' said Bartholomew. 'But I suspect that was because his week was up, and Tysilia had already abandoned him for her next victim.'

462

Michael frowned thoughtfully. 'On the morning of his lecture, Heytesbury said that Cambridge "no longer held any attractions" for him. I wonder if he was Richard's replacement for a while.'

Matilde nodded keenly, pleased to be able to provide at least some useful information. 'He was. But she confided in me that men who drink a lot do not make good lovers. Poor Heytesbury was dismissed well before his week was up.'

'Well, Tysilia need not worry about escaping from St Radegund's any more,' said Bartholomew. 'She no longer lives there. Bishop de Lisle has removed her to the leper hospital.'

'Has he?' asked Michael, startled. 'Does she have the disease, then?'

Bartholomew shook his head. 'But it is clear her mind is impaired, and she is pregnant for a third time in a very short period. Leper hospitals not only house lepers; they are a haven for those with other incurable diseases, too, including weaknesses of the mind. It is also cheaper than St Radegund's, and the Bishop is apparently short of funds at the moment.'

'Insanity?' asked Michael bluntly. 'She does not seem to be any more lunatic than most of the people who freely walk around Cambridge's streets – including certain Michaelhouse scholars.'

'I suppose we should feel sorry for her,' said Matilde. 'But she treated poor Brother Andrew shamefully, and it led to his suicide in the King's Ditch. It is hard to feel compassion for someone who is so completely dedicated to her own selfish desires.'

'I feel compassion for Faricius, though,' said Bartholomew. 'The poor man only wanted to express what he really believed, but academic bigotry silenced him. And I feel compassion for the Michaelhouse lad who was killed just for greeting Brother Timothy in a cheerful manner. And for Simon Lynne, murdered because he was walking down the street in the misguided belief that all his troubles were over.'

463

'Simon Lynne is a good example of why liars are a danger to themselves,' said Michael. 'He told us untruths, and we later disbelieved him when he claimed he had an identical brother and that his aunt was Mabel Martyn. He was being honest, but we already had him marked as a liar. I might have been able to protect him if he had been open with me from the start.'

Matilde looked up at Michael. 'Over the last two weeks, you have lost two Junior Proctors. What will you do? I cannot imagine that you have many willing volunteers lining up to take their places.'

'No,' admitted Michael. 'Although there is one man who has offered me his services. I am seriously tempted to accept them, because at least I know that *he* will never organise clandestine meetings behind my back, or plot to have me murdered.'

'Father William?' asked Bartholomew, horrified. 'You would appoint that old bigot to a position that will allow him to persecute anyone who fails to comply with his own narrow set of beliefs? And what about the realism-nominalism debate? It will never die down with William accusing all the nominalists of heresy.'

Michael shook his head slowly. 'The fire has already gone out of that particular issue. When Heytesbury left, only one Carmelite turned up to hurl a clod of mud at his back, and a passing gaggle of Dominicans did no more than laugh at the mess it made. I even saw Dominicans and Carmelites standing side by side to watch the mystery plays in the Market Square yesterday. They are at peace again – for now.'

'And what brought about this abrupt change?' asked Matilde suspiciously. 'Only a week ago, they were prepared to tear each others' heads off in St Mary's Church.'

'Lent is over,' said Michael. 'The sun is shining and the spring flowers are out. People are happier. And there are no more of those silly meetings of Walcote's; they hardly poured oil on troubled waters. Lincolne's death has helped, too. The Dominicans believe that one of Lincolne's own

464

students made an end of him, and consider justice to have been done for both Kyrkeby and Faricius. I cannot imagine how they arrived at such a conclusion, personally.'

Bartholomew said nothing.

'And once I appoint William as my Junior Proctor, I shall be able to relax again,' continued Michael, leaning back and holding out his cup to Matilde to be refilled. 'I am expecting a large consignment of cheese in a few days, and I want to be able to appreciate it without rushing off to see to students with broken heads and bloody knuckles. William can do that.'

'Cheese?' asked Bartholomew cautiously. 'This would have nothing to do with Heytesbury's deed, would it? Richard claimed you wanted it signed so that you could dine on fine cheese and butter. Do not tell me he was right!'

'Of course that was not why I wanted it signed,' said Michael. Then his large face broke into a grin of happy anticipation. 'But it is certainly one of its advantages.'

historical note

THROUGHOUT MEDIEVAL TIMES, CAMBRIDGE WAS FRAUGHT with disputes of one kind or another. Some occurred when the townsfolk took exception to the influence and sway held by the University in a town that was really very small by modern standards; others happened when specific factions within the University took against each other. A number of these are recorded in historical documents, including a very serious contention in 1374, when the Dominicans and Carmelites were on opposite sides of a theological debate. One John Horneby was the spokesman for the Carmelites. Riots and civil disorder followed, and even the Pope was drawn into the argument.

The religious Orders comprised a large percentage of the student body in the University, although it did not mean that their students were saintly men dedicated to a life of learning or devoted to the service of others. Many were sent to Cambridge to acquire a basic education before taking positions in the King's courts or high-ranking posts in the Church – indeed, some Orders were obliged to send a specific percentage of their friars to one or other of the universities. It is certain that some of the alliances formed in the friaries formed the basis of an 'old boys' club', where favours were given to former acquaintances.

The Franciscans, in particular, were often accused of preying on the younger students and encouraging them to join their Order. Some of their converts were as young as fourteen, although most were in their late teens. It is not unreasonable to suppose that controlling large bodies of active young men was extremely difficult, and that this alone led to at least some of the trouble with the other Orders and the town's apprentices.

Cambridge in the fourteenth century was a small but busy town, with relatively good road and water communications. By the mid-1350s, it had eight Colleges – King's Hall, Michaelhouse, Peterhouse, Gonville Hall, Trinity Hall, Bene't College, the Hall of Valence Marie and Clare – along with a number of hostels and several friaries. Entry to the town was controlled by two gates (Barnwell and Trumpington) and two sets of bridges (Great Bridge and Small Bridges).

The Great Bridge had a turbulent history. There had been a crossing of the River Cam at this point since prehistoric times, and a newer, stronger bridge had been erected after William the Conqueror had raised his motte and bailey castle in 1068. By 1279 the bridge was in a poor state of repair, and a tax was levied on the townsfolk to pay for a new one. When the money was raised, the Sheriff simply declined to build a new structure, and instead made superficial repairs to the old one. Evidence indicates that any remaining funds found their way into his own pocket. Complaints about the state of the bridge continued until well into the fifteenth century, and it was common practice for soldiers from the Castle to remove parts of it so that would-be travellers were obliged to use the soldiers' ferries.

The University, founded in the early years of the thirteenth century, grew in importance and influence throughout the Middle Ages. Among its most notable public occasions were its debates, and many were held in St Mary's Church, which was the only building large enough to house everyone who wanted to attend. They occurred at regular intervals throughout the year, and it was considered a great honour to be invited to speak at one.

Contemporary accounts indicate that some subjects were more popular for these occasions than others. The possibility of life on other planets did not seem to interest medieval scholars much, and little is recorded of their speculations on the matter. When life on other worlds was considered, it was usually in the form of parallel universes – that is that there are universes identical to our own that exist simultaneously. The possibility of encountering little green men was apparently not something that inspired much serious discussion.

It is not possible to say whether the debate that raged in the fourteenth century between the realists and the nominalists ever led to violence. It was, however, a highly contentious issue, and dominated almost every aspect of teaching, from theology and natural philosophy to rhetoric and grammar. It was an old argument, originating with Aristotle and Plato, but it was revived in the 1300s by the Franciscan scholar, William of Occam. Occam was a student of the Oxford master Duns Scotus (the derogative word 'dunce' is derived from his name), who was a leading proponent of realism. Occam disagreed with his teacher, and spent a good part of his life in Europe being criticised by various popes. He died somewhere around 1349, possibly from the plague.

The debate did not die with Occam, and a group of like-minded scholars began to gather in the Oxford college of Merton. Men like William Heytesbury, Richard Swineshead and John Dumbleton were leading thinkers of their day, although little of their work has survived. Heytesbury's *Regulae Solvendi Sophismata*, however, is a remarkable text, covering a wide range of philosophical issues as well as defining uniform speed and uniformly accelerated motion. These definitions were used and accepted by Galileo. Heytesbury and his colleagues even developed the mean speed theorem, which is perhaps the most outstanding medieval contribution to mathematical physics.

Not much is known about Heytesbury, other than that he was bursar of Merton in 1338, and that he was old when he became Chancellor of Oxford University in 1371. These dates alone indicate that he lived a long and successful life.

John Clippesby and Thomas Suttone were members of Michaelhouse in the 1350s, and Ralph de Langelee was its Master. Thomas Kenyngham, one of Michaelhouse's founding members, had ceased to be Master by 1354, and had probably resigned. The University's Chancellor was a man named William Tynkell.

In 1354, records show that the Prior of the Dominicans was probably William de Morden, while other Dominicans at around that time include Henry de Kyrkeby, Robert de Bulmer and Thomas Ringstead. Ringstead was a professor of theology in 1349, and was Bishop of Bangor by 1357. He died in 1366, leaving his Cambridge convent £20 and a couple of religious books.

The Warden of the Franciscans in 1354 was probably William Pechem, while John de Daventre is mentioned in a document dated to 1348.

The Prior of the Carmelites at the time was William de Lincolne. John Horneby became an important man in the Carmelite Order, and was a Regius professor of theology. The Carmelite Order arrived in Cambridge in the 1290s, where they built a church on Milne Street (probably near where King's Chapel stands today). Humphrey de Lecton was the first Carmelite to earn a doctor's degree in Cambridge. If he were buried in the town, it is likely to have been in a graveyard in the conventual church, although he was probably not honoured with as splendid a tomb as the one described here.

With the blessing of the King, Ralph de Norton was elected Prior of the Austin community at Barnwell in 1349, after his predecessor died of the plague. His election was contested five months later by a man called Simon of Seez, who had been granted the position by the Pope at Avignon. This led to some lively politicking on Ralph's part, but that is another story. Ralph had two brother monks called John and Simon Lynne, while a man named William Walcote was also a Cambridge Austin canon in the 1350s. The canons ran a small hospital, the chapel of which was dedicated to

St Mary Magdalene. This still stands, and is the pretty Norman building on the Newmarket Road.

Throughout the fourteenth century, records indicate that the small Benedictine convent of St Radegund's had something of a reputation for licentious behaviour. One Mabel Martyn was Prioress in the 1320s and 1330s, while Eve Wasteneys is recorded as Prioress in 1359. The nuns were poor, and had lost a great deal in a devastating fire in 1313, but this does not excuse some of their behaviour. In 1373, 1389 and several times in the 1400s, the convent was visited by various officials, and the nuns were warned about their 'extravagant and dissolute lifestyles'. According to the officials' reports, nuns were allowed to leave the priory when they pleased, and men visited them at 'inappropriate hours'. By 1496, only two nuns remained (one of whom was said to have been of 'ill fame'), and Bishop Alcock of Ely expelled them and used the estates and buildings to found the College of St Mary the Virgin, St John the Evangelist and St Radegund the Virgin, which, almost since its inception, was known as Jesus College. So, although the nuns in this tale might appear flagrant in their intentions, this part of the story may not be as far-fetched as it may seem.

Go back to the beginning

Discover the first three chronicles of
Matthew Bartholomew

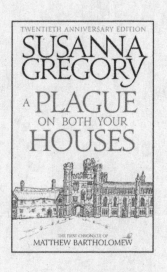

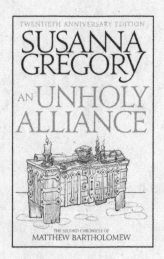

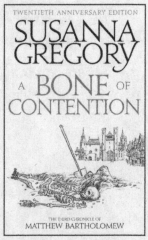

Out now

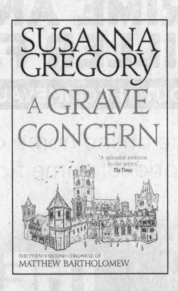

SUSANNA GREGORY

A GRAVE CONCERN

'A splendid addition to the series'
The Times

THE TWENTY-SECOND CHRONICLE OF
MATTHEW BARTHOLOMEW

Identifying the murderer of the Chancellor of the
University is not the only challenge facing physician
Matthew Bartholomew. Many of his patients have been
made worse by the ministrations of a 'surgeon' recently
arrived from Nottingham, his sister is being rooked by the
mason she has commissioned to build her husband's tomb,
and his friend, Brother Michael, has been offered a
Bishopric which will cause him to leave Cambridge.

Brother Michael, keen to leave the University in good
order, is determined that the new Chancellor will be a man
of his choosing. The number of contenders putting
themselves forward for election threatens to get out of
control, then more deaths in mysterious circumstances
make it appear that someone is taking extreme measures to
manipulate the competition.

With passions running high and a bold killer at large, both
Bartholomew and Brother Michael fear the very future of
the University is at stake.